Marguerite Reilly

by

Elizabeth Lake

THE CLAPTON PRESS
LONDON E5

First published 1946 by:
Pilot Press Limited45 Great Russell Street
London WC1

Republished 2019 by:
The Clapton Press Limited
38 Thistlewaite Road
London E5 0QQ

ISBN: 978-1-9996543-1-3

CONTENTS

TO MY MOTHER

PART ONE: ACCESSION

1

These were the circumstances of our heroine's birth.

One Sunday morning after High Mass, Mary O'Connor came slowly and thoughtfully out of the cool darkness of the church into the smoky autumn light, a spot of holy water glistening on her white forehead. She felt herself watched and turned her head to meet the eyes of a young man who was talking to Father Farrell. She smiled at the priest and her smile seemed to include the stranger, Patrick Reilly. He fell in love with her.

After that he watched for her in church every Sunday and waited on the steps or in the porch until she came by. In time they were introduced by the priest and he heard her speak. Her voice was musical, a rich blend of a South Shields accent and an Irish brogue. He began to escort her home, talking hesitantly about the sermon, about Father Farrell, about anything which might interest her, shy of asking about herself, accepting her easy laughter and lack of embarrassment as a sign of good breeding. Every night he prayed that he might marry her. Gradually he felt that he could win her.

From Father Farrell he learned that she was a sea captain's daughter and therefore his social superior. He imagined her station to be far more exalted than it was and he loved her for it. The more out of reach she seemed, the more mysterious and beautiful she was, the more he was haunted by her image; tender, dignified and in need of his protection.

When the answer came to his prayers he looked on it as a miracle. There was no miracle. The sea captain was poor, he had always been poor; the boats in his charge had always been small and humble. Despite his angry boasts about former fortune, old O'Connor was a widower with little concern for the position of his family. Four unmarried daughters were on his hands, handsome enough girls, especially Mary, but young men of their own or a better class expected some kind of a dowry. Mary was not his favourite and he was quite willing to hand her over to the first man who wanted no money with her and who was earning a steady wage. Patrick might be a manual worker but he had no dependents. Besides, Father

7

Farrell recommended the young man highly, spoke of him as serious and industrious, and said that he had it from the manager of the steel works—another Irish Catholic—that he was likely to be made a foreman very soon.

Nine months after their first meeting, Patrick married Mary. She was seventeen and he was twenty.

Their life together went smoothly. She was not what he imagined her to be, but it made no difference, because he neither saw it then nor at any time in his life and continued to treat her as someone whose gentle refinement must be protected from a rough world. She was energetic and gay. She sang popular songs as she worked; she joked with the tradesmen; she teased Patrick about his seriousness and laughed at him for buying books. It was not his steady character which had won her but his handsome face. She was glad to escape from her father's violent tempers and her eldest sister's domineering ways. She enjoyed having a home of her own and a husband who thought her perfection, and her love for him contained respect, gratitude and a warm, uncomplicated physical sympathy.

When he was twenty-one Patrick's own abilities and Father Farrell's entreaties secured him a foremanship. Two months later his first child, Margaret, was born.

2

Margaret was self-reliant, active and interested in everything around her. From the first months she displayed strong reactions, with a solemn expression and shining intelligent eyes as though working out the deepest mysteries of the universe. Later, as consciousness came, she was aware of only the delights of her surroundings. There were no sudden fits of screaming and few tears. The highly polished brass in kitchen and bedroom, Our Lady's blue lamp which flickered by her cot, her father's luxuriant silky auburn whiskers and her mother's jolly songs were magical and exciting.

Contentedly she reached the toddling stage. The arrival of a little brother, Michael, pleased her. Her jealousy was tempered by her interest in the small baby. He was his mother's darling but she was the apple of her father's eye and knew she always would be. Later came Thomas, surly and fretful. After an interval came Elizabeth, bright and with tiny pointed features. Margaret took them all under her wing, fussed over them and played with them. She considered herself to be on a different level from the babies, halfway between them and the parents.

The children were nearly always together. They slept in one small room. They went for short walks, to the end of the street and back again, Margaret in charge and Elizabeth in the pram. They played on the doorstep or pavement when it was fine, by the kitchen fire when it was wet or cold. They were well fed, well clad, they were seldom ill and the neighbours admired them. They were never bored for they entertained each other. Their mother would laugh, sing, tease, scold and cuff. Their father would kiss them in turn when he came home from work, ask what they had done during the day, listen gravely and help them with their evening prayers.

As soon as she was old enough to kneel for a long period without wriggling Margaret went to Sunday Mass with her parents. She enjoyed this because it distinguished her from the other children. The service itself seemed long and for the most part lacking in variety but it was punctuated by two moments which never failed as drama. The first was when it came to kneel again after a long period of sitting down and suddenly a great thunderous rumbling sound would echo through the church. The second was when everything was hushed and silvery bells rang gently and everyone bowed their heads low. And when that was over she could look forward with mixed feelings to the final moment when the organ started up with a throbbing puffing roar, so alarming that she could feel her hair roots tingle and the gooseflesh rise as she walked down the aisle. After Mass she found herself the centre of attention and often Father Farrell gave a holy picture or a sweet.

On Sunday afternoons they were all allowed into the parlour (never used at any other time), and while her father played simple tunes on the piano and the little ones amused themselves by crawling and squatting and clambering onto the plum-coloured chairs, Margaret explored the inexhaustible mysteries of carpet and furniture with her eyes and looked out of the window.

On Sunday evenings there were baths by the kitchen fire, the little ones splashing and screaming with pleasure, Margaret sober and officious. When they were clean and ready for bed their father arrived back from Benediction in time to tell a holy story before prayers. This story was always of some miraculous happening.

9

Miracles seemed the easiest way out of difficulties to Margaret and when she thought of St. Bridget with her pails suddenly filled with milk, flowers springing up in snowy footprints, loaves being multiplied, a poor family finding a meal on the table, a beggar watching his penny turn into gold, she longed to be a saint so that she might do such things. When the story was over she always asked her father to do a miracle for them and, smiling, he always refused.

"Well, will Father Farrell?"

"No."

It seemed to her that life continued like this for a very, very long time and then it seemed that it had always been like this with all of them there in this house. The fact was that a lull in the regular appearance of a new child had been caused by a stillbirth and a miscarriage. Memories of the arrival of the other three had faded in Margaret's mind, memories of her father's long silky whiskers had gone too, and she believed him to have been always as thickly bearded as he was now. The only change was that things became a little smaller and simpler. She would come home from a walk and notice that some piece of furniture had shrunk and that its shape was really quite easy to grasp. This process continued in jerks until there were many less mysteries to be solved in the house and until the last stronghold of massiveness and obscurity, the piano in the parlour, fell before her own increased size and comprehension. But these changes did not modify her feeling that her life was timeless and therefore the greatest change, when it came, was all the more abrupt and pointless.

Patrick's right leg and arm were smashed in an accident at the foundry. One afternoon a workman walked through the open front door, with never a word to the children playing there, straight into the kitchen where Mary Reilly was ironing. His fingers tapped the table and his voice was hoarse. "Mrs Reilly. There was an accident at the works."

She stopped him. "Paddy's dead," she said. She put her iron carefully back on its stand and pressed the palms of her hands over her face.

It was not as bad as she had feared. The man explained.

"As long as he's alive," she said, "it will be all right."

He was carried home in great pain and Margaret heard him groan as they took him up the narrow stairs. She was told he was ill and she must stop the others from shouting. She was not allowed to go to him. She sat in the kitchen frowning and fidgeting. Her worry was like a pain. She was angry with her mother for not allowing her to go to him. What right had her mother to do such a thing? She, Margaret, could have been useful and looked after him. Disobeying orders, as soon as her mother's back was turned, she went quietly upstairs, cautiously opened the door and saw him lying with his eyes shut, looking much the same as usual.

Patrick bore the pain well and never complained. For him the virtue of good health had never been the sensation of well-being but the capacity to work. His enforced idleness made him anxious about the future and his pain gave his brooding a morbid tinge. He was tormented by the thought of what would happen to his family. He had not been satisfied with their present position. To mark them off from other working-class families, because he had married someone whom he considered to be of gentle birth, he had had a parlour, the children called him "father" and he called them by their full names. No coarse expression or slang was allowed in the house and when he was at home there was an air of solemnity, almost formality about their behaviour. He never mixed with the neighbours and he imagined that his wife did so only because she had a kind heart. The loss of his weekly wage, the dwindling away of his savings meant squalor, a drop in the social scale and the abandonment of his ideal of "refinement". The children would not be able to go to good schools as he had hoped. Prayer comforted him but he could make no plans. It was his wife who thought of scheme after scheme.

He was lamed for life. His right arm, though healed, would never be strong enough for heavy steel work. When he got up his long face was white and drawn and there was a deep crease between his arched brows. Mary brought Father Farrell to see him, for the priest had been like a father to him and brought him up when his parents died. She urged Father Farrell to have a word with the manager of the steel works. She went with him. Between them they secured good compensation, a rare enough thing in those days. Then the priest offered him a job from the owner of a chain of dairies who wanted a manager for Liverpool. The pay was small but they could have a flat above the shop rent free and if the business prospered there would be an increase in salary.

Patrick accepted at once. To be in trade was a step on the road to respectability. Mary hated the idea and begged him not to go. She was busy getting him a light, caretaker job at the foundry. She was not interested in status and found it difficult to understand her husband's horror of this light job. What did it matter if it was a comedown after being a foreman? They could manage. She was reluctant to leave South Shields because a great part of her happiness came from talks to the neighbours, nods from people in the streets, visits from her family and the look of every corner of her own home.

3

Margaret sided with her father. If he wanted to move then the move was right. She was outraged to see her mother argue with him. He had had an accident and he was ill. He was also infallible. She felt protective towards him, and because he felt protective towards her mother she felt in some way more important than her mother; she felt she was like a third parent and must be taken into their confidence.

The idea of moving was thrilling to Margaret and so were the journey and the tales of a shining, white dairy told by her father to cheer her. But her heart sank when she saw Liverpool, vast, unfriendly and damp, and she wept when the dairy turned out to be a dark, poky shop in a narrow back street.

The tiny rooms above it never saw the proper light. There was no parlour. The piano, the plum-coloured chairs and other prized pieces of furniture had to be sold. The children felt cramped. They were told it was unsafe to play in the street and spent much of the day on the wooden staircase and the landing. They were told that the neighbours' children were rough and coarse and they must not mix with them. They were packed off to bed very early, Margaret included, to be out of the way. Patrick, preoccupied with the future, over-conscientious and thorough, worked late each night, seated at the kitchen table, counting and recounting long columns of figures, worrying about the muddle left by the last manager and laboriously writing letters in a fine, copper-plate hand to his employer.

As soon as it could be arranged, Margaret, now eight, was sent to the local Catholic school by her mother, not for what she could learn there but to be out of the way. Michael was sent there too. Margaret had already learnt to read and write from her father and she became fluent. She took little interest in lessons and books and she knew that her father did not approve of this school, a poor school. Something held her back from joining in the games of her companions. She sensed the anxiety at home and she felt apprehensive and on her guard.

In the morning, before school, she dressed the others, tidied their bedroom and swept the floor. After school she ran errands and sometimes stayed up to look after the shop if they were shorthanded. Customers were amused by her serious, businesslike manner and occasionally gave her a few pence for herself. These she gave to her father. She grew pale and nervous. To comfort her, her parents told her they might go back home one day. She was sharp enough to detect the doubt in their minds when they spoke of this but she made herself believe it was true.

When she was nine another brother, John, arrived. The flat was far too small to hold a fifth child, a tiny baby who could not fit in with the others. It was winter; the rain never stopped and from morning till night most of the family were huddled together in the kitchen. For three weeks Margaret stayed away from school to help. Mrs Reilly was tired and cross, she had not wanted another child and she resented him being there. She loved her first four children, Michael especially, but for those who came later she had scarcely any affection.

It was now impossible to keep the place tidy. There were always wet things steaming in front of the fire, piles of unmended clothes on chairs and the baby needing food and attention. The children grew quarrelsome and began to look dirty and uncared for. Mrs Reilly, tormented by varicose veins, scolded all day and nagged her husband in the evenings.

"If we were poor I could put up with it," she said, "but you've been doing well and there's money put by and here we're stuck with the family increasing all the time."

Patrick invested his compensation money and other savings in a milk business in Newport.

4

"Will we be going back home?" was Margaret's first question and she was told no, but it would be better than that. It was true.

There were five good-sized rooms above the shop and a sitting room behind it. The houses opposite were low and therefore the rooms were bright with a wide stretch of sky to be seen from every window. Patrick delivered the milk himself in a pony-driven cart and the children sometimes went round with him.

They prospered. In time there was a new coat of paint for the cart. Later a man was employed to deliver the milk while Patrick concentrated on increasing custom. Mrs Kenny—Mrs Reilly's favourite sister and on whose advice they had taken the shop—began to figure in their lives. She was prosperous; her husband owned a sweet shop in Cardiff. Boxes of sweets arrived regularly for the children; there were outings and visits. She took a great fancy to Margaret, who was called after her and who resembled her in appearance. Her personal influence on Margaret was never great but the fact that she had a rich relation, an enormously rich relation, as Margaret believed, confirmed her feeling that the Reilly's were not an ordinary poor family. The squalor and poverty in which they had lived had been an unhappy accident, it had been unreal and wrong.

Mrs Kenny arranged with the headmistress of St. Joseph's, the Catholic High School of Cardiff, that Margaret should go there daily and lodge with her aunt. Her aunt's house seemed the height of luxury and elegance. The Kenny's did not live above their shop but had a whole house to themselves with a short drive in front and two tall, dark trees, so that there was a gate to open as well as a door. There was a maid and Mrs Kenny did very little work. The drawing room floor was not only covered by a flowery carpet but rugs were laid over that. On each side of the fireplace were small tables covered with what seemed hundreds of objects, not for use but for decoration; statuettes, china trays, silver boxes and many other things. The mantelpiece, draped in red plush edged with pom-poms, held a further variety of ornaments, including a black clock like a Greek temple. A massive, oblong table by the window was covered by a shining silky brushed green plush cloth and supported a large plant in a shining brass pot which caught the red dancing reflection of the flames in the fire.

Aunt Kenny's wardrobe—they always called her Aunt Kenny—seemed unlimited, and she looked majestic to the child as she advanced across the floor, her trailing skirts zig-zagging behind her. Having no children of her own she made a great fuss of her niece. She took her out shopping and bought her a blue coat, a fur cap and muff to match and a pair of soft, black leather boots which took a button-hook and many minutes to do up or undo.

At St Joseph's Margaret found herself at a loss. The other girls had done history, geography and arithmetic before whereas she had to learn these subjects from the beginning. None of the other parents were less than shopkeepers—and by that they did not mean little shops in back streets—and they never served in their shops themselves. Many girls were the daughters of professional men and they spoke differently from the others, with only a trace of the Cardiff accent.

Pride, hitherto dormant in her character, now dictated all her actions. She said her family was very rich and when, unfortunately, one of the girls said she knew Mr Reilly's shop and it was a very small one and he delivered the milk himself, Margaret replied without hesitation that he had only delivered it for a short time because the man was ill. She added that, just for the moment, her parents were in a small shop, but they had had a much larger one, a great store, and soon they would again. They were very high born. She soon believed this herself. Her memories of the house in South Shields, where she had been so happy, turned it into a mansion, even more imposing and full of things than Aunt Kenny's house. The sea captain grandfather, whom she had rarely met, was no longer a coarse old fellow without a penny to his name, but an admiral dressed something like Nelson. She did not remember her father as a steel worker; he had worked in a steel works, she told herself, but he must have been a manager or even the owner. His long, chiselled face with its slender nose was a hundred times more aristocratic-looking than the faces of any of the fathers she had seen, and it convinced her that she came of an exalted family. The accident in South Shields had been the beginning of his bad fortune. She never questioned her parents about their early life.

In other ways she began to lie. At first it was half-deliberate but soon the dividing line between fact and fantasy became fainter until it almost disappeared. She grasped that prestige was attached not only to what parents were but to many other things as well and she was never going to appear at a disadvantage. If a book was mentioned she would claim to have read it. A girl said she had been abroad and Margaret said she had too, often. She became clever at evading further questions and yet convincing her hearers that what she said was true. She did not care for lessons but pride drove her to long hours of homework every evening until she had mastered what the others already knew. She gained ground steadily. The nuns were impressed by her piety and application. The girls admired her self-possession and something independent and wilful in her character.

When she went home at weekends she set about advancing the rest of the family in the world and she corrected their speech and deportment. The boys would not learn and called her bossy. Elizabeth was an apt pupil.

Things were getting better and better. A daily woman helped with the housework. A young girl served in the shop. Patrick Reilly, always in his best suit, sat in the parlour behind the shop doing accounts and sometimes went out to see customers or the farmers who supplied the milk. Mary Reilly now put aside the black useful clothes she had worn in Liverpool and appeared in brighter colours and newer fashions. There were new carpets, new curtains and a new piano. There were visits from other prosperous people and a parlour upstairs to receive them in. There were excursions in the pony-driven cart on Saturdays or Sundays.

All this seemed right and proper to Margaret. The Liverpool days receded like a long-past nightmare; perhaps they had never happened. Yet sometimes at the thought that she had once been at a poor school, dream or no dream, she would feel the blood rise to her cheeks and pulse in her neck and she would tell herself again and again, "It's not true." If such a thing had happened to her she could not, would not blame her parents and therefore it must somehow have been her fault. She must be vigilant or she would be caught out again. The others too must be on the watch and that was why she drilled them so. Yet while she guarded her manners and speech and especially her carriage, because she had heard one of the sisters say, "You can always tell a lady by the way she holds herself," she was reckless with money and possessions.

Pocket money and presents given to her by her aunt she handed on to the others. A fine new doll's pram she swapped for a whistle. She was impulsively generous, she felt proud to be in a position to give. One of the children only had to say they wanted something for her to promise to get it for them. With a look of great self confidence she would affirm, "I'll see that you get it. You can leave it to me."

She forgot these promises quickly. She was the same with the girls at school and with strangers—the exchange of pram for whistle was done with a boy in the street—almost anyone could get something out of her if it were hers to give, and often if it were not. She would hand over Michael's toys to Thomas, Thomas's toys to Michael, Elizabeth's dolls' clothes to a girl at school and so on. The end would always be the same, tears and recrimination between the boys, angry protests from Elizabeth, and Margaret would call them selfish and babyish and wonder why they got so upset about possessions.

She did not show off in the usual way. She never pushed herself forward and she spoke quietly. But when the occasion arose she boasted and promised, believing that what she said was true, believing that she had unlimited powers and that she could deal with any situation and any person. She must, she must, she must. No one else would do it for her. She did not want anyone else to do it for her. Her brothers and sister found her interfering and domineering. Elizabeth, self-contained and sly, handled Margaret carefully and obeyed her more in appearance than in fact. Thomas became grumpy with her and gave in in the end. Michael relied on his charm but did not get his own way.

With varying success Margaret set out to make them long to get on, to make their chests fill with family pride as they walked to church, brushed and washed under her supervision, on Sunday. They never felt safe with her; it was as though an adult were present at their games. At the height of the fun she might say, "Oh, what a horrid expression to use!" or "How can you slouch like that?" She was unconscious of this. She had very little idea of what other people were thinking. And if it had occurred to her that the others were irked by her presence she would not have been altogether displeased. Wasn't it natural that they should when she was so much more grown up than they? She assumed people liked her and never gave it a thought. She was not in need of affection. People must be aware of the Reilly status, that was all she asked of them.

A new brother had arrived. Mrs Reilly looked after her two younger children well but only from a sense of duty. She confined herself to the necessities, seldom comforting them when they cried and following their progress with little interest. Her husband told her that each child was a precious gift from God.

17

"I could have done with four gifts better than six," she said.

Even her four eldest children, whom she loved, she found tiring, and she never seemed to have the patience to listen to their confidences or to talk to them about things in general. It was to their father they turned for sympathy and advice. He was an oracle to them with his long silences, his grave expressions and his slow, definite statements. Everything he said was held to be wise and true and not one of them ever dreamt of disagreeing with him. Each one knew that after religion, education was the greatest thing in life because their father had said so. Even Michael would have stated that this was his belief although there was nothing in his actions which bore it out.

Margaret was pleased with life. She had made her mark at St. Joseph's. She enjoyed herself at Mrs Kenny's. She enjoyed herself at home for weekends and holidays. She put on many airs and graces, holding her back very straight and her head high. She became the best friend of the local Catholic doctor's daughter, Sarah, and through her the doctor and his wife made the acquaintance of Mr and Mrs Reilly. She noted with satisfaction how her parents mixed with the most respectable, well-dressed Catholic citizens after Sunday Mass, how the priest spoke to them as great favourites and thanked them for donations to charity and how he shook each of the children by the hand and patted Michael's bright curls. She felt proud when Sarah said, "Your mother is very pretty and your father is much handsomer than mine."

One occasion marked the height of her glory and was long remembered. She was allowed to stay up for Midnight Mass for the first time. By contrast with the dark night the interior of the church was as bright as heaven itself, each candle a star and each facet of the ornate candlesticks reflecting a hundred lights. The priests wore vestments of brocade and velvet, crimson, light gold and dark gold. The attendants were in the whitest linen and lace. She had no ear for music and could not sing in tune but the singing conjured up celestial choirs. The frosted figures of the crib spread over rocks of brown paper below a tinsel star, the kings, the shepherds, the Holy Family, the ox and the ass.

They drove home afterwards in the doctor's carriage, leaving clear, thin lines in the newly fallen soft unblemished snow. The shabby carriage and aged horse were princely to Margaret. Wide awake, conscious that here she was driving home with the loftiest personages of the congregation, her satisfaction was like a fire inside and she felt no chill draughts. Half-hypnotised by the scene she had just left, by the regular sound of the horse's hooves and by the sight of the hushed, white street, she sat silent and oblivious of the conversation.

5

Patrick Reilly fell ill, one of the first victims of a typhoid epidemic. As he lay in bed rumours spread that it was his own infected milk which had given him the disease and custom fell off. The business was placed in the hands of a temporary man and, partly out of a wish not to upset Mrs Reilly, partly out of slackness, he pretended that things were not doing too badly. Hoping that, given time, his words would prove true, he did nothing. He neither cut down his purchases of milk nor did he make any effort to counteract the rumours by personal calls.

In those days typhoid was treated by starving the patient until he recovered. After twelve weeks of this Patrick was weak and emaciated. Some of the bad news came through to him and he worried. Long before he should have done he rose to look through the books. They told a dreadful story. He hoped he had made a mistake. Day after day he shut himself in the parlour behind the shop examining accounts and receipts. His head was dizzy and mental effort wore him out. He realised that he was in debt and that next to nothing was coming in. He had a long talk to the manager and, looking more resigned than angry, he gave him notice. He did not know whether milk could carry the germ and, because he was scrupulously honest, he did not assume his own had not done so.

He drove out in the cart to see customers. His ill-health made him speak slowly and diffidently and his own doubts were obvious. Customers were sorry for him but their confidence was not restored. He cut down his purchases of milk. He took round the deliveries himself—there were only seven families to supply—and he dismissed the girl in the shop. He was not hopeful but he failed to cut his losses while there was still time. He feared that his well-born, delicately nurtured wife could not stand the blow. He asked no one's advice, he answered no questions from the family. Every week he lost money.

When the time came and he was forced to sell up there was nothing left.

The children were told just enough about what had happened to make the coming move seem reasonable. There was no question of paying for schooling now and Margaret would have to leave St. Joseph's. She would not be staying with her aunt either because her mother would need her in the house. Besides, now that he was no longer prosperous, Patrick was touchy about accepting favours.

One favour he had to accept was a job for himself in the sweet shop. For the moment there was nothing else and he was in such poor health that he felt unable to go looking round for employment. "He has a fine head on him," Mrs Reilly told her sister and Mrs Kenny promised to urge her husband to take him into the sweet business as a partner as soon as he had learnt enough about it.

The family moved into a wretched house in a dark alleyway with the few pieces of furniture which had escaped being sold, the worst pieces of course. Mary Reilly's natural resilience came to her aid. Patrick, in spite of everything, was comforted by his religion. It was Margaret who suffered the most. She could hardly bear to look at her father. To her eyes he seemed transparent, like a ghost. She hated to think of him serving behind a sweet counter. She was more worried about the effect of their change of fortune on him than on herself and every evening when he came home she ran down to meet him, staring at his face and rushing into his arms to comfort him and reassure herself. Her moment of glory was past, at least for the time being, and her pride made her break with it completely. She neither saw nor corresponded with Sarah. If she met any of her former school friends she pretended not to notice them and hoped they would not know who she was.

The ground floor of the house had once been some sort of warehouse and was not habitable. A narrow staircase led up to the first and second floors, two rooms on each. A sickly, musty smell hung over the landings, an odour of cats and mice and bugs. In rainy weather the front walls were damp and water dripped through the bedroom ceiling. There were cobwebs and dust and beetles. Margaret shared a room with Elizabeth and the baby, the boys shared another. In the evenings, when the others were in bed, she kept asking her parents, "How long will it be before we have our own shop again? We will have one quite soon, won't we?" Her mother took little notice, her father tried to reassure her.

Her education was on his mind and he spoke to his sister-in-law. Mrs Kenny was told of a convent in Devon where Margaret could go free of charge on the recommendation of the headmistress of St. Joseph's. It was an orphanage, the nun admitted, but some of the girls had one parent and the teaching was better than was usual in such institutions. Patrick decided that this would be better than the local school. The country air would be more healthy than the air of the Cardiff slums and convent girls would certainly be more refined than the children of the neighbourhood.

When Margaret heard what had been decided she begged her parents not to send her away. Her mother was short with her and said the decision was none of her making. Her father urged her to go for his sake and promised to have her home as soon as possible. It was decided that Elizabeth should go too.

Life at the convent was hard. Margaret found herself separated from her family at a time when she felt most anxious about them, especially her father. She also discovered that the place was an orphanage and it seemed the depths of humiliation that she, who had both parents living, should be there.

There were no small comforts to cheer her and many hours of silence and boredom in which to worry. The day was long. All the older girls, and that meant all those who were more than seven years of age, rose at six o'clock, heard Mass, and then returned, hungry, to make the beds and sweep the dormitories before they breakfasted. Breakfast, like all other meals, was taken in silence and consisted of bread scraped over with dripping and a cup of something hot and unpleasant. It was the most melancholy time of the day and she would brood over the great space between then and the next meal, dreary hours of sweeping, dusting and sewing, broken by a short catechism lesson. After dinner came half an hour's walk and then more sewing until the next meal. Sometimes a short lesson in grammar and writing broke the monotony of the afternoon, but most days held no such distraction. Silence was observed during sewing and work, in fact silence was broken only during walks and one short recreation.

The older girls did embroidery which was sold in London shops and helped to pay for their keep. The younger ones did hem-stitching. All were dressed in dark, grey, prickly dresses, handed on from one child to another. Over these they wore black aprons which were removed for chapel and walks.

As the weeks went by and each day seemed like the last, but always more intolerable, Margaret began to despair. She missed her family. Elizabeth she saw only in chapel because the little ones were kept separate. Often she let her work fall into her lap and sat idly staring ahead of her, biting her nails. She discovered that most of the girls never went home for the holidays, never went home at all, had no homes, but stayed on and on in the convent until they went out into the world to work, or else, if they were very holy, became lay sisters. She felt trapped. In a panic, she ignored the letter written on the blackboard for all to imitate, and wrote in her own words to her father. He must make sure that she and her sister went home when other kinds of school had their holidays. Her life was awful but she would try and bear it for his sake. She felt better after she had written. Once her father realised what it was like he would be certain to do something.

The sister in charge took her to one side. She was told that such a letter would cause her parents pain and that she was a selfish child. It was not sent.

In time a letter came from her father. She was not allowed to read it. During recreation she was taken over to a bench at the side of the room and sat there while it was read to her. All were well at home and sent their love. She must look after Elizabeth, work hard and remember them all in her prayers. There was no word of how they were getting on, no mention of whether they would be moving out of the alley. She asked if any part of the letter had not been read. Ignoring the nun's look of anger, for Margaret was never afraid of anyone, she went on, "I do wish I could read it myself." She was ordered to go back and join the others at once.

She could blame no one. If her father had decided this he must have done so for good reasons. And yet she was furious to be so shut in. Sometimes she felt a resentment against her mother and Mrs Kenny. More often she hated the nuns for having deceived her father and led him to believe that this was a good school. Days of brooding gave her mouth a set line which she never lost. One motherly nun who tried to gain her confidence she repulsed. She needed no sympathy or help. If only she were free and with her family she would be strong enough, ready enough to do anything.

She did not get on with the girls. They mistook her preoccupation with the family for aloofness. Her lack of interest in her present life was insulting to those who had never known anything better and made what they could of it. When they asked if she was going into service she answered, "No, never!" with such indignation that they thought her stuck up.

"But we had our own carriage," she explained, "and servants and a house with *two* parlours."

The vision of a fine house, maids in uniform and luxurious rooms consoled her and she abandoned herself to dreams of the past. How could these girls bear the thought of domestic service, let alone look forward to it? She was sorry for them because they had no parents. She prayed for them and she gave them any possessions of hers which they coveted.

At long last the two sisters went home. The family was still in the alley and Patrick Reilly was still working in the sweet shop. Margaret's extreme happiness to be with her family once more reconciled her to the sordid house, their obvious poverty and her father's thin worn appearance. When he came in she flung herself into his arms and stayed there a long time, her head pressed against his chest, her arms round his waist, conscious that she loved him better than anyone else in the world.

She kept asking, "Need I go back? May I stay at home now? You can't say it's for my education."

"Well, don't tell your father that, Maggie,' said Mrs Reilly, who was not in the least interested in education. "Promise. It would only make him unhappy."

She did not want the two girls at home. The two youngest were now in their room and it was also used for cooling and storing sweets. For the moment they slept together in a narrow iron bed in the kitchen and this was inconvenient.

They returned to the convent. Elizabeth cried. Margaret comforted her by telling her that she had made her mother vow over a holy picture that it would not be for long and that this time would really be the last. The first time she had felt shut in a trap. Now she knew that what had come to an end once would come to an end again. Two long, tedious months dragged by, months of chapel, meals, housework and sewing, sewing, sewing. She tried to apply herself but quickly saw that she would never be good at embroidery. She hated fiddling work and she hated having no say in what she was to do. Now that her despair had gone and she knew she would eventually be free she could give herself up to plans, she could think of great schemes in which she would do the organising and give the orders. She would start a shop and the others could serve there. She might go abroad and seek her fortune—but that would mean leaving her father, and he must be always near her. Her mental energy and enterprise were cramped by her daily tasks and her dreams and fantasies grew stronger and richer until they were the more real part of her life. And these visions were never very detailed; they were bold, rough sketches of a fine house, a ship on the sea, an enormous store in the High Street with indistinct figures of the family. Her father and herself, detached from the others and together, were more carefully filled in. The visual quality was not so marked as the sense of movement. She could feel her fancied movements so strongly that her companions could observe her arm rise or her head turn for no apparent reason. She felt herself walking up the long drive to the family mansion, pacing the deck of the ship, moving from one department to another in the great store.

Elizabeth, who had now joined the older girls, was deft and neat. She did everything well. Even in convent uniform she looked elegant, spruce and aristocratic, with her oval face, arched eyebrows, slender nose and glowing, light pink complexion. There was no doubt that she was a beauty.

Margaret had had less luck with her physical inheritance. Her face was less finely drawn than her sister's. The features were regular and strong and the unusually level deep setting of her dark grey eyes combined with her straight thick eyebrows to give her a look of determination and self-reliance. Her brown hair grew strongly off her broad flattish forehead, forming a square outline which dipped back at the temples. In bright warm colours she could look handsome but in the drab grey her coarse downy skin had a mottled look and her tightly scraped-back hair emphasised the broadness of her face and the squareness of her jaw.

6

When Margaret went home there was another baby, Kathleen. She was a pale, thin, little thing, left between feeds to the indifferent care of one of the boys while Mrs Reilly made sweets which were sold in her sister's shop and "home-made butterscotch". There was good news. In a few months the Reilly's were going to open a sweet shop of their own, at first as a branch of the other one. From now on Margaret was to stay at home and help with the sweet-making. Elizabeth was to stay also. A room had been taken for them two doors down.

Margaret tried hard to do her new work well but she had no hand for it and day dreams made her unreliable. Finally her mother allotted to her the fetching, carrying and washing-up of pans and trays. The butterscotch, when cooled, was cut and heaped into a big tray on the kitchen table. Then the four eldest children sat round, wrapping each piece in silver paper, one of them occasionally jumping up and showing a glittering strip to the baby who watched with fascinated eyes.

Margaret found her father looking much better. His face was smoother, there was colour in his cheeks and his skin was clear, almost luminous. She spent as much time as she could with him. Every morning she accompanied him to the sweet shop, helping to carry the boxes of sweets. He limped slowly, his shoulders still hunched from the time he used crutches, his long, soft beard falling onto his chest.

He treated her as his chief assistant and confidant. He told her of his determination that all his children should have a good start in life. He said that soon now, they would have a shop of their own again and more money coming in. The first thing to be done then was to find a good school for all of them. He dwelt on the idea of "refinement". (There was no fault to be found with the two girls on this score; they had evolved a curiously mincing lady-like way of moving and talking; they articulated each syllable with great precision and never shouted). It worried him to see how rough and noisy the boys had become, fighting with the other boys in the alley, shouting in the sing-song Cardiff accent and using expressions he did not care for.

She listened attentively and understood what he meant. She was entirely in agreement with him. He told her that his dearest wish was that one of the boys should be a priest. On the other hand, he did not want any of the girls to be a nun, although if any of them had a vocation he would certainly not oppose it. He told her that being the eldest daughter was a vocation in itself. She had a responsibility towards her mother and the other children. She must never forget this and if anything were to happen to either of her parents she would have to fill their place.

This made her feel important and pleased her at first. Later it hung heavily over her and made her want to start earning and show her mettle to prove to him how right he was to trust her. She resented having to do odd jobs for her mother. It was wrong; it was a waste of her powers.

Patrick wanted to spare his wife any worry but it never occurred to him to spare his daughter. He was unaware how infectious his anxiety was and how vulnerable a child could be. He seemed hardly conscious that Margaret was a child. Because he loved her the best he tested her constantly. Her manner was becoming anxious, she could no longer laugh and play with the others and he saw nothing but good in this. Sometimes her natural high spirits broke out and she raced Michael along the street or rushed up the stairs, and then she suddenly checked herself and frowned.

Ever since his accident Patrick had been consumed with fears for the future and every trifle worried him. Often a look of displeasure crossed his sensitive face in spite of his self-control. Since his typhoid and ruin he felt deep pessimism, which he never expressed, a sense of battling against heavy odds, and this made him more religious and serious than ever. In the first years of married life his lack of humour had been modified by his wife's gaiety. Now, although he remained romantically devoted to her, he smiled wanly at her sallies. And like this smile, everything about him seemed forced and conscious, from his carefully combed hair and beard to the stoop and the limp, as though he knew very well the total picture which he presented to the world, a picture of suffering and dignity. Margaret saw him as he wished to be seen. Everyone respected him and some were in awe of him. Mr and Mrs Kenny found it difficult to be natural in his presence, for his behaviour to them was always formal and correct. He was a man of strong principles but, firmly convinced that every member of his family must be honest and good, unaware of Margaret's private fantasies because she was careful when she was with him, he never stressed truthfulness to her. Rather he feared that her environment might coarsen her and therefore he stressed refinement. And she interpreted this word in her own way, in many different ways as time went on.

One Sunday morning the family were preparing themselves for High Mass. The four eldest were upstairs, Margaret supervising Michael and Thomas, Elizabeth, always ready in good time and neat as a pin, sitting on the edge of the bed swinging her legs. In the next room Mrs Reilly was putting on her best clothes, the bright clothes she had worn at Newport. Downstairs Patrick was polishing his children's boots.

He felt dizzy as he crouched on the floor, watching the hand which held the brush move backwards and forwards, backwards and forwards, as though it were something over which he had no control. There was a tickle in his throat and then a sudden jerk from lower down. He caught his breath in an attempt to stave off a cough, afraid of a recurrence of a coughing fit because it was painful and left him feeling weak. The breath choked him until he could hold it no longer. He opened his mouth and let it flow with a gasp. There was a pause and a feeling of relief.

Coughs came, terrible uncontrollable coughs, each one a spasm, each one torn from farther and farther inside him until it seemed as though his stomach must be forced up. Yet although the area from which the coughs jerked up grew and grew, the tickle itself remained elusive, untouched, somewhere in the middle of each spasm and nowhere at all. A quick flash of ideas came which did not seem his own but advice from someone beside him. The dust on the floor, the smell of boot polish, his hunched position, surely these were aggravating it. He tried to stand and straighten himself but his limbs made no response and he found that he was lying on his side. The coughing continued.

He saw his wife come in and approach him. She was saying something. Her lips moved. Her words never reached him, blotted out by the sound of his coughs, a deafening sound which resounded inside his head and then came, like an echo, to attack his eardrums from without. He tried to reassure her by signs, by a smile, by raising a hand. She came over and knelt beside him, her bright, plump face creased with concern, her grey eyes open wide. He felt her slip an arm around him and try to drag him to a chair. The pain increased. Each cough seemed to open up afresh a long, deep wound stretching from his throat far down into his chest.

Suddenly it stopped. The tickle seemed to melt and came gently, without pain or effort, up into his mouth, transformed into a salty stream. He fumbled with his handkerchief because he had tasted blood before. Peacefully and sleepily, hearing his wife's voice as a faraway, indistinct, soothing. impersonal murmur, he put the handkerchief to his lips. It was soaked at once. Dreamily he noted the bright, frothy appearance of the blood and saw it flow onto his beard and spill off onto the floor as he turned his head, or rather as his head turned of itself, for now only his hands obeyed him. He shut his eyes.

The four children came down the stairs in the way they often did, Michael hopping on one leg, shouting that he wouldn't change legs until he reached the bottom, Thomas imitating him, Elizabeth giggling at them and Margaret telling them to hurry up. No sounds had reached them from below for they had all been talking in the bedroom and when they opened their door all was quiet in the kitchen.

Mrs Reilly rushed out and barred their way with her stout figure. "Tom and Lizzie get back upstairs," she ordered and then, as though their looks of surprise were some kind of impertinence, she shouted, "Do as you're told. Back you go at once. No questions. And stay there till you're told."

White-faced, angry, she stood between the others and the kitchen door. "Now, Mick, will you run and fetch Father Paine?"

Michael looked sullen; he hated errands. "I must put my boots on... And what will I say to him?" She moved at once and gave him a hard slap on the cheek. "Do as you're told. At once."

As her mother moved forward, Margaret caught sight of the scene beyond and tried to run in to her father. She was pushed back roughly .

"I've never met such children," said Mrs Reilly. "What devils you are. And you can go and get the doctor to your Da."

7

Margaret was fourteen at this time. During the days that followed her father's death her sense of loss was tempered by the feeling of importance and excitement which many children experience when they find themselves in the centre of unmistakably dramatic events. She felt that the limelight had suddenly been turned on her and everything she did was watched by a thousand interested eyes. She would sob until her throat was dry and then she would feel elated and want to talk or show off to someone.

She dwelt with something like pleasure on the last day of her father's life; her race to the doctor's in her felt slippers through which she could feel the shape of the cobbles; her talk to the doctor's wife and the look she must have had as she told her of what had happened; her return home, running and panting; the scene in the kitchen. This last had been the most vivid and stirring of all, with the blood on the floor, her father's pale face and the priest praying by his side. She quickly altered it in her mind; there was more blood and it was redder, her father's pallor was green; the priest's black robes were transformed into rich vestments and he had many white-robed attendants; there were many tall candles and the smell of incense mingled with what she termed "the odour of sanctity", a scented emanation from her father. She added incidents. In fact her father had never recovered consciousness but now she saw that his eyes had opened and he had looked at her and smiled, because he knew he was going straight to heaven, and solemnly given into her care her mother and the children.

She enjoyed the funeral because it seemed to her no ordinary funeral, just as her father had been no ordinary man. All through it she behaved in accordance with her idea of what was due to him and to herself. She held her back straighter than ever, letting her head drop reverently forward and keeping her eyes half-shut. No expense was spared by the Kenny's and everything was done in great style. But Margaret did not know who paid and she assumed that it was a tribute from the church and congregation to her father's sanctity. Wreaths were sent by people she had never heard of. She heard praise of her father on all sides.

The anti-climax which followed the funeral threw her back into unrelieved misery. Everything was over. Her heart was broken and could not, would not, mend. She cried a great deal. Sometimes the tears stopped, giving way to dry, uncontrollable sobs and then she would fall into a state of exhausted, thoughtless calm. But the sight of something associated with her father, and there were so many things in the house which brought him sharply to mind, would set her crying again. During this time she thought she would like to die too. She longed for a sudden sad end like his.

After her days of crying came days of brooding. She thought over everything he had said to her on their morning walks to the shop. She was certain now that he knew all along he was going to die. He had had a premonition or, more likely, an apparition from his favourite St. Joseph, who had told him of his coming death. That was why he had kept telling her about his wishes for the future of his children. Now she was melancholy and alone. No one else in the family knew of her father's ambitions and shared them as she did. Elizabeth might understand but she was too small. In any case, Margaret did not want anyone else to share them. It was dreadful that her father had died while he was poor. People might now think of him as a poor man, like other poor men, whereas he was not really that at all.

She hated her mother. She never admitted this for it had no place at all in her picture of herself. No, she saw herself as her mother's friend and comforter and she tried to see her mother as overwhelmed by this terrible bereavement. But when she saw her mother going about her daily tasks exactly as she had done before, cooking in the same way, washing and ironing as she had always done and making those wretched sweets, and even humming and looking cheerful while she did it, she was seized with rage and, with a face like a thundercloud, talked relentlessly about her father until tears had come into her mother's eyes and she herself was sobbing. Then she felt a little better but the fury remained.

She considered it would have been more fitting to fast, to eat dry bread and water, to put all the children into deep mourning, to do anything unusual in the nature of a sacrifice to mark the occasion. When the children laughed and played she would stop them and set about depressing them and making them feel guilty. To the rest of the family she seemed intolerable and inexplicable. She kept urging her mother to dispose of things which belonged to her father because it upset her to see them. Yet when Mrs Reilly finally sold his clothes, Margaret flew into a temper and told her it was wrong to do such a thing. They should have been given to the poor.

"And who is poorer than us, I'd like to know?" said her mother. Margaret found this question stupid and unpleasant. Although they were poor for the moment, they were not members of "the poor".

It was the local priest who consoled her during long talks after confession. He spoke to her of her father's saintly character and his words confirmed her belief that her father had gone straight to heaven. He had become a sort of presence to whom one could pray, like a second guardian angel. As he had borne such a striking resemblance to the thin-faced bearded saints on the crudely coloured holy pictures which she collected, she thought it might not be long before he performed miracles and was canonised. This had the effect of restoring to her not only her father, but also her self-esteem and sense of the family's importance, so rudely punctured by her mother's natural (which she called "ordinary") behaviour. A saint was higher than a prince or a cardinal.

Mrs Reilly had shed many tears of genuine sorrow. She had loved Patrick and she missed him. There had been no comfort for her in the splendours of the funeral and thoughts of his sanctity. But she had seven children on her hands and little money coming in. There was much to occupy her practical mind and she wasted no time in discussions with Margaret. She acted quickly.

She stepped up the sweet making with machinery provided by the Kenny's. Her boiled sweets were sold in the market place twice a week off a barrow. The toffee was sold not only in the shop but a fair quantity was sent up north in big boxes where it was called "genuine Doncaster butterscotch". She organised her children as though she were running a factory. She bought her raw materials in bulk at reduced prices and soon learnt where to go for the best value. She did her own accounts.

She had no qualms about accepting charity and took as much as she could get. She paid many visits to her relations, to the priest and to the sisters at the poor school. She knew how to tell a sad story and they had cause to be sorry for her. The result was that some sort of school was found for the three youngest boys where they could be out of the way, free of charge, for the moment. Elizabeth was packed off to live with Aunt Kenny. Only the two eldest and the baby were left with her in the house.

Margaret disagreed with all these arrangements. What annoyed her most was that she was not consulted although she told her mother again and again that her father had said that she would be like a second parent when he died. She felt pretty certain that the place where the boys had gone was an orphanage and they would learn nothing. She was shocked to hear her mother say to Aunt Kenny, who had offered to pay for Elizabeth to go to St. Joseph's, that schooling was a waste of time and she would rather have the cash itself or the value of it in some other form. She made a strong protest, quoting her father once more. Mrs Reilly was angry and amused. "Sure will you never stop telling me what your Da said and what he did not say?"

With four of the children provided for and money coming in from the sweets Mrs Reilly managed. Her life began to change. For the first time she felt free to do as she pleased. Fond as she had been of

Patrick, she had always had to mind herself when he was there. Now if she had a bit over she did without new clothes and kept it to pay for a glass or two of beer at the pub. She soon made friends there who drank and joked with her. Women of the neighbourhood, with whom she had always been friendly, but who had been considered unsuitable company by Patrick, could now drop in for a cup of tea and a chat in the afternoons. They were mostly Catholic Irish like herself, good-hearted and gay, fond of gossiping and telling fortunes with the tea leaves, where they saw dark strangers, trips over the water and unexpected presents. They were all poor and mostly cleaners, but they often gave their old clothes and toys for the children and always lent a hand with the sweet making and wrapping.

Margaret liked these women and listened as credulously as her mother to the fortunes, but at the same time she felt that they were not "refined" and would never have come to the house in her father's time. She struggled to retain a picture of her mother as gentle and ladylike. She made excuses for her. Of course her mother knew perfectly well that they were coarse, but she was too kind and polite not to ask them in.

Reluctantly she enjoyed the jokes and the talk. Reluctantly she found some pleasure in turning the handle of the sweet machine and watching coloured fish drop onto a tray. She hated wheeling the barrow through the streets to the market in her ragged clothes. The barrow was heavy and she must concentrate to keep it balanced. Once in the market she felt more sheltered and could not help responding to the friendliness of other stallholders. She gave sweets liberally to their children. Often she took her sweet-selling seriously, thinking of making money to further her plans and, carried away, she shouted herself hoarse to attract custom and gave orders to Michael not to idle.

Then suddenly the sight of a well-dressed person or a cultured voice awoke her pride and she thought with shame about her present life, noting how harsh her voice was, how grimy and rough her hands, how ragged and dirty her clothes. She told herself that the life she was leading did not count, that it was a period of marking time between her past life with her father (now changed beyond recognition into a life of continuous prosperity and elegance) and some future time when she would earn a lot of money and mix with aristocratic and refined people.

At last she found someone in whom she could confide. Sister Aloysius, headmistress of the poor school where Elizabeth went, came into her life. At first she went to see the nun with messages from her mother. Later she visited her on her own initiative. Sister Aloysius was interested in the Reilly family; Elizabeth was quite the cleverest pupil in the school; she had seen Patrick once or twice and was struck by his appearance; now Margaret made a strong impression on her. She questioned her about her education and her life and she felt sorry for her. Margaret did not want sympathy but she believed the nun could help her. She was also taken with the pale face, white hands and gentle voice. When she learnt that she was the daughter of wealthy parents, who had given up her life to teaching the poor, she looked on her as the finest example of "the perfect lady". She revealed her consuming desire to better herself and her family. She spoke to her of her father and said she knew he was a saint.

The nun listened and advised her to be patient. She grew fond of her, lent her books and encouraged her to read. She gave her a French grammar and told her to study it.

By the time she was fifteen and a half Margaret had waded through many of the milder classics, she could read French and speak a little. Because Sister Aloysius was half-French and told her about the country she longed to go there. Her longing changed to determination. She could think of nothing else. She must leave Cardiff, the scene of all her misfortunes, she must get right away and start afresh and then everything would be all right. On her own, in the world, she could do wonders. She was vague about what work she would do and how she would make money but she felt boundless self confidence. And even though her family might need her, what could she do for them so long as her own position did not improve?

She brushed aside the suggestion that she should be patient. What was the use of being patient? What was it for? She pressed Sister Aloysius to do something for her now. She was quite old enough to leave home. She had been for years. She begged, she implored, she pestered. Any sort of job in France would do so long as it was not domestic service.

Sister Aloysius wrote to a cousin of hers and asked her if she would take Margaret as an English teacher to her children.

"And please don't tell her what I am doing now. Please say nothing about the family," Margaret insisted.

The cousin, Mme Chantabrie, wife of a wealthy wine merchant in Bordeaux, replied that she would be willing to take an English girl. Mrs Reilly gave her consent because she knew that her daughter would go whether she had it or not. Mrs Kenny was asked to lend the money for the fare.

"I shall pay it back, of course," said Margaret. "I shall soon be earning a lot of money and I only want it as a loan."

8

When she was just sixteen Margaret left Cardiff. The world was opening before her and she must be a success. Any sadness at leaving her family was soon banished by the excitement of travel. To be on her own in a train, a speeding, puffing train and then on a boat, above the heaving waves, made her eyes shine and her heart beat hard.

She watched the other travellers. It was the women she was interested in, their clothes and their manners. The more she looked at them the more she was struck by her own shabbiness. She had put up her hair to look older and wore it piled on top of her head under one of her aunt's hats. She realised that she did not look grown up, but ridiculous, and everyone was treating her as though she were a child. The hat was wrong; her hair was wrong; her clothes were terrible. She studied every well-dressed lady she saw in order to learn what sort of clothes you ought to wear and how you should wear them. On the boat she pressed her face against the glass which divided her from the first-class passengers and stared at two ladies who wore long travelling coats trimmed with fur. She saw that their hands were gloved and that they took small steps and made birdlike movements. She resolved to imitate them.

In France the ladies were even more elegant. One in particular caught her eye, a tall thin fair lady, busy saying goodbye to a number of people. What polished gestures she made. This scene might have been rehearsed for days! What a host of attendants she seemed to have, burdened with rugs and cases, and with what deference she was treated by all! Such a person must be extraordinarily happy. Margaret herself had no rug, no gloves, no paraphernalia, nothing but a purse in her pocket and one small, shabby box with some awful underclothes in it. By the time she reached Bordeaux her excitement was at its height but the knowledge of her disadvantages weighed on her.

At the station she was met by so well-dressed and sweet-smelling a lady that she imagined it must be Mme Chantabrie herself. It was the governess Mme Dufour and she held out a hand and introduced herself. The coachman relieved Margaret of her shameful box and handed her into a closed carriage. As they drove through the town she took no note of the streets but stared at the governess as though in a dream.

From the outside the house looked nothing out of the ordinary but once the front door was opened all was splendour. Great gilt mirrors multiplied a profusion of tall plants. A magnificent, sparkling chandelier hung low. A flowered carpet with a rich, red background looked as though it had been poured over the curving staircase. There were doors to right and left. Menservants in special clothes moved from one door to another. There were many distant noises and such an impression of activity that you would have thought it was a feast day.

A maid advanced from a distant door, over the marble floor, to show her to her room. Mme Dufour accompanied her as far as the first landing and explained that she would come and fetch her as soon as she was washed and changed. Margaret followed the maid along passages and up more stairs, all carpeted. She could not believe that anyone lived in so marvellous an establishment. To be only a servant in such a house was to be fortunate.

The room allotted to her was one of the smallest and barest in the house, but she found no fault with it. She marvelled at the way all the furniture matched down to the smallest detail of edging and handles. Only her box looked out of place. And then, of course, she herself looked wrong. If only Sister Aloysius had said something about clothes. If only someone had told her. If only her skirt was longer and if only her boots did not show.

Mme Dufour had told her to change but she could not change. She had nothing to change into. She could take off her coat and that was all. This was her best dress, bought second hand a year ago and now too short. She had brought no others with her because, even in Cardiff, her other clothes were appalling. She washed carefully, did her hair as best she could and looked at herself in the long mirror.

She looked poor, she looked as though she came from the Cardiff slums.

It made no difference to her that her face was attractive for she would far sooner have been hideously ugly but in the right clothes. In fact her face looked awful to her, so childish and not at all aristocratic. As for her hands, they told a tale of sweet making and trundling barrows, with their ragged, black nails which would not come clean, and their rough skin.

She opened her box and bundled the grey-looking, patched underclothes and nightdresses into the bottom drawer, thankful that no one need ever see them. She hung her coat in the wardrobe and placed her hat on the bottom shelf. That was all there was to go in there. She sat on the bed and waited.

After a long time Mme Dufour came for her. Margaret had decided to say nothing about her clothes until someone else did. She was sure that the governess despised her for them, but at all costs she must show no embarrassment. "You can always tell a lady by the way she holds herself," she remembered. "It is not fine clothes that matter." As she was shown down the stairs and along a wide corridor, she held herself straight, took tiny steps and held her hands together in front of her.

Mme Dufour stopped outside a tall, ornately framed door and knocked. She opened it and gently pushed Margaret in before her. The room was vast and scattered with little tables, footstools and small upholstered chairs. Everything was flowery and feminine as though in wait for a rush of short visits from elegant ladies. By the fire sat a lady in silk and lace bending over some embroidery, concentrating on it as though her life depended on the quick completion of the work. She looked up at them for the briefest moment, motioned them to come nearer and continued with her work. Like the lady on the platform this person's movements had a wonderful well-rehearsed quality.

It seemed to have been pre-arranged that Mme Dufour should question Margaret in Madame's presence while Madame simply listened. The interrogation was lengthened by the translation of questions and answers into English and French. The governess had forgotten much of her English and her nervousness had obliterated Margaret's few words of French.

What was her age? What were the circumstances of her parents? What schooling had she had? Had she any experience of teaching children?

Margaret told the truth about her age and, while the translation was going on, prepared herself for the other answers. Her father was dead, she said, and her mother was therefore left badly off and had to take in a little sewing to help out. While her father had lived they had been extremely well off, for he was a merchant. Naturally they had lived in a large establishment outside Cardiff with carriages and servants and all the usual things. Her grandfather had been an admiral, that was her mother's father. Her other grandparents had died before she was born but she knew them to be landed gentry in Ireland.

Mme Dufour glanced cynically at the girl. Margaret, her level eyes looking bright and honest, her hands unmoving in her lap, continued. She had been educated at St. Joseph's, that was the very best school in Cardiff. She had done very well at her lessons and had always been first at everything. Naturally she had no experience of teaching, because until her father died, and that was under two years ago, none of them dreamt that they would ever have to earn a living. However she had experience of children because she was the eldest of a large family. There was a pause. No one made a comment.

Mme Dufour explained her duties. The first thing to remember was that she must speak nothing but English to the children whether they understood or not. She would take meals with them upstairs, accompany them on their walks and look after them all the time they were not actually having lessons. She would be present at their lessons and during that time could do their mending. On Sundays they lunched downstairs with their parents and she would go with them. She must try to interest the children in English and see that they had a good pronunciation.

"How many children are there and what are their ages?" Margaret asked boldly. The two ladies looked a little taken aback. There were three children, Jacques, aged twelve, Angélique, aged ten and Marie-Louise, aged seven.

The interview came to a close without one direct word from Madame, no enquiries about her relation, Sister Aloysius, no mention of the long journey, no hope that Margaret might be happy, nothing. Quietly and firmly Margaret was led from the room.

Then came the introduction to the children, far more alarming than the adults. Whereas Madame and Mme Dufour had given nothing away, the children looked her up and down with their black, worldly-wise little eyes and the conclusions to which they came were written large all over their smirking faces. As the door closed behind her she could hear them laugh. She remembered her father's admonition never to humiliate anyone (in spite of which she had succeeded in making many people feel small) and she decided, "They have very bad manners." This consoled her.

For the first few days her sense of inferiority, of *looking* inferior while not really *being* inferior at all, made her long to show them that she was as good as they were. Whenever possible she reminisced to the children about her own childhood in the great mansion and wooded acres of her merchant father. At the same time her delight in her new surroundings made her wish to please in order to be kept on and so she put up with things she disliked. The children treated her as a servant and asked her to fetch things for them because, until she came, a servant had always looked after them when Mme Dufour was not there. Indignantly she did their bidding.

She soon realised that it was Mme Dufour who would pronounce the verdict on her. This lady, always dressed in black, always calm and calculating, was neither kind nor unkind and neither liked nor disliked the English girl. Dispassionately, she weighed up the advantages of having her in the house, watched her with the children and watched the children with her.

Margaret was a quick learner. By listening carefully to what was said during lessons she improved her French and increased her general knowledge, besides noting that Mme Dufour, like her father, had maxims to which she adhered. To her, actions were either *comme il faut* or not *comme il faut* or, on a slightly higher plane, *distingué* or not *distingué*. These were sentiments with which Margaret could sympathise, closely related as they were to her belief in "refinement". She echoed them in the presence of the governess. When, in time, the matter of clothes was raised she could say with perfect sincerity and no trace of a smile that she was sure that whatever Mme Dufour advised would be *comme il faut*, and Mme Dufour was pleased.

It was decided to provide Margaret with two dresses and to deduct the cost from her wages. Further discussion revealed that she had no corset and since it was impossible to look well without a tiny waist, these also had to be found. Finally they thought it wisest to fit her out completely, shoes, gloves and all, and she was told that there could be no question of pay besides for a very long time.

9

Margaret was transformed. Madame's maid showed her how to do her hair. Her well-developed bust showed to advantage above a pulled-in waist. The grey dress for every day was by no means plain in cut. The blue dress for Sundays and occasions was a mass of braid trimmings, tucks, pleats and gathers. The skirts were pulled tight across the hips in front but were voluminous at the hem. The sleeves were enormously full at the shoulder and very tight at the wrist.

She learned to the full the importance of clothes. She was not at all vain and never became so because at home they had always said that Elizabeth was the beauty, Michael was the handsome one and that was that. She loved to be well dressed because the clothes were the label of one's status and made all the difference to the attitude of others. With the right clothes came a heartening sensation of self confidence. Without them the social fight could not be successfully waged. The three children behaved more carefully towards her. The servants were more respectful. Everyone might know it was Madame who provided the clothes but it made no difference. Once Margaret had them on it was her prestige, rather than Madame's, which gained. And, of course, it was not long before she had fully re-clothed her family and herself in her past life and would say of a dress which she saw on Angélique or Marie-Louise, "I had a dress very similar to that when we lived at Newport."

In her new clothes her naturally domineering nature could assert itself. She no longer fetched things for the children and they were soon taught to obey her. At the first sign of impertinence from them she put on a stern expression and said, "I expect you to behave in a way becoming to children in your position." This English sentence, which they did not wholly understand, they soon learnt by heart and treated as some mystic formula which had the approval of Mme Dufour.

Margaret never liked the children, probably because they had hurt her pride when she was most vulnerable and she remained unrelenting in her criticisms of them to herself. They seemed to her deceitful, pleasure-loving and heartless. She lectured them constantly on the need for self-discipline, kindness and truthfulness (she never considered herself other than truthful and, if taxed, would have said that there was a vast difference between her exaggerations in order to uphold family honour and the ill-natured petty deceptions of her charges). As the result of much badgering they acquired a faint appearance of these qualities, especially in her presence. They respected and feared her and were very glad when she was absent from the nursery.

She was not at all happy about her relations with them. She liked to discipline but she also liked to love. She had found no difficulty in believing that she loved each member of her family and many girls at school most of the time. Often she had felt a strong impulse to give them pleasure or to comfort them when they were sad. Always she had enjoyed being appealed to. She found Jacques self-absorbed and cruel, Angélique vain, rude to servants and hysterical, Marie-Louise a sneak and show off.

However, at a conscious level, it made little difference to the children whether she loved them or not. They were not interested in affection. They disliked each other and were indifferent to Mme Dufour. They assumed that they loved their mother and there was much talk of *"votre chère maman"* from the governess. Most people assumed that Madame loved the children and that, had it not been for her many engagements which she did not enjoy but which she had endured with a good grace for the sake of her position, she would have had them close to her all day. When Madame paid a short visit upstairs and sat gracefully on a chair while the children gathered round her, she smiled graciously at Margaret and told her how happy these moments were.

Margaret believed her and admired her in every way. Madame was related to Sister Aloysius. Madame was obviously a devout Catholic because among the flowers and plants of her splendid sitting room there nestled (as in shrines) crucifixes, rosaries and holy pictures. Madame was also *distinguée* and a model of elegance and although she was sometimes unapproachable her manners were perfect.

Madame began to like Margaret. She was pleased with her religious nature, with her level eyes and upright carriage, with her firmness with the children and above all with her naïve, unspoken admiration of Madame herself, so much more flattering than the calculated tributes which Mme Dufour never failed to pay. It was pleasant to see herself as the ideal of this young girl.

Soon Madame liked to have Margaret with her when she was going for a drive or shopping. She did not treat her as an equal or as a servant. Her tone was one of affectionate condescension and the subjects of which she spoke were general: clothes, the houses which they passed and books. There was never a word about the children. At first she left Margaret outside while she went into one of the smart shops she patronised, but later she took her in with her, not always of course, so that each time she did so it seemed a favour.

No one could have called Madame a beauty. Her nose was too long and curved downwards, her eyes were small and asymmetrical and there was a rough, scraggy look about her neck. Everything about her was sparse and thin, from her hair to her voice and she had no particular liveliness of mind or temperament on which she could fall back as an attraction. She experienced no very heightened form of pleasure although she surrounded herself with all that might evoke it. In spite of this she remained contented by performing every act with correctness and a sense of ritual. The daily round of her life remained absorbing to her, like an actress in an unending play, where picking an object off a table or looking out of a window must be done "in character". And here was a girl who was convinced by the performance, who saw behind each gesture a rich unstated mass of feeling and imagination, who never noticed Madame's physical defects and who thought her near to perfection. As time went on she saw more and more of her when she was not visiting or receiving visitors. Naturally there was no question of taking the girl into company.

Margaret learnt many things about fashion. She discovered that just as Bordeaux seemed so much smarter than Cardiff, so Bordeaux itself was greatly inferior to Paris. Madame, a Parisian by birth, prized only those things which had come straight from the capital and found everything around her dreadfully provincial.

Monsieur was to be seen on Sundays only. He was a large, red-faced, black-haired man with a thick moustache and wiry hair in his nostrils and on the backs of his hands. Margaret, who still admired only those who looked pale and saintly, found him very coarse. He rarely came up to see his children and when he did he never knew what to say to them or to her and stood with hands behind his back and feet apart staring at them. He was, in fact, smiling, but the length and depth of his moustache concealed the movements of his upper lip. *"Eh bien?"* or *"Alors?"* he would ask once or twice to make conversation. Sometimes one of the children would say something, sometimes there would be no answer at all and, smiling his invisible smile, he would leave the room.

During lunch on Sundays he gave himself up wholly to eating as long as there was something on his plate, and between courses he crumbled bread, held his glass to the light, smelt it and mumbled to the servants, as though getting through a meal was quite a business and there was no time for trifling conversation. Only Marie-Louise was at all garrulous and most of the meal was silent.

10

When she was eighteen she called herself Marguerite and from now on we shall call her Marguerite too. This made no difference to the employers and pupils because they had always addressed her as *Meess Marguerite*, but Mrs Reilly was surprised when she saw the French name at the bottom of the letter and it was not until she had seen it several times that she herself adopted the new spelling.

Marguerite's face had lengthened and this was an improvement. Her brown hair was glossy, abundant and well arranged. Her wardrobe had increased. In the top drawers of her dressing table were beads, brooches, artificial flowers and several pairs of gloves, nothing of any great value, and all handed on from Madame. These were prized as the appurtenances of the well-dressed woman. Marguerite knew how to wear a hat at the correct angle, she studied the fashion magazines from Paris and she managed to look dashing although she lacked neatness and as often as not had something held up by a pin.

She had educated herself by studying the children's textbooks and glancing through books in the library. She chose a book entirely for its binding and for that reason plodded through the red leather editions of Molière, Corneille and Racine, making very little of them.

She became sufficiently familiar with the names of famous authors and the titles of their principal works to pass herself off as cultivated and she picked up useful phrases from the literary periodicals on Madame's table. When the occasion arose she could say the right thing. This was all she wanted to know. Literature did not interest her for its own sake because she had no questions about life which needed an answer, having taken over a set of ideas and principles from her father which she had never once reconsidered. There were simply a few details to fill in, a few pieces of worldly knowledge and these could best be learnt by observing the behaviour of someone like Madame. Conversation she looked on as an exercise in behaving according to fixed rules, certainly not as a means of providing oneself with new ideas and stimulation. Her picture of life was satisfactory and unshakable.

The children were well under control. Her relations with Mme Dufour were most cordial because there was a sad story of early widowhood in the governess's life and Marguerite, a sympathetic listener, sat through many an account of the circumstances of the bereavement with a look of great interest and compassion on her face. Besides, there was no question of jealousy between them because Mme Dufour was anxious to secure a place in a noble household and therefore it mattered little to her whether the Chantabries liked Marguerite or not.

Marguerite was worried about her family. She was earning very little and she felt that it was up to her to provide the money to educate the boys and take her mother away from the alley.

Sensing that something was on her mind Madame asked her lightly if she was contented, expecting, of course, a flow of assurances and gratitude.

Marguerite was moved by Madame's interest. "I'm very happy," she replied. "Everyone has been kind to me and if I had only myself to consider I should be glad to stay here as long as you liked. But I have to think of my family. It's a matter of money. You see I must help my brothers and sisters."

Madame laughed. "They must learn to fend for themselves. After all, you will most likely marry and have another family to think of."

Marguerite was surprised. "Oh no, Madame, I don't think I shall marry. I have never imagined I would. My father expected me to look after the others. When he was dying he looked at me and begged me to look after them. I promised him I always would. So it

43

would be quite wrong to have another family until they were provided for. Besides, I know my father wouldn't have wished me to marry and if you had known him you would understand. He was not like other men at all."

The suggestion of marriage disconcerted her, causing a rush of strong emotions she could not understand. The idea was hateful, repulsive and wrong, and yet it was pleasing. There would never be another man like her father. She looked reproachfully at Madame. "He was a real saint. He really was. It's not just what I think. Everyone thought so. They all said so, including the priest."

There was a silence during which Madame thought it wiser to say no more.

Marguerite continued. "So you see I must try and earn as much as I can because my mother is very badly off at the moment. She is such a delicate, refined lady. The blow of losing her husband was too much for her and she has six children on her hands."

"But you said they were all at very good schools."

"Oh yes, they are. Our relations are very rich and help a great deal."

"In that case I think you might feel satisfied."

"Madame, my father did not believe in accepting charity."

Madame reflected; she wanted to keep Marguerite with her and the children had improved under her influence.

"I want to take a diploma," said Marguerite. "I've heard you can take a teaching diploma and then you are a qualified teacher or governess. If you'd give me permission to attend classes and sit for the examination I should feel that I'm doing something. And then when I was qualified I could start earning."

"You must understand that your keep and clothes are quite an expense. You're doing very well indeed for a girl of eighteen. Why, in the noblest houses in France you wouldn't do half so well—I have been very generous to you. It's my nature. My friends are always laughing at me for being extravagant and generous. Of course I quite see that you would feel your future secure, and although I couldn't possibly afford to pay you more at the moment, I might pay a little towards your classes and I'm quite willing to allow you to work for the diploma without deducting anything for the time you are not working for me."

"And then when I have the diploma?"

Madame laughed. "Ah, that's looking rather far ahead. We shall see then. Mme Dufour may be leaving at the end of the year and in that case you might take her place. That would mean a rise in pay."

She did not say just how much the increase would be. She also failed to mention that it would mean quite a saving for herself because Mme Dufour was being paid for teaching three children and refused to take a penny less, although Jacques was now at college, where Marguerite would be paid for teaching two.

Mme Dufour left to educate a future duke. Marguerite took her diploma, became a proper governess and was given a large bedroom and more money. What she earned she saved and then fresh worries beset her. How was she to spend the money? If she sent it to her mother what would her mother do with it? Could she be sure that it would go on the boys' education? Elizabeth now had a scholarship to St. Joseph's and Michael was too old to do anything about, but what about the three boys in the orphanage? Would her mother have them at home and let them go to a good Catholic school in Cardiff? If they were day boys she could just manage the fees, but would her mother be willing to let them live at home? It was no use sending money unless she was sure. Letters were no way of persuading her mother. Mrs Reilly was extremely non-committal as a correspondent, found it a great strain to write a letter at all, and fell back on such phrases as "We are all well here and send love", "Glad to hear you are keeping well" and "Busy as usual".

As the money accumulated the worries increased. Signs of dissatisfaction were observed by Madame who now found Marguerite indispensable. There was another talk. This time Marguerite did not attempt to say what was really on her mind because it was not possible to admit that she did not trust her mother.

"I'm very worried about my mother," she said. "It's a very long time since I saw them and they miss me. I'm particularly worried about my little sister Elizabeth because she looks on me as a second mother. I feel I really must see them soon."

A day or two later she asked for a holiday. "My father would never have wished me to be separated from them for so long."

Madame hummed and hawed. She was sick and tired of this wretched family who, by all accounts, seemed to spend their time writing sentimental letters. If Marguerite did not go she would become impossible. If she did go she might never want to come back and it would be very tiresome having to find another English girl who would probably not be half so suitable. She was put out. "If you go I feel you may not return."

Marguerite saw her advantage. She had long planned to bring Elizabeth abroad and start her on the road to earning. She had always felt that it was up to the girls to raise the family. And if Elizabeth came then one of the boys could go to Aunt Kenny, and that would mean two provided for. Now was her chance. "Of course I shall come back. I've been so happy here and I'm hoping to bring my sister back with me. Perhaps you know of someone who might like a young English girl of good family?"

"But I thought she was only a child."

"Oh no," Marguerite lied, "she is sixteen. I dare say I did make her sound younger because I always remember her as I last saw her and that's over two years ago. She could be a treasure in a house like this. Brilliant at her lessons and wonderful at sewing and embroidery. And she's very refined."

Madame could do with someone who was good with her needle. In this one respect Marguerite had been a great disappointment to her. Also if it were arranged that Elizabeth was to come back with her, Marguerite would be bound to return. She did not hesitate for long.

"I shall take her myself," she said with a sigh. "But of course, there can be no question of pay. She will be in a good house and it will give me pleasure to bring two sisters together."

"You are the kindest employer in the world," said Marguerite.

It was agreed that she should be given three weeks' leave and half her travelling expenses. Madame was amazed at her own generosity.

11

On Cardiff station Marguerite knew that here she looked a very fine lady. Porters approached her as a sure customer and she played up to this, saying as though it were a mere whim, "I shall carry my luggage myself, thank you. It is very light." She was economising in every way in order to have as much money left for the others as possible.

Her first evening at home was upsetting. She had anticipated many touching and tender scenes, taking it for granted that nothing could be so wonderful as to be back with the family once more, imagining the happy faces of her brothers and sisters as they crowded round her, forgetting that they were nearly all away.

But as soon as she reached the slummy area in which her mother lived her heart sank and by the time she stood outside the dirty streaked front door and looked up at the small grimy windows with their torn yellow curtains, her depression was like a dull headache. By contrast with the splendours of the Chantabrie residence, this miserable place looked a hundred times more squalid than before. The picture she had painted of her mother to others had ended by becoming almost reality for her and therefore she felt that her mother had steadily been sinking to these depths while she was away. And not only had she sunk but she was happy.

The slim, hour-glass figures of Madame and her friends had become the norm of the feminine form for her and she saw her mother's stout waistless uncorsetted shape with distaste. Her ears, now accustomed to the thin precise sound of French and well-turned sentences, were appalled by the broad richness of her mother's accent, a vintage blend of Irish, North Country and Cardiff, and the spontaneous, untrimmed phrases which rolled out. She even disapproved of her mother's vitality and high spirits and would have given anything to see her languid, sad and pale.

None of the others appeared. Surely her mother should have made a special effort to assemble them for her return.

At first, of course, mother and daughter embraced again and again, and there were tears of maternal joy and pride in Mrs Reilly's eyes. But later, when she addressed her daughter as "Maggie" she was told sharply, "Please don't call me that, mother. My name is Marguerite now. It is necessary for my work." From that moment they were not at ease with each other.

Marguerite was sorry to see the sweet machinery and the display of pans and trays and wrappings. "I had forgotten the place was full of these," she said disdainfully.

She ate very little of the supper prepared for her. She seemed constantly on the lookout in case her clothes got dirty, looking at the seat of her chair before she sat, gathering her skirts round her away from the floor. However she felt tired and not at her strongest and therefore decided to postpone serious discussion until the next day.

The following morning she got down to business. She questioned her mother closely, sitting bolt upright on one of the kitchen chairs and looking as stern as a judge.

Where was Michael? She had expected that he at least would be at home. Was he usually away like this? And what had happened to the baby? Had she been sent away too, and if so, where, when she was so young? She had been certain that she would find at least Michael and the baby. It was strange to find her mother alone like this, with none of her children. Were the boys still at school and what were they being taught there? Did they write at all? Might she see their letters?

Mrs Reilly, who had brushed aside questions the night before with a cheerful, "I'll tell you all about it tomorrow," as though she had the best of news, was on the defensive.

"Sure and Michael's only away for one night. He's always at home at other times but this time he was working over on the other side of town and he stayed the night with his boss."

"What sort of work is this?"

"Oh, it's a fine job, some sort of building work, I think, and it'll lead to a great trade."

"What sort of building do you mean?" Marguerite hoped against hope that it might be something like surveying or doing accounts.

"Well wait till I see now... Of course he's starting only, but I think he can turn his hand to most things, a bit of bricklaying and tiling and of course painting and that. He's real clever with his hands and the lad likes it and that's the great thing."

It was not the great thing so far as Marguerite was concerned. "You mean he's just a building labourer. I'd hoped he might do something better. And where's the baby, Kathie?"

"Well, the nuns advised me to put her into a good school. It's a fine place, a grand school and she'll be learning everything there."

"I suppose it's an orphanage."

"Ah, no. It's not that at all. Why, half the children have a parent alive, they say, and the other half will all be having uncles and aunts and relations, not like real orphans who haven't a soul in the world."

"Have you been there?"

"I've not. But I've been meaning to go all the time."

"Who took her there?"

"One of the sisters."

"But she's so young to be away from home."

"Sure she's very advanced for her age and doesn't mind a bit. The nuns tell me she's happy and full of fun."

It was the same with all the questions. The answers were unsatisfactory. Her mother was satisfied with what she had done and defended herself, not out of a feeling of guilt but out of a good-natured wish to avoid a quarrel. Nothing could make her see how wrong she was. Michael was a worker and he hadn't a chance now. The other three boys were probably not learning a thing and the poor baby was in some institution where she might be lonely and miserable and certainly not being taught the first steps in how to get on. Marguerite was indignant and baffled. There was too much to do, too little time and money to do it, and no co-operation from her mother.

In the late afternoon she visited her aunt. Mrs Kenny was full of admiration for her niece's appearance and plied her with questions about her life, the house she lived in, Paris fashions, what Madame wore and what sort of furniture she had. Marguerite was vague about the furnishings. "Oh, everything's very elegant, don't you know? Large rooms, all antique stuff. No, I don't know which period, but a very good period, the best. And many different styles too, and plants and flowers everywhere. There is nothing like it in Cardiff." On clothes she was more specific. "Yes, much fuller here, and pulled in there, and not so much bustle and more padding just there. A little shorter, I think, and plainer colours, coffee colour and tobacco colour."

"You won't know Lizzie, Maggie, any more than she'll know you," said Mrs Kenny.

"I'm called Marguerite now, owing to my work, you know. And it think it would be better to call Elizabeth by her proper name. I always do. It sounds better."

Elizabeth arrived home for tea, flushed from running, surprised and delighted to see her sister. She was prettier than ever and Aunt Kenny kept her in good clothes. She threw her arms around Marguerite's neck. "What lovely clothes you've got! And what thin gloves! You do look a swell."

"Where did you get that expression from?" said Marguerite, but she was pleased with her sister's appearance.

During tea Elizabeth prattled excitedly; she had won a prize for needlework; she was first in class; she was voted the best at acting and had been given the part of Cinderella in the end-of-term play.

All this was very well, thought Marguerite, but it seemed very childish and she wondered whether she could pass her off as sixteen. In a country like France, where the tiniest tots were sophisticated, what would she seem?

After tea she told them of her scheme, expecting no opposition.

"But she's not fourteen yet," said Mrs Kenny. "It's too young to go away from her family and earn her living in a strange country."

"It will not be like earning her living. She will be in a very nice house and with little to do. She will simply be a companion to the children. As for leaving her family, I really can't see how you can say that when she will be with me."

"What about her schooling? I thought you were a one for education. She's doing very well where she is and the nuns say she can train to be a teacher later on, and that's a really good career and one your father would have liked."

"I know best what my father would have liked. She will never have an opportunity like this again. It's a house such as you never see in Cardiff, everything is so elegant and just right. And once she's been there she'll be able to go anywhere and hold her own. And as for her education, well I'm a qualified governess now and I can teach her, and besides that she'll learn French and there are all the books you need to read there."

Elizabeth listened round-eyed. She was cutting such a figure here that she did not want to go away, but on the other hand Bordeaux sounded exciting. She was given no chance to express her feelings for no one consulted her.

The struggle between Mrs Kenny and her niece did not last long. Each tried to drag in Mrs Reilly but she refused to take sides because she did not care which of them had Elizabeth and she would rather have had the girl herself to help with the sweet making. All she wanted was to be left in peace and she longed for the day when Marguerite would leave Cardiff once more. Mrs Kenny kept visiting her sister and talking to her. She also tried to work on Elizabeth.

There were other struggles too. Michael was obstinate.

"But Michael, if I were to find the money," Marguerite insisted, "surely you would like to go to classes and then do clerical work. Or you could be a shop assistant in some nice draper's. There are many openings of a refined kind if only you would look for them. And I would do everything to help you in the way of clothes."

Michael said nothing and looked at the floor, his handsome face clouded.

"But you can't possibly want to be an ordinary labourer? What would father have said?" She was up against a stone wall and so, for the moment only, she washed her hands of him.

Then there was Kathleen she had her on her mind and decided that she must go and see her. It was a day's outing and when she arrived the nuns seemed reluctant to let her see the child. She should have written to make an appointment. She quelled them with a rather overbearing manner, angry at the suggestion that she should go all that way in vain and a trace of indignation remained when her little sister was brought into the parlour. She found the child pale, unhappy, bewildered and ignorant about most things, including her family, just able to read and write, anxious and so shy that she could talk only in a hoarse whisper. Kathleen had never realised she had such a grand sister and more out of a feeling of the unexpectedness of life than a feeling of sadness she began to cry and could not stop.

Marguerite felt sorry for her and put an arm round her little hunched shoulders. She meant to comfort her and give her some reassurance but she found herself lecturing her about her Welsh accent and awkward manners. "Now do stop crying. I shall see to it that you leave here very soon and you will be given very good opportunities. But you must pull yourself together and make the best of them." Her voice sounded harsh and stern because she felt that Kathleen, aged five, did not grasp the importance of what was said to her.

She left her more bewildered and anxious than she had found her and yet all the way home she kept worrying about her, pitying the poor little thing, wondering if her clothes were warm enough, if she had enough to eat, if the nuns were kind and how she could arrange for her to be somewhere nice. She could see that the child needed love and attention but it never occurred to her that she might have displayed a little more affection during the visit.

It was as though she always relegated the expression of her real feelings of sympathy and affection to a future date. She must put them all on their feet first and she must spare no efforts to improve their position. And then when they were all settled there would be ample time for love and companionship, then she would do everything to make them happy. There could be no question of happiness until the status of the entire family had been raised.

She paid a long visit to Aunt Kenny and took her by surprise with a sweet conciliatory manner. "I have not been fair to you, Aunt," she said, "but I want you to know that I realise how kind your intentions have been and I am most grateful for all you have done for Elizabeth and myself. I know you will be sorry to part with Elizabeth and though it may seem selfish of me to take her, believe me, I am only doing what I think best. I know, too, that you have done quite enough for all of us and I should not ask any more favours of you, but who else is there to turn to? I am thinking of Kathleen. She is so young and it's not right that she should be far away from everyone in an orphanage. You know what these places are like. They probably teach her nothing and I could see that she was unhappy. I wonder if you would consider having her here in Elizabeth's place. It's no use asking mother to have her at home. She is too busy with sweet making and she hasn't any money." This was soon arranged to her satisfaction.

There were still the three boys to be seen to. The place with Aunt Kenny, which Marguerite had meant to allot to John or David had now gone to Kathleen. They were too far away to visit and discussions with Father Paine always led back to the same orphanage, because there was no other sort of boarding school which cost very little. A day school was out of the question because her mother would not have them at home.

"But Maggie—I mean Marguerite," said Mrs Reilly, "how can I have them here unless they work? It takes me all my time to keep myself and buy clothes for them. And then I have to pay for Mick and for Kathie's clothes, and it's as much as I can do to find the rent and a little bit more. And with three boys in the house I'd have so much to do there wouldn't be time for sweet making. If it was likely you'd be making enough to support the lot of us, clothes and schooling and all, it might be different, but all you can do is pay for the schooling and I'd have to find the rest. And where'd I find it?"

For the moment Marguerite had no choice but to leave them where they were. She wrote to them and sent them some warm underclothes. She must decide where to send money in future so that it would be spent in accordance with her instructions. She toyed with the idea of her aunt. That was no good because Mrs Kenny would be bound to tell her sister; sooner or later it would slip out.

There was Sister Aloysius. She had difficulty in persuading her but succeeded in the end. "It will be a real act of kindness if you do this for me. Then I know it will be spent as I say. I shall give you instructions each time and then you can write and tell me what is needed most."

Now that everything was arranged, not exactly as she would have liked, but as well as could be hoped for at the time, and now that the first impression of her mother and the alley had been softened, she relaxed. One final sum, allowing for Elizabeth's fare and her own, showed that there was thirty shillings over. She made a present of it to her mother and did it properly, with no conditions and no telling her what she should spend it on. She was reverting to the idea of her mother as a gentle helpless soul and she knew that she had bullied her.

Living with her family again, thinking of nothing else night and day had filled her with many conflicting emotions. Different impulses took hold of her. Sometimes it seemed all important that she should have her way in everything, that she should establish herself as unquestioned controller, not for her sake but for theirs. She knew what should be done and she alone could do it. At other times she wanted to give pleasure, to make a present, to agree at once without fuss. She had seemed unkind to her mother, she thought. She must not hurt her feelings more than necessary. But of course it had been necessary. Marguerite never reproached herself for a past action. She could do no wrong and should not be questioned. Her father's mantle of infallibility was now on her shoulders.

She returned to Sister Aloysius and begged her on no account to say where the money came from with which she was to buy clothes. It might upset Mrs Reilly dreadfully to think her own daughter had not sent the money to her directly. "You can say it's from charity. From someone who knew my father. This will hardly be a lie."

The nun smiled. "Very well. What a pity it is you were not a general."

Now that Kathleen's future was at stake, Marguerite took trouble to please her aunt. She saw her daily and consulted her about equipping Elizabeth. Together they visited the shops, compared the quality of different articles, reckoned the cost and made decisions. Many hours were spent experimenting with Elizabeth's hair, all three laughing at the results. Something had come over Marguerite and she laughed easily at any little joke. She was light-hearted because she had done all she could do.

On her last Sunday at home, her mother, the Kenny's, Michael and Elizabeth accompanied her to High Mass. They went to the local church which she had known so well when her father was still alive and which had been the scene of his funeral. During the offertory her eyes filled with tears. For once she abandoned her rigid self-discipline and allowed herself to cry, burying her face in her hands as though she were deep in prayer.

For a moment she wondered what she was about? Why was she going away? Why was she taking Elizabeth with her? Why did she do any of the things she did? These questionings did not come as words for she was never analytical. She did not seek answers. But, because she was still very young, her natural resemblance to her mother and Michael broke through the image she had made of herself in her father's likeness, and she knew what it was like to be them. She knew what it was like to be slack and glad of any small pleasures which came one's way. She almost knew what it was like to be unambitious. And she knew what it was like to be herself as she had been before the offertory. She did not oppose these two pictures and she passed no judgements, but the experience threw her off balance. Her fantasies of the past and dreams of the future temporarily lost their force. For once the present was stronger than either and a sudden glimpse of what was actual and real could hardly be borne.

12

During the journey Marguerite rehearsed Elizabeth and kept her at it. "Think of yourself as sixteen," she said. "Don't walk like a child. Take small steps and try not to stare around you. Look as though you're used to this sort of life, and remember, you are never to say anything about the family to any of them. Leave that to me."

Elizabeth was like a child in fancy dress, over-excited, conscious of everything she had on and wondering what impression she was making. Men always seemed to be staring at her. They hovered round her on the boat and first-class passenger men looked through the glass at her. On the train to Bordeaux the three men in the compartment looked as though they could eat her. She did not realise the implications yet, but she was a beauty. Her oval face was angelic in its perfection of feature, her large blue eyes were puzzled and excited beneath their heavy top lids and thick black lashes, and her small curly mouth looked childish and uncertain. Her colouring was typically Irish, a fair bright complexion and black hair and black brows.

Marguerite had looked handsome enough to receive many courtesies when travelling but the effect Elizabeth had on the opposite sex was devastating. Even old porters stared at her. The coachman who came to meet them was tongue-tied. Marguerite never observed much unless she had deliberately set herself to notice something for the purposes of self-education, and with her head full of a thousand projects, all that reached her of the general admiration aroused by her sister was a faint awareness that people were being kind.

As they drove to the house there was last-minute advice. "Be very respectful to Madame, but not humble. We come of a very good family and are every bit as good as they are. Don't fidget and do keep your hands still. It's best to hold them together in front of you whether you are standing up or sitting down. And you mustn't sit down unless Madame tells you to. Try not to stare at everything as you have been doing. You must realise you have every advantage really. When I first came here I had no one to tell me anything and I had no gloves and a dreadful short dress which showed all my boots." When they arrived she took her straight to see Madame. After years of appearing to have nothing better to do than wait for other people she knew the advantage it gives you if you pay flying visits and say you must dash off to do something else, so washing and unpacking were left so that she could say that they must hurry off to have everything done before dinner.

There was no need to worry, for Elizabeth could act, and it was Madame who looked amazed and at a loss when they met. Elizabeth stood with her hands clasped together, calm, demure and graceful, her eyes fixed on the flower in the carpet by her foot, respectful but not ill at ease, exactly like the heroine figure in an illustration to one of the sentimental magazine stories of the period. They were told to sit down and Elizabeth sank gently onto one of the small armchairs and looked neither to left or right while Marguerite asked after Madame, Monsieur and the children and then described the journey and begged Madame to excuse them as there was so much to do.

Elizabeth sailed along the passages, listening with envy to the swish of her sister's skirts and glancing slyly at her surroundings so that anyone who might be observing from some hidden corner could not accuse her of staring. She was shown into the nursery. Angélique, now thirteen, and Marie-Louise, now ten, eyed her with interest. There was a brief shaking of hands and she was whisked away.

She adapted herself to her new environment quickly, one might say instantaneously. Her French was soon fluent and easy, although her vocabulary remained small for a time. The children found her very entertaining and a welcome change from her stern, serious sister. She taught them a number of games they did not know before and she herself joined in with enthusiasm. They all developed a passion for dressing up and acting and she was never at a loss for a subject which might be an everyday occurrence, like going out to tea, or an historical scene such as the burning of Joan of Arc or Alfred and the cakes (which was quite new and fascinating to them), or a fairy tale. She understood Angélique's vanity because she, too, was vain and she found Marie-Louise's craving for attention the most natural thing in the world and let her show off to her heart's content. After all, it was only a matter of a very short time since she had been openly a child herself and so it was hardly surprising that the atmosphere in the nursery was now gay and conspiratorial against the adults of the house.

When adults were present she grew up in a flash. Madame was pleased to see the children so happy and she was more than delighted with her new *Meess's* needlework and gave her many delicate things to mend and embroider. At the same time Madame was not altogether happy about her and she often wondered if it was wise to have such a beauty in the house; for the girl's beauty was very noticeable, demanding recognition like a bright, freshly painted picture. The menservants stared at her and the women servants made comments. Monsieur, who was not at all flighty, broke his habitual silence at Sunday lunch when he first set eyes on her, and though he did not address a word to the girl herself, the fact that he took part in the conversation at all was the greatest tribute to her appearance. Madame felt uneasy when he went up to the nursery and finally made a practice of accompanying him on those rare occasions.

There was something else too which was not quite right. The child's acting was a shade too good and it would have been better for her if Marguerite had not given her advice. If she had seemed embarrassed and stared and fidgeted, if her eyes had betrayed a naïve admiration for the grandeur of her new surroundings Madame would have liked her better, for after all it was Marguerite's naïveté which she had found so endearing. Elizabeth lacked the level look and upright carriage of her sister but always seemed relaxed with her small head hanging forward above a long neck, like a drooping flower on a slender stalk, from which position she would look at people through her lashes. This bent head was really no affectation but simply the mark of the recent convent girl. Her arched eyebrows and the downward curve of her mouth gave her, unknown to herself, a supercilious air and sometimes Madame would wonder whether she was secretly criticising her and feel that there was some covert impertinence going on which she could not pin down.

It was no wonder then that Madame was not generous and neither paid her new *Meess* a penny nor bought clothes for her. There was the excuse that the clothes she had arrived in were adequate but Madame also knew that better clothes would have enhanced not only Elizabeth's beauty (and this in itself could have been borne because Madame had long ago reconciled herself to the fact that she was plain) but also her natural elegance, pose and style. The new *Meess* would have looked far too *distinguée* with just a little more dressing.

Elizabeth thought Madame stingy. She had expected at least two new outfits at once and she had been looking forward to them enormously. She grumbled to her sister; after all, Marguerite had had them and many other things besides and she didn't work half so hard, and she didn't have to keep sewing all day; all she had to do was to give a few lessons and be with Madame. Marguerite, who always longed to give people anything they wanted, asked Madame's permission to hand over her grey dress to her sister, saying that it no longer fitted her properly. Madame hesitated and then graciously consented, deciding that the dress was out of date and would be bound to look bulky on the girl because she was smaller and slimmer than her sister.

She had not reckoned with Elizabeth who now studied the fashion magazines with extra care. In a few days the dress was re-modelled and a perfect fit, a piece of silk cadged from Angélique was sewn into the skirt so that it rustled. When Elizabeth appeared in her new outfit at Sunday lunch all eyes were on her. Madame felt she had been deceived.

There was trouble when Jacques came home for the holidays. At fifteen, despite his narrow shoulders and hairless face, he felt quite a young man. During the previous holiday he had complained to his mother that he was too big to be upstairs with his sisters who were mere children and that really his parents ought to allow him to be downstairs now like any adult. Now all this was forgotten and he said no more about the subject. Screams of laughter would come from the nursery morning and afternoon and whenever Madame walked in she would find the four of them dressed up, Elizabeth dazzling as usual, in the middle of a performance. Oblivious of any criticism they would continue quite gaily in her presence until Angélique whispered to her one day that she must not come in to watch them any more because now they were rehearsing a proper play and intended to give a proper performance downstairs on her mother's feast day. She also added that her mother should ask as many guests as she could.

This would never do. Madame could not have Monsieur and a mixed gathering watching Elizabeth for half an hour or so. She mentioned the matter to Marguerite. "I don't want to offend you but you will understand that it is not quite fitting that the children should act with your sister in front of guests. The children may act on their own if they wish and I shall let them do a little play, just a very short one. But it would look very odd if your sister appeared. I didn't want to say anything to her and so I should be very glad if *you* would just say a word or two about it to her. As though it was your opinion. In that way she will not be offended." Marguerite thought Madame the soul of consideration.

There was no play, for without their *Meess's* talent the children felt uncertain of success. Jacques was told that he was old enough to be downstairs and encouraged not to go to the nursery. His holidays came to an end and everyone, except Elizabeth, was calm again.

Elizabeth was angry. She knew perfectly well it was Madame and not Marguerite who had stopped the play and she was disappointed because she had wanted to shine in public. She felt dissatisfied with her life. She was growing up at a great rate and the company of the little girls was boring. There were many things she wanted, gloves, purses, beads and other ornaments, all of which Angélique had in abundance. Angélique had been prevented from lending or giving her anything and she herself earned no money to buy things with. Every penny that Marguerite earned was put aside for those in Cardiff. It was unfair. She complained to her sister.

"No, you mustn't ask Madame to pay you," said Marguerite, "leave it to me and I shall say something about it when I think it is a good moment." There was no good moment but, egged on by Elizabeth, Marguerite asked. Madame refused flatly.

Then it occurred to Elizabeth that the Chantabrie house was not the only one in Bordeaux and there must be many families who wanted an English girl. While Marguerite was giving a lesson, she slipped out of the house and boldly presented herself to Mme de Sarne, the mother of two little girls who sometimes came and played with Angélique and Marie-Louise, and asked her if she would take her to look after the children. Mme de Sarne had a son of eighteen and a husband with an eye for the ladies. One look at Elizabeth convinced her that a *Meess* was unnecessary and loyalty to her class led her to call on Mme de Chantabrie the next day and inform her of what had happened.

Madame was furious. She accused Elizabeth of ingratitude and deceit. "Ever since you came here," she said, "there has been something not quite right about your attitude. Many times I have been on the point of saying something to you but I always hoped that you would see your faults in time and also I knew it would upset your sister if she thought I was not satisfied."

Elizabeth was collected and injured. "What have I done wrong? What wasn't right about my attitude ever since I came? I can't think of anything. I've always done exactly as I was told. Perhaps I shouldn't have gone to Mme de Sarne without asking your permission, but I wasn't ungrateful. I am very grateful to you. I should be very sorry to leave here and the only reason that I looked for something else was that I must earn some money. It's not for myself but for my brothers and little sister."

This was too much. Madame shouted, *"Cette famille!"* and told her to leave the room.

There was a cloud over her for some time after that. At first she didn't care whether she was sent away or not, for after all, life at Aunt Kenny's and St. Joseph's had been quite nice, but one day she heard that the family were going to Italy for a holiday and she was careful to give no further offence.

13

Monsieur, Madame, their two daughters, their two governesses and many of the servants installed themselves in a villa in Bordighera. It was late spring and from her window Elizabeth could see a clear blue sky, a still sea and masses of bright flowers. Up to the nursery came sounds of festivities below, festivities from which the two children and the two English girls were excluded. Guests came to the house every day, clients or potential clients of Monsieur, minor nobility and merchants, with their wives and grown-up children. There were parties and outings. Madame wore splendid toilettes.

It was too much for Elizabeth. The sound of carriages and the glimpses of guests being handed out made her long to go downstairs and see what was going on.

"You are always going on about the advantages and opportunities we have here," she said to Marguerite, now always in the nursery because Madame never required a companion, "but all I ever see here are the two children and the only rooms I'm ever in are my bedroom and this one. Even on Sundays we don't go downstairs now. We're shut away from everything. We're treated like servants. Worse, in fact, because the servants are always down there with the guests."

She would think of excuses for going downstairs and offer to fetch things, until Madame once found her at the bottom of the stairs and told her coldly that she must ring for the maid if she needed anything.

When the sisters took their charges out for walks they left the house by a side entrance, secured from the sight of the drive by trees and high bushes. In spite of this one of the guests, Ottavio Montori, observed Elizabeth through a gap and from that day he was always coming to the house. He would come with messages from his family and with flowers, he would angle for invitations, he would try to please and entertain his hostess and Madame was flattered. Then when he found himself in her good graces and well received he began to speak of her children and often suggested that it would be delightful if his little brother and sister could meet them and play with them. Madame began to wonder if Ottavio were thinking of an alliance with Angélique and it was quite possible, for both families were in the wine business. A meeting between the children of the two houses was arranged and Elizabeth accompanied her two charges.

The sight of her seemed to inspire Ottavio. He threw himself into the children's games with the greatest verve and told stories and made jokes without tiring. Then as they were leaving he darted to her side and asked her if she ever had an afternoon to herself. Not understanding a word of what he was saying because he spoke French with a marked Italian accent, she assumed it was some sort of farewell and gave him a friendly nod.

A talk between Mme Chantabrie and Signora Montori revealed that no one had been thinking of a betrothal. Naturally Madame did not mention the subject at all but she gave many openings which might have led to something and was soon convinced that such an idea had never crossed the other lady's mind. She was puzzled. Ottavio continued to pay calls and seemed stranger and stranger. Sometimes she would see him standing in the drive staring up at the top windows, sometimes when he was in the drawing room he would keep jumping up and dashing into the passage whenever he heard footsteps. For a short time Madame believed that he had fallen in love with Angélique and said nothing as yet to his mother, but on thinking it over she was led logically, step by step, to see what had really happened. She sent for her *Meess* one day when Ottavio was there and watched his face. What she saw made her furious.

"Your sister is not *sérieuse*," she said to Marguerite. "A certain young man who comes to this house every day is interested in her. If she had not given him encouragement he would not go on like this. Please speak to her about it or I shall have to."

In future when Ottavio called he was told Madame was busy. He hovered round the house, he watched the windows, he tried to waylay Elizabeth when she went out, but he never succeeded in being there at the right time. He became desperate, wrote her an impassioned note and bribed one of the maids to give it to her.

Elizabeth was flattered and alarmed. She had no intention of answering because Ottavio had made little impression on her and in any case even if she had wished to continue the correspondence she could not have done so for she had no experience of bribing messengers, no money to bribe them with and if she had posted a letter to the Montori she would have been afraid that Madame might go there and see the envelope and recognise her writing. More letters came.

Meanwhile Marguerite had decided to raise the distasteful subject of Ottavio with her sister although she felt it was quite wrong because Elizabeth was much too young to know what all the fuss was about and if only Madame had not thought her two years older than she was this would never have happened. Briefly and unemphatically she mentioned her conversation with Madame and, glad that that was over, did not ask Elizabeth to comment and spoke of something else. She had many family matters on her mind and Ottavio was the least of her worries, in fact she was not worrying about him at all. Every week she wrote to Sister Aloysius, to Mrs Kenny, to the boys, to Kathleen and her mother. Each reply she received she studied carefully. She spent many hours making plans and budgeting, sometimes feeling optimistic and sometimes feeling that nothing could ever come right if the boys were not taken out of that wretched orphanage and put somewhere where they would learn something. Their letters were full of bad spelling and grammar and their handwriting was unformed. Thomas seemed to be delicate and nearly always had something wrong with him. Michael never wrote at all and there was no word from her mother of what he was up to.

She would never have given another thought to Ottavio if she had not found a letter of his in one of Elizabeth's drawers. She read it on the spot, hurried to the nursery, threw the door open and said sternly, "I want to talk to you, Elizabeth. You can leave the children for a moment. Come to your room."

There was a storm. Elizabeth was not ashamed, cowed or apologetic. On the contrary, she was furious that her sister should have looked through her things, and refused to believe that Marguerite was merely searching for a pair of gloves she had lent her. As for the letter, she shrugged her shoulders, and when more letters were discovered she remained unmoved.

"I didn't write them, did I?" she said. "How can I help it if someone writes me a letter? How is it my fault?"

"You must have encouraged him. Did you answer him?"

"No I did not. I did nothing at all. And I don't see why you should treat me like a child in front of the children. I don't go to your room and look through your things and I don't see why you should go to mine."

"I'm sure you must have done something, but it's no use going on about it now. You must let me do what I think best. I shall have to say something to Madame otherwise she'll get to hear about it from the maid and then we'll both lose our jobs."

"I shouldn't care. I'm not paid anything."

Marguerite went to Madame with a sad expression and a confidential tone. Her sister had told her that Ottavio was pestering her with letters. The poor child was very upset. While anxious to avoid any fuss she did want Madame to know that it was through no fault of her own. They would be very grateful for Madame's advice.

Madame still disliked the affair and still mistrusted Elizabeth but there was not the faintest excuse for reproach. "I shall see to it," she said drily. A talk to Signora Montori led the Signora to speak to her son. Ottavio flew into a rage and wrote a farewell letter to Elizabeth; she had deceived him; she had betrayed him; she had treated him as a joke; she had made him look ridiculous in the eyes of his family and friends; it was a base action to show his letter to others; it was vile; he would like to kill her; he never wished to see her again.

Marguerite was shown this. "What shall I do?" said Elizabeth.

They did nothing and there the matter ended.

From that time on Marguerite kept an eye on her sister and meditated on the perils which beset the path of beauty. She observed how men looked at the girl in the street. She watched the menservants and any male guests and she exaggerated their reactions and her sister's lightness. She also noticed that Elizabeth was extremely dissatisfied with her present life and perhaps on the point of taking some unwise step without consulting anyone.

"Do you know of anyone who would take Elizabeth as a governess?" she asked Madame. "She is very clever and good with children. It is not that she wants to leave, but she is ambitious and anxious to earn some money."

Madame laughed. "The only person who would take her as a governess would be a widower with children. And do you think that would be quite suitable?"

Back in Bordeaux there were more incidents. Now that Elizabeth looked more grown up scarcely a day passed without a new conquest. On the walks with the children men followed her, men of all ages and classes. The bolder ones went so far as to wait outside the house and look hopefully up at the windows when she had gone in. Every Sunday in church she was followed by many pairs of eyes. A cousin of Madame, an elderly friend of Monsieur and a school friend of Jacques all fell in love with her. As for Jacques himself, he followed her about like a dog and sulked when he was kept away from the nursery.

There was no need for Madame to fear, as she did, that Elizabeth would run off with some member of her family and disgrace them. There was no need for Marguerite to suppose, as she did, that her sister's head would be turned by admiration. Elizabeth had her head well screwed on and was straitlaced.

Until she came to France she knew nothing about the facts of life. She had seen her mother pregnant many a time and the facts of birth were clear to her, but no one had ever told her how one became pregnant in the first place. In the Convent she had not thought about such things. She had never happened to be present when whispered and embarrassed speculations went on among certain groups. Her aunt was most careful about what was said in the child's presence. Her brothers were in awe of her and would never have breathed a word about it. But a book in Madame's library aroused her suspicions. With no word to Marguerite and filled with dread she collected clues and pieced the whole thing together. When all was clear she was horrified and disgusted. But for a while she tried to forget about it.

By the time she returned to Bordeaux these emotions had hardened into a lasting attitude. She believed that contact with a man was not so much immoral, for when it was sanctified by the sacrament of marriage it could no longer be called that, but degrading, repellent and wholly out of character for someone as dainty and ladylike as herself. She saw other dainty and refined creatures with husbands and imagined what they must suffer. Perhaps, as some later date, she might find it just possible to marry some wealthy member of the highest aristocracy, but even then it would be a heavy sacrifice to position and wealth, for in all circumstances marriage would have an unpleasant side. Would the delights of a title, the attendance at great balls, the rides in a splendid carriage dressed in the height of fashion be worth the secret shame?

And even though other people married, she was different. She had always felt different. At home, because she was the prettiest and the youngest of the first four, who made a group together, the only group which counted, she was treated as a little flower. Every day people called her fancy names. "Little Princess", "Lady Fair", "A Daisy". In nearly every eye around her she had read admiration and love. And when she had met her own eyes in the glass she had seen love there too. In the orphanage, where all the others were treated as nothing, she was singled out by the mother superior, she was produced for visitors. All this struck her as perfectly natural and inevitable. She never boasted about it. She hardly gave it a thought.

Now that she knew more, she realised that she did not want to be desired, although she continued to expect admiration. She took pleasure in her appearance and her surroundings. In the hurly burly of her mother's house, she had always folded her clothes carefully, put her little possessions tidily away in places known only to herself, made a fuss if anyone touched her things or borrowed a ribbon. Around herself she must have her belongings just so, and be a self-contained, organised little unit on her own. She had always been acquisitive and careful with her pocket money, sometimes lending it at interest to Michael. Now she thought and dreamt of clothes with great emotion. Fine clothes she must have, not to please men, but because they were her due, they were aesthetically necessary to her.

She was far from flirtatious. As her attitude towards sex became rigid and defined so she found the attentions of men distasteful and never encouraged any of her followers by the slightest sign. What she most prized were compliments from her own sex and she was amazed that Mme de Chantabrie and Mme de Sarne did not love her. Such a thing had never happened before.

Like her sister she was ambitious to secure a social standing but there was a difference in their ideas and plans. Marguerite believed in refinement as a moral virtue, a virtue extolled by her late father who was a saint. Elizabeth believed in refinement because she had a horror of anything coarse or vulgar, as of a loud noise or unpleasant smell. Marguerite dreamt vaguely of some well-appointed house where her mother, her brothers and her sisters would all live together in an atmosphere of refinement and affection. Elizabeth dreamt of some small, exquisitely furnished, very feminine apartment, filled with pictures, ornaments and flowers, where she would live alone, or perhaps with another lady, a lovely creature like herself, and receive visits from admiring people. And her vision was not vague. She could see just the sort of chairs she would have, just how she would arrange them. At the same time her religious upbringing and her sister's teaching had made a deep impression on her and she considered it her duty to pay her share towards the education of the others and the comfort of her mother.

Madame could not make up her mind what to do. Now that Angélique was nearing the age when suitors might ask for her hand it was unfair to allow her to be constantly in the company of someone very much more attractive than herself. Yet if she dismissed Elizabeth, Marguerite might go too.

In another six months the position would be impossible. Meanwhile, it could be borne and therefore it was perhaps wiser to do nothing.

14

The situation was solved, to no one's satisfaction, by two sentences in a letter from Mrs Reilly:

"I'm getting married to Mr Edgar Hughes. Do you remember him he was very good to Michael."

These sentences, unheralded, unexplained, written in the usual uneven hand, coming after the usual uninformative phrases, could scarcely be believed. Marguerite read them again and again, stared at them and then went right through the letter from the beginning, trying hard to think of some interpretation other than the literal one, some little omission which would explain away the whole thing. This was impossible for no statement could be balder. When she handed the letter to her sister the full meaning of the words was sinking in and she trembled.

Elizabeth read calmly and thought for a moment. "I know this Hughes. He's the builder Michael was with." Looking up she saw Marguerite's bright eyes and bloodless face and she felt frightened and said no more.

There was a silence. When at length words came, they came in a torrent. "How could she think of such a thing, Elizabeth? She must be mad. She can't mean it. Our mother could never think of such a thing. After our father. *Our father*. Elizabeth, you remember him, you remember what he was like, so good, so patient, such a gentleman, such a saint. You remember how they all said he was a saint, and he was a saint, too. I know it because I knew him well and the priest told me so after his death. And how he loved mother! There was never a cross word in the house when he was there. You remember how calm he always made everything. He was perfect, I

66

don't think he had any fault at all, I don't believe he ever committed even a venial sin. No one who was ever married to him should ever marry again, you couldn't think they would ever want to, they couldn't want to. Elizabeth, we must stop her. She must *not* marry again. Do you think she means something different? How do you read it? What do you think she means?"

There was no pause for an answer. "Do you think someone else is getting married to this man and she's written it wrong? But why should she tell us about someone else when we don't even know the man? And then she'd have seen her mistake and corrected it. You know how long she takes to write a letter and how she always goes through it afterwards looking for spelling mistakes. She *must* be stopped. We must go back at once and stop her. We must write straight away. We must post off the letter at once." She was silent for a moment, making a great effort to reason. "No. That would be useless. It would be quite the wrong thing to do. We must take her by surprise. If we're actually *there*, on the spot, we can stop her. If she knows we're coming and if she knows we want to stop her then she'll hurry."

Elizabeth's words, which had sounded in her ears while she spoke, now reached her consciousness. "A builder! A common builder! Oh, Elizabeth!"

Alone in her bedroom she tried to regain control of her feelings, to express them in words, accurately or not it didn't matter, to cover them over with reasoning. She imagined that the sacred love she felt for someone who was now with the blessed in heaven had been outraged and her suffering was righteous. But quickly these high-flown considerations wore themselves out despite her efforts. And her first love for her father, strong in her from the time she first walked, her personal love for a handsome, bearded man who seemed wiser, cleverer and more distinguished than anyone else in the world, came back to her with overpowering strength. She experienced again the sensations of flinging herself into his arms after a separation, of walking beside him to the shop, of hurrying down the stairs to meet him when he came home. But these sensations were made sombre by the knowledge that they would never happen again. She felt no longer outraged but wretched, desolate and alone. She would always be alone. She had been alone since his death, she had chosen to be alone. No tears came. She felt empty, dizzy and made of some light substance, a sort of thin container enclosing a dark void. For minutes her suffering was so extreme that unknown to herself she moaned.

She walked up and down, rubbed her dry hands together and steadied herself. Back came the arguments, the rights and the wrongs, and it was a relief to keep them churning over and over in her mind. Whose fault was it? Mrs Reilly, Michael, Mrs Kenny and Mr Kenny were blamed in turn. Her mother's friends, those women who came in every day, had had a hand in it too. Her picture of her mother changed from one moment to another; now she was weak, always taking the line of least resistance, unaware of the higher things in life; now she was the refined unhappy widow, unable to cope with so many children and such poverty, sacrificing herself and her higher nature to their needs; now she was a monster of heartlessness, deceit and cunning.

As for Hughes, she hardly gave him a thought, he was some nonentity, some miserable outsider who had made his way into the family but who would never count. It made things worse, of course, that he was a common builder but whoever he'd been, if he'd been rich and high born, if he'd been royalty itself, her mother still should not have dreamt of marrying him.

In time she prepared a story for her employer. Pale, upright, in an even voice she said, "Madame, I must ask you permission to go home at once. The reason is quite unexpected and I am sorry I could not give you longer warning. But my mother is about to marry again and naturally I must go home for the wedding. She is most anxious that I should be with her at such a time. I don't know the future husband very well but I am told he is a wealthy merchant."

Madame remarked that she looked very distressed. Marguerite admitted only a little. "It *is* rather a surprise to me." The last thing she cared about at the moment were signs of sympathy from Madame, for that lady held no further interest since she was not a protagonist in this particular drama, and her answers to other kind enquiries were short and impatient.

There was a delay. Madame tried hard to keep Marguerite, producing endless reasons why she must stay just one more day and then just one more. Each day increased Marguerite's agony, each reason given seemed more ridiculous and trifling than the last, and she now began to loathe the sight of the person who tried to hold her away from Cardiff. She no longer cared what impression she made. If it had not been for the fact that she had not been paid yet and must have the money, for even at a time like this money still counted and she was not going to lose what was owing to her, she would have left at once. She made no pretence of taking an interest in anything to do with the Chantabries, she forgot to do things, she lost things, she failed to answer when spoken to, until at last Madame thought it wiser to delay no longer. She knew Marguerite would not be likely to return despite the flow of promises she made whenever asked. She parted with her fondly, gave her some dresses of which she had tired and at the last moment kissed her on both cheeks.

Something strained and yet so determined in Marguerite's face touched her. "I have become very attached to you," she said, "there will always be a place for you here when you need it." She shook hands with Elizabeth formally.

15

During the journey Marguerite had worked indefatigably on Elizabeth's feelings and had finally inspired her with much of the indignation and sorrow which she felt herself. They left their luggage at Cardiff station and hurried home.

Picking up their skirts they made their way down the cobbled, litter-strewn alley to the house. The door was shut, which was unusual, and there was no knocker. Marguerite tapped hard with the handle of her umbrella. There was no answer. Looking up they saw that the window was shut and without curtains.

Marguerite went next door. "Where is my mother?" she asked the woman.

"What, it's Maggie!" said the neighbour. "How are you, dear? Fancy seeing you. Haven't you grown up and what..."

There was no time for this. Marguerite interrupted by repeating her question. Knowing, dreading what was coming she listened. Mrs Reilly was gone. She was Mrs Hughes now and living in Stanley's Row in Riverside. She didn't know the number of the house but they could tell it because it had a big yard down one side.

They hurried out of the alley and halted at the main street. "She knew I'd try and stop her. She deliberately deceived me," said Marguerite.

"Shall we go there?" said Elizabeth.

"Of course not. *He* will be there and we don't want to see *him*. I must see her alone." She had scarcely slept during the long journey. She had taken nothing but one small meal and several cups of tea and coffee. She had paced up and down the deck for hours. She was exhausted and despairing. Usually she could make a decision at once but now she was stuck.

Several of the passers by wondered when they saw two such very well-dressed girls in this area who were standing and staring at each other in silence. One man, who had perhaps glimpsed Elizabeth's profile, came over to them. "Are you lost, Miss? Can I tell you the way?"

"No, thank you," said Elizabeth, for Marguerite was oblivious of her surroundings and the question. "Marguerite, do let's go somewhere. Everyone is staring at us. We could go to Aunt Kenny."

"No, I don't want to see her either. She is just as bad as the rest of them. She said nothing, nothing at all in her letters."

"But we must go somewhere. Where will we stay?"

"Very well, we'll go to Aunt Kenny."

It was tea time, the fire was bright and the big table by the window was laid. Mrs Kenny was contented and without a care in the world and when she heard first the gate click open and then someone coming in the front door she assumed it was Kathleen whom she was expecting. It was a great surprise when her two eldest nieces walked into the parlour, and as she saw the expression on Marguerite's face all feelings of comfort and satisfaction vanished. Yet, as though by pretending that this was just a pleasant, unexpected visit she could make it so, she continued to look cheerful and went over to embrace them, first putting her lips to Elizabeth's soft cheek and then, plucking up courage, advancing towards Marguerite.

Marguerite stepped back and held out her hand. "We are just back," she said. We went straight home and found no one there. Perhaps *you* could tell us what has happened."

"But I thought you knew. Mary said she'd written all about it."

"She told me she was going to get married. She never said when it was going to be. Perhaps she was married when she wrote it. When was it?"

"About six days ago."

"That must have been almost immediately after I got the letter. She might just as well not have sent it." Her anger had been with her too long to boil over again and in a way she was glad to have her worst suspicions confirmed. It gave her a strong case.

"Now come along to the fire and make yourselves comfortable. You look..."

Marguerite made an impatient gesture. "And who is this Edgar Hughes?" she said, revealing her contempt for him by pronouncing his name in a mock Welsh accent.

"A builder."

"I know that. What else is he? What is he like? Is he a Catholic?"

"I'm not sure, dear. I think perhaps he isn't."

"Oh. Not a Catholic. Then what is he?"

"Well, dear, I'm not sure. It might be a Baptist or something like that. But don't worry about it. It's really quite all right. They were married in a Catholic church. He was quite willing for that. Your mother insisted. They really were married in a Catholic church."

Marguerite sat down on the nearest chair, gloating. "A non-Catholic! A non-Catholic! How shameful!" A few years of being a governess had made her assume a stern commanding tone whenever things were not to her liking and she addressed her aunt as though she were one of her charges. "And why didn't you write and tell me about this? Why did you never say one word?"

Mrs Kenny did not like being spoken to as though she had done something criminal but, seeing how upset her niece was, she controlled herself and argued gently. "Now, Maggie dear, think. I left it to your mother. If you were going to get married you wouldn't expect Elizabeth to tell your nearest relations, would you now?"

The door, which had remained ajar, opened wider, and in came Kathleen, smiling and fully expecting the usual nice tea and pleasant chat. Being a sensitive child and easily frightened she was subdued at once when she saw the grave faces around her. Marguerite went over to her, kissed her quickly, handed her over to be kissed by Elizabeth and then, taking her arm as though to lead her away at once, asked, "Is there anywhere where she can go?"

"Well, dear, it's better for her to be in the warm and I've got the tea ready for her here and I think..."

"Very well, let her stay." Turning away from Kathleen, who cautiously approached a chair by the fire and sat down gingerly hoping to be inconspicuous from now on, she continued, "Why didn't you stop her? How could you let her make this marriage? You must have known about it beforehand."

Mrs Kenny had thought the marriage a good idea but now was not the time to say so. "It was none of my business."

"Surely as a Catholic you should have stopped the marriage?"

"Quite a number of mixed marriages are a success, and they were married in a church and the priest says that so long as it's a Catholic wedding and the children are brought up as Catholics it's all right."

"My father would never have thought so. He detested mixed marriages. You know he did."

"I don't think the subject ever came up, dear."

The subject had never been raised between Patrick and his daughter either. "Well I *know* he detested mixed marriages."

Elizabeth was crying into a scented, lace-edged handkerchief, one of the many titbits Marguerite had passed on to her. She looked like a little girl again with a smut on her forehead and a fallen lock over her shoulder. Mrs Kenny felt sorry for her, sorry for both of them. As she left the room she was overcome with sorrow for herself and her poor sister Mary and when she returned with the teapot she was crying too. Kathleen, impressionable, looked into the fire and cried noiselessly. Marguerite, dry-eyed, resented this display. "Elizabeth, do stop that snivelling. It will do no good. And what's the matter with you, Kathie?"

After tea, a little refreshed, Marguerite began to make fresh plans. The marriage was over. There was no more she could do to stop it. Later perhaps it might be put an end to somehow. "At any rate, it's a good thing Kathie's living here."

"No, dear, I'm afraid she isn't. Not any more. She has just come over for tea. Hughes took a great fancy to her and..."

"Well we must stop that. She must come back and live here. Naturally none of us can remain in a non-Catholic household. Kathie must come back with you."

"I'd gladly have her but he's an obstinate man."

There was worse to come. "And is Michael with them?"

"He was but he's gone off into digs somewhere."

"Where?"

"I don't know. He didn't tell Mary."

"Is he all alone in digs?"

"He's taken Thomas with him."

"Thomas? Thomas? But I thought he was at school."

"I think Mary thought he was getting too big for there and he came back with her and Michael but Edgar didn't want the boys in the house and they've gone off."

"She didn't even tell me Thomas had left school. Every week she sent me off a letter and there was never anything in it. Well I'll see about the boys later. But Kathie must stay with you."

While Marguerite and Mrs Kenny talked and Kathleen listened to what was to be done with her, Elizabeth cried again. She was more sorry for herself than for anyone else. To be whisked away from the luxury of Bordeaux to the dreariness of Cardiff was terrible. This parlour she had once thought so fine was really very dingy and had a hateful stuffy smell. There were no fresh flowers here, only one dusty plant. She had no home. They couldn't stay with Aunt Kenny for ever and even if they could she didn't want to. She was very tired and after breaking a long fast she felt sick.

16

When Mrs Hughes and her daughter met, each knew there would be a battle. They embraced, Mrs Hughes told her daughter she was looking well, showed her into the kitchen and put the kettle on to make her a cup of tea.

"It's great to see you. Where's Lizzie?"

"With Aunt Kenny. We're staying there."

"And when did you arrive?"

"Yesterday."

"And why didn't you come here? There's plenty of room."

"We went straight home and found no one there. We never thought you would have moved so soon."

These were preliminaries and each now prepared herself.

"Mother, why didn't you tell us the date of the wedding? Why did you wait till the last moment to tell us?"

"I didn't know myself until the last moment."

"You must have done. You must have made arrangements at the church, with the priest and all that. I don't believe you."

"It was all such a rush and there was so much to do and you know what I am about letters."

"But you *wrote* and you said nothing. You didn't want us to know. Your news was a great shock to us. Naturally I could hardly believe it. I had never imagined, I had never dreamt it possible that you could think of marrying again."

"You never know what'll happen."

Marguerite saw a pile of underclothes and socks ready for mending, obviously belonging to Hughes, and this ugly reminder of the completeness of the new marriage nauseated her. It was like watching her mother commit sacrilege. "Mother, how could you have done such a thing?"

"There's many a person who married again."

"But not like this. Mother, what do you think father would have said?"

"And wouldn't he have wished me to have a bit of comfort?"

"You know quite well father would never have wished you to marry a non-Catholic. He would have thought it a sin."

"I won't have that talk from you. I'm as good a Catholic as anyone."

"Father's whole life was his religion. *All* his friends were Catholic. He *never* made friends with a non-Catholic. He expected us to be like that. As he was dying he talked to me about religion. He wanted one of the boys to be a priest. And now when the boys come back to this... this Baptist house or whatever it is, do you suppose it will be good for them? It will be a bad example to them. And it's no wonder Michael and Thomas walked out from such a place, and it's no place for a child like Kathleen."

"You've no call to lecture me about religion and duty like that. The children will be Catholics like they've always been and like I am and didn't I place them all in good Catholic schools and isn't it to me they owe their religion? As long as I'm here it's a Catholic house. And the children will be better off now. I'll be having more money for them."

"Better off? How can you say that? My father was a gentleman and now they'll have a common working man for a stepfather."

Mrs Hughes laughed. "And what was your father if not a working man too, and a lot poorer than Hughes here!"

"He was *not*. I know he was poor when he died but poverty isn't what counts. The greatest families in the land can lose their fortune. Money isn't everything. He was a gentleman, you had only to see him to know it. He was refined and educated."

"The only education he had was at the poor school and I don't know if he even had that."

"Mother, how can you tell such wicked lies? How can you speak like that of my father? I won't stay and listen to you."

"You can do as you please, but I know better than you do what education your father had."

"*I* know what my father was. I know all about him. I knew him better than anyone else knew him because he told me everything and I understood him. And when he died he left you all in my care. You don't seem to realise it but he did. And ever since then I've been doing all I can for all of you. If you'd only waited. I was planning to come back to Cardiff and live with you. Every penny I earned I saved for you and the children. I never spent a thing on myself. I don't say this to boast because you know I don't care about money for myself, but I do want you to *see* how I would have helped you and so there was no need for this marriage. You've only thought about yourself. You've never seemed to care about the family at all. You've let Michael become a common labourer and now he's been turned out of the house with nowhere to go except some awful lodging-house, and Thomas, poor Thomas, straight from school, straight from an orphanage where you put him, comes home and is pushed out too. They haven't gained much by your marriage to this common man, have they?"

"Don't talk of Edgar like that. You've not even met him."

"Very well. But you've let us all down and you know it."

Mrs Hughes' Irish blood was up. The bit about religion and the late Patrick she had expected because she knew Marguerite was crazy about the subject, but the accusation that she had a hand in turning out the boys was too much. She had done everything to keep them with her, she had insisted that they should be with her before she married and it was only because Michael and Edgar would quarrel about nothing that the boys had gone off in a huff, and now Edgar swore he'd never have them back. This was very much on her mind and she had been wondering how to get her sons back. She slapped her daughter hard on the face.

"I've not let you down. I've done no such thing. If Mick had kept his temper he'd be here in a fine home and with a good job. And Thomas, too. They'd no cause to go off like that. I thought I'd be getting a fine home for all of you. I've slaved for the lot of you ever since your father died. You were enjoying yourself in France and you

75

were too fine to make sweets and you were too grand to wheel a barrow and you didn't like this and you didn't like that. And so it was myself that had to make them. From morning till night I was working hard, and not the easy work that you've been doing either, but real hard work at all hours of the day. And where did the money go? On clothes for the children, on the rent, on a bit of food, on a bit of coal. Many's the time there was scarcely a bite and no fire. If I was ill, then there were no sweets and nothing coming in, and I never wrote and asked you for anything, did I? And you're always grumbling about the children in orphanages. And where else could they be for nothing? And you say I should have had them at home. And what sort of home do you think it would be for them? They'd have been starving and cold. Do you know how much money I made from the sweets? Do you think it would have paid for the lot of them? Wasn't it the best thing to put them in an orphanage and wasn't it myself who begged the nuns and priests to take them and didn't they say it was a wise thing to do? But you've always criticised and looked down your nose at all I did. If I had a bit over once in a way and bought a bottle of beer (and sure where's the harm in it?) you'd be looking at me as though the end of the world had come. It was the only bit of comfort I ever bought for myself. I haven't had new clothes for so many years that I couldn't tell you when it was I bought any until Edgar gave me some for the wedding. And then you can come in here, dressed up to the eyes, and with plenty more clothes in your trunk, I'm certain, and you can talk to me about sacrifices and you say you didn't spend a penny on yourself. Sure if any of us were given these things free and a fine house to live in and great meals and servants and all the rest we'd not be needing to spend a penny on ourselves either. And then you say you were making plans, and wasn't I making plans too? The two boys are in a good place. Didn't the priest say it was? They're a lot better off than they were in your father's time and we hadn't enough money to go round. And Mick's learnt a good trade and he could have had a good home and a good job if he'd wanted. That's what they want, to earn their living like anyone else. You want to make them full of fads and ideas like yourself so that they'll be fit for nothing. You want to rule everyone. Didn't you take off Lizzie with you just to have her under your thumb, when she was doing well at school and had a fine home with her aunt? No. You couldn't leave her alone, you couldn't stop interfering with the lot of us. And your poor aunt who's done nothing but good, you've been ordering her about and criticising her. Who's the head of this family I'm asking you? Who's the mother and who's the daughter? There's a good home now for all of you."

For the moment Marguerite's fury had abated. She didn't mind the slap as an insult to herself, although she hated to see her mother do anything so "common". She saw that her mother had had a hard time and had meant to do her best. But she also realised how impossible it was to make her see things as she wanted her to, how impossible it was to make her feel guilty for her dreadful action, how little she understood. Bewildered, she said automatically, as though the phrases had been in her mind for some time and must be spoken, "This will never be our home. I shall never live here. Elizabeth will never live here. It is not a suitable house for Kathie and she must go back to Aunt Kenny."

"Must? Who are you to say must? I'm her mother and she's staying here with me."

Marguerite's heart felt heavy. Her compassion switched from her mother to Kathleen and she had a vision of the child as she had seen her in the convent parlour, timid, wretched, with questioning eyes and answering in whispers. "You may be her mother, but you didn't seem like it before. You put her away in a home when she was much too young to go. You never even went to see her, did you? Did you ever pay her a visit? Did you ever write to her? When I went there she didn't seem to know she had a family at all. I don't believe she knew who I was. And she was so miserable. It was I who got her aunt to take her, not you. How can you talk of being her mother? If this Hughes hadn't wanted her here you'd have let anyone take her off your hands. Send her back to her aunt."

The accusation struck home. Mrs Hughes was upset by this bit of unexpected realism. "Go and give your orders to someone else. I'm not taking any. Go away now. Go away, Maggie. You can make this house your home whenever you need it but you must stop your nagging. Go away now."

They were standing close together and with a sudden burst of violence Mrs Hughes pressed both her hands hard against her daughter's side and drove her towards the door.

"Mother, you've broken my heart," said Marguerite and left the house.

17

At fifty-two Edgar Hughes was still a handsome man. His short, thick figure was well proportioned and muscular. His curly auburn hair and beard, his red face and his blue eyes gave him the look of a sailor. His first wife, a thin nagging woman, had been dead for some years, and his only son, with whom he had quarrelled, was living in North Wales with an uncle. Tired of being on his own at home he was quick to feel the delights of female company and he fell in love with Mary Reilly soon after meeting her. To him she seemed a great beauty, and she was in fact very good-looking, for her plump face was firm and unwrinkled and her bright complexion was enhanced by her almost snow-white hair. She was matriarchal without looking old.

He came across her in her local pub, because he had a job in that part at the time, and long after the job was finished he still came over to meet her there and pay for her drinks. Carried away by a feeling of warmth in the presence of her gaiety and vitality he asked her to marry him. She held out at first, clinging a little to the memory of Patrick. Then, because whatever she might have been once, she was unromantic now, she accepted. There was no question of love on her side. She was tired of living alone in poverty, she was the sort who liked to have a man about the place, and she wanted somewhere she could have her children, especially the two eldest boys, with her.

The relationship was not smooth. She felt that she was doing him a favour by sacrificing her independence and she looked on him as stupid, for his intelligence was all in his hands. He thought he was doing her a favour, taking on a widow with seven children who professed a religion he had always been taught to mistrust. Even during the courtship, if such can be called, they quarrelled when drunk. But she felt comfortable with him; she did not care what he thought. She had curbed her tongue in Patrick's day and now she could say what she liked. She had drunk very little when she was with Patrick because, although he never rebuked her, his own total abstemiousness was a deterrent. Now she could drink as much as she pleased. Besides, she could have any of her cronies in to see her.

Edgar promised to have the two boys in the house and to leave Kathleen where she was, but two days after the marriage there was a row between the boys and their stepfather. He accused them of slacking in their work, for both were working for him and they walked out. He was jealous of them, especially of Michael, and he did not want to share his wife's affection with them. Kathleen he took a fancy to. She was shy, timid, not at all her mother's darling and young enough to become attached to him. He set out to win her over, giving her presents, sitting her on his knee, talking a great deal about giving her a good home at last and always treating her with gentleness and kindness. It was useless; she hated him. His temper terrified her, although it was never directed against herself, and she was sickened by the smell of beer and tobacco in his beard.

When Marguerite came to see her, Mrs Hughes was having doubts about the marriage. In spite of the larger house and big garden, in spite of the extra money, she was not happy. She missed her Michael and worried about him. Edgar had earned well before the wedding but he drank more and more and there were days when he was hardly fit for work.

After her daughter had left, Mrs Hughes' anger abated. She had a good cry and determined to make it up. The girl was only doing what she thought right and she was a good daughter in her way. She must go and see her and put things right.

An appeal for sympathy and help from her mother could not be ignored. Marguerite could never resist a direct appeal from someone she believed herself to be fond of and they were reconciled. Her aunt and Elizabeth had expected that there would be a scene when they left the two of them alone in the Kenny drawing room. Marguerite had declared many times that she would never set foot in the Hughes' house again and that she would never do another thing for her mother. They had seen her firm mouth and square jaw and they had believed her.

But after the interview Marguerite was calm and smiling. "Poor mother," she said to Elizabeth, "we must go and see her often. And we must go there next Sunday when Hughes is there and meet him. Naturally he's angry that we have done nothing about him, and he'll only take it out on her. Poor soul! She was acting for the best. We cannot cut ourselves off from her and she needs our help." She spoke as though it had been Elizabeth's idea that they should.

She felt strong now. The worse Hughes was the better she felt. She had all the allies, including Michael, who had never sided with her before. Everything she did looked generous and forgiving. In time she might arrange for her mother to have a legal separation.

"Elizabeth, we must be very tactful for the moment," she said as they approached Stanley's Row.

Edgar was uncombed, dirty and gloomy. He had been brought up as a Baptist, and although he no longer went to service, the Baptist Sunday was still oppressive. His wife was not allowed to have her friends in or go for an outing. Kathleen was kept away from her toys and the piano.

He did not rise as his stepdaughters entered and could scarcely bring himself to murmur a greeting at the sight of such waists and bosoms. He was fanatically against the current fashion in ladies' clothes. The slightest *décolleté* struck him as indecent and often he held forth in an obsessed way about the nakedness of actresses and society women. These things could lead only to unbridled promiscuity. The sight of paint or powder on the female face roused him to fury.

Marguerite and Elizabeth were neither painted, powdered, nor wearing *décolleté,* but their waists were nipped in, their bosoms swelled in a fine curve and their skirts were pulled tight across their hips. They had put on their finery to inspire him with awe. They had meant him to realise that they were the product of quite another kind of marriage, they and their mother were of another class. They had meant him to feel inferior. They were condescending and cold.

Throughout the meal he held forth about the wickedness of foreign countries and the dangers which beset young girls who travelled on their own. No matter what attempts were made to change the subject he returned to it. Not even Marguerite's sarcasm could stop him. "I suppose you have travelled a great deal, Mr Hughes?"

His biblical turn of speech was new to them for they were not familiar with the full version of the Old Testament, having been brought up on the New Testament and *Stories from the Bible*, which outlined the principal tales of Abraham, Job, Joseph and others. They found him ridiculous and a little crazy.

"We can do nothing with *him*," said Marguerite afterwards, laughing happily at the thought. "He's one of those who can't take in anything. He is quite uncouth. Did you ever hear such nonsense? But we must stay in Cardiff for the sake of mother and the others. We cannot have them under his influence. He'll ruin them all if we go away."

"Oh, why did mother do it?" said Elizabeth. "Such a coarse, horrible man. How could she? It was so wrong. Do you think we should try to convert him and change him?" Her sister's talk of religion and moral wrong had penetrated.

Marguerite roared at the suggestion. "Of course not. It would be far worse if he were a Catholic. Then the marriage would be far worse, don't you see?"

"But I thought you said mixed marriages were wrong and..."

"Of course they're wrong. But this one is wrong in every way and it would be silly to try and make it better."

"Mother should never have done it." Elizabeth's blue eyes watered as she thought of the matted hair and beard, the filthy hands, the collarless shirt. "I could hardly believe it when I saw him."

"Poor mother," said Marguerite. It was no use Elizabeth recalling to her how she had felt at first. She never worried about inconsistency and her attitude had changed. From now on she looked on her mother as one of the children who had somehow strayed into the wrong home. "Poor mother."

18

Marguerite was nearing twenty-one and Elizabeth would soon be sixteen. They had little money left.

"We can't stay with Aunt Kenny for much longer," said Marguerite, "and of course there's no question of living with mother. We must decide what to do."

Elizabeth had already made up her mind; she would return to St. Joseph's and live in as a pupil teacher. "You have a teaching diploma," she said, "you could be a teacher in any school."

The idea did not appeal to Marguerite. History, geography, arithmetic in particular bored her and for other subjects she had little enthusiasm. She had not enjoyed her governess days. Also, teaching in a school restricted your world; you did not live in fine houses; you met nobody of interest.

She decided to train as a nurse at Cardiff Infirmary. Life during training might be tedious but once she was qualified she could take private cases, earn good money and move from place to place. She went to see the matron on the very day she took this decision. She made a most favourable impression and was taken on without delay.

During her first year in the Infirmary much of Marguerite's time was spent scrubbing floors and washing dishes, but she became the favourite of the sister in charge and was taken off these menial tasks sooner that the other probationers. She did well. It was her character rather than her aptitude for the work which made her a good hospital nurse. She was never deft or neat, and with her many preoccupations she was often forgetful, but she had the right touch with people. A disciplinarian herself she had a clear grasp of her position in relation to the authorities, the patients and the probationers. She was never slack and she respected the timetable; there was never any need to reprimand her for loitering, giggling or making eyes at doctors and male patients. She always looked busy and responsible.

By the time her second year was under way she had made her mark. The way she wore her uniform on duty, her French clothes off duty, her hair style, her refined pronunciation and use of French words and her grand manners were noticed by those in authority. They took it for granted that she came from a rich, travelled family. She naturally encouraged this belief and took care that nothing should be known of her mother's circumstances. Elizabeth was the only member of the family ever produced in public. Many of the girls training with her were rough and coarse and she described them to herself as "ordinary". Automatically she became one of the small group of "ladies" who spoke of nursing as a vocation and were occasionally asked to tea with the matron. Within this group she not only held her own but was considered a leading light.

While securing the favour of the authorities she was not unpopular with subordinates because she did them many good turns and never reported them for slackness. She was strict with them herself but in her dealings with them never brought in a higher authority. It was not in her nature to do so because she considered that she alone could deal with anyone. The sufferings of the more serious cases touched her and she took endless trouble to ease pain. The patients were quick to feel the warm-heartedness and generosity under her firmness and they loved and trusted her.

The work was hard and the hours were long but she had enough energy left to see to her family. Her spare time was filled with visits to her mother (when Hughes was likely to be out, of course), lectures to Kathleen on her speech and manners, visits to Aunt Kenny in order to discuss family plans, consultations with Elizabeth and entreaties to Thomas and Michael.

Michael was employed in the market place at one of the stalls. This setting particularly upset her because it recalled the lowest days of her life and brought home to her how little her brother had risen. Many of the stall holders remembered her and while unwilling to ignore them completely she felt compelled to reply to their greetings with guarded politeness. She would edge her way to Michael's stall, constantly glancing over her shoulder to see that none of her Infirmary friends were about, her face expressing a mixture of affection and disapproval as she saw his blue eyes and curly hair behind the piles of vegetables. The meetings were always unsuccessful. She would be nervous and distracted. In conspiratorial whispers, which were difficult to hear among the shouting and bustle, she urged him imperiously to leave his present job, take a course in some subject or another—this varied each time—and make new efforts to better himself. Always she would insist that he should leave his present lodgings, alleging that she had been told it was a disreputable house. Her quiet but impassioned harangues would often be interrupted by a customer and while he was being served she would tap her foot with impatience. Michael, despite his dullness, could sense that she was afraid of being seen with him; he was always obstinate and non-committal.

Where Elizabeth steered smoothly past the difficulties of her family, Marguerite tied herself in knots with fantasies and explanations. It was more difficult for her, of course, because whereas Elizabeth was willing to admit the existence of the Kenny's and Kathleen if necessary, Marguerite would own to none of them, and in fact pretended that her family were not in Cardiff at all. This led to explanations of why she herself had decided to train in this town, why Elizabeth was also working here, to the matron and sisters who took an interest and expected to be told something about her life.

There was something so fanciful about her stories that no one quite believed them. Yet, because she looked so upright, all were certain that she must have excellent reasons for concealing the truth—and of course no one had the faintest idea of what the truth was. Elizabeth, because all her friends were Catholics, could produce the piece about her stepfather being a non-Catholic if questioned about her family, and this would hint at a tragedy and make the questioners feel that they had been tactless and that she was wonderfully brave to have left home for religious principles. But the staff of the Infirmary were mostly Protestants and had Marguerite fallen back on this she would have appeared very bigoted indeed.

Had she been able to say once and for all that her family lived abroad it would have been the way out, but she could not depart too far from the facts because at any moment one of the many people she had known in Newport and Cardiff might appear. Therefore she spoke vaguely of having lived here once, of having travelled with her merchant father, who now, after the model of M Chantabrie, was said to have been connected with the wine trade, a big importer. Her mother's whereabouts shifted frequently and so did her income. She had a way of forgetting a previous story but made up for it by fearlessly bluffing her way out of a corner.

She never thought out her plan of action or her motives in these matters sufficiently clearly. Elizabeth knew what she was up to but Marguerite was not a realist or even reasonable where her family was concerned. Elizabeth thought it wiser to avoid lies and had a regard for the truth. Marguerite resented the existence of her stepfather so bitterly that she would have thought it a far greater crime to own to him than to tell a thousand lies.

She was increasingly conspiratorial with her family. One sister or brother would be drawn into a plot and told not to say a word to the others. She now never told anyone what was really in her mind. When she asked her aunt for a loan (for now that the fight with Hughes was on she sank her pride in this respect) she never gave the exact reason why she wanted it, even though that reason would have been perfectly acceptable to Mrs Kenny. She intrigued with and against every one of them, driven on by the unformulated desire that each one should trust her only, that she alone would hold one end of all the threads. Thomas was to persuade Michael to go and see the priest with him and the priest must urge him to go to evening classes, but neither Thomas nor the priest must let Michael know that she had asked them. Her aunt was to tell her mother that the wisest thing would be to have a separation from Hughes; she must also find out something to his discredit ("There must be many such things," Marguerite affirmed airily) and threaten to expose him if he did not hand back Kathleen. Michael was to make it up with Hughes and go back home in order to keep an eye on what was going on there.

Her great strength lay in her ability to cut her losses and move on. If a plot failed it was dropped and another one set on foot. Even when there were indications that it might be successful, she might tire of the delay and start something else. She urged each of her brothers in turn to become a priest, and to each one she solemnly swore that her father had singled him out for this honour. She even made the long journey to see John and David to try and persuade them. It was no use; with the exception of Thomas, all the boys disliked the idea of priesthood, and Thomas, in a silent, surly way was determined not to be led by her.

PART TWO: NUPTUALS

1

Marguerite insisted on seeing the manager personally. Her imperious manner and good clothes decided the timid clerk to let her have her way. She sailed into the manager's office and stood in front of his desk, her face half-shadowed by a large hat heavily adorned with velvet ribbon, flowers and feathers. "Good morning. I've come to see you about a debt."

Geoffrey Boyd, owner and manager of Boyd's Drapery Stores, was wealthy, handsome and in his late thirties. He had good manners and rose at once and looked pleasantly towards the young lady, finding what he could see of her face to be interesting. She would be one of the wealthy customers, of course, but perhaps in difficulties for the moment. "Please sit down. The name?" He smiled.

She returned the smile perfunctorily; it came and went in a flash. "The debt is in the name of Hughes, Mrs Edgar Hughes, my mother. One of your pack men came round yesterday to collect the weekly amount and she was unable to pay him. I think this has been going on for some time and he said something about reporting the case. I believe she is very much in arrears and I want to settle the whole account now."

Still smiling, he nodded to conceal his surprise. Pack men? They went only to the poor, the very poor, to those families who paid off a small amount at a time, sometimes only a shilling or two a week. He stopped looking for the name in the book before him and looked through another. Hughes, Mrs Edgar. One of the poorest customers in one of the poorest parts of the town. He eyed Marguerite's clothes. A draper himself, he could tell a good piece of material and a well-cut dress.

(Marguerite was wearing one of the dresses Madame had given her as a parting present, originally the work of a Paris *couturier*, and though it was many years old by now it had been skilfully renovated by Elizabeth. Over it she wore a fur-trimmed jacket, borrowed from Elizabeth who had made it for herself.)

"Ah, yes. Here we are, Miss Hughes."

"My name is Miss Reilly," she said indignantly, sitting straight on the edge of her chair and looking hard into his eyes. "How much is there owing?"

"Two pounds fifteen and six."

She opened her purse with a gloved hand. "Very well."

"There is no hurry."

"I'd sooner pay it off now. I dislike being in debt." She counted out the exact amount and handed it over.

He never took money like this. He should have said that the cashier downstairs would see to that. He meant to say it. He was about to say it. Then he felt it would sound wrong in this case, it would be discourteous. Meekly he pulled the money towards him and put it in a drawer. "I'm sorry if the man was rude."

"Oh, no, not at all. Please don't think that. He's always been very nice. I shouldn't like you to think otherwise. My mother says he was always very considerate." In a firm voice, in an accent she had evolved for herself and which was always changing, she continued, "Mr Boyd, I'm going to ask you a favour. I know it may sound off. But please will you refuse to accept any orders in future from my mother unless she pays cash."

He might have been a naughty child from the way she spoke. He might have been personally responsible for tempting her mother to buy things she should not have done, and perhaps he was, for it was he who had come to Cardiff from the north and introduced this credit system, it was he who had mobilised a fleet of pack men to poor houses with tempting samples and persuasive tongues. He felt annoyed and at a loss. When conducting business interviews he always did an act, not for the fun of the thing, but to keep the tone on the right plane. He now raised his eyebrows and looked amused. "Well, Miss, er, Reilly, it's a very unexpected request. You're asking me to refuse a customer. I don't think I can do that."

"I daresay it is unusual. But in this case I am the one who pays and therefore the *real* customer. You shouldn't refuse me."

"But Miss Reilly, how can I do it? If your mother comes into this shop and orders something, are the assistants to tell her they have orders not to sell her anything? And how are they to know her?"

"She's not likely to come to this shop. I don't think she's ever been here." Her voice was scornful, suggesting he knew this perfectly well and was hedging. Her mother was one of those who never move from their neighbourhood into the glittering centre of the town. "She bought everything through the man. If you could arrange that the pack man never called again."

She was within her rights here. He could hardly go on sending the man to the house if he had been expressly asked not to. He turned the full charm of his front face towards her with the look of one who is doing a great favour. "Very well, Miss Reilly. I shall see to that for you."

"Thank you so much. And may I have my receipt?"

A week or so later Marguerite was walking down the High Street. It was a drab morning. People were on their way to work and she kept to the edge of the pavement to avoid being jostled. A trained nurse now, she was on her way home from a case. She was walking to save the fare, for although she now earned good money there was never a penny to spare.

The family fortunes were not rising. The Kenny's had gone to Canada and therefore the chief source of help had dried up. Hughes had drunk himself into a state where he did little work. He was no longer his own master but did jobs for another man whenever he was fit for it. The pony and cart, the house with its yard and garden and stacked timber had all been sold. Mrs Hughes, once more in a slum, was hard up all the time and tried to keep things going by buying on credit and letting bills mount up. Michael had married his landlady's golden-haired daughter, Jennie, and had a baby already. Kathleen, who now had a scholarship to St. Joseph's, always seemed to be in need of clothes.

It was Marguerite who paid for Kathleen's new coat. It was Marguerite who arranged for David and John to go up north to their O'Connor relations so that they would be out of the orphanage and away from Hughes, and it was she who provided their fare and part of their clothes. It was Marguerite who paid for Thomas to take a secretarial course, for he was earning next to nothing as a shop assistant and wanted to better himself. It was Marguerite who paid for food and clothes for Michael's baby because she could not let it go cold and hungry, although she disliked the mother. Fortunately Elizabeth helped too now that she was earning well as a fully qualified teacher. She paid the rent of the flat where they both lived, she gave something towards Thomas and she used her needle cleverly on her sister's clothes and her own.

She saw a motor-car coming towards her. They were rare enough in those days and she forgot her preoccupations and stared at it with interest. To her surprise and delight it came to a halt beside her with a great grinding sound and a jerky bump, and there was Geoffrey Boyd in the driver's seat, smiling at her broadly. "Miss Reilly! It is Miss Reilly, isn't it? Good morning. Where are you off to? May I drive you?"

She had never been in a car before. It excited her, just as train journeys and channel crossings on steamers excited her. Her restlessness was partly satisfied when she found herself in some great, chugging, noisy thing, moving marvellously rapidly from one place to another. She gladly accepted the offer. Boyd shouted above the rattle and the roar.

"So you're a nurse."

"Yes."

"Are you just off to work?"

"No, I've come off night duty."

He put her down outside the door. He watched her unlock it and go in, waving to him a friendly final goodbye. He would have liked to run after her and say something, anything. He felt he had behaved discourteously in the office and owed her an apology. He wondered which floor she lived on, and did she live alone there. It was a boarding house in a good residential district. He felt reluctant to go. He felt unsettled and impatient.

A few days later she ran into the car and the driver again. It was the car she was glad to see. It was not by accident as she supposed. Every morning Boyd had been hunting for her up and down the High Street. Once more he offered to drive her home and once more she gladly accepted, mounting the high platform with happy anticipation. Now she knew the pleasures of driving, and in fact, her dreams of the family future had lately had the addition of a fine motor-car.

"You look tired, Miss Reilly. I hope you're not working too hard. How long have you been on night duty?"

"About a month."

Having to shout so loud made it impossible to express his concern for her in his voice, and with his face screwed up against the wind he could reveal no sympathy by his expression. Besides she was not looking at him. Her hair in wisps about her face, her bonnet driven to the back of her head, she was looking ahead, exalted, in a dream.

She thanked him with great friendliness, bedraggled and flushed and smiling, but as she spoke she looked not at him but at the car. How wonderful it would be to have such a thing and to drive it oneself. She could sit in the front with Michael and Elizabeth and Michael's baby, Patrick, could be at the back. Boyd would have liked to suggest driving her home the following day, any day she chose, but his courage failed him.

Back in the office he found that she was on his mind. That morning she had walked in so well dressed and so self-assured, she must have been up working all the night before. The two pounds fifteen and six she handed over as though there was plenty more money in her purse must have come out of her hard-earned wages. He looked up the Hughes address in his book and stared at it. In the afternoon the impulse to go there was too strong to resist. Hardly knowing why he went and wondering what he would say he called on Mrs Hughes. Experience with every type of customer gave him words. He smiled charmingly.

"I'm Mr Boyd of Boyd's Drapery Stores and I thought I'd just drop in because I was passing this way, to let you know your daughter has settled the account. Of course I suppose she's told you, but just in case she hasn't."

"That's very kind of you indeed, sir," said Mrs Hughes.

"There's another matter I wanted to discuss, but please don't let me keep you out in the cold."

"If you would like to come in. There'll be a cup of tea going."

"Just what I most fancy," he said, "if it's not too much trouble."

He trumped up something about the pack man. He said he was anxious to know if he had been polite. He had not meant the man to press for payment and if there was any unpleasantness he would like to know.

Mrs Hughes, afraid that the pack man might lose his job, assured him that there had never been any unpleasantness. As she spoke he looked around the kitchen as though searching for a clue. There was no trace of Miss Reilly, no photograph of her as a child. Perhaps she seldom came here.

"You have a large family, Mrs Hughes?"

"There's seven of them."

"And the daughter I met, where does she come in the family?"

"She's the eldest."

He might have guessed it. Mrs Hughes had the natural expansiveness of the Irish and told him much of the family history. So her name was Marguerite and she had travelled, gone off abroad on her own at sixteen. Her story interested him but learning it like this was no use. He must see her, he must know her, he must hear her speak about herself. He took a great liking to Mrs Hughes. How very like her daughter she was and what a fine-looking woman.

When he first met Marguerite the thought of flirting with her had crossed his mind because he always flirted mildly with his lady customers. But her stern face, the lordly way she gave the name Hughes and the story that name told him in his account book baffled him. Then again, if the second time he had seen her she had been as well dressed as ever and on top of her form, she would again have made an impression on him and he would simply have thought, "Splendid girl that. A bit alarming."

But the sight of her tired, almost aged face, her dragging step on the grey, morning pavement and the plain dark nurse's cloak was too much for him. It went to his heart like a sudden pang. He was filled with pity and the feeling allied to pity which is a realisation of what someone else's life is like, an experience of it at second hand— usually illusory and in this case wholly so for he magnified Marguerite's sufferings and struggles. His imagination was fired by the idea of women like Florence Nightingale, as though the nurse's cloak could enfold heroines only. At that moment he knew that he must pull up and speak to her or his morning would be clouded. He had recognised her from a distance, for there was something very characteristic about her which had struck him at once, and as he began to slow down to reach her, carefully estimating the distance between them, the ever clearer vision of her worn face had engraved itself into his mind. He would never forget her as she looked then, her lips pressed tight and hollows under the eyes.

When he next encountered her and drove her home he mentioned that he had visited her mother, hoping that this would disclose to her the intensity of his interest, and yet making light of it to avoid embarrassment.

"I had to go that way and so I thought I'd look in, just to show it was all right about the bill. And also I wanted to make sure the pack men hadn't worried her. I know what it is to be pressed for money. My family were always hard up." This was not true.

Marguerite saw nothing strange in the visit. She might have done the same thing if she had been in his position for she was often seized by an impulse to oblige a stranger. She thought him considerate and refined; refined because his clothes were well made, his face was long and pale and his broad north-country voice did not jar on her as the Cardiff accent did. Her father had had a north-country accent.

It was not until her case was finished that he could bring himself to ask her out to tea. Now that she was no longer on night duty he had no qualms about keeping her from sleep.

"He must be sweet on you," said Elizabeth when she heard of the drives and the invitation.

"Oh, no," said Marguerite with conviction, "not at all. I think he's very lonely, you know. His parents are dead and he's not been long in Cardiff. He came from the north, you see, and so he knows no one. I think it's because we come from the north too."

This put an idea into her head, but not the obvious one. Elizabeth was pretty and Boyd was lonely and therefore would be bound to fall in love with her and it would be a most suitable match. Elizabeth had many suitors but none was so rich and none possessed a motor-car. Boyd, who was such a nice man, and his car, would be kept in the family.

Over tea she would speak of nothing but her sister. "She is so beautiful. You wait until you see her. And she is very charming and clever. She would be wonderful in a house."

In Elizabeth's interests she thought it wise to give him a proper idea of the family—he had been introduced to it at the wrong end unfortunately—and she disclosed to him how, though they might seem poor now, her mother was the daughter of an admiral and her father had come from landed gentry in Ireland. He could not tell how much of this to believe and he saw many weak points in the story. Usually, snobbery irritated him but in this case it was different. She was no ordinary little social climber. He looked credulous and sympathetic.

He did not fall in love with Elizabeth. He did not even like her. Compared with Marguerite she seemed insipid and affected, although she was the more upright of the two and every bit as determined. Any glimpses he caught of her well-organised character did not strike him as admirable, but jarring and calculating, out of place behind those heavily lidded eyes and the pink and white skin.

"Hard as nails under all that pretty stuff," he told himself. With him, as with the sisters at the Hospital, Marguerite got away with the lies and inconsistency because she looked adventurous and strong, because she created an impression of honesty with her straight brows and level eyes. They made excuses for her. With such a person it was not the actions which counted but the motives, and these could not be petty or self-interested. Always she gave the impression that she was battling, and always it seemed that the battle was waged for the sake of others.

To please Marguerite, Boyd said he found Elizabeth delightful and she thought her plans were going well. Because of this and because of his imagined loneliness she had no hesitation in accepting invitations, or asking him to employ Thomas in the shop, or arranging to buy clothes for the children at wholesale prices. It was a relief to have found someone who could be asked to help the others. But the fact that he knew all about the family did perhaps make it impossible for her to see him as a love object. The fact that he was happy with Mrs Hughes and even with Edgar was not altogether to his credit in her eyes.

All benefited by the acquaintance. All were taken for rides in the motor-car. Kathleen received many bright half-crowns.

2

For some time Geoffrey Boyd could not decide what he wanted from Marguerite. He wanted her to love him, but if she did, what would he do then? Anything other than marriage was out of the question for her, and in this case nothing but marriage would suit him. But did he really want to go as far as marriage? Did he want anything other than to compel her to notice him, to admire him and to love him, to look on him as someone wonderful, which she obviously did not. He admired her and he loved her. She stirred all his most generous impulses and to find himself so chivalrous increased his self-esteem. He had an exaggerated idea of the importance of her good opinion. But she must admire him for what he was, with no fantasy. He could see she had some idea of him as a generous, lonely soul and this was not enough.

He began to think that if he married her then she would love him. He might settle down and get a grip on his life. He might drink less; that would be easy. He might, perhaps, escape at last from the bouts of melancholia which pursued him; that was unlikely. He had thought of marrying before, marrying someone of good class in order to consolidate himself because he was a self-made man. He had never known poverty but his father had been a small draper whereas he himself now owned three large stores in three different towns.

From the class point of view Marguerite would do. Her family background was odd, to say the least, but she herself had such style, such airs and she spoke so well. Anyone would take her for what she claimed to be. He would be proud to be seen with her, he was already. How splendid she looked in the car, perched straight-backed on the high seat, her large hat held on by yards of tulle, wrapped over and over and tied under the chin in a full bow.

She held his interest and he enjoyed himself out with her. They went for excursions in the car, out into the countryside, down to the sea, and she sat, unreactive to beauties of scenery, but exhilarated by the movement. They went to the theatre, in the best seats, and she blossomed out and became very grand; they were "the cream of Cardiff society". They went to the best restaurants and there she pronounced the names of foreign dishes with the most French of French accents. He saw her looking plain, handsome, animated, tired, cheerful and worried. He imagined he knew her well. Each new trait fitted logically onto what he had already constructed. Everything about her seemed inevitable and all of a piece. Everything about her moved him, even the great web of lies and fantasies she wove around the simplest fact. However peculiar her actions he could explain them to himself in such a way that she remained intact.

He saw her as the very opposite of himself; he told no lies to himself; his actions were straightforward; he was analytical and yet he never knew his motivation. He had set out to make money and he had made it. He was his own master, could do what he liked and he was dissatisfied. How satisfied she would be when she had achieved her ambitions! He drank, he had women, he had an entry into Cardiff society, for what it was worth, he could move to London whenever he chose, but nothing seemed of any importance. At any time, for no reason, a feeling of overwhelming depression might take

94

hold of him. She was never bored with any of her different activities, she put everything she had into each action. Life never lacked meaning for her; it was one continuous drive ahead. And though heaven might be her ultimate goal, there were many goals here and now to be aiming at.

He found himself clinging to her as to a rock. She liked him and included him among the people whose interests she had at heart. She was domineering and unaware of what he was like. She drew him into her schemes for the family. He confessed to a weakness for drink and she took him in hand. He even began, "I get these moods of dreadful depression," but he could see from the look she gave him that she was ready to be sorry for him but unable to understand. And it would have been impossible if she had understood, for only those who had similar experiences could understand, and they were no use to him.

After wavering he proposed. Marguerite was surprised, having hoped until then, with little reason, that it was Elizabeth he wanted. She never liked refusing a request. Seeing him saddened by her hesitation she felt sorry for him.

"But you know I couldn't marry for some time. There's all the family to be seen to."

"You can see to them just as well when you're married, in fact better. You'll have more time and money."

The idea of marriage was strange to her and made her uneasy. It was not shocking as it had been in Bordeaux but it played no part in her dreams.

"But Geoffrey, there's the question of religion. I could never marry a non-Catholic."

Reluctantly he promised to go to the priest for instruction. He would have preferred a sudden conversion on the spot to save himself the bother, but only a look of genuineness would satisfy her.

She raised other objections and he dismissed them. He pleaded and played on her kindness. They became engaged.

The fine, expensive engagement ring on her hand gave her no pleasure. It conjured up none of the rosy thoughts that another woman might have had. She responded to the enthusiastic congratulations of her family with mechanical smiles and any old phrase which came into her head and seemed appropriate. With a wish to do the conventional thing, she introduced her fiancé to her special friends, all of whom were either members of the hospital staff or former patients.

Being engaged seemed to make little difference, thought Geoffrey. He could hold her hand and kiss her. He could even put his arms around her and feel close to her. But always he came up against her lack of enthusiasm, her impersonal quality and her wish to be kind. It was to be a six months' engagement. Sometimes he was glad of the time but more often he felt that if he could not do the thing quickly, do it on impulse, it would dwindle away to nothing.

Once married, he believed, she would become physically attached to him. She was not fundamentally cold like Elizabeth. Her face disclosed a warm and passionate heart. But until marriage she would remain as she was, passive, unweakened, and dispersing her emotions so that few reached him. Besides, he wanted to see her rich and free from cares. It was his wish to do something for her, to help her, which had driven him into love and which still dominated him.

He deceived her, of course. He continued to drink heavily. He saw and had other women. He pretended to be coming slowly and steadily round to Catholicism, although he well knew that a thousand priests could have worked on him for a thousand years without making the slightest difference.

Meanwhile Marguerite continued with her cases. They were mostly surgical and although she dealt with them competently she longed to specialise in midwifery. At this time, nursing enthralled her. It suited her temperament to live for ever in an atmosphere of crisis and emergency and to be the key person in the situation. Each of her patients she felt to be in her hands. She was the person who could save them and not the doctor. Her attitude to authority was changing. She paid lip service to it in the form of matrons and doctors, but she respected only the Church and her father. Apart from them she felt that no one was her equal, not with pride, for she never told herself she was wonderful, but with an ever-strengthening confidence and feeling of isolation.

Her great love for the moment was Patrick, Michael's baby. Not only was he the eldest son of the eldest brother and therefore the Prince of the family, the future ruler, but he was also called after her father. He was the only member of the third generation yet and he charmed her. She would trump up any excuse to go and see him, often cancelling an outing with Geoffrey. She loved to play with Patrick. She talked ridiculous talk, smiled and made funny faces. She did anything to make him laugh, rushing across the room, hiding behind a chair, suddenly shouting, "boo!" And when he chuckled she roared back at him. She sang out of tune to him. She bought him presents. It seemed right to her that his every whim should be indulged. If correction was needed—and for the moment it was not—she was the only person who could judge. She looked on any strictness from his mother as cruelty and coldness. She would have liked to take him over altogether and she interfered as much as she could.

"He looks so intelligent," she said, gazing into his blank, blue eyes. "He is the image of my father," she said, and no one else saw the slightest resemblance.

Geoffrey often had to visit his stores in other towns or go up north to buy cloth in bulk, and at these times Marguerite almost forgot he existed. She felt relieved and free to spend as much time as she wanted with Patrick. When Geoffrey was with her she tried to be pleasant but she often appeared restless and distracted.

One evening she found him waiting for her. He was unusually surly, bored with Elizabeth's well-meant attempts to keep him amused. He was pining for a drink. "You're very late," he snapped.

"I had to go along to Michael's. I knew you'd understand."

"But you're hours late. Did you realise how long you were keeping me? Did you realise we won't have time to eat before the theatre? If you're going to be late like this you should at least let me know beforehand and then I could have something to eat."

"I'm sorry. I'm very sorry."

Seeing Elizabeth about to slip into the other room tactfully she called her back. "Oh, Elizabeth, you should just see Patrick! He's really talking now. He said, 'Oh, dear.' I had to laugh. I do wish you'd seen him." She went on to describe the child's other achievements.

Geoffrey suddenly rose from his chair. "When will you be ready? There's not much time," he interrupted.

"I'd better go and tidy then."

She went off with Elizabeth and he could hear her voice, probably still talking about the boy. In a fury at the time she took he walked to the mantelpiece and stood looking into the fire. When she returned he turned round in a flash and shouted at her. "You took your time. We shall be lucky if we see more than the last act. What on earth were you doing?"

She flushed at being spoken to like that and said nothing.

Alarmed by her expression he changed his tone. "This engagement is getting on my nerves. Thank goodness it'll be over soon. In two months we'll be married and I'll have you to myself."

She seemed not to be listening. She was obviously thinking of something quite different. Her look of anger had gone and her vague eyes were staring at the picture rail above his head.

He raised his voice. "You do want to marry me, don't you?"

"Yes, yes." Because he had been angry and spoken roughly she was less sorry for him. This freed her to speak as she felt. "But Geoffrey, I've been thinking. Two months is really a little soon for me. I'd meant to speak to you about it. You see, I can't give up this case. The old lady is very ill and it may last some time. And then, I must try and get the boys down here."

"But you can do that afterwards."

"I know. Perhaps I can. But you see, the old lady begged me not to leave her. She's used to me and I know her ways and I wouldn't hand her over to one of these young nurses who do things anyhow." When speaking of her profession, Marguerite always sounded as though she were a hundred.

"You could find a nurse you trusted in that time, couldn't you?"

"She wouldn't like that. I promised her."

"You had no right to. And since when have you bothered about keeping promises?"

She looked surprised and a little hurt. Only a little, he noticed with mortification, because her mind was on something else. There was no way of getting at her.

"Geoffrey, what would you say to another six months? Then I could have everything done, and we could go right away after the marriage as you suggested. I wouldn't have anything to worry me then."

"Oh, yes you would. I bet you would."

"After all, there's very little difference between two months and six. You wouldn't mind, would you?"

Without replying he ushered her out.

3

"You must meet Nurse Calder," said one of the nurses at the hospital to Marguerite. "She's so charming. You would love her. Do come to tea on Sunday."

Nurse Calder, small, frail-looking, white-faced, with pinched nostrils and a country voice, was in fact just what Marguerite admired. Of good family, a great friend of the matron's, she had trained many years ago and was now working in London.

Marguerite listened attentively to what she had to say. She learnt a great deal. In London one could earn much more as a nurse. It was not just a matter of wages but presents at the end of the case and that sort of thing. One could get in with specialists, Harley Street men, and be sent to the houses of the most eminent people, even royalty.

In a solemn voice the sister explained. "Nurse Calder has nursed a relation of the Queen."

Marguerite put on her grandest manner and made a successful effort to impress.

Nurse Calder took a very great fancy to her. "Now you, Miss Reilly, with your languages and travelling, could do very well in London. I could give you introductions to several people. If you really wished to become known to some of these doctors I've mentioned, you might come with me on some case in the future."

Before parting they exchanged addresses and promised to correspond.

That evening Marguerite spoke to Elizabeth. "You know, if we could only get to London we could do so much. You could teach there and I could nurse. They say there are very good cases going and one can earn much more. In time we could get the rest of the family there. Of course I shouldn't like to leave Patrick. Jennie's no good and he's so fond of me."

"What about Geoffrey?"

"Ah, yes. I mean this would only be temporary of course. Just for a year or so. Just long enough to get them on their feet. We could take a small house, in a good residential part, the sort of place where we could have people like Nurse Calder to tea. We could let most of the rooms. That would pay for the rent. Then we should be rent free and both earning well."

She walked up and down the room, restless, excited, unsettled. "I tell you how I see it, Elizabeth. We would take Michael with us and his family. Then Jennie could look after the house and we should have the baby there with us. We'd soon find some nice job for Michael. And until we did he could be helping with the lodgers and doing odd jobs and that sort of thing. After all, we must have someone there with us because we should both be out all day and I might be away for months on a case."

Elizabeth was amazed and guarded. "I could hardly give up St. Joseph's. For the moment I'm very content here."

"How can you say that when you are so ambitious? You surely don't want to be a teacher at St. Joseph's all your life. Now one of those nice Sacred Heart Convents…"

"But Marguerite, you talk as though you weren't going to get married at all!"

"Geoffrey's so understanding, such a dear."

The idea had taken hold of her. Why hadn't she thought of London before? Of course she had thought of it but not so clearly. And the thought of letting rooms had appealed to her ever since she had reckoned what her own landlady must make. Cardiff was just a provincial town. She had never liked the place and it had terrible associations.

The date of the marriage was approaching. A few months now and it would be done at last, thought Geoffrey. Noticing her increased preoccupation with something other than himself he became more and more restive and difficult. He was in a highly emotional state, desperate to hold her and trying to fit in with her. He tried keeping away for days at a time to make her all the gladder to see him. When he was with her he made every effort to appear interested in her relations. But all the time he kept fidgeting. His long fingers never stopped moving. He looked worn and grey.

It was Elizabeth who noticed this. "I think Geoffrey doesn't look very well," she said, "you really ought to be more considerate to him. He seems upset to me."

"Oh, it's his work," said Marguerite. "He gets very tired because he works so hard. Such a big business is a great responsibility. And then he does drink too much."

For some time Geoffrey had been in the habit of dropping in on Mrs Hughes, when he couldn't see Marguerite, in the evening. He had abandoned his old friends because he didn't want to see them, and it gave him some comfort to sit in the Hughes' kitchen and feel like one of the family. Quite naturally he slipped into drinking with Edgar; he liked the man.

On this evening he found Mrs Hughes worried. "Oh, Geoffrey, you must stop this idea of Marguerite's about going to work in London. And she means to take them all away from here. And here I'll be left without any of my children, and Michael going too and taking his Patrick with him."

This was the first Geoffrey had heard of it. "To London? But there's no time for her to do that."

"Isn't that what I was saying to her?"

"And what did she say?"

"She said there would be time enough and she was so taken up with the idea and the grand opportunities there'd be. I wondered had you quarrelled?"

Agitated, Geoffrey was on the point of leaving the house and going round to Elizabeth to find out more. But seeing Edgar come in at that moment, he greeted him, produced some whisky from his pocket and together they settled down to drink.

Marguerite never came here in the evening as a rule. This evening, however, anxious to find a matching button for Patrick's little coat at once, she rushed in to search her mother's work box. She found the three of them around the kitchen table. The sight appalled her.

"Mother, what is all this?"

Mrs Hughes had had just enough to make her happy and smiling. "Oh, nothing, dear. What would it be?"

"Are you drunk too?"

"Sure nobody's drunk."

"Yes they are. You all are. Look at you all. Geoffrey, how could you?"

Geoffrey stood up and grinned at her. He was not so drunk as he looked but it amused him to worry her. He rose and bowed. What was she doing here? She'd told him she would have to be with a patient till late. "What an honour, an unexpected honour to see you."

He left the kitchen and went into the parlour where he sat at Kathleen's piano and tapped out a tune with one finger, taking no notice of the child, who had been sent in there out of the way, while drinking went on. He wanted to irritate. He wanted a scene. He didn't care how it ended but he must have a scene, and it must be alone in here with her, not with the other two. He heard her come in after him. Good. He kept his back to her and tapped away, thumped, bent over the notes.

"Geoffrey, how long have you been doing this? How long have you been coming here and giving them drink?" She caught sight of Kathleen and checked herself. "Kathie, go into the kitchen."

"They told me to do my homework in here."

"Well go back to the kitchen now." Closing the door behind her she went on. "What will the child think? What an example! How could you do this behind my back? You know what a struggle I've had against Edgar's drinking. I could never have believed it."

"When are you going to marry me?"

"Answer me. How long have you been doing this? You know what I think of Edgar. How can you come and make friends with him, a man in your position?"

"When are you going to marry me?"

She came near him. "Mother said you often came to see her. I thought that very sweet of you. I never imagined what really went on."

"When are you going to marry me?" He was still tapping.

"How can I marry a person who drinks? How can I have another of them in the family?"

He jumped up and faced her. He took hold of both her hands and stared at her. "Maggie Reilly. Yes, Maggie. I said Maggie. That's what your mother calls you when you're not there, and so does Edgar and so do I, and it's a much better name than Marguerite. I told you I loved you. I asked you to marry me. Do you want to marry me? Do you mean to marry me? Do you want me to love you?"

"No. Not if..."

He went white. "I knew it. Why couldn't you say so? What have you been up to all this time? Aren't you engaged to me? Didn't you say you were going to marry me?"

She was exasperated and tried to free her hands. "I didn't know you were like this."

"Listen to me, Maggie Reilly. What's all this about you going to work in London? You never said a word to me about it. I came in here this evening and your mother told me. And then you wonder why I drink?"

"I can't forgive you. With Hughes of all people."

"Forget the drink and answer me. What are these plans about London? Were you going to tell me? Were you thinking of postponing the wedding again?" He put his face close to hers, knowing she would hate it, knowing she would recoil from the smell of drink. He felt he hated her. He had always been benevolent towards her but now he wanted to hurt her. He had made all the effort and she had let him down. Ever since he had known her, it seemed like years ago, he'd tried to make something of it, of himself. She was the only person who could help him, he had told her so again and again, but she never listened, she never took anything in. She didn't care what became of him. She hedged and made promises and you never knew where you were with her.

"You must answer me now. I want to know once and for all. All the time you were engaged to me you should have been busy with a trousseau and ideas of a home and furniture and all those things. It's those things I want, they will make everything seem real to me. But instead of this all you'll talk about is this wretched baby, your brother's baby, as though you couldn't have babies of your own to care about and if it's not the baby, it's the boys up north or your old patients. I thought your unselfishness very fine. I thought you'd give a bit of it to me. But I'm the only one you don't bother about."

He found he was shaking her. He didn't care. "I don't know what you think marriage is. Do you ever think about it? No. I'm sure you don't. Or is it that there's something wrong with me? I'm not good enough for you. I'm only a business man. If I were some bleeding aristocrat, one of these foreigners you're always talking about, you might hurry up the marriage a bit." He knew that wasn't true but what did it matter? "I want to know, are you going to marry me or not? And if you are will you marry me in two months as we arranged?"

She was angry, she was sorry for him, and above all she disliked having to give a straight answer. "Geoffrey, I'm very fond of you, but I've always said to you, I said it from the first, that perhaps I shouldn't marry. I've all the family to think of, and until they're all settled..."

"But they'll never be settled. First one of them will have a baby and then another and then another and there'll always be someone you think you ought to look after. Do you mean to marry me?"

He looked so wretched. "Yes," she said slowly.

"In two months' time?"

"Well there's so much to do and..."

"Yes or no?"

"Shall we say six months?"

"No. Two months or never. And decide now."

"Very well. Two months."

Then he let her lecture him and promised anything she asked. He would keep away from Edgar. He would cut down the drink. He had been in the wrong. He should never have done it.

He felt he had lost again. He had appealed to her pity and she had wanted to comfort him. She would say anything and then she would try and postpone it again.

4

Now that a tinge of hate had crept into his love it was more obsessive and passionate. He went to see her mother constantly, but not in the evenings and not with drink, to ask if any more had been said about London. He had talks with Elizabeth, whom he still disliked, and asked for her help. He forced Marguerite to go to the shops with him and look at furniture for their future home. He drove her to houses for sale and made her look over them. He badgered and pestered. What was her time off? When could he next see her?

Marguerite was hard put to it to make excuses for going to see Patrick. Sometimes she said he was ill and made her family swear to bear her out. Sometimes she said her hours were longer than they were and, still in her cloak and bonnet, slipped along to Michael's wretched house, looking over her shoulder to see if she was being watched. It wasn't that she feared Geoffrey, but the degree of his unhappiness alarmed her and she wanted to avoid hurting him.

Egged on by Elizabeth, who was all for the match, she took pains to please him. She tried hard to think of the marriage. She tried hard to take an interest in a new home.

There was a month to go. Geoffrey was off to Bradford to buy cloth. A letter arrived from Nurse Calder.

"Mr Rathbone has asked me to take a nurse with me. I wondered if you would care to go? You would be the night nurse."

The patient was a viscount. The house was a large country mansion. Mr Rathbone was one of the most noted surgeons of his time.

The night before Geoffrey was to leave for the north, Marguerite accompanied him to see *The Mikado*. To give him pleasure she expressed great enthusiasm for this work, and in fact she believed that she loved it. The Japanese costumes were the height of what she termed "daintiness" and something in the music seemed to go with them exactly.

She had dressed up for the occasion. Her cheeks were flushed and her eyes shone. She had never looked better.

Talking animatedly during the interval she observed Geoffrey's good humour and lack of tension. Now would be the right moment to mention the case.

"It would only be for six weeks or so," she said. "This nurse cannot find anyone else suitable and I should like to oblige her. Then as soon as it was over we could get married."

Geoffrey's face darkened at one. "My goodness! Do you *want* to go?"

"Oh, no. I don't want to go at all. I would much rather not really, but this poor nurse is so anxious..."

"Marguerite if you go that'll be the end of it." In a frenzy he rose from his seat and pulled her up by the arm. "We must leave here. We can't talk here."

"But I want to see the rest of the show."

"No, no," he pulled at her hand with all his strength. "If you're thinking of going off like that, I'm not going to sit through this show. What do you want to go for? Are you trying to get out of the marriage?"

He was shouting and she was afraid of what the audience might think, for there they were, the two of them, standing in the middle of a row, among seated people. She saw faces turned towards her. Her eyes kept meeting other eyes. "Geoffrey, please sit down. Please stop shouting. I shan't mention it again. I promise I won't go. If it upsets you I won't go."

He sat down. "What do you want to go for? That's what bothers me. It's one of your peculiar reasons, something to do with getting more money, something to do with the others. And why should you be thinking of that when you're going to marry me? What's in your mind? What are you hiding?"

"I was only asking you, Geoffrey. I asked you." She felt he should have been grateful for that. She never asked anyone's permission. This was a great concession. She saw his twitching mouth and moving fingers and misery and terror in his brightened eyes, but she minimised his reactions. He was peeved and worried, she thought.

The reassurances she gave were wholly inadequate. It would have been better had she given none. The thinness of her kind smile and consoling words increased his feeling of insecurity and mistrust. And yet he must control himself. Another scene, another opening for frankness and she might postpone again or even decide not to marry him. Again and again he made her promise not to go, useless though it was.

"You have promised me," he said as they parted.

"Yes." She looked at him with tenderness, glad that this ordeal was over at last. She was tired of it and wanted a rest. The street lamp showed up the dark hollows beneath her eyes and recalled to him the moment he fell in love with her. She was a wonderful woman, he thought, unlike anyone else he had met. Once married her real character, now unbalanced by many worries, would show itself.

When Geoffrey had gone she felt free. She spent her off-duty time with Patrick, bathing him, teaching him words and believing the sounds he made to be an exact imitation of what she said, looking on him with the most complete and uncritical love. She was extraordinarily happy.

Elizabeth and Mrs Hughes thought that Marguerite was at last looking forward to the wedding. She seemed in a dream. She was even more absent minded than usual. As she contemplated Patrick's chubby limbs, luminous in the firelight, she thought of the case. The great mansion, the noble patient and the famous surgeon seemed to beckon to her. It might lead to anything: to great earnings, to a house of her own in London where she could put Patrick. She would pay for a good school. He would be taught to speak properly. He would not be left to imitate the Cardiff accent all around him. She must send a reply to Nurse Calder in two days. What a pity it must be "no", but she must refuse.

Geoffrey's troubled face receded. She saw him as he had often looked, jolly, good-humoured and patient. Such a dear! So understanding! Tired, elated, muddled, not following any train of thought to its logical conclusion, unimaginative about the feelings of others, on an impulse, she wrote two letters. The first, to Nurse Calder, said she would arrive in three days. The second, to Geoffrey, explained: "Unfortunately the nurse really cannot do without me. She seems to be under the impression that I promised to go and she can find no one else suitable at such short notice. I know you will understand my position. After all, it will be for a very short time. As soon as it is over I shall come back to Cardiff and we can be married at once. I shall write and tell you the exact date as soon as I can so that you can make all the preparations."

5

There was much to do. Another nurse had to be found to replace her here. Many instructions had to be given to Patrick's mother and they had to be repeated, drummed into her head. There was packing and it must be carefully done to avoid creasing the spotless starched aprons, collars and caps. Her uniform must be perfect. Then came the excitement, the exhilaration of finding herself on a train once more, going to somewhere new on her own.

It was not until she reached London and paused between trains that she discovered the letter to Geoffrey still in her pocket. She posted it.

Her new place was all she had expected. The large, white house looked down onto a long, curving drive, smooth lawns and tall trees. Nurse Calder embraced her as though they were the greatest of friends. She was made comfortable. The housekeeper, respectfully, showed her to her room. There were maids, footmen and a butler. Outside a host of gardeners and under-gardeners trimmed edges, grew rare plants in hot-houses, mowed and rolled. It was in some ways like the Bordeaux house but the Chantabries owned no landscape and it was less gaudy and more hushed. How long it was since she had been in such an establishment! It was like returning home. She belonged to such a life. It reminded her of her father's way of life before his ruin.

It was an ideal case. The patient had been successfully operated upon, was therefore recovering steadily and not really ill. At first there were frequent dressings and heavy lifting, but soon her night would be a peaceful vigil. Later it would be possible to doze off comfortably in an armchair while waiting for the bell. Then there would be time to get to know the influential Nurse Calder and many other pleasant things.

She missed the baby. The thought of Geoffrey made her a little uneasy. Otherwise Cardiff life seemed very remote.

A letter came from Elizabeth, written in the shorthand style she affected:

"Mother asked me to write because too upset herself. Dear Marguerite must be brave. Have very bad news for you. Geoffrey in serious accident. Afraid no hope."

Here, fearing that Marguerite would come out at once if she thought Geoffrey still breathing, she thought it better to tell all.

"Geoffrey dead. Know there is nothing can say to comfort you but have been praying for you and poor Geoffrey. Am offering daily Mass for both. If shock not too great and if can continue where you are, am sure would be best. Here in Cardiff will only upset you. Would advise you stay where you are. If would give any consolation could come and stay near you."

Marguerite left for Cardiff at once. Finding Elizabeth out she hurried to her mother's house.

"But I didn't know he was in Cardiff, mother. I thought he was still up north? Did you know?"

Mrs Hughes hedged and then came out with it. She cried, shook her head and wrung her hands. (Sudden deaths and accidents had been the subject of her talk with cronies for the last few days. "I can't bear to think of it. I can't bear to talk about it," she had repeated and then they had settled down to hear the details from her all over again. Shaking their heads they made philosophical remarks of a consoling nature. They had been horrified and they had been pleased).

For the moment she forgot what she knew of her daughter. She assumed, as is so often the case, that for this once she would behave as she expected her to. And she decided that when Marguerite broke down, giving way to dreadful grief at last, she would be there, maternal and comforting, to say the right things to her.

"I didn't want you to know, Maggie. I thought it would only be upsetting you more but he came here that evening. Yes, he came here. He'd been round to your place and he'd seen Elizabeth and he found you'd gone and he'd been drinking. He was in a terrible state, angry and swearing and he kept saying he'd be doing something desperate. Oh, Maggie, Maggie, I felt he'd be doing something of the sort. I knew it."

Marguerite went white. "But mother, wasn't it an accident? It must have been. But he knew I was away. I wrote..." She thought and put her hand to her forehead. "But if he was back in Cardiff he may not have had it. Mother, did he say anything about my letter?"

"No, dear. I'm sure he'd had no letter."

"And why was he in Cardiff?"

"He said he knew you'd go. He said he'd been worried and hurried back to see you. He wanted to stop you."

Marguerite was frightened. They had been standing, one on either side of the big scrubbed table, and now Mrs Hughes hurried over to her daughter's side. But Marguerite wanted no sympathy. She moved away to be able to think. It was not herself she was sorry for. She stood still for some time.

Tears poured down her cheeks. "Oh, mother! Oh, mother!" She was bewildered and apprehensive. "Mother, I hope it was an accident. I hope he didn't die in a state of mortal sin. If he'd been drinking, mother, if he'd been drinking, he wouldn't have known what he was doing. Did it seem like an accident? Elizabeth said it was an accident. Where did they find him? What did they say?"

"I'd meant to keep it from you, dear. I'd not wanted you to know."

"Tell me what they said."

"The car was right up against the wall and the front all broken as though he'd gone straight at it."

"If he was drunk he might not have seen it. We must pray it was that, mother. We must pray for poor Geoffrey."

He had been such a cheerful character. It was dreadful what drink could do to a man. If only he had followed her advice and given up drinking. Poor Geoffrey. She felt sorry for him. No feeling of guilt, no remorse came to her. She wished she had been in Cardiff because she might have stopped him. She did not see herself as the direct cause of his despair. He must have been unhappy—were there business reasons? If only she had been there to comfort him. He was such a nice character, such a gentleman and so considerate. She believed she had loved him deeply and she had been away when he most needed her, when some terrible trouble had overtaken him. Many theories crossed her mind. She was not the cause of his trouble but she might have alleviated it. Naturally he had turned to her. Now she would gladly have married him on the spot, not out of love but out of compassion. Now she would have protected him as though he were one of the children.

Trying to control her sobs, she sat down, put her hands together and bent over the table. Silently, but with moving lips, she repeated to herself the Our Father and the Hail Mary.

6

To Kathleen, her sisters' lives were eventful and exalted. The peculiar version of the Geoffrey episode which she had pieced together from snatches of conversation, the fine motor-car in which she had ridden, the glimpses of handsome young men who came courting Elizabeth in vain, and the tales of foreign travel, were things in a book in which her name was never written. The praise of both her sisters which she had heard from the nuns at St. Joseph's, praise for those wonderful intangible qualities, personality and charm, which could never be acquired, which came just by luck, and the romantic passion which many of the girls felt for Elizabeth, confirmed her belief that her sisters were something quite apart from her. Some kind of glorious accident had happened long before her birth, something splendid which included her father. They were not really related to her at all, nor to her mother, nor to the boys; not in the way that people were usually related to each other. She would never have dreamt of comparing herself with them if the comparison had not been flung daily in her face at home and at school. She knew she seemed undistinguished, plain and common.

What bothered her was that there was nothing she could do which would make her count. She knew it was not in her power to please the family. She was first in class. She was the best at maths. She was brilliant at music. When the priest came and asked them funny, catchy questions such as, "If a cat and a half eats a rat and half in a minute and a half, how long would it take ten cats to eat ten rats?" she alone of all the class spotted the catch. In her reports "excellent" was written against every subject except sewing and drawing. But apart from one or two mistresses at school no one praised these abilities. No matter how hard she worked, no matter how well she did at school, not a single member of her family thought any the better of her.

When she tried on a little mild boasting with Marguerite she found indifference. In theory, Marguerite loved her and was sorry for her and when the child was not there she would go so far as to plan something to please her. But when Kathleen was present, Marguerite found herself irritated by the pathetic aspect of her personality. When taking her out for tea for a treat she kept scolding. "Pull yourself together. Do get out of the habit of gaping. Why do you look so frightened? If you sit like that you'll get round-shouldered." Kathleen, with all the bitterness of the unloved, would become ten times worse and hunch herself up and let her eyes fill with tears. Another thing which maddened Marguerite was Kathleen's love of accuracy. She would listen attentively and with great concentration to Marguerite's tales of their ancestry, and then, wrinkling her forehead, she would shyly point out some discrepancy, not out of cynicism or a wish to trip up, but simply to get it clear in her own mind.

When Kathleen tried to interest Elizabeth in her achievements she found the gracious, impersonal sweetness which Elizabeth extended to everyone. And although this was not what she wanted, although Elizabeth gave her nothing whereas Marguerite paid for her piano lessons and gave her presents, she was grateful for this sweetness and preferred Elizabeth by far.

Kathleen had very little in common with her sisters. She was not ambitious, she was interested in learning for its own sake and she had little family or personal pride. Sounds and ideas meant a lot to her but visually she experienced little. She was so accustomed to poverty, dirt and untidiness that she never felt the need to conceal her background. She never tried to make a show. Where Elizabeth, tidy and clean, could pat a cushion, move a table, pop a vase of flowers onto the mantelpiece and transform her dingy little furnished room into something inviting and feminine; where Marguerite, untidy and unmethodical, by a stroke of bravado, such as flinging an embroidered shawl over the table, or rolling the shabby cushions in her dressing gown, could create an impression of grandeur among the chaos in a second; Kathleen, working hard and doing her best, would always leave things scrappy and scruffy-looking. If she laid the table, laboriously and conscientiously, the knives and forks would be all awry and unsymmetrical. When she did out the parlour, going right under the piano for dust and moving all the furniture, taking hours, she ruined the effect by leaving a duster on a chair or a pile of dirt in a corner. She had an unfailing way of driving her mother to distraction.

It was not wholly her fault. By nature she was left-handed but they had made her write and do all the usual things with her right hand. So she became awkward and fumbled and everything felt wrong. She dropped things, broke things and took a very long time over any manual task. There was a barrier to surmount before the message from her brain reached her fingers. But this never happened when she played the piano, for then the fact that her left hand was so good made her able to tackle pieces which the other girls shirked.

Most of the time she didn't care how she looked. Side by side with a hundred daydreams of being beautiful was the boredom of having to think about details of appearance. With her mind on something much more interesting she would draw a comb roughly through her long, thick hair. She pulled her clothes on anyhow and it was no unusual thing for a stocking to be inside out. People nagging her about how she looked did no good, it simply made her reason fatalistically, "If I was the kind who was meant to look nice then they wouldn't be going on at me like this all the time. And if I'm the kind who wasn't meant to look nice then there's nothing I can do about it."

After an unusually insulting remark she might be seized with a dread of looking repulsive and, on her toes in front of the cracked kitchen mirror, she would stare at the white peaky face. Her slit of a mouth was like a straight line of fine pencil shading. She had the arched eyebrows and slender nose of Elizabeth. Most features, taken separately, were like Elizabeth's, but the total effect was very different. To console herself she would fish in her memory for anything kind that had ever been said about her appearance, by a crony of her mother's, by one of the nuns, by Aunt Kenny, and even by Edgar: "Her eyes are very expressive." "Her eyes are so intelligent." "She has a very fine head of hair on her." "Such a sweet expression and that's what counts."

Among all this she managed to carve out some intense enjoyment for herself through reading and playing the piano. Tales of travel and adventure, the ripples of Mendelsohn's Spring Song, the mellifluous simplicity of Schumann's pieces for children were treats which she could look forward to and remember. She enjoyed her lessons and loved doing sums. Her school companions took little notice of her and left her in peace. Hughes often gave her presents, very handsome presents indeed, when he was in funds; a real leather satchel; a set of pencils in a two-storeyed pencil-box; a music case. The trouble was that they had to be paid for with a kiss. "Now give me a kiss, Kathie," he would say as he bent down. Screwing up her eyes she would touch his beery whiskers with her mouth.

Marguerite had left Cardiff first. After the Geoffrey episode she had resolved never to leave Cardiff again. Kathleen had heard her talking to her mother in the kitchen. "No, mother. I'm really superstitious about it now. I think it brings bad luck." But the limitations of Cardiff and further correspondence with Nurse Calder had made her change her mind and now her headquarters were in London. She often came to see them, but she was always so rushed, had so much to do, was so much more interested in seeing Patrick, that she never paid more than a flying visit to the Hughes' house.

When she heard that Marguerite was coming, Kathleen would get in a panic and try to tidy herself up. But when Marguerite was actually there and nothing worse happened than the usual complaints about accent and appearance, Kathleen would cheer up and gaze at her sister with interest and amazement. Marguerite always had a new dress; her voice had changed, or rather with a new accent went a new timbre; she was very particular about words and no longer said "Isn't" or "Won't" but "Is not" or "Will not" or "Is it not?" or "Will you not?"; she used French words; she had a little laugh which was not meant to be humorous exactly; she began her letters in French and ended them in a flowery French way. She was unpredictable. She might kiss Kathleen warmly on arrival and display the greatest affection. She might take no notice of her at all. She might start nagging her and not stop until she had to leave.

Elizabeth had left Cardiff two years later. She wanted to be on her own and held out against joining Marguerite in London. A little Portuguese girl at St. Joseph's idolised her and begged her parents to allow Elizabeth to accompany her back to Lisbon. The Da Feiras wrote to Elizabeth, offering to pay her passage out first class, and all expenses, and asking her to stay with them for as long as she liked. Memories of the delights of Bordeaux came back. She would be glad to get away from a young solicitor who was making himself ridiculous. She accepted. But once in Lisbon she realised that it would never do to stay with the Da Feiras as a governess. The way the father, uncles and brothers eyed her boded trouble. She also discovered that there was a large English colony there and that the English language and customs were all the rage. Joining the English Ladies' Club she made friends with a Miss Simpson and moved into her flat. Here she found herself very comfortable, worshipped by her friend, earning good money by giving private lessons, the darling of a small, refined circle and in a position where no word of scandal could be breathed of her.

Kathleen was sorry when she went and envied her. Coloured postcards of peasants with mules on a dusty road under a blue sky, or sailing boats in a blue harbour, arrived for Mrs Hughes from time to time. These Kathleen collected and put in an album.

With the two eldest girls out of Cardiff, Edgar seemed happier. Whether it was their departure or not that did it, Mrs Hughes could not be sure, but he pulled himself together, cut down the drink, looked for work and earned more. They were able to leave the slum and settle in rooms above a small general shop at the corner of a narrow street. This shop became the bane of Kathleen's life. Every evening (for they kept open until eleven if necessary) she would have to sit there, hour after hour, in the flickering light of a hissing, fan-shaped gas jet, trying to get through her homework despite the frequent calls of customers. On Saturdays, when her school friends were enjoying themselves, she would be tied to the shop for the afternoon, longing for a clear half-hour when she could get on with her latest adventure story.

She knew her mother resented her having any interests at all and simply wanted to get as much work out of her as she could. With no wish for revenge but with great bitterness she brooded on her mother's harshness, sometimes dwelling on one terrible episode which had taken place years before.

One evening, ecstatic and triumphant, she had carried home a long-coveted prize, a huge book, *Children of Many Lands*, filled with coloured pictures of strange landscapes, houses, people and animals. From her mother there was no sign of pride or interest. "Now leave that, Kathie, and go and get the corn for the chickens, for I've to go along to poor Mrs Sullivan who's so ill." Her head was swimming with impressions: little kimono-clad Japanese sitting on the floor in front of painted screens or standing in queer, raised shoes among blossom trees; little fur-encased Eskimos, huddled in igloos, or lying by a hole in the ice waiting for a seal; little befeathered Red Indians squatting by their wigwams; these and many other scenes which she had never before imagined.

"I'll teach you to disobey me!"

With a start Kathleen looked up into her mother's comely, furious face. The book was flung into the kitchen fire. The pages went brown at the edges before bursting into flame. The cover, with its large, gold lettering still visible, seemed to resist, smouldering, yielding only inch by inch. The riches which had been hers and which she had barely explored had gone for good.

7

Kathleen made a friend, a boy, Dick Treherne. It was soon after she came to the shop. He was two years older than herself and lived in the same road. Every Saturday he came in for his weekly copy of *The Boys' Friend*, which she thought the least interesting of the magazines. Under her influence he took more notice of *The Magnet, Chums* and *Pluck,* for she let him read these at the counter for nothing. With animation they discussed the boy heroes and villains and speculated on the outcome of difficult situations in future instalments. They got into the habit of cycling together (for Edgar in a fit of generosity had given her a bicycle) every morning as far as the crossroads at the bottom of the High Street, after which she would go on to St. Joseph's while he went off to Cardiff Higher Grade. Like herself he had a scholarship.

With him her conversation flew easily. Both of them were born and bred in Cardiff, they had the same accents and associations, so no thought of criticism ever arose. His homework finished, he often came into the shop to help her with hers and chatted to her. His family was very poor. He told her, thinking she might not like it, that his father was a piano tuner. "He must have a perfect sense of pitch," Kathleen said with admiration. "To be a piano tuner you've got to have a perfect sense of pitch. No one's got it at school, not even the teacher."

When she was older he asked her to join the Ladies' Swimming Club, for he was one of the leading lights of the Men's Swimming Club, so that on mixed evenings they could swim together. After hesitation she timidly asked her mother if she might be away from the shop on those evenings. To her great surprise there was no opposition, on the contrary there was encouragement. Mrs Hughes was a woman who liked young people to be courting and that sort of thing and she thought the better of Kathleen for having been invited out by a boy. She laughed, looked jolly. "Well now, Kathie. I'd never have thought you'd be getting a boy so soon."

Later on, Dick asked Kathleen to join the Band of Hope Club, a social club attached to his church, for he was a Protestant, where there were dances and whist drives. Again Mrs Hughes was all for it; if Dick, tall and good-looking, took any interest in her miserable-looking daughter, well, so much the better and good luck to him. She was sympathetic and conspiratorial. Edgar looked on dances, socials and coming home late as the devil's work. Many an evening she assured him that Kathleen was in and had gone upstairs to her room. Many an evening she slipped down and put the key under the mat.

When Kathleen's school days were over she became a pupil teacher at St. John the Baptist's, a Catholic poor school, and worked for her teacher's certificate. Dick, who had left school some time before because his parents needed his earnings, started as an errand boy and then secured a job as clerk with a shipping firm. They continued to meet daily.

He began to praise her looks, much to her surprise. "I've never seen such thick hair. It looks fine with a small face, I always did like dark, thick hair." She discovered that she had a small waist, that she was a good dancer because she was light on her feet and had a sense of time and a good memory for the steps of such things as the Barn Dance and the Lancers. She was a good swimmer too and blossomed out. As Dick earned more so he took her to new places, and now that she was earning she could afford to buy a few clothes. Not that she wanted anything fancy or had much taste, but it was a joy to have a new dress, a proper dress, not something made out of oddments by her mother or some very old, ill-fitting thing sent by her sister.

The pleasures of Cardiff opened up before her. There were dramas at the Theatre Royal, stirring pieces like *The Silver King*, *The Sign of the Cross* and *A Royal Divorce*, plays in which actors roared and ranted and actresses swooned and trembled. She accepted them wholeheartedly as masterpieces and identified herself with the heroines. Then there was the Park Theatre where she saw musical shows like *The Dollar Princess, The Merry Widow* and *The*

Quaker Girl, watching the statuesque ladies with admiration and learning by heart the best tunes. At the Empire she saw Dan Leno, Little Tich, Eugene Stratton and, her favourite, Vesta Tilley. Here she and Dick roared with laughter at the jokes and listened solemnly to the sentimental songs. Less often and as a great treat they would go to a Gilbert and Sullivan.

Whenever Marguerite came, Kathleen asked Dick to keep away. "You never know with her. She's got such funny ideas. She might not like me to go out while she's there."

When Dick was promoted to pay clerk, with what seemed the enormous salary of five pounds a week, he suggested marriage and she accepted. "We won't say anything about it, though. Not for a time," she said. To her, marriage was a release from home and a continuation of these jolly times and the pleasant friendship with Dick.

As Dick's savings grew, so did his wish to buy furniture for their future home. Together they went to sales and chose what they wanted. They decided that Roath would be a nice place to live for it had a large park with an open-air swimming pool where there were regattas in the summer and firework displays on Guy Fawkes night. Near the park were avenues of newly-built houses, very modern red-brick houses with gardens. "We'll live in one of those," said Dick.

At last Kathleen had to tell her mother. Mrs Hughes was delighted, kissed her warmly and gave her advice. She was against long engagements and she believed in early marriages. "I was only seventeen myself," she said. "I must write and tell the others."

"Couldn't we wait a little before telling them?"

"Perhaps that would be better. We'll tell them when it's nearer the time."

It was agreed that the wedding should take place at the beginning of Dick's Christmas holiday so that there would be a few days for a honeymoon. The landlord was seen about a house at Roath. The furniture was collected and could be moved in at any time. Everything was prepared.

"You know, Kathie, I think I must write and tell your sisters," said Mrs Hughes. "They'd be sorry if we didn't say a thing."

"But Maggie might..."

"Sure Maggie'll be delighted and wanting to come up for the wedding."

A letter arrived for Kathleen:

117

"*Chérie,*

I was very surprised to have your news from mother. My best wishes and congratulations. Are you not very young to marry? I had not expected it. Is it not a very short engagement? You do not say whether Dick is able to support you or not. Mother says he lives in your street so I imagine his parents are not well off. What does his father do?

I hope you will do nothing hasty. This is a very important step to take. I shall try to come up for a few days and then we can have a long talk about everything.

Ta soeur qui t'aime bien,
Marguerite

The bold, slanting writing suggested great haste. With no margins the words seemed to dash from one side of the page to the other. Kathleen felt apprehensive. In her rather wailing, singsong Cardiff voice she kept repeating, "But she sends best wishes and congratulations, Mum. If she sends best wishes and congratulations that means she must be pleased, eh, Mum?"

"Sure she's very pleased and why wouldn't she be?" said Mrs Hughes uneasily.

It was the "few days" which worried Kathleen. The shadow of a visit from her sister clouded her horizon. And then the letter seemed to demand a reply. After consultations with her mother and Dick she sat down to compose a letter. It took her the whole evening and it was only after tearing up several attempts that she thought it would do. She was not really satisfied even then. "I'd better tell the truth. It's always best in the end," she said to herself; then, "I believe in telling the truth," she thought, trying to hide from herself her inability to think up something else and her terror of what would be said if she was found out in a lie. After all, what was there to hide, when she came to think of it? Wasn't Dick earning a big wage and wasn't his father in a most respectable profession?

About ten days later Marguerite arrived. In her nurse's cloak and bonnet, explaining that she had taken the train straight after night duty, she could scarcely be persuaded to take a cup of tea, and then with the cup and saucer in her hand walked up and down the kitchen anxiously awaiting Kathleen's arrival.

"Oh, Kathie, thank goodness you came at last. I have been waiting so long."

"But I never get home till now."

"Well, never mind. Never mind about your tea. There is no time for that. Oh, very well, just have a cup quickly. You can have something to eat when we get back." She gave her a sharp look. "Kathie, is that the only coat you have? Have you no other hat? Let me see your dress."

Kathleen obeyed.

"Now finish that tea and try this on." She pulled at the stiff clasps of her case (there was always something the matter with her possessions) and almost broke it open. Pulling the clothes out onto the floor, she shook out a crumpled jacket. "No, it is no good. It is too large in the bust. The colour is awful with your dress."

Rummaging through the clothes she thought rapidly. "I know, I shall wear it. I shall change everything. I must be quick. Mother, I must change here now. Would you lock the door in case Edgar comes in."

Kathleen was watching, apprehensive.

"Kathie, stop standing there staring at me. Tidy your hair and clean your hands. You can keep that dress on. When you are ready I want you to put on this cloak and bonnet."

"Me? Oh I mustn't. They're only for nurses."

"Never mind. We are going on a very important visit and we shall be late if we do not hurry. You will look far tidier in this and it is sure to fit you."

"Oh, Marguerite, I don't like to. I don't feel it's right. It isn't right for me to wear that. Really."

The plea was unavailing. In the street Kathleen felt she could die of shame to be wearing these things, walking round in broad daylight in this unbecoming fancy dress. She prayed she might not run into anyone she knew. She wondered what she would say if she met Dick. I feel such a fool, she thought. Forgetting her preoccupation with the clothes she began to wonder what was happening.

"Where are we going?"

"To the hospital."

"But why?"

"On a visit. I want you to meet the matron."

At this Kathleen hung back and seemed on the point of running away. "Oh, Marguerite, please, please don't take me there in these things. I shall feel such a fool and whatever will she think? She'll know I'm not a nurse. Whatever will..."

"I can explain to her. You had to look tidy. You have no idea how much better you look like that. Now Kathie, I want you to make a good impression. There is no need for you to say a great deal, but do answer up when she asks you questions. She is a very great friend of mine and such a sweet person. I can trust you not to let me down in front of her I am sure. Will you promise not to let me down?"

"But whatever will I say? Why will she ask me questions? Is it to tea we're going or what?"

"No, just for a very short visit. She wanted to see you because I told her you would like to be a nurse and she was very pleased." Seeing Kathleen about to protest, she went on quickly. "I had so much trouble to arrange this appointment. You can imagine how difficult it is to see to all this from London. But I am always thinking of your future and I felt it was worth taking the trouble." She smiled and shook her head. "Now I do not want any thanks or gratitude. All I ask is that you should answer up well."

"But I never wanted to be a nurse. I never said..."

"There will be plenty of time to think it over afterwards. We can have a long talk about it later and you shall tell me just what you want. I had to do this in such a rush, you know. There has been so little time for a good talk. But I thought such an opportunity should not be missed. I should never have forgiven myself if I had not tried to do my best for you."

Unable to make head or tail of this, with faint stirrings of gratitude in her breast and worn down by her sister's repeated entreaties, Kathleen promised to do nothing which would let her down. Along stone passages, up stone stairs, she followed meekly, stopping still when Marguerite met some old friend and exchanged greetings and enquiries, hoping to goodness that all these nurses and sisters would not suddenly pounce on her and denounce her for wearing the uniform. In the presence of the matron at last, she raised her eyes to the stern face and the stiff, grey hair, feeling how wonderful it must be to be strong enough, as Marguerite was, to think such a person sweet. She blinked when the Matron's eyes met hers and averted her gaze first to the floor and then to pictures of royal patrons on the walls. Marguerite, matrons and royalty seemed all much the same thing, eminent and all that, but one was happier left to oneself.

Meanwhile Marguerite had rushed forwards and shaken matron by the hand, speaking without fear. "How happy I am to see you, dear matron. It seems such years since I was here last. And I am longing to hear all the news." All sat down and the conversation continued. Marguerite laughed, made little jokes, private jokes which would mean nothing to anyone who was not a member of the hospital staff, and often brought a smile to the matron's lips. Then when she thought the time was ripe she turned round towards Kathleen and said a few words about her.

"And so your sister wants to be a nurse?"

"Oh, yes, matron, she has always wanted to be a nurse. But of course she was too young to train before." Marguerite noted matron's glance at the bonnet and cloak. "She has on this uniform because she is acting as a nurse to some children for the moment, just by way of training."

"I see. And why do you want to be a nurse?"

The cold, dry voice unnerved Kathleen. She didn't want to be a nurse. She had never dreamt of such a thing. To be in this institution with a lot of overpowering sisters on top of one was the last thing she wanted. It was impossible to imagine what would make her want to be a nurse. What made people want to be nurses? She turned, helpless, towards Marguerite who was watching her intently. She tried to think of something and feeling that inspiration might come at any second she opened her mouth. It stayed open and no words came. She must look an idiot. "I want to be a nurse because... because..." Her lips trembled with embarrassment.

"She would like to look after the sick," said Marguerite. "She is a little shy. She has always been shy. But *I* know she has a real vocation for nursing for she has often spoken to me about it. And then, having a sister who was a nurse made her very keen."

Matron was silent for a moment, then turned to Kathleen as though expecting something more from her. She took a paper off her desk and held it out. "You must fill in this form. Not now. Then let me have it back and we will consider the application."

When they had left the hospital well behind Marguerite voiced her indignation. "Why did you say nothing? How could you sit there with your mouth open? Kathie, you have no spirit. You must learn to pull yourself together. You make a terrible impression on people and it lets *me* down. You should think of that. You should learn to think of others."

At home, as Kathleen was slowly reading the form, Marguerite snatched it from her. I shall fill it in for you. I know what to say and all you need do is sign it."

"But Marguerite, it says I must be there for three years. I can't do that, can I? Not when I'm getting married so soon. How could I?"

"We'll arrange about that later. After all, it is far better to have a long engagement. You are very young, too young really, to make such a decision now. You never know, you might regret it later. In three years' time you would be at a very good age for marriage."

"But what would be the point of training if I was going to get married?"

Marguerite took this question as a sign of weakening. "Yes, it would be a pity to throw away such a training. It is such a fine profession. As a nurse you can get to travel about and travel to different countries. Think of the opportunities. You know you are very lucky to have such a chance. There are many girls who would give anything to be allowed to train."

"But I *want* to marry Dick."

"Of course. Naturally. I quite see that. But the longer you wait the better. And you know three years in hospital would be such a useful experience. Many nurses marry when they leave hospital. Many of my friends are married. But they all say they would not have missed their training for the world."

Kathleen was hardly listening. The thought of three years had put her in a panic. Mustering every ounce of courage she could find, she shook her head. "No, Marguerite. I don't think I'll sign it. I'd rather not."

Marguerite's cheerfulness melted away and she looked sad and stared hard at her sister. "You are so ungrateful. I have never known anything like it. It is only your good I have at heart. What difference will it make to me whether you train or not? I travelled down here, dead tired. Did you know I had no sleep last night? I would have liked to take the day off. I would have given anything for a good sleep. But I thought of you and I knew I must get to Cardiff for this appointment no matter what it cost me. And now I shall have to go back to London not knowing what is to happen. I shall be worrying myself sick about you. You never think of me. You are going to make me very unhappy, you know."

Kathleen's eyes clouded with sympathy.

"Now please sign this and be sensible," said Marguerite, cheering up. "It will make me so happy. And after all, what is there to signing it? Matron may reject the application. It commits you to nothing. It is just an application form, nothing else. You will have plenty of time to think it over."

Kathleen signed.

In her haste to dash away Marguerite had not time to search for an envelope. "Promise me on your word of honour to post it. Say 'I promise'."

"I promise."

"Goodbye, *chérie*. You have been very wise. I am so glad. Now you must write and tell me all that happens. I shall be most anxious to know." Two kisses on each cheek showed the degree of her satisfaction.

Kathleen broke her word of honour and the form was never posted. Hoping that her deception would not be discovered until she was married and beyond the reach of her family, she waited, at first uneasily, then later, as nothing happened, with increasing relief.

8

A fortnight before the wedding she came home to find her sister had arrived. She was so overwhelmed by this that she went dizzy and pale. Trying to vow to herself to be firm this time, she bent her head, as though waiting for the inevitable reproaches. To her surprise not a word was said about the hospital. Marguerite seemed in the most affectionate and effusive of moods.

"*Chérie!* I so wanted to see you. And you look so much nicer, so much neater! What a very sweet little dress you have on, is it not, mother?"

"But I had this dress on the last..."

"Now, *chérie*. Talking of clothes—I know you must have been thinking about them, and I have too. I have been making plans. It was all a secret. I am going to give you a real surprise. What do you think of coming up to London with me for a week? By a lot of wangling—you would laugh if I told you how I did it—I've managed to get the week off. I know there are any number of things I *ought* to do, for you know my time is precious these days, but I am going to spend it all with you. I'll show you round and we'll go shopping together. How would you like that?" She took Kathleen's tongue-tied blush as an assent. "I knew you would. Is it not a great surprise? You will be able to visit London at last. Well?"

"I hadn't thought of that. I think I've bought all I want already. I don't need much and I was thinking I'd buy other things later on. Mum says..."

"Now, *chérie*. You must say 'mother' and not 'mum'. I think I told you that before. But to get back to what I was saying. You have so little choice here. In London there are the most wonderful shops! You never saw anything like them. And I believe things are cheaper, that's if you know where to go for them. There are all sorts of clever little dressmakers, French, of course, tucked away just off the big streets. It will be such a treat for you. We'll find plenty of time to do other things besides shopping. We'll do all the sights, the Tower of London, the Houses of Parliament, the Changing of the Guard, all that sort of thing. And then we'll go to the theatre. Now what would you say to that?"

"I *have* been to the theatre. I often go. There are very good shows here. They say it's the same companies in London. They say it's the best companies. We go..."

"What grammar, *chérie*," No, no. The best companies never come here. You can only see them in the West End." She made a wide sweep with her arm. "Ah, you should see the West End, Piccadilly, Kensington! You will enjoy it so much. How you must be longing to get there."

Kathleen was silent. She was satisfied with Cardiff.

"Now, *chérie*," Marguerite's smiles vanished and her tone became colder and firmer. "I think we should leave early tomorrow so as to have plenty of time."

"But I have to go to work tomorrow..."

"I have talked about that to mother. We have it all arranged. Mother's going to tell them you had to go to see your sister who is ill." Seeing more protests coming, she made an impatient gesture. "You had better do your packing tonight. Just a very few things. You'll hardly need anything. I can fit you up when you are there. When you've finished your tea I shall go up with you and tell you what to take." Her face softened and crumpled into a ridiculous smile, the smile she used for her favourite child. "Mother, how is

Patrick? And the others? Maureen is such a little pet, but she's not a patch on Patrick. He's so sweet, not at all spoilt. I'm going over there for the night. As soon as this packing's done I must fly. I must see him before he's put to bed."

"But aren't you going to see Dick? You've never met him yet," said Kathleen.

Marguerite frowned and looked blankly down at the table. "Oh. Well... Yes, yes of course. If you run along and bring him over now, I can wait a minute or two."

9

Kathleen arrived at the station in good time and hovered anxiously at the entrance to the platform. People brushed past her, a porter answered her brusquely. "I'm plain and insignificant," she thought, "they all treat me as though I don't count."

She kept trying to reassure herself about the future. Dick had begged her not to go; he was sure her sister was up to something. He had implored her to be sure and come back on the day she had promised. "But it's only for a week and it's different this time. She just wants to give me a treat and it's so kind of her that I can't say no. Of course I'll come back."

Marguerite arrived, out of breath, with hardly a minute to spare before the train went. "Kathie, why did you not get in and keep a place?"

"I didn't know what to do." The expostulations continued as they ran along the platform.

During the journey Kathleen looked at her sister. Marguerite must be quite thirty now. It seemed a great age but a fine age to be, an age when your family left you alone. She was very good-looking. Kathleen was too young to bother herself about faint signs of age and, in fact, although there were lines on Marguerite's forehead and by her mouth, she was more handsome than before. There was something imposing and theatrical in her face. There was something so intense in her expression, so concentrated, that it always came as a surprise when one heard her careful articulation and low voice. She looked so important, so in the thick of things, thought Kathleen. It was exciting and uncomfortable to be with her.

Impressed by Marguerite's effusiveness of the day before, always in search of a friendly word, recalling tender scenes between loving sisters in novels and plays, anxious to discover that she was not really looked on as a nonentity, Kathleen leaned forward and said hesitantly, "Isn't it good for Dick to be earning so well at his age? Mum—mother—says he's very steady."

"Yes, yes." Marguerite turned her head and looked out of the window. She was thinking of other things.

The snub was still rankling when they reached London. The crowded, noisy, smoky damp station gave Kathleen a dismal first impression of the capital. She had been expecting a magnificent terminus something like a giant conservatory, a second Crystal Palace. By nature she reacted and moved slowly and she now found herself so hustled that there was no time to grasp what was happening. To keep up with her sister's pace she had to run, gulp down the tepid, greasy coffee, swallow lumps of the stale sandwich before she had time to chew them properly and be for ever picking up and setting down her luggage. And all the time Marguerite gave her no look or word to show that she was glad of her company.

Meekly, Kathleen did as she was told but she became increasingly sullen and resentful. Growing bolder she made one or two snappy answers. To her surprise Marguerite let them pass. This seemed even more humiliating, to have someone not care what you said to them as long as you did what they ordered.

Brooding over the wreckage of her tiny little edifice of self-esteem, Kathleen found herself pushed onto a tram. She looked out onto grey streets and drab houses, much the same as those in Cardiff but unsoftened by familiarity. No sumptuous room had been prepared for her. She was to share Marguerite's room and bed in a small boarding house off Baker Street. This alarmed her extremely, for although Marguerite was her own sister, she was so formidable and there was such a lack of understanding between them that it was like having to tuck in with some forbidding stranger. She would have given anything for a minute to herself. "I shall never sleep at all. Not for the whole week," she mumbled quietly, half-wishing to be heard. No one took any notice.

After a hasty, unappetising meal in a nearby restaurant, a long lecture, so rapidly delivered and confused that she could not follow it, a cup of cocoa made too strong and lumpy by Marguerite, Kathleen was allowed to go to bed. She slept lightly and fitfully, in her wakeful patches feeling cramped, not daring to move and pining for the solitude of her room at home. A lumpy mattress and small draughts creeping under the untucked blankets maddened her. Marguerite liked to make a show but she was indifferent to comfort.

The next morning there was breakfast in the dining room with the other lodgers. Here Marguerite kept up a great flow of conversation, appeared at great pains to please all except Kathleen and seemed very popular. Then there was the introduction to the landlady, "such a sweet woman, such a dear." Then there was a friendly word for the maid, a warm and considered enquiry about an ailment.

Back in the bedroom, the cupboard doors were flung open, displaying a confusion of clothes, several dresses bundled onto one hanger, others thrown over the bar, a mixed pile of shoes down below. "Now we must see what suits you best." A dark red dress was selected at length. Kathleen, tired of slipping things on and off, declared that she was satisfied.

"Yes, this suits you very well, Kathleen. If you really like it you can have it."

"Oh, I only want to borrow..."

"Of course you must keep it if you like it."

By pinning and rough stitching the dress was made to fit. It felt precarious. A broad-brimmed hat was fixed to Kathleen's head with two enormous, green-tipped hat pins. She was told to put on a pair of black shoes. "Now I shall take you round Regent's Park," said Marguerite.

Trudging round the lake in narrow, pointed shoes which hurt, moved by the lines of light on the water and the pretty ducks, Kathleen thought nostalgically of happy walks in Roath Park with Dick. How freely they had talked; how understanding he was; how interested in everything she had to say.

Marguerite paid for meals. "Now choose whatever you like, Kathie." She paid for tickets to the Zoo and for their fares. Kathleen found this expenditure dreadful because they were neither of them enjoying themselves. She felt heavily indebted to her sister, oppressed with gratitude and made a great effort to show it.

"What a lovely place," she said when they were in Hyde Park on the following day. "I'm very glad to see this."

Marguerite looked pleased and smiled benevolently. "Yes, you can never have seen anything like this in Cardiff. You know, after you've been in London for a little while, you'll find you never want to go back."

When they had walked a little further, she continued as though the conversation had moved on several stages farther. "After all, *chérie*, there is nothing there at all. There are no opportunities. One has no chance of meeting people. Now we will sit here and watch the people riding. This is Rotten Row. The most fashionable place. I have nursed many of the people who ride here."

Kathleen watched the riders with melancholy respect, never taking her eyes off the scene in front of her, like people who have paid to go into the theatre and therefore must look at the stage whether they like it or not.

"You know, Kathie, in nursing you meet the most interesting people. You would love it, being so fond of books. One comes across writers and artists and, er, thinkers."

"Would they ever talk to their nurses?"

Marguerite gave a short, condescending laugh. "Of course. I've had such wonderful conversations with my patients. It's all up to you. If you show you are educated and refined they treat you accordingly."

The days, packed with sight-seeing and shopping, dragged horribly for Kathleen. She longed for the delights of idleness, of drifting and of being alone or with someone you didn't have to live up to. Too much incident, if untinged by sympathy or some personal feeling, was more boring than anything. Mixed with boredom was apprehension. Everything Marguerite bought her increased her anxiety. After all this kindness how would she ever be able to refuse to do what her sister wanted? And what did she want? Why did she never talk of Dick and the marriage?

"Now this afternoon I'm taking you to see a great friend of mine, Miss Tracy. You'll like her so much and she is very interested to meet you."

As they paused, in a Kensington street, outside a door which bore the title *Tracy and Borrows Agency*, Kathleen was full of misgivings. "What is an agency?" There was no reply.

She was shown into a room, divided from an office by a glass-topped partition. She had had a surfeit of unfamiliar faces, unfamiliar voices. It seemed a dull, unending dream. "This is the sister I was telling you all about."

She was now unreceptive to new impressions. Everything was much of a muchness. A vague face smiled vaguely. A hand held her hand. Miss Tracy.

Marguerite and Miss Tracy were on the best of terms. They called each other by their Christian names and referred to mutual friends. After much light talk and laughter a form was produced.

"I filled this up for you," said Marguerite, "all you have to do is sign."

"But what is it?" said Kathleen.

"Just a form, dear."

Miss Tracy looked surprised. "Didn't she know ... ?"

"Of course, of course. She's always so shy and nervous that she forgets, you know. Poor Kathie. I've told you about this so often. Now here we have all your qualifications, you see. And then down here you just have to write your name." She nudged her with her elbow and gave her a stern smile. "There's no need to read it through now. You know your qualifications as well as I do." She fixed her with an imploring look.

Suspicion and stubbornness fought with a wish not to make Marguerite look silly in front of her friend, not to "let her down". Marguerite's full sleeve was half covering the paper. Kathleen read what she could. Under a heading 'Languages' was written "Fluent French. A little German and Italian." She felt pressure on her foot and taps on her arm and saw Marguerite, her face turned away from Miss Tracy, making signs with her lips. Confused and despairing she signed.

"What was it? Why hadn't you told me before?" she said angrily as they walked down Kensington High Street. Anger brought unbecoming red blotches to her white face.

"Just a list of your qualifications, dear."

"But why should she want it? What are you trying... ?"

"Do not get excited, *chérie*. You see, if ever you should want a really good position, you could always go there. One never knows what will happen and I thought it such a good opportunity to get your name onto their books while you were here."

"I don't want a place. I never..."

"Not at the moment, dear. But you never know when you might need it."

"I haven't signed that I've accepted a job or anything?"

"Goodness, no." Marguerite laughed heartily, as though the suggestion was ridiculously amusing.

Suspicion was fainter but still present. "But it said something about French, German and Italian. It said fluent French. I can't talk any of them."

"You must have been mistaken, I think."

"I'm certain I saw that. Really."

"I have a form there too. It must have been mine you saw. You've got it mixed."

She knew that was nonsense. She might be very green but she couldn't be fobbed off with such a silly explanation. Black surliness came over her.

"It's not true. You tell me not to let you down. That's all you ever say to me. And then you take me somewhere and I have to sign things and I don't know what they are or what's happening. If I'm not told anything, I'm bound to let you down and I don't care."

Marguerite laughed kindly, like someone who, though perfectly in the right, is going to humour the other person out of sheer good-heartedness. "Poor *chérie*. I'm afraid I've taken you round too much. But it's so delightful doing these things with you. What happy times we could have together if you were in London!" She suggested that Kathleen should have a nap in the afternoon while she herself paid a dull and long overdue visit. She drew the curtains, patted the eiderdown around her. "Now have a good sleep."

To be alone at last was bliss for Kathleen. Shutting her eyes she stopped feeling puzzled, "She is really very kind," she thought. "She means to be kind. But living in a different sort of world naturally I don't always understand her." Comforted, she dozed off.

When Marguerite returned she found Kathleen very much refreshed. She kissed her fondly. "Poor Kathie. You must have been dead tired. I've such a surprise! Guess where we're going tonight? To *Gipsy Love*. Someone gave me seats for the stalls."

After elaborate preparations, Kathleen found herself sitting in a very low-necked dress with a hobble skirt, in Daly's Theatre, among a throng of perfumed ladies with their escorts. This was a great experience, the one time when she thought she understood the glitter and splendour which her sister pursued. Set to music, lit up, these people in the audience were like a musical play themselves. The interval was the insertion of another short show in the main entertainment. Never had she heard a more delicious, animated buzz of conversation. And the miracle was that everyone looked so kind and sweet, smiling affectionately at friends, saying "excuse me" with the greatest courtesy as they passed one.

Before the curtain had gone up with a gentle purr, she had felt embarrassed and out of place, but she was carried away by the acting and singing and by the time the curtain fell she was flushed with pleasure and had forgotten her troubles. Marguerite was wonderfully conversational, talking to her as though she were Miss Tracy or the Matron or one of those people. She had nursed a member of the cast.

"He is such a delightful man and has the sweetest wife and the prettiest little girl. And they are very good Catholics too. I had a very happy time there and I often go and see them. It was he who gave me the tickets for tonight. When I was there I met a great many actors and actresses, most of the famous names you have heard. And they are not at all fast or anything of that sort. Sometimes in the evening they sang. You would have enjoyed it so much, Kathie, because you're so musical. How I wish you had the chance to meet such people. With your piano playing you'd be a great success."

Kathleen was listening attentively. "What songs did they sing?"

Marguerite racked her brains. She was no stickler for accuracy. "Every sort of song, Gilbert and Sullivan, Schubert, Mozart, Verdi, Poggioli, Roselli, Chopin, everyone!"

"Did Chopin write songs? I never heard of Poggioli and Roselli."

"Did you not? They are quite the rage. But then, in Cardiff you are out of touch with that sort of thing. Anyone as musical as you are would get such a lot out of London, operas, concerts. What concerts there are at the Albert Hall! I often go there. Nothing gives me so much pleasure." Marguerite's eyes were shining and her gestures were large. She was holding forth in the most classy accent Kathleen had ever heard from her. In fact, she was in a state of elation, in a dream, going through all the movements of what she considered a typical member of this sort of audience. She reminisced about other cases, some real, some a fantasy, some a mixture of both. She lowered her voice when she mentioned "nursing" but let it rise richly as she spoke the names of people distinguished by birth or fame.

After the show was over and they were undressing, the glow remained with her and she held Kathleen spellbound with her tales and descriptions. Believing that at last she had something in common with her sister, that music would bring them together, Kathleen went happily to sleep.

However in the morning her attempts at earnest discussion of favourite composers and tunes were cut short. "Now this afternoon," said Marguerite, "we are going to see Miss Tracy again. You said I never explained things beforehand so this time I shall make you understand. There is a French lady, Madame de Sercier, a very sweet person and very well connected. Miss Tracy took quite a fancy to you and told her all about you and she wants to see you. How's your French?"

"Do you mean you want me to *speak* French?"

"Yes, this lady does not understand English."

"Oh, I couldn't. I'm sure I couldn't."

"Kathie, you make no effort at all. You must try. Surely you could say something?"

Kathleen looked anxious and helpless.

"Well, I shall have to tell Madame that you're very nervous. I'll have to do the talking. Then when I look at you like this you must say "*oui*". She gave further detailed instruction, outlining an ingenious system of signals. "And do look bright and alert. And smile and look cheerful. You always look so miserable."

Although Marguerite appeared to believe that everything was now fully explained, Kathleen was as bewildered as ever. Easily giving up in the face of obstacles she soon ceased to try and discover more. Her suspicions were aroused once more, but unable to clarify them, she let herself sink into passiveness and mental apathy. She dragged herself along pavements and past shop counters, looking neither to right nor left but staring at the ground, always a yard or two behind her sister. She didn't listen any more to what was said; tears often came into her eyes, never rolling down her cheeks, but staying to blur her vision; her hands kept moving for no reason; she kept muttering inaudibly; often she opened her mouth as though about to speak and then shut it. At the back of her mind there was some idea that all this would show how fed up and reluctant she was. But these subtleties were wasted on Marguerite who was walking ahead the whole time and could not see them, and was in any case not one to watch people's faces closely and study their slightest action.

After the happy hopes raised by their conversation at the theatre, Kathleen found the reversion to being ordered about and not listened to intolerable. Often shrewd and capable of following a train of thought through to the end so long as it did not lead to action, when there was a definite stand to be taken her mental activities became paralysed. With her family she was always having to fall back into this fog and torpor. Sadly she realised that only with Dick was she really herself.

All this silence and sullenness infuriated Marguerite. In a thoroughly bad temper, whispering "Do pull yourself together," she pushed her sister roughly into Miss Tracy's room. Then, in a second, recovering her presence of mind, she smiled at all present with sunny politeness. There was handshaking between the four of them, murmurs of *"enchantée"*, *"ma soeur"*, nudges, meaningful looks, smiles and all were seated. The French lady, in heavy mourning and wearing an enormous hat like a mushroom, asked questions. Marguerite, with much gesturing and facial expression, replied. Miss Tracy and Kathleen looked on and tried to guess what was being said.

Half an hour passed like this, half an hour during which cups of tea were brought, Madame de Sercier grew tired, Miss Tracy grew bored, Kathleen became more and more apprehensive and despondent and Marguerite never flagged. The word *"dommage"* occurred several times at the end. Then all rose and after further shaking of hands the French lady left.

Marguerite seemed disappointed but said no more about the incident for the moment.

The next day all her thoughts were centred on a "really smart dress" for Kathleen. Shop after shop was searched for the right thing. "Something you can wear every day and which will always look right." There was something on her mind and she showed signs of strain and agitation. At times she looked unhappy. The right dress was found.

Back in her room she paced up and down and put her hands to her hair, playing with strands until they loosened and fell and she looked strangely dishevelled. "Oh, Kathie," she said at last in such a breaking voice that Kathleen looked startled.

"Kathie, I am so worried about you. I have tried so hard to do something for you. Your future is on my mind. You cannot think how unhappy I am."

"Please don't worry about me. I'm so sorry."

"How can I help it? You are so young, too young to realise what you're doing. I know Dick is very nice and all that. I'm not saying anything about him personally, but think of his background. His prospects may be good but his parents are not at all our class." She saw before her the figure of a humble, shabby man with a grey moustache who had tapped maddeningly on one note in the house of a patient—a piano tuner. "Not at all our class."

Her strongly-made eye teeth often gave her a snarling look when she smiled and added to the interest of her face. Now she was not smiling but her lips were drawn back, square and fanged. Never ceasing to pace over the threadbare carpet like an animal in a small cage, she continued. "You were too young to remember our father. But, *chérie*, I've told you all about him and how things were then. And you must try and imagine how mother was, how she is really if you know her properly. You have only known her with Edgar. But Edgar is not our class at all, you know. If you were his daughter I could understand you wanting to marry Dick."

Kathleen protested. "But Michael's only selling vegetables off a barrow and Thomas isn't more than a shop assistant. Dick's much better than that. He's a clerk and he's earning twice as much and his prospects are..."

"*Chérie*, do try to understand. It is not a matter of money. I do wish I could make you see that. It's his whole background. After all, he's had no schooling."

"He has. He got a scholarship."

"Perhaps, perhaps. But then his home influence! Now Kathie, you really must listen to me. I only want to do what is best for you. If you're fond of this boy there is no reason why you should not marry him later. But first of all you must see something of the world. You should have an idea of what you're giving up. These happy times we have had together, travel, opportunities."

Kathleen felt she would gladly give up the 'happy times'. "I think I'd rather marry now. I have thought about it. Really."

"How could you think about it properly when you know nothing better than Edgar and the shop? Any of us would have married rather than stay there."

Marguerite's words flew on. Over and over again she said the same things as though by mere repetition her sister would be worn down. Moving her hands the whole time, displaying a great mobility of expression, sometimes looking excited and happy as she talked of plans, sometimes looking the picture of despair as she dwelt on missed opportunities, she began to outline her scheme.

Unfortunately Madame de Sercier was not returning to France for three weeks. But she was willing to take Kathleen on as governess and there was no reason why Kathleen should not go on ahead to Paris and wait for her there.

"It is the most beautiful city in the world. You would enjoy it so much. I'll pay for your fare and your *pension*. I know you would love it."

Marguerite's displays of emotion were never embarrassing. Lost in her feelings she had no trace of self-consciousness. She was putting all this on to win over Kathleen, but at the same time everything she said and did was heartfelt. Kathleen felt torn between her desire to spare her sister this suffering and a longing to get back to Dick, settle down and be sheltered from further scenes. At the same time she felt some satisfaction at having provoked such emotions, she felt more important. At first she cried quietly and then, seeing that whatever she did was out of the picture she made some cocoa, found some bread and cheese and prepared a snack. She was dying of hunger.

The next day Kathleen's resolution, such as it was, was tried to the utmost. All morning the talk continued in the bedroom. Every time the servant tried to get in to clean it she was told to come back later. The room looked as though it, too, had taken part in the storm. Clothes had been pulled out of the cupboard and chest of drawers, sometimes to be offered as presents to Kathleen, sometimes to demonstrate the sort of thing she ought to wear when she got to Paris. They now lay over the two upright chairs, the brass end of the bed and the armchair which sloped to one side because a caster was missing. A few oddments lay on the floor. The curtains had not been fully drawn back, although there had been hours to do it in and, apart from a broad strip of light down the middle, the room was in shadow. It was cold but only the grey embers of the day before lay in the fireplace.

"Let us go to the station now," said Marguerite suddenly. "Leave today."

Kathleen, thinking this meant that she was to leave for Cardiff, packed her bag and prepared herself.

She heard Marguerite say "Victoria" to the cab driver. The damp leather seat seemed to perspire. The horse's hooves clacked monotonously. The rain was coming down in a steady drizzle. She felt her heart breaking. Her throat was dry. She could hear

Marguerite still talking, on and on, never stopping. She hated her. She hated all her family. She thought of Dick. She had never loved him more. He was not just her boyfriend now, he was her lifeline.

Tears rolled down her cheeks. Her sobs grew louder and louder and she shook all over. "No, Marguerite. I won't go to Paris. You can't make me. If you get the ticket I still won't go. If you put me on the train I shall get off it at the first stop."

She could hear words, reasoning, pleading, menacing. She shut her ears and clung onto two simple ideas. "I won't go. She can't make me."

Back in the boarding house, back in the room with the bed still unmade and everything in confusion, she felt she was now to pay some fearful penalty, as though Marguerite might beat her or kick her. She didn't care. She had learnt that nothing could make her go to Paris and nothing would keep her away from Dick. No storm broke over her head. Marguerite spoke coldly, contemptuously for a very short time and then was silent. So far as she was concerned that was that. No more time was to be wasted on this particular venture. There were many other things calling her. Bored, irritated, she walked round picking things up and putting them into drawers and the cupboard. She wished her sister would go. There was only one more day before she would be off to Cardiff but she felt she couldn't face another minute of her company.

Kathleen, nervously waiting for some final burst of fury, believing that this calm could only be temporary, could scarcely believe her ears when she heard.

"*Chérie* I have been wondering whether you should not go back to Cardiff today. I've just remembered there are several things I must do, and I really will not have any time for you. Your bag is packed and it would be a pity to have to undo it and do it all over again."

"Yes."

"*Chérie*. I must fly in half an hour. I will not be able to go to the station with you. I can give you the money for a cab. Why not go now?"

"Yes." She rose from her chair, walked slowly over to her case. Something more should be said. This ending was too chilly. "Oh, Marguerite, thank you for all you did. Thank you for the lovely dress. I'm very grateful, really I am."

Marguerite smiled without interest, went over to her, pecked her on each cheek and holding her arm led her firmly to the door. "I'm very glad you liked it. Goodbye."

10

Kathleen, safe but overcome, worrying about hurting Marguerite's feelings, leant on Dick's shoulder and ended her tale. "I think she has washed her hands of me."

This proved wrong. Marguerite had decided that if the girl was going to get married, then the thing should be done properly. It must be made clear that she had a family behind her. Who to? Marguerite had the vaguest idea about that—perhaps to the hospital, to patients, to Cardiff in general. There must be a Nuptial Mass and a slap-up meal to follow. Collecting all the money she could lay her hands on she hurried up to Cardiff.

The family was not represented. It was impossible. Mrs Hughes refused to go without Edgar because she dreaded the consequences. Michael was not very presentable and in any case it would be so dreadful if he brought his wife. Mr and Mrs Treherne were not asked and neither was Dick's sister. Thomas was up north with the other boys. Elizabeth was in Portugal.

Invitations were sent to select friends; sisters at the hospital, doctors, several former patients, a young solicitor who had been in love with Elizabeth and still kept up with her sister. The wedding breakfast was to be Marguerite's party, a Christmas party, for it was only three days before Christmas day. Kathleen was to wear a dove grey tailor-made with everything to match. Dick and Kathleen were allowed to ask two guests, Dick's friend from the office and his fiancée, who would be best man and bridesmaid.

Dick's protests were quelled by Kathleen's pleas. "Please let her do as she wants. It will be best in the end."

Marguerite's favourite priest, the local priest who had known her father, performed the marriage rites and celebrated the Mass.

Marguerite had nursed the proprietress of the Park Hotel and there the reception was held. In a long panelled room where a bright fire blazed, sixteen people assembled. Everything was of the very best. There was a fine roast turkey, golden brown and shining on a

137

silver dish. Two waiters attended, wearing long white aprons and carrying snowy napkins over one arm. The Christmas pudding came in covered in a purplish blue flame. Oranges, mince pies, nuts, dried fruits and different kinds of sweets in silver dishes were placed along the centre of the table. There were champagne and port. There was a great iced wedding cake.

After the meal was over and all were mellowed, Kathleen's shyness went. The bridesmaid, who had a clear soprano voice, was pressed for a song. To Kathleen's accompaniment she sang "I Know That My Redeemer Liveth" for she was a Protestant. Then came "Hearts of Oak" from the best man. Later Kathleen played a solo, Mendelsohn's Spring Song. Other guests performed.

The clapping was loud. All were animated. The pianola was put on again and again. The tunes were mostly solemn and included the Marches from *Lohengrin* and *Tannhauser*. From time to time, with beaming faces, the proprietor and his wife came in to see if anything more were needed. Marguerite sailed among her guests, pressing them to eat and drink, joking, laughing and happy.

After the wedding party Marguerite hurried over to see Patrick and his little brother and sister, taking with her the remains of the feast in paper bags. She laid the food out prettily on plates, decorated the table with holly and coloured paper and sat with them, smiling calmly while Patrick stuffed himself.

"He'll be sick," said Jennie.

"He will not," said Marguerite. "Who's a sensible boy? Who's quite grown up now? Who's going to write to his Auntie?"

She took the night train to London.

11

Kathleen still felt an apprentice at running a house. But since Dick could afford it she had a woman in to do the rough work. She had learnt to cook and now some dishes always came right. She was still slow; peeling vegetables, stirring the gravy and mixing the pudding took her hours. When there were several things to think of at once she felt flustered and pressed her lips together. However, fortified by Dick's affection, patience and admiration, her touch was growing surer.

The house was a mansion to her, so large that two rooms remained unfurnished. Marguerite had come that morning for the first time. Kathleen had seen her from the window, taking jerky steps along the gravel, hampered by a tight skirt, and she had wanted to laugh.

"Kathie, what wonderful news!"

"Yes, isn't it?"

"How long have you known?"

"Well I wasn't sure at first because I've often missed one before. But I think I must be about three months gone."

"Are you taking care of yourself?"

"I'm all right except for my teeth."

She had chatted on about how she felt and what Dick had said and how pleased he was. "Shall I show you the house?" She envied neither of her sisters. Sometimes she even felt sorry for them. However grand the places they went to, they were never theirs. And how dreadful it must be to have to bother about what people thought and servants thought all the time. She was safe here. No one could get at her. She led Marguerite into the parlour and pointed out the piano. "All the furniture's paid for. Dick believed in paying on the dot." She took her up to the bedroom and showed her the view from the window.

It was a suburban view with small detached houses half-hidden from each other by hedges and recently planted trees, trees with slim trunks and thin branches which trembled in every breeze. It was a bright day in May and the leaves were strong and sparkling. Town-bred, the two sisters looked on this as the country, but country softened and made bearable by houses, carts and people. Their eyes, accustomed to variety and change in urban landscape, the new coat of paint, the fuller shop window, the brighter lighting—saw open country as much of a muchness unless there was some sea there. The great seasonal changes of ground and trees had passed them by when they went on excursions. For the first time, this year, under Dick's guidance, Kathleen had observed, with cries of "Fancy!", lengthening twigs, unfolding buds and small green shoots pushing through the soil.

So that when Kathleen said, "And down there it's all fields and that," she was not surprised at the tonelessness of Marguerite's, "Oh."

"Mind you, we're near the town. It doesn't take long getting in. And the air's so good here. They say it's the best air."

"What will you call it? Have you thought?"

"William, that's if it's a boy. And I've got a feeling it will be a boy. So has Dick. He says..."

"Why William? There's never been a William in the family, has there? Why not Michael? That's a lovely name."

Kathleen was firm. "Dick says he wants it to be William."

"What is this about your teeth?"

"They ache so much I can't eat a thing and sometimes I think they're poisoning me. I get so sick. But that might just be natural."

"Have you seen anyone?"

"No."

Marguerite had attended a lecture on the ill-effects of bad teeth in pregnancy, the fatal effects on the babies. She thought of one or two sentences so fearful that they must have sprung from her imagination rather than from her memory. "Kathie, you must do something about them at once. Why did you leave it so late? You ought to think of these things for yourself. I'll arrange it now. We'll go to Mr Walker. Such a nice man. A great friend of mine."

Now Marguerite had returned and was telling her to get ready and go with her. Kathleen, surrounded by her own kitchen furniture, the four plain chairs tucked neatly round the scrubbed table, the dresser where she had screwed in cup hooks so unsymmetrically that Dick, laughing, had taken them all out and put them in again, the china bordered with a bright floral design, felt calm enough. "Very well."

As she shut the back door she felt a little sad. Walking past her own lawn and flowerbeds, then past hedges and the corner of the Park, leaving them behind, she felt more exposed. In the tram she twisted her mouth backwards and forwards. "Marguerite. What did he say? If he has to take them out what will I look like? I'll look terrible. I'll look like an old woman without any teeth. He won't do anything today, will he? I must think it over. And I haven't seen Dick to say anything to him. Whatever will he think? Will it hurt?"

The frosted glass and the smell of the surgery seemed to shut her in. Mr Walker, tall and with a black moustache, appeared to be waiting for her. She stared miserably at his fat, firm hands. She heard Marguerite apologising for being late. It was so good of him to take so much trouble. He answered politely in a small gentle voice.

He smiled. Unwillingly Kathleen felt she must be grateful to him. They were all trying to help her. A little of what Marguerite had been saying in the tram now came into her mind. It seemed very convincing. It was really very kind of them. Marguerite had given up going back to London for her sake. Mr Walker had meant to go somewhere this afternoon but he had stayed just for her. Some mothers who didn't have their teeth seen to had their systems poisoned and the babies were born with diseases. Sometimes they had stillbirths. The thought of self-sacrifice made an appeal. Mothers giving up everything for the sake of the baby.

She opened her mouth, embarrassed by the proximity of a strange, respectable-looking man, and tried not to breath. She kept swallowing back her saliva.

After the examination Mr Walker said a few reassuring words to her and then spoke at greater length to Marguerite. Suddenly Kathleen felt angry. Why didn't he tell her what he had to say? Why did everyone treat her as a half-wit—that is, everyone who was a friend of her sister's? He was saying that there were abscesses, decay and infection. He advised taking them all out. Marguerite was nodding.

"The front ones too?" asked Kathleen.

He smiled benevolently. "I'm afraid so."

"Couldn't you leave them? Isn't there something else you could do to them?"

He shook his head. "I was explaining to your sister that the infection..."

"Not the front ones. They hardly hurt at all. If I could just keep those." They were small, white and even. Dick loved them.

Marguerite looked exasperated. "Now, Kathie. Do stop worrying. Think of the baby. Mr Walker says they're infected. Now, dear, do you think you could be very brave and have them out without gas? Not that it hurts really."

Kathleen shook her head, her mouth felt dry and she couldn't think of words, shook her head violently and wrung her hands.

"In your condition you should really not have gas. It will hardly hurt at all. It will all be over so quickly."

"No. No." She had had teeth out before, only one at a time, and it had been torture enough then. She jumped out of her chair. "No, Marguerite, no." Apprehension was like a large, grey stone in her stomach. She looked round for the door. "I'm not well. I feel sick. Really, honestly, I feel awful. Not today. Some other day."

They tried to calm her. Mr Walker firmly helped her back to her chair. Marguerite kept talking. They left the room and stood outside the door talking so softly that she could not catch the words. The daylight behind the frosted glass was bright and her staring eyes smarted. They came back and stood beside her. "You shall have gas, dear," said Marguerite. "I quite understand, *chérie*. But it will be your own fault if it disagrees with you. However, I think it will be all right. You'll feel nothing. And you'll be ten times better when it's done. I'll stay here with you. I'll see that you are all right."

As though to gain time Kathleen got up and walked about. She picked up her hat from the floor and put it onto the table. She took off her jacket. Mr Walker left the room and Marguerite helped her to loosen her skirt and her corsets. "You're sure it's for the best? Well, I suppose he must know. And if he says—then it must be right. It would have had to be now or later, wouldn't it?"

Prepared, in the chair, she prayed. She was not religious in an orthodox way. She and Dick had often speculated and doubted, and although he had joined the Catholic church to marry her, both of them frequently missed Sunday Mass. But she always believed in something, and at this moment she believed in all she had been taught. She prayed hard. It was a vague prayer, not that her teeth might be spared, not that her health might be all right, but just that someone above would watch over her and comfort her.

With the feeling that the air had intensified, become green and compressed, and was now pushing against her temples and the back of her head, she floated away.

She saw the High Street, filled with traffic and people, more crowded than it had ever been before. She herself, although present, was not really there. No one pushed past her and no one saw her. She was disembodied. Everyone was hurrying and moving. Nothing but motion filled their lives; they were not going from anywhere to anywhere, they were just moving; they were not saying real words or making real sounds, there was just a movement and rush of noise. And the traffic was the same, whizzing in both directions, with the honk of motor horns and the swish of trams and the clop-clop of galloping hooves.

There was a lull, a feeling of whiteness and then voices. The voices were dim at first and, as she opened her eyes onto a misty world, she thought she had imagined them. But with a rush they came close to her and they were voices she had heard before. The mist before her eyes dissolved. Long-backed chairs, a table, a door, all dark brown, all shining through fine grey dust, sprang up. They seemed very large and towered above her. There was a clock ticking out of sight. There were some thick, dirty lace curtains.

She felt a heaving under her ribs and a movement up towards her throat. She shouted, "I'm sick. I'm going to be sick." Dizzy, apologetic, she thanked them. She was so ashamed of herself that she could think of nothing else. It was terrible to be sick in the presence of a strange man. "I'm sorry. I'm very sorry." She fought hard to keep it down.

At last, lying back on the musty-smelling sofa, she shut her eyes, half-expecting to find herself in the High Street again. Her head was swimming and surely there were all the noises and the movement. She couldn't quite hear them, she couldn't see them at all, but she could feel them. She remembered there was somewhere else too, somewhere she might find herself. The house, her house. And there was Dick. He might be in it with her.

She knew what had happened. What would Dick say? What would he think? He would always be kind and he would always love her. But what would he think? Her mouth was aching now and full of blood. She moved her tongue. There was nothing there, nothing but huge soft wet throbbing cavities. She visualised them as some dark, gigantic, infernal, mountainous landscape. She began to cry. Marguerite drew up a chair beside her and took her hand. "*Chérie,* he's getting something for you. I knew you should not have gas. In your condition it is unwise..."

Kathleen turned her head away, in towards the musty velvet, until a strand of her soft, dark hair lay over the fringed edge of the antimacassar.

12

The agony of finding Kathleen gone, he did not know where, the hour of waiting for return, the fruitless search at her mother's, made Dick feel nothing but relief when he saw her at last. She too had been wondering where he could be, imagining he must be searching for her, too sick and dizzy to know what to do. She was lying on the bed and her face was deathly pale.

At first Dick had no idea what had happened. Ashamed of her torn gums, Kathleen kept her mouth tight shut and looked at him with eloquent eyes. Marguerite explained and his relief turned to fury.

"You might have left a note," he said. "You might have said something to me. You had no right to do such a thing without consulting me."

It was Marguerite's fault, not Kathie's. She had always been an interfering, domineering heartless unimaginative creature. He loathed her. His head was cool and his thoughts were clear. He said what he had long wanted to say.

"Please leave the house. You've done quite enough interfering and from now on I shall be very grateful if you don't come back."

When he had seen her out, not out of politeness but to make sure that she went, he returned to the bedroom. The anxiety in Kathleen's large, filmy eyes made him careful not to look at her mouth. She must not feel ashamed of being without teeth. He must notice nothing.

Unfortunately the mouth was too torn and sore to bear false teeth. Mr Walker, in his haste to extract all the teeth in one go, because the patient could not be under gas for long, had gone as fast as he could. There was not time for the careful manoeuvring of crossed roots and awkward angles. It would be a very long time before dentures could be worn.

Ashamed to smile, her slit of a mouth now crumpled and pinched, Kathleen resigned herself to soft food and a feeling of deformity. Sometimes she consoled herself by saying it was a fine sacrifice to the baby's health. Sometimes she saw it as the result of a wicked conspiracy against her and was filled with heavy hatred. The conspiracy had been against Dick too and that was intolerable. In time, as their life remained much the same, as the outings to theatres and seaside continued, she thought less of her mouth.

Her composure was short-lived. Her life was returning to normal. She was beginning to look forward to winter when the baby would be born, to the following spring and summer when they would be playing with it and putting it in the garden. Dick fell ill. Soon they knew that the heart was involved and the outcome would be fatal. The doctor thought it best to tell Kathleen all, fearing the effect of the sudden unheralded loss of her husband on her pregnancy. Dick had long had a weak heart; an attack of rheumatic fever in childhood had started it; rapid growth and swimming had strained it.

During the first months of marriage she accepted his love greedily and used it to blot out her life before. She was like someone accustomed to the greatest poverty who suddenly finds money and spends it all on drink to forget the years of struggle. This new, protective affection which had by such good fortune come her way was a means of forgetting the world and cutting herself off from further trials. She clung to the house; she clung to herself; she clung to Dick. She used him to avoid making her own decisions. It was he who chose the furniture. It was he who decided what to have for dinner. She consulted him all the time and he was kind enough never to consult her unless he had already made up his mind.

The daily round, the jokes at meals, the nicknames given to people and things, comforted and reassured her. She saw herself as a sad, frail little thing with a protector at last. Lost in this aspect of their life she saw Dick in rough outline only, an ideal husband character. He was patient, kind, even-tempered, generous and reliable. He planned treats and brought home presents. He looked for a smile on her lips and colour in her cheeks. From his six-foot height he bent down to enquire, "Are you happy? Are you enjoying yourself?"

There was a little more body to her picture of him because they had been children together and therefore she knew his tricks of speech, the sound of his step and other small things peculiar to him. Also she realised with pride that he was tall and good-looking. But when she recalled the times they had had together, when they were adolescent or after they were married, she did not think of how he looked, how he spoke or of anything characteristic of him, she dwelt only on those words and gestures which revealed his attitude to her, some act of kindness he had done for her, something about her which he had praised.

In time, although she still shrank from sex, she turned a little away from herself, her troubles and her needs. One hesitant step and then another led her towards his personality. She was on the point of seeing him more clearly when he fell ill. Then he became for her the noble, suffering character, the uncomplaining, brave, ideal patient. Her desire to help him gave her no freedom to know him better. Besides, knowing he was about to die, how could she have had the heart for it? All the same, the few months of love and companionship had left their mark. For once self-pity was pushed away and nothing mattered but to make Dick happy while she could.

The seeds which he had planted and tended were now in full bloom but he could not see their brilliance from the bedroom window. The baby, stirring so violently that they joked about having a footballer, he might never see. He might never see her in her dentures and his last impression of her face would be the childish look of the bewildered eyes and the shapeless, crumpled lips, combining to make her ageless, timeless and unreal.

Trying not to think of what would become of her when he was gone, she dipped into their savings and bought him anything he fancied. Her family came to see him. Edgar in particular kept coming with grapes and flowers. Finally Marguerite appeared.

Dick wanted her to go away. He had told Kathleen not to write to her. "I won't have her fussing round and upsetting you."

Marguerite was on a case when she heard the news. First the night nurse had told her fortune and there had been an ace of spades reversed very prominent in her hand. Then came a letter from Mrs Hughes. Marguerite, forgetting the many times the cards had failed, forgetting also the letter which had given details, told Kathleen a strange story.

"I had a strange dream. There was someone, a man, in trouble. And then I had a strong premonition. It was as though I heard your voice asking for help. And then this nurse told my fortune. With me you know it always turns out to be true. I always know when something is about to happen. I have a sort of gift. She said a member of your family is ill, not a blood relation because you are clubs and he's diamonds, but probably a relation by marriage." There was not a word of truth in this, the ace of spades having been interpreted as some railway disaster. "He is desperately ill and he needs you. It's a house just outside a big city, but not London, and it has a garden. I knew at once. I knew before she told me. I always feel these things."

They were downstairs in the sitting room. Kathleen was impressed by the story but anxious to prevent Marguerite from going upstairs. She believed her sister was one of those who possess second sight.

"It was very good of you to come. I don't want to seem rotten but it might be best if you didn't see Dick. He doesn't want to see people."

Marguerite took no notice of this. She had long forgotten his angry words. Criticisms of herself were banished from her memory in a matter of seconds. She saw him and stayed. She bought herself a bed and installed herself in one of the unfurnished rooms.

Now in a professional relation to Dick and therefore to Kathleen she was at her best. After a few days he was glad to have her there. She became fond of him because she always tended to love those who were dangerously ill. She bought him books and read to him for hours. She bought Kathleen wool to keep her occupied with knitting. She went to his office and extracted sickness benefit from the firm. She paid for the doctor. She was tactful, too, and when he was temporarily better left them alone. When he was bad she stayed by him all night.

Kathleen was surprised and lost her dread of her sister. She even believed that Marguerite was fond of her, had really always been fond of her but unable to show it. After all, her attempts to prevent the marriage had probably sprung from affection. When Dick was sleeping Marguerite would come down and ask her to play something on the piano, something quiet. "I am so fond of music," she said and Kathleen believed her. She would ask to be shown round the garden. She kept talking about the baby and the fine future they would make for it.

"I misjudged her," said Dick. "She's a very fine character really."

13

It was no wonder then that, when all was over, Kathleen allowed herself to be taken to London, handed over her furniture to her sister without a murmur, handed over the insurance money, and moved with her to a house in Kensington which they ran as a boarding house. She had six weeks to go now.

Every morning she walked slowly round Kensington Gardens. It was mid-November and under the bare, black branches the ground was covered with dark, rotted leaves. There was a smell of wood smoke in the air. The lack of colour seemed ugly to her, for she had learnt only the first lesson in the appreciation of nature, and reacted only to the brightness of young leaves and flowers. Dull melancholy filled her.

The end had not been the worst part because she had expected it for so long and there had been relief in the tears shed during the funeral. But now that Dick had gone for ever, security had gone too. The strong nesting instinct, which often comes in late pregnancy, was a torment to her. It was pointless to try and make the small back room, allotted to her in the boarding house, look nice. A lodger might want it and she would be moved. It was like camping, she could settle nowhere. Catalogues with coloured illustrations of pretty nurseries had made her dream of a frilled cot with a soft rug beside it, and she had longed to spend some of the insurance money freely as a grand gesture of motherhood. But Marguerite had interfered, producing a shabby, rickety, second-hand thing in which to put the infant.

Words of resignation came into her head, for she liked sayings and quotations and believed them to be compact repositories of centuries-old wisdom. "One must take it philosophically"; "it was meant to be and you can't alter fate"; "I'm one of the world's unlucky ones". But always she ended with an angry complaint. "Why should I be cheated out of everything?"

Sometimes, indoors by the fire with a hot cup of tea, she felt hopeful. "After all, I have my health." The baby was something to look forward to. It would love her. She saw a tall, handsome, protective son, as kind and considerate as his father.

When her lying-in was past she walked once more around the gardens, now wheeling a little girl in a pram. It was a very fine pram, the best you could have, the gift of Marguerite's patient.

Resignation and melancholy had gone. It was now love and hate; love for the baby and hate for Marguerite. The baby was good and resembled her father; she never cried; she slept and slept. When Kathleen suckled her she was overwhelmed by the strength of her attachment to this small creature. Her character was not maternal for she was in search of a parent figure herself, but for the first months her physical devotion to the child was instinctive and real. It was the strongest and simplest feeling she had ever had. It was independent of her past or any picture of herself. The sight of the small, transparent eyelids and the downy hair made her dreamy and happy.

Marguerite had been hard during labour. "She didn't even get me a cup of tea." Marguerite had not sent for a doctor to give her stitches although she was torn. Marguerite had ruthlessly made her get up sooner than she should because a lodger came for the room. Marguerite had moved her with the baby to the damp back basement room with its iron-barred windows and smell of mouldering floorboards. She knew Marguerite expected the child to be called after her but angrily turned a deaf ear to all her hints.

"I shall call her Elizabeth," Kathleen had said.

Besides looking after the child, Kathleen was expected to be at the beck and call of the lodgers. One of them, an Indian medical student, terrified her. He would come into the kitchen when she was feeding the baby and stand smiling with his black eyes fixed on her naked breast. Once when she was dusting his room he grabbed her hand and pulled at the front of her blouse. She complained to Marguerite, who was out all day.

"Nonsense, Kathie," said Marguerite. The student had been recommended by a doctor she wanted to keep in with. "You are making it up. You're exaggerating. You imagine things. In any case these foreigners are different, you know, and you are bound to misunderstand them. In future make sure he's out when you do the room. There's no need for any of them to come to the kitchen. Be firm and do not allow them in."

"But Marguerite, it's true. He's an awful man."

"Marguerite looked at her as though she were a nitwit. "If you find him so very awful, all you have to do is keep out of the way."

"Couldn't you give him notice?"

"No, of course not. We need the money, *chérie*. What would you live on if it were not for the boarding house?" She always spoke rapidly to her sister, never looking at her for more than a second, as though all conversation between them were inexpressibly boring and a waste of time.

Kathleen found the money position mysterious. They were always hard up and often she had nothing with which to buy lunch. The insurance policy had been worth a hundred pounds. Marguerite had taken all this and the furniture. Besides, Kathleen was earning her keep by helping with the house. Why should she be treated as a pauper? Marguerite was definitely queer about money and one could not describe her as mean. She would give one things, never quite what one wanted—just as she had promised to provide the cot and it was this miserable-looking thing—but often new and expensive. However if she could possibly avoid it she would never hand over cash. And if she had to provide cash in order to prevent one starving then she counted out a small amount with a frown and grumble. And if you had any money she always wanted to take it from you. She must have the handling of it.

Kathleen suspected that some of her insurance money was now paying for Michael's children. When she voiced her suspicions, Marguerite made no attempt at denial but was scornful of her.

"Of all the people I ever met, you are the most selfish, Kathie. You hang on to every penny like... like Shylock. When have I ever grudged you anything? Whenever you needed anything you only had to come to me and if I had it, it was yours."

It was difficult to be consistent with her. The hatred remained but on the surface Kathleen often felt gratitude and admiration. When Marguerite came back with a tasty piece of roast chicken, stuffing and all, wrapped in paper, for Kathleen's supper, and Kathleen realised it was her own lunch she had brought home, she would have liked to thank her properly. But Marguerite never wanted to be thanked. She did everything so brusquely. When she brought home a toy for the baby she threw it onto the table without comment, unless of course the baby was awake. Then she would dangle it over the cot and make funny noises and laugh.

When Kathleen complained of having only one dress Marguerite gave her her best one. "Here you are. And do stop grumbling!" It was unpleasant to be given things like that. It was better to be given nothing.

Then Marguerite was unpredictable about the lodgers. One day she might say, "Poor Mr Williams. He's very hard up, so I told him not to worry about the rent for the last few weeks. He may try and make it up later but it does not matter. Now what a sad story he has! Such a refined man too and very well educated. You know he was in a very good post when..."

Yet if Kathleen suggested letting someone off the rent, for she too was tender hearted, there would be trouble. Marguerite would tell her she had no business to think of such a thing.

"Kathie, we cannot afford it. That man is only making a fool of you. He can pay very well if he wants to. It's a good thing you're not the landlady or we should never have a penny."

She would hurry upstairs to deal firmly with the defaulter. And even then one never knew what the outcome would be. She might return with the money or without it, furious with the man or full of sympathy for him. Whatever happened she would not admit that Kathleen had been right. "Why could you not have explained the matter properly, *chérie?* You are always so muddled."

One day Marguerite returned without her nurse's cloak. It was bitter weather, and although she was erratic in her reactions to climate, sometimes wearing the heaviest coat in the hottest weather, sometimes a silk dress on a chilly day, this time she was shivering and her teeth chattered. Kathleen was certain she had seen her go off in her cloak that morning.

"Why did you leave it? You look frozen."

"Oh, Kathie," said Marguerite. "I gave it away. I was coming back along that terrible road and there was a poor woman holding a baby. You should have seen its hands and feet, blue with cold, and it was crying. It was crying with cold. I had nothing else I could take off, and the cloak was so nice and large. I put it round the mother and baby, you know, folded it right over so it would keep the wind off it. It was such a pitiful little thing, not six months and exposed like that. If you'd seen it!"

"But that cloak was worth pounds and you need it. And supposing the woman sells it and buys something for herself, the baby will be no better off."

Marguerite shook her head. These considerations were not new to her. She had not thought of them but she knew them. In cases like these she refused to let them modify her impulse. It was difficult to say how much she saw, what stage of reason and counter-reason she had reached at a given moment. She felt impatient now, still seeing the mean street and the frozen child. Looking away from her sister, leaving the fire at which she had been warming herself, she walked briskly over to the window.

"I know, Kathie, I know. If that child had only half an hour's warmth it's worth it."

14

The more Marguerite succeeded as a nurse, the more interested she became in her profession. As a midwife she was outstanding. Her reputation was known to several eminent obstetricians and she was recommended to their patients. She never lacked work. She became accustomed to living in fine houses and being treated with respect and her interest in these things decreased. It was the type of case rather than the type of house which now interested her, and often if she felt the family was poor she refused to take full fees. She was firm with the mothers, highhanded with the rest of the household and tenderness itself with the infant.

Completely unscientific in spite of her training, never bothering to examine her reasons for taking a certain course and never dreaming of giving a proper explanation to anyone else, she worked by intuition. Often she sensed what kind of a labour it was going to be. Her hands could feel the exact position of the unborn baby in a second. After the birth she could sense whether the infant was ill or well. Sometimes she would diagnose an ailment right outside her sphere. One of her patients, a lady of intelligence who had grown fond of her, always maintained that she should have been a doctor and not a nurse. But Marguerite would never have mastered the amount of exact and detailed knowledge necessary to a medical degree. She would have lost patience and she would have invented her own facts. She must always have been an inspired quack, a medicine man.

During her earlier cases she had been at pains to impress those around her. She had believed that no one would pay any attention to you unless you claimed birth and education. Now, conscious of her standing in her profession, she was businesslike and impersonal. Those tales of her exalted ancestry, which had once been poured out during the first week at a new house, were told no more. Not a word was said about her background. She appeared and she took charge. She stood no nonsense from night nurses or assistant nurses. The case must be in her hands and everyone must do things her way. If she disagreed with the doctor she did not tell him so but ignored his instructions and acted on her own initiative. She threw herself into nursing each new patient with great devotion. That was why they liked her. Nothing was too much trouble. She was not the kind to grumble when they rang the bell.

She made no friends for purely emotional reasons now. All the ladies she visited frequently were of use to her, or else she was of use to them. They might, like Miss Tracy, run an agency. Or they might be nurses of standing like herself. Or they might be former patients who wished to keep in touch with her, because they had confidence in her and her forceful methods had undermined their confidence in any other nurse, and wanted to make sure that she would come to them when any member of their family fell ill. With these acquaintances those fluffy parts of conversation, those pieces of ritual which she had so prized in Bordeaux, were rarely needed. Usually, unless there was something to be planned, to be decided, she said nothing. While the others spoke of things in general she would either sit with a polite smile on her face and a vague look in her eyes, or else, forgetting where she was, she would give way to her restlessness and walk over to the window or leave the room without explanation. Very occasionally, something about the people she was with or the room would place that particular gathering under the heading "A special occasion" in her mind. Then, regardless of relevance, she would launch out into high-flown descriptions of foreign lands and the houses she had been in. Many found her disconcerting. Fond patients fell back on phrases: "Such a character!"; "Quite eccentric!".

Looking at her strong, expressive face, many thought that they would soon get to know her, that there would be confidences and intimacies, and they were wrong. Her face moved people, it went to their hearts, all the more so because there was nothing sentimental in it. She appeared on the verge of giving out endless, unembarrassing love. This was deceptive. When she knew that she would have to go on seeing a person for some time she scarcely reacted to them at all.

At the same time, her relations with the world at large, that is with complete strangers, met on trains, in trams, on a bench in the park or in a shop, grew in intensity. The fact that they would appear once and no more made her strangely receptive to them. She listened to them, sympathised with them, felt for them and gave them advice. Often she worried about them long after they had passed out of her life. She hardly noticed their faces or understood their characters. She could not have described them in any but the vaguest terms.

She put everything into making each casual contact flower. For the moment she would long to make the person happy. She was the first to give up her seat in a crowded bus. She pushed over the sugar basin or searched for a menu for someone at the same table in a restaurant. She carried suitcases for people at railway stations. She was always attentive and considerate to those she did not know. She opened her purse for every beggar who passed. Any hard luck story would find her producing half a crown or more. And even though she often sensed that she was being hoodwinked it made no difference. But when it happened that some stranger crossed her path several times, she would lose interest, find their personality oppressive, and try to avoid further encounters. Kensington Gardens was full of old ladies who had once poured out their woes into her sympathetic ear, and now received from her only the briskest of nods as she hurried by.

And with this taste for a rapid turnover in human contacts came sudden longings for completely new surroundings. To be abroad, not in Bordeaux but somewhere she had never been before, to hear a new language and to see a new kind of life seemed necessary to her.

Towards the end of a case, when the strain and crisis were past, no matter how happy she had been there, no matter what advantages the place offered, she would have given anything to leave the house at once and never see anyone there again. She felt particularly restive when returning to the same house for the second or third time. While the mother of a child helped into the world by Marguerite, then nursed for mumps and now for measles, might be saying, as the rich will say, "Nurse Reilly is so devoted to us. She always comes when I want her. And she does so adore John," upstairs Nurse Reilly would be fretting. So uninteresting an illness would appear a waste of her time. Finding John unspeakably tedious she would be trying hard to think of a convincing excuse to hand over to another nurse.

If it had not been professionally wise and correct to return to the same families she would not have done so. But when a doctor said that so-and-so would have no one but Nurse Reilly and she must oblige them, then there was nothing for it but to look obliging.

15

Shortly after the birth of Lisa, Marguerite was summoned in the middle of the night—she had had a phone installed in case of emergencies. Now began a case after her own heart, the birth of a premature baby.

The father, Mr Jamieson, was a wealthy banker. The mother was what Marguerite styled a "society lady", a description which she gave to any lady with a high income and a fair number of friends. The house was furnished in every style; the Queen Anne room, the Italian room, the Chinese room, and so on. The large entrance hall was a Landseer Tudor, with oak panelling, antlers, iron lamps, antique chests and the suggestion that at any moment gun dogs with hanging tongues and ears would come bounding over the brown carpet. All this greatly impressed Marguerite, who loved variety. In the future she maintained, "Mrs Jamieson had the finest taste of anyone I met."

With the excitement she always felt when someone was about to be born, Marguerite set about undoing all the preparations made by the temporary nurse and arranged everything as she herself liked it. The order which she found soon turned to chaos, but the sort of chaos she could work in. She spoke to her patient as though she were a child and kept up a flow of lively, bewilderingly inconsequent remarks. When Mrs Jamieson, sick and dreading her second confinement, complained of a pain, Marguerite laughed, "Oh, that's nothing yet." But as soon as the poor lady had resigned herself to the fact that she was in the hands of one of the hard kind, she found her nurse full of compassion and doing everything in her power to make things easier for her.

Marguerite decided that a bath would be a distraction and hurry on the slow labour. She rang the bell, ordered it and made preparations. When all was ready she changed her mind. Perhaps as it was a second child things might speed up too much without warning.

From the moment she arrived, the apprehensive stillness in the bedroom vanished. There was movement and there were constant surprises. At one moment she agreed to send for the doctor. At another she refused, saying it was far too early and, in any case, she could do everything herself. She would talk rapidly and unceasingly for ten or fifteen minutes. Then suddenly she would go over to the window and, holding back the heavy brocade curtains, stare silently down at the street. Often she picked up a book, a different one each time, and scanned the first few pages. Sometimes she darted out of the room.

Mrs Jamieson felt it was like having ten nurses instead of one. Between pains she tried to decide whether Miss Reilly was always like this or whether it was all a carefully planned and subtle way of entertaining and distracting. However, she had complete confidence in her.

Marguerite, diagnosing correctly that instruments would have to be used, sent for the doctor. With a gleam in her eye she watched the last stages, bullying, cajoling, encouraging, biting her lip and jutting forward her head. She worked hard, she never let go her high pitch of concentration. When the child arrived she triumphed. It was as though she had produced it herself. For a short time it would be entirely hers.

But there was no question of relaxing or resting. The child was terribly small, it weighed two and a half pounds and it was incomplete. It had no nails on fingers or toes. It was too weak to suck. She could see from the doctor's face that he thought its chances small. She felt angry with him. Outside the bedroom door she didn't listen to his words, until she heard, "Well, I'll leave it to you, nurse."

She removed the cot to her room at once. There was no time to be lost. Although she had not been to bed for well over thirty hours she couldn't sleep until the baby had taken something. She tried everything. It couldn't take the breast, the sucking instinct had not arrived and even if it had where would it have found the strength? She made a very large hole in the teat, but although the milk dropped through it into the mouth, it simply lay on the tongue. She soaked pieces of cotton wool in milk, hoping that the sodden, woolly texture would lure the infant into sucking. For some reason she was anxious that it should suck and help itself. In the end she used a pipette with which the milk could be expressed almost down into the throat.

She kept to no regular feeding times because too little would be taken that way. It was a very slow process and nearly every half-hour in the daytime and every few hours at night she returned to it. By degrees some nourishment was pumped in. Then a little sucking was induced. The tiny, wrinkled, wretched, red little thing looked more lively. Its thin, wavering cry grew a little richer. It stirred a little. There was a slight movement in the hands and feet.

Everyone agreed that she had saved it. "My babies always do well," she said. Her passion for it eclipsed her other thoughts. Even Patrick was out of her mind. She had meant to make the mother feed it as soon as possible but finding that the delay had diminished the already inadequate flow of milk, she kept to diluted cow's milk. As the little thing, now referred to as Basil, progressed, so the doctor prescribed two patent foods to be mixed with sugar in a certain proportion. Marguerite laughed scornfully. "They all say that," she said to Mrs Jamieson.

The patent foods were procured. Every time the doctor came he found them prominently displayed on the table. As soon as he had left the house they were put back in the cupboard until his next visit. Mrs Jamieson found herself drawn into conspiracies and intrigues. "No, you must not take that," Marguerite would say, whisking away the medicine prescribed by the doctor. "You should try walking round the room. I do not know what he means by trying to keep you in bed so long." Before the doctor arrived there were instructions. "Now you must say you did as he told you. You took the medicine. One must humour them."

There was a fight brewing. Nanny, who looked after the eldest child (Alan, aged two), fully expected to take over the baby as soon as he was out of danger. Marguerite, having heard her agree with the doctor's ideas on food, decided that the woman knew nothing. She was determined that little Basil must be saved from her incompetence or else he would perish. As the matter was so urgent she stopped at nothing. In a short time everyone on the third floor was in one camp or the other.

Mrs Jamieson, still weak and resting for half the day, didn't know what to believe or what to do. As she described it afterwards, "It was like having a Borgia in the house."

Marguerite began by commenting on Alan. "He looks very pale. A child of that age should have less clothes on. Why does she give him all that pappy stuff to eat? What good does she think it will do him, making him walk round the park weighed down by that coat? He has not the strength. His shoes are too tight." She did not confine herself to the truth. She hinted at dishonesty and cruelty. She won over the under nurse and used her as a spy.

Tearfully, Nanny came into Mrs Jamieson's room to complain. After a scene with Nanny, the under nurse followed also in floods of tears. Then the housekeeper, who was against Marguerite, complained that all her arrangements for nursery meals were being tampered with. All were tense and suspicious, except Marguerite who had never been more buoyant.

Marguerite made many allies among the staff by tending cut fingers and colds and shaking her head and looking serious as she listened to tales of previous illnesses. Having thrown doubts into Mrs Jamieson's mind about Nanny and Basil (for she suddenly announced that Basil was very ill) she made her promise that there should be no question of the baby going to the nursery for a very long time. He was kept in her room and, apart from his parents, no one but herself ever saw him.

The room became a sacred shrine. Only one of the maids she trusted was allowed to do it out and she must make no noise and be very careful about dust. If she found a servant from the other camp in the passage outside, she would give an exasperated sigh. "Must you make that noise? Is Basil always going to be disturbed just when I've got him off to sleep?"

She would ring for the maid and send her to the nursery with a message. "Would they please make less noise and consider the baby?"

Marguerite insisted with some cause that the under nurse should be her assistant and thought up a hundred ways of keeping her occupied. Every time Mrs Jamieson came in from a walk or a visit she dreaded what would greet her. Someone was crying or grumbling. Marguerite had a story, told rapidly and difficult to follow.

"Really it was too bad of Nanny. And it's not the first time. Poor Basil needed his milk. I had so much to do. I could not heat it myself. So I asked Elsie. But of course she would not let her. She wanted her to do up Alan's shoes! Poor Basil was crying his little heart out. He was so hungry, the poor mite. I had to leave everything. And then of course there was no help from Mrs Pritchett either."

"I'm sorry, nurse. Nanny says as it was her half-day..."

"Her half-day!" Marguerite roared with false laughter. "She is so anxious about her half-day that she would sacrifice anyone for it. Have I ever considered half-days or that sort of thing? If I had kept to my hours and half-days, what would happen to poor Basil? What would happen if he were handed over to someone like that? To do up Alan's shoes!"

In the end Mrs Jamieson always sided with Marguerite, not without doubts of course. But the nurse had a more persuasive manner and she never wept like the others. Besides, she had saved Basil and the family thought her wonderful in her way.

Marguerite ate with the family. Sometimes in the evening she appeared in full evening dress and spoke airily of France, Italy, Spain and Germany and the delights of travel. At other times, usually when they would have liked her to dress on account of the guests, she would say she had no time and appear in uniform, taking no part in the conversation and interrupting it as soon as it got going. "Was that a cry? Do you think Elsie is up there?" She might hurry out and not return for a while. Her soup would have to be kept warm. She would be a course or two behind. The mildest rebuke would be construed as a display of indifference towards the fate of the baby.

When every member was fully engrossed in the battle, when Nanny had given notice and the housekeeper threatened to do the same, Marguerite threw in her hand. The old restlessness had come over her. Basil was safe now. To Mrs Jamieson's surprise she urged that he should go to the nursery. Perhaps she was sorry to see anyone lose their job.

"Nanny's very good with the children," she said. "She's such a dear. It will be so nice for the children to be together. Poor Alan keeps asking for his little brother."

In a week she had gone and the life of the house became calmer and duller.

PART THREE: JOURNEYS

1

The Portuguese food and climate suited Elizabeth. She was not so slim and flower-like as she had once been, but at twenty-eight she looked young and yet in her prime. Her cheeks were full and firm and rosy and her black hair and eyebrows had a bright gloss. Her waist and hips were kept neat by careful corseting. By contrast her shoulders seemed beautifully rounded and padded. Men still paid her many attentions but she had become skilled at dealing with them. A cold glance, a steely glint under her sweetness, a touch of the firm schoolmistress, soon put them off. And if they continued to sigh for her, at least they did not approach her twice unasked.

She had become intensely religious and had even been on the point of becoming a nun. Perhaps this was due to the infectious passion of Catholicism in Iberia. Perhaps it sprang from her increasingly acquisitive disposition, a wish to lay up treasure in heaven. Nearly every morning she rose early and went to mass and communion before breakfast, coming home through the narrow streets while the air was still fresh, meditating on holy things, a black lace veil falling down to her shoulders. In her room were holy pictures, statues and several beautiful crucifixes of ebony and silver. Below a small shrine to the Sacred Heart she said her night prayers, kneeling on a red-cushioned walnut *prie-dieu*. This had been given to her by a pupil who was now a nun and whom she often visited. She had many favourite saints and she was learned in the dates of feast days. She lit candles to Saint Anthony whenever she lost anything. Often on her way back from a lesson she slipped into one of the big churches to pray. She loved the large old dimly lit churches, with the clusters of yellow candle flames burning as though in a dark fog in the side chapels, with the distant gleam of bright metal from the high altar, with the heavy cold-water font by the entrance.

She was extraordinarily like her father. Not only her appearance but her reactions were similar to his, although she had not known him very well and rarely thought of him now. She, too, always appeared to be watching herself, to be aware of how she seemed to others. She, too, was more conscious of salvation than damnation, and that was why she found Edgar's frenzy about immorality so ridiculous. Her father never thought about such things as the indecency of dress, and though her convent days had left her modest, there was no anxiety in her about sin. Like her father she thought of heaven as her future abode, she would simply have to adhere to certain rules of conduct—rules which she knew she was by temperament unlikely to break—to reach it. It would be an elegant place into which she would fit at once. It was as though she were already one of the blessed.

Finding herself far away from her family, meditating on virtues and duties and determined to do all the good she should, she asked herself whether it was not time to do something for the others. Marguerite was wonderful, of course—wonderful was how she described her to others and wonderful was what she sincerely believed her to be so long as she was at a distance—but all Marguerite's care went to Michael and his family and, to a lesser extent, to the two youngest boys. Perhaps poor Thomas was being left out of it. Thomas often wrote to her for he still adored her. His writing had not improved and his English was faulty. While employed as an odd-job man at the Park Hotel he had hurt his arm. It had been crushed by a beer-barrel and he was not well. She wrote to Marguerite:

> "*Chérie*" (she had copied this word from Marguerite),
> "*Have heard from Thomas. Sorry about arm. Hope not serious. If he could take course English lessons, particular attention grammar and spelling could find him something here. Will send money for lessons of course. Also accent. Know it is difficult for him but could you do something about accent. So broad. Even here might be noticed. Very nice type English person out here.*
> *So please, chérie, course in grammar, spelling and speech. Must stress this last. Handwriting not good but less important. Please could you see to it soon. Course of one month and could come here. Will find him good post.*"

There followed a few pious phrases. She had some misgivings. He might disgrace her in front of her English friends with his Cardiff ways and he could be so stubborn. But then his stubbornness had only been directed against the others, she had always been able to deal with him. If necessary she could keep him out of sight for a short time. She wrote further instructions to Marguerite and waited.

When Thomas did arrive she was very happy to see him. She had not realised how strongly the fact of being a member of a large family had made her miss the others. She had forgotten how much they meant to her. Taking him to a little café where they would meet no one she knew, she studied his face. His features were regular and he had no coarseness. His voice was soft. As she watched him she saw resemblances to the rest of the family, especially to her father, herself and Kathleen, the ones with oval faces and arched brows.

"And how do you feel?" she said and she did not wait for an answer. "Much better, I'm sure. The climate here will do you good. Does the arm still hurt? What are these pains you wrote about? What exactly happened to the arm? Now tell me about your English lessons. Did you make progress? It is just a matter of grammar, very simple really. But sometimes these Portuguese are very cute and might catch you out." She did not want him to feel she was belittling him. "I have had some regular little terrors to teach, and how they tried to trip me up! Miss Simpson can't put you up for the moment but later on I'm hoping we shall arrange that."

She spoke as fast as her eldest sister, but much more graciously. She had always planned what she was going to say, keeping notes in her head—point one, point two, point three. She expected no interruptions. Often she repeated herself, not out of vagueness like Marguerite, but because she was used to teaching children and foreigners and supposed that unless you said something many times it did not sink in.

She told Miss Simpson that her brother had arrived. "He's in lodgings now. I felt I couldn't burden you with another Reilly, dear!"

She worked on him and coached him, going through her text book on English grammar with him, making him do all the exercises. Tactfully but persistently she urged him to modify some of his vowel sounds. She was particularly partial to the thin "O" and she liked words such as "pass" and "grass" to be pronounced as "parss" and "grarss". It was not long before he was presentable and ready for a job.

Thomas soon earned enough to support himself. He tutored two boys for half the week, and this kept him away in Estoril for three nights, and gave English lessons on his other afternoons.

"Poor Kathie," said Elizabeth, when the news of Dick's death reached Lisbon. "What will she do now I wonder? And what will happen to the baby, poor little thing?"

Later a letter came from Kathleen, written in a fit of pique against Marguerite, giving a description of the little girl and saying she had called her Elizabeth. Elizabeth was touched. "She sounds the sweetest pet. I'm longing to see her." She was very glad it was a little girl. They were less noisy than little boys and one could dress them up and make them pretty. It would be nice to have a little niece whom one could influence and who would adore one. Because Kathleen had written—in all good faith but quite inaccurately—that it resembled her pretty sister, Elizabeth wanted a hand in its upbringing. Perhaps, too, she considered that Marguerite had taken over quite enough of the young ones for the moment.

It happened that Jacinta, the little Portuguese servant girl, had a way of not turning up on certain days. When questioned she explained that she had to be at home then to help her mother wash the sailors' clothes. It was special washing off a ship which put into Lisbon harbour from time to time and came from England.

"The next time this ship is in," said Elizabeth, "I should like a word with the captain."

To her delight the ship, a coaling vessel, actually came from Cardiff. This meant that her mother could send her over many articles which were much more expensive in Lisbon, in particular tea. She and Thomas soon became on good terms with the captain and visited the boat whenever it came in, smuggling what had been sent over for them in their clothes and walking bravely past the customs officials on the quay, while Elizabeth gave them a bright smile and perhaps exchanged a few words. She was very good with the crew, not too condescending and with a word for them all. She was able to do a few errands in Lisbon for the Norwegian captain and he was not indifferent to her beauty.

When war broke out, she wrote at once—a letter addressed to both Marguerite and Kathleen.

"England hardly place for young baby. Cannot tell what situation may be. Would be far better here."

Permits and passports had been introduced and a visit to the consul convinced her that there would be difficulties. Armed with a bottle of the finest port and other presents she went to the captain as soon as she heard that the boat was in.

"You'll think me terrible, I know," she laughed and looked at him through her lashes. "I want you to smuggle someone over for me. Yes, I mean it, a person. In fact two people, although one of them hardly counts!"

He appeared not to know whether she was joking or not. Laughing and smiling she continued, with no fear in her voice, no anxiety. "Yes, seriously, Captain. I will explain it to you. My sister has a tiny baby and she is longing to leave the country and come over here to me. And now it has become difficult to arrange things, and it really is most urgent that she should be here before the winter. One doesn't know what will happen about food. Of course I mean to pay you just what it would cost on a proper boat."

He seemed about to protest and she chose to pretend she had misunderstood him. With mock alarm she continued. "Oh dear! Did I say the wrong thing? Don't think I find your boat inferior to a passenger boat. This is just the sort of boat I should choose to travel on. Much more fun!"

Without pausing she became more serious, but with no strain. "And if anything were to happen I would take the blame. You must put the blame on me. Now what I think we might do is..."

2

Kathleen was not told the whole story. She knew she was going over to Portugal on a coaling boat, but apart from that she thought it would have been a journey in the ordinary way and that any papers needed had been seen to. After weeks of waiting with packed luggage in her mother's house, word came that the boat was in. To her surprise she was hustled on board, hurried down to a small cabin below and told not to come up on deck.

She was becoming used to not understanding what was going on around her, she was resigned to the fact that there was always something odd in arrangements made by her sisters, so she did not try to puzzle out what was happening. She sat down on the narrow bunk, put the baby on her lap and played with her. She could hear the coal clattering down and heavy shoes hurrying up and down ladders. After a time she heard the engines start up, and looking from the porthole, she saw the water moving sideways.

It was not until they were well out to sea that she was allowed up on deck.

"It's a good thing that baby of yours doesn't cry," said the captain and she thought he was referring to being kept awake.

Because she was the only passenger and even more because she had a baby everyone was nice to her. When the wind blew hard, she left the baby sleeping and walked about the deck watching the agitated sea. When the weather was fine, she sat outside and put the baby down on a shawl. When they ran into really bad weather off the Bay of Biscay, her appetite was none the worse and she discovered that she was a good sailor. She was timid of people but a rough sea held no terrors. It was too much like the adventure stories she had devoured in her mother's shop and she stayed up to watch the waves break over the side.

The most wonderful sight was the entry into Lisbon. It was all she had hoped and more. At first she could see it only through her porthole because a little boat with official-looking men had come up alongside and she had been hurried down below. But soon they went off and she was allowed on deck again. Above the blue harbour, houses rose tier on tier. The colours were brilliant. Under the strongly blue sky the roofs stood out bright red, the purest, most even red, the colour of a glowing coal. And in the sun they looked so hot that she felt her finger would burn if she touched them. Many of the walls were covered in glazed tiles, tiles dyed clear, rich colours: yellow, green, red and most frequently blue, the bluest of blues, a blue with no hint of green or purple. The quays were filled with movement and the sounds of voices and engines and the clatter of loading and unloading.

Some men came near the ship and shouted over to the sailors. She had never seen men like them in London or Cardiff. But their tight trousers, red sashes, brightly checked blouses and tasselled caps, like old-fashioned night caps, were like the chorus of a musical show she had seen. As they moved the green tassels danced.

In the captain's cabin she found Elizabeth, Thomas and Miss Simpson. How well they looked, how glowing! They seemed to have taken on some of the colour of this place.

"Dear Kathie," said Elizabeth kissing her, "and look who's here, little Elizabeth. What a long name for such a tot! What do you call her? Just 'baby' I suppose. She doesn't seem to be any the worse for the journey."

She took the baby from Kathleen, showed her to the others and kissed a small, fat hand. "What a darling! This is your Auntie. And this is your uncle. And this is another Auntie. I hope you don't mind being made an Auntie so suddenly, Stella dear?"

She handed the baby back and went on brightly, glancing at the captain as though he were very much in the know. "Now I don't want to alarm you Kathie, but we have been up to such awful things! I really couldn't tell you all our misdeeds, could I, Stella? But what I want you to do is this—I know it will sound quite absurd—unpack all your clothes and give them to the washerwomen to take off with the sailors' bundles. Now the hard things, like boots and so on, we'll leave in the trunk and see about later."

Kathleen did as she was told. As they walked along the quay Elizabeth took the baby in her arms and Kathleen walked with Miss Simpson. As they passed the officials at the end Elizabeth held up the baby, nodded to them and said in Portuguese, "Don't you think she's a bit young to be taken to see the boats?"

The officials laughed but were a little mystified. They had seen all three people go by and one of them was Elizabeth whom they knew very well by sight, and they now saw four people and a baby coming away. Perhaps the others had joined them when they were not looking or perhaps they had not noticed how many there were. They let it pass.

Safely away from the quayside Elizabeth handed back her little namesake. "The little pet is quite a weight."

They walked on at an easy pace until they reached a large square where the trams stopped. Kathleen was hoping she would not wake and find that all this had been a dream. She must take it all in before it vanished. Her eyes lingered on the palm trees and strange plants to which she could not give a name, on a splashing fountain round which some barefoot boys stood idly, on women who swayed past, carrying baskets on their heads, not holding on to them at all, but just letting their hands rest comfortably on their hips. How did they do it? One of these baskets, large and boat-shaped, was full of live, clucking chickens, held in by a net.

"It's very interesting here, very pretty," she said to Elizabeth.

In the tram she craned her neck to see everything that went by. In Cardiff and London she had moved from one place to another unseeing, uninterested. Here it was different. She must miss nothing. She saw warm sunshine pouring over the city, casting inky shadows onto pavements, lighting up buildings and faces, turning windows into beacons, giving the plainest stone a look of life and maturity. She saw more bright tiles, precipitous streets, brown-faced people, a broad avenue with strange trees and large shop fronts and everyone seemed to be both animated and easy going.

Elizabeth was sitting beside her. She was so beautiful, so kind and so gay. She was the very opposite of Marguerite. It was a great blessing to have such a sister. It was odd not to have thought of her more often during these last years. There she had been all the time, someone to turn to and trust.

Elizabeth gave a little sniff and shiver for the salt smell of the sea had penetrated every thread of Kathleen's and the baby's clothes. "Do you know, Stella, I believe we're taking two fish home with us, a big one and a very little one!"

Kathleen laughed. She thought she had never heard anything so witty.

"And now, Kathie," said Elizabeth, "I think the time has come to tell you, you have been smuggled. And so has the baby. What a way to begin life!"

While Kathleen was thinking this over, Elizabeth leant forward to Miss Simpson and tapped her on the knee. "I was saying, how will this little thing end up if it starts life by being smuggled?"

3

Lisbon fulfilled its first promise. Kathleen was happy. The town itself continued to give her pleasure. She liked to think of guide-book details. "It is built on seven hills, like Rome. Fancy! How extraordinary!" She liked the exotic dress of the peasants, the sloping streets, the funiculars and the bridges which spanned the narrow valleys so that you could look over and see the people walking beneath. She liked to see the dead, embalmed kings in glass coffins. She could never take these things for granted, for Cardiff and London were the norm—to her they seemed exactly alike. And therefore she would often say, "I can't get over those palm trees" or "I can't get over the cactuses everywhere" or "I can't get over the mules and oxen carts" or "I can't get over the siesta". And to be unable to get over them was wonderful.

Life in the flat was pleasant. The other three set off for work after breakfast and she was alone with the baby and the maid for the greater part of the day. When it was fine, and it was fine so often, she sat on the balcony which ran outside most of the rooms because they were in a corner house. High up on the seventh floor she could see a big area of the city, somewhat cut by the high houses. It amused her when she let down a basket on the end of a rope for the street vendors to place some of their wares in it. It amused her to see a cow being milked before your very eyes in order to provide the pint you needed.

At second hand she enjoyed Elizabeth's social life, enjoyed it much more than if it had been her own. Elizabeth was queen of the English teachers and had the pick of the banking, titled and retired Brazilian world as her pupils. When they gave parties and dances she was asked. Many an evening she dashed home to change and when she had put on her best dress, she threw a wrap over her shoulders, called Kathleen in and asked her to hold hairpins and fetch and carry, while she herself sat in front of her mirror and arranged her hair. She talked to her and described the house she was going to and who would be there. Sometimes she said kindly, "And we'll see if we can't get you asked next time."

Kathleen, who would have liked to be a fly on the wall at these gatherings but dreaded not knowing what to do on grand occasions, would answer. "Don't bother about me. I wouldn't enjoy it. I wouldn't shine like you do."

After a time they decided that Kathleen must earn and Elizabeth offered to hand over to her the more backward pupils, the beginners who would need the simplest instruction. Jacinta must be trained to look after the baby.

Here a slight trouble arose. Not understanding Portuguese well and hazy about pronunciation, Kathleen had several misunderstandings with the little servant girl. The first serious brush was when, wanting Jacinta to take the baby onto the balcony, she waved her hands and shouted, *"Atirar, menina per cima balcon!"*

Jacinta's eyes grew frightened. *"Não pod. Não pod."*

Irritated, Kathleen insisted. To make her meaning plainer she threw her arm out violently towards the French windows. *"Menina, atirar, balcon!"*

"Não pod."

Angrily, Kathleen went to pick up the baby herself. Jacinta threw herself at her feet and clutched her knees. *"Senhora! Senhora! Jesus! Maria!"* Her large black eyes stared out dramatically from her pretty, golden face. She clasped her hands together as though in prayer. Seeing Kathleen with the baby, she rushed to the windows and barred her way. For the rest of the day she dogged her steps and would not leave her. Kathleen thought she had gone mad.

In the evening Elizabeth solved the mystery. "She thought you wanted to throw the baby over the balcony. You do look very wild, you know, sometimes, Kathie. I've told her you're not the unnatural parent she takes you for, but she's very suspicious."

Elizabeth never nagged like Marguerite, there was no harshness in her manner, but she fussed and fussed. At first Kathleen scarcely noticed it but after a time it was like having a mosquito constantly by her ear. Dropping her eyelids, sighing softly, raising one corner of her droopy mouth to show it was humorous, Elizabeth would say gently, "Kathie, dear, are you really going out without gloves because you don't believe in them, or was it just absent-mindedness?" or "Do have a look at your hair in the mirror, dear. Is that wisp the latest style?"

Then there was the question of religion. Kathleen went to Mass on Sundays and Holidays of Obligation, observed fasting and abstinence and left it at that. Elizabeth wanted something more.

"Kathie, dear. I am going to make a special novena. I really feel you should join me. It would give me great pleasure. There, I knew you would. Now you must be up at six tomorrow and we'll go along together. It will do you good not to lie in bed so late."

For Christmas, Elizabeth gave her a crucifix and a missal. Kathleen tried to be grateful but she felt disappointed. Thomas had become very religious too and his duodenal ulcers had made him increasingly taciturn with everyone but Elizabeth. He was teaching English to some young novices for the priesthood and was now interested in theological questions.

On most evenings Elizabeth was out with friends and Miss Simpson was at the English Ladies' Club. Kathleen, hoping for a little conversation with someone, always found Thomas deep in a religious book or Boswell's *Life of Johnson*, for which he had a passion. He either took no notice of her or said, "Shut up. Leave me in peace, can't you? What do you want now?"

No one treated her as an equal. When praising the baby's intelligence and precocity they often betrayed some surprise that this marvel should be her child. And she began to accept this attitude to herself and to look on little Lisa (they had to call her Lisa for the sake of Jacinta) with awe and respect. Her physical attachment for the baby gave place to a desire to sacrifice herself for it. Any money she could save she spent on expensive and unnecessary toys, going shabby herself and doing without many little luxuries she would have enjoyed. Lisa was to be a second Elizabeth, someone who went to parties while you stayed at home, someone who had whims which were always right and must be gratified, someone who out of the goodness of her heart would occasionally say something nice to one as a gracious favour.

And Lisa, like all children, sensitive to her mother's attitude, became tyrannical and exacting in a pleasant way. She never cried or made a scene and she put up with her aunt's firmness when she had to, but she took it for granted that she would usually have her own way and everyone would love her. Imitating her aunt, she made eyes at people who came to the flat and set out to win them and extract presents from them. She was too young to have such thoughts in her head but there was a vague consciousness that she was one of the elect and her mother was not.

4

Elizabeth realised that her present way of life could not go on for ever. She was in her prime now and never lacked work. Her youth and beauty secured her the interest of her pupils and made her position unique among English teachers. But a time would come when this would not be so. Lisbon was full of elderly English teachers. They continued to earn enough to live modestly but their lives were dull and they themselves were pathetic. Besides, although Portugal was a very pleasant country, she was English (the Reilly children always thought of themselves as English and not Irish) and she did not want to live away from her country indefinitely. It was in England she would have to establish herself eventually.

There was a very splendid match in the offing, and if the man had been English she might have made greater efforts to get him. He was a banker's son, Honorio Ribeira, a cousin of one of her pupils, and whenever she encountered him his black eyes glowed, he saw no one else in the room and he looked in despair when she walked away. He had sent her flowers and notes. He had declared his love. She could not be sure whether he had intended to propose for he was always tongue-tied in her presence and she took care never to be alone with him. One could create a scandal so easily and she was cautious. He was rich, presentable and a good Catholic. If she was married to him she would remain in this society forever, but in a better position that she was in now. But despite the sight of the elderly English-teaching spinsters, she still had a horror of marriage, and though she liked the Portuguese, a foreigner was still a foreigner.

It was the beginning of 1916. Marguerite had written that there were excellent jobs to be had in London now. If one had languages one could earn as much as six pounds a week in the censorship, and one worked with such a nice type of lady now, ladies from the best families were in every office. One met all sorts of useful and interesting people.

Not until she had made up her mind did she let anyone know that she was thinking of leaving. Then quickly, within a fortnight, she arranged to hand over her best pupils to Miss Simpson, her less promising ones to Kathleen, and told them of her plans. She found it natural that they should all be very upset to see her go and she felt sorry for them. She spoke of patriotism and the future.

She made sure that Ribeira should hear of her coming departure from someone other than herself. He hurried to his cousin's house when he knew she would be having a lesson. He asked Elizabeth if he might have a word with her alone.

"Miss Reilly. Is it true you are leaving?"

"Yes, I'm afraid so."

"For how long?"

"I cannot tell."

"Miss Reilly, please forgive my impertinence but I must ask you a question."

She looked forgiving and said nothing.

"Are you—er—have you a fiancé, Miss Reilly? Is there anyone in England you are... ?"

She shook her head and laughed gently. Emboldened he begged her not to go, urging the terrible dangers of war.

"You know I have loved you for a long time. You never replied to my letters. I was hoping you might. Now I know there is no one else I wish I had time to speak to my family about you. I would like to take you home to see my mother."

He wanted to propose but he did not want to do anything which his family might oppose. He wanted to question her about her family, she could see that. He was hoping she would volunteer some information. He was trying to get her to make a move.

She had never egged him on or flirted yet and she did not do so now. She knew that if she tried hard she could have him. His caution did not surprise her. In any case her vanity did not suffer, could never suffer, it was a hardy plant, carefully nurtured all her life. She gave him Marguerite's address and permission to write.

5

In London, Elizabeth did not find everything to her liking. The climate was dispiriting after the warm brightness of the south. Marguerite was extremely offhand, never lived in her boarding house herself, had filled it with the strangest lodgers—Elizabeth thought—and could offer her sister only the dingiest and darkest of rooms. She never asked her about her life during the last years. She never assumed she had done well. On the contrary she expected her to be overwhelmed with gratitude for being rescued from Lisbon and found a job in the censorship. She also expected her to collect the rents, see to any complaints from the lodgers and be prepared to rush up and down between Cardiff and London with messages and parcels for Patrick and their mother.

"Marguerite," said Elizabeth after ten days, "I think I shall find a room somewhere else. Kensington is a little far away for me."

"Just as you like. Just as you like," said Marguerite without concern or surprise. Something had driven her to get Elizabeth away from Lisbon, to break up that little family nucleus out there, and now she did not care whether she saw anything of her sister or not.

She found her cold and selfish and she had never cared much for the society of the girls. She preferred Michael, John and David, especially Michael. He was with the army out in France and seldom wrote. David and John had also joined up and never wrote a line. She wanted Michael's children to come to London but Jennie was still obstinate. Her off-duty time never amounted to more than a couple of hours and she could not get up to Cardiff.

She often sent Elizabeth a summons to come to the hospital. It was always to ask her to do something.

"Now look, why do you not go up to Cardiff and see mother?" she said, or else, "Why do you not take the night train on Saturday. You could be back very quickly. Then you could see Jennie. *You* are so persuasive and I'm sure she would let you bring the children back. You could get her to decide there and then, on the spot. Do it quickly so that she has no time to argue. And then you could go back to Kensington and be with them."

Elizabeth was firm. She would undertake to help the family in her own way and at her own time, but she was not going to be drawn into these rushed schemes of someone else's. She resented Marguerite's assumption that life in the censorship was so slack and easy that you could take time off when you liked and no one noticed. Her answer was always, "I'm very sorry, *chérie*, but I couldn't possibly spare the time."

Marguerite had discovered that being an assistant matron did not altogether suit her. It was a great honour to have been chosen to supervise the nursing of wounded officers in one of the big London nursing homes. But having some responsibility and not enough was irritating. There were so many fiddling details to remember. There were forms and regulations. She preferred to work in her own way, on inspiration and impulse. The matron admired her but was often forced to rebuke her for forgetfulness. The staff liked her but found her erratic. Besides, it was all surgical work, to which she had never been partial, and surgeons and physicians had to be obeyed to the letter in an institution like this. If only she were matron herself she would dispense with all this formality and over-respect for medical men.

At the same time she was glad to be in the thick of the war. The idea of soldiers and officers excited her. Military bands had always sent her hurrying to the window to look out. Now, the sight of the big recruiting posters, the marching men in khaki, the troop trains puffing out of stations with waving arms and grinning faces cramming out from every window, made her feel that life was rich and precious. There was constant change. Anything could happen. Great numbers of people were moving from one occupation to another, from place to place. Englishmen were going to other countries and foreign soldiers were coming here. Women were doing all kinds of new jobs. It was as though her own restlessness had seized the whole world and now everything was like her. War meant a constant state of flux. Strangers became friends and friends suddenly went away and did not come back.

She had adopted the conventional attitude towards the patients, "the boys." Like other nurses and sisters she approached them humorously: "Now, what do you mean by running a temperature? This will never do. We cannot have that sort of thing here!" All assumed that this was how wounded officers liked to be spoken to. Many of the officers thought so too and it gave some satisfaction to know by heart which bright cliché a nurse would use and by which funny name a part of their anatomy would be called.

Walking briskly down between rows of iron beds, looking important and efficient, Margaret would hurry on the nurses with frowns and gestures, and say a word to each patient with a set smile on her face. This meant that her expression changed from moment to moment, automatically, unconsciously. A great part of her time she forced herself to concentrate on routine and pushed feeling away. The physical tragedies, the loss of a vital limb or eye, did not leave her unmoved. But there was little time for pity and to be sorry for everyone *en masse* had never been her way. Her pity had no sense of proportion. Some man with a small injury might arouse her deepest compassion. Another with a greater injury might leave her cold. "He's always sorry for himself. He makes no effort." And living among these broken bodies she still found that some unimportant little misfortune related by a stranger in a teashop would move her most of all.

She continued to collect lame dogs and protégés whom she later tried to palm off onto other people. She did not observe the rule of showing no favouritism at work. When a little probationer took her fancy with some tale of a brother at the front, she sided with her, quite unjustly, against the staff nurse.

Off duty her heart was always full and her eyes showed it. Under her straight brows, with wrinkles at the corners, they looked out, grey, intent and arrestingly level. It was as though she had always known that the real part of everyone's life was tragedy and now that was becoming plain to a smug world. An unconscious "I told you so" exhilarated her. On the rare occasions when she spoke to Elizabeth of things other than family worries she would say, "Life is very sad, very sad indeed," with a look of satisfaction. Was it now proved that others than Reilly's had their ups and downs? Was the selling of sweets off a barrow in Cardiff market place now all cancelled out? Whatever it was, there was something in the present situation which was like balm.

And all the time she said she hated war. "How tragic! To think of all those lives being lost! When I think of those wounded men!"

It was not long before Elizabeth had found a lady friend of "good class" from her office with whom to share a flat, and it was not long before this lady friend was devoted to her. Filled with patriotic fervour the two of them went to first-aid classes and did spare time nursing. Elizabeth was deft with dressings and quick to learn. Her sweet expression and neat appearance made a good impression on all who worked with her. "What an angel she is. How kind. The men adore her," they said, and once more she found herself lapped in the soft warmth of general admiration and love. She felt virtuous, too, when she thought that she had given up the comforts of Lisbon to do her bit.

But she grew tired. The long hours at the office and the extra work in the evenings and on Sundays drew lines on her soft skin and there was a tinge of grey under the pink. She lost weight and there were shadows beneath her cheekbones. Her fussiness became more nervous. Little things irritated her. Other people's lack of efficiency jarred on her. If a wounded man tried to hold her hand as she tended him she felt outraged. Coming home late at night and observing that the charwoman had left dust on the table she would be on the verge of tears.

She kept away from Marguerite as much as possible. When they did meet, usually over a cup of tea in some crowded restaurant, they both talked rapidly and jerkily, jumping from one subject to another and not listening. Elizabeth believed she loved her sister. Marguerite had no thoughts about her sister at all. At one of these meetings Marguerite was distraught.

"I've just had the most terrible news from mother. You must go to Cardiff for me. Jennie has run off with someone, some man—I

175

always knew she would. And do you know what's happened to all those poor children? She's taken Maureen with her and sent all the others to her brother—he's a miner. Elizabeth, we *must* get them away from him. Those poor children! And Patrick, who was so refined, a real Reilly!"

"Do you know his address?"

"No. That's what I want you to find out. You can go along to Jennie's mother and get it out of her. Mind you, I'm not sorry Jennie has gone, she was no good, just a man-chaser." (This, of course, was quite unfair. Jennie had loved Michael for his curly hair and blue eyes and she had tried to be a good wife to him. He had always spent a large part of his small earnings on drink. He had let her and the children go short. Since he had been in the army he had sent her only one letter and no money. Any complaint she made to the Reilly's was treated as a malicious lie. Anything she did for the children was either ignored or criticised.)

Elizabeth fiddled with her spoon. "What a tragedy, *chérie!* How terrible! It's such a pity I have no time. I would love to help you but..."

"You can make time, surely! I'm tied to the nursing home. In my position I cannot budge. After all, what is the censorship? And all this St. John Ambulance work..." She looked down on untrained voluntary nursing. "It's nothing really. You could easily take a day or two off. It's not often I ask you to do anything for me."

Elizabeth frowned and her blue eyes hardened. "*Chérie*. I've told you I cannot spare the time. I know best about my own affairs. And really I'm not at all sure what you would do with the children in London. Who would look after them? Neither of us has the time. And isn't it a dangerous place?" She sweetened her tone and looked softly at her sister. "It's all very sad, I know, and please don't imagine I don't realise it every bit as much as you do. But at a time like this we must try and make the best of things as they are. It's no use wishing to do the impossible. After all, *chérie*, this uncle may be a very good man. It's certainly kind of him to take them. Leave them there until things are settled. If it's money you need I could always..."

Marguerite did not look at the person she was talking to if she disagreed with them. She now fixed her eyes on a distant waitress and followed her movements closely, turning her head right round, so that Elizabeth could see only her profile. "I was not asking you for money. You can keep it. I'd thought you would help me out in a fix but I see you're thoroughly selfish."

Elizabeth sighed. "That's no way for one sister to talk to another. You are being most unfair. And how can you say you never asked me for money? Many times in Cardiff I helped you out. Really, Marguerite, I've thought for some time that you were becoming very odd. I know the strain and responsibility..."

Marguerite could not tolerate criticism. She disliked being discussed. She rose without another word and went away.

This incident upset Elizabeth and when she was alone in her room she cried and prayed. It was all part of the war she hated. Men were being killed and marriages were breaking up. Nothing seemed stable. She longed for an ordered world where she could find a niche for herself. Tension and change did not exhilarate her as they did her sister.

It was not possible to do anything for the children for the moment. Marguerite corresponded with the uncle and sent money. The thought of Patrick, now thirteen, in a mining village tormented her. She imagined him as sensitive as her father and appalled by his present surroundings. The few letters he wrote were cheerful enough and she explained this away by telling herself he was being wonderfully brave and trying to spare her feelings.

6

The next big piece of news from Cardiff was the death of Edgar. He had been ill for some time and once or twice Marguerite had thought of taking a week off to nurse him. She had almost felt sorry for him at last. But now he was gone she was overjoyed. She sent sympathy and condolences to her mother, spreading herself over four pages, every word seeming heartfelt. And the fact that she was delighted did not make her sympathy any the less genuine. On the contrary, her happiness left her free to say to herself, "Poor mother. What a hard life she's had."

As her realisation of what this meant increased she went about in a kind of trance. A load had been lifted from her and her mother had been restored to her. It was as though Edgar had never existed, she was Patrick Reilly's widow now. To any nurse or sister who came her way she gave a kind smile and cheerful word. She was easy going, gently and considerate. She wrote an affectionate note to Elizabeth.

"*Chérie*," she said to Elizabeth when they met the next day, putting her arm round her and kissing her. "Poor Edgar! I'm so upset about it. But mother says he died very peacefully—in his sleep. Perhaps it's all for the best. After all if he had lived he might have been in great pain! Poor mother! It was very good of you to come here so soon." (They were in her office at the nursing home). "It was very sweet of you *chérie*. Especially when you are on such important work and must have had such a fight to get them to allow you to come. I've been thinking. We cannot leave mother down there. She must come here. She can stay in the Kensington house and run it for us. She was always such a wonderful manager. What happy times we shall have, *chérie!*" Her grey eyes were shining and the ridge between her brows had nearly disappeared. "Poor Elizabeth!" She kissed her again. "How tired you look. Do sit down. That chair is the most comfortable. You are so thoughtful. It was sweet of you to come at once. You cannot think how nice it has been for me to have you here, *chérie*. I am so glad you came to London. It has made all the difference to me!"

This statement did not come as a surprise to Elizabeth, for she had always believed that Marguerite would one day realise how greatly she prized her. At the same time she was glad to hear it said.

Marguerite continued. "Between us we can look after mother and make her happy. At last we can give her some sort of a home. She has earned it, poor soul. How she slaved for us! She has had such a hard life, brought up in the lap of luxury and then losing it all." Her eyes were swimming but not through grief. "We can all have a home together. And when things are more settled—when all this is over," she waved her hands as though the desk and chairs represented the battle front, "the children can come too. With what we are both earning we can easily manage. They can go to good schools."

Elizabeth did not commit herself but now was not the time to betray caution. She looked up at her sister. "Yes, it would be splendid to have mother here. We must look after her now. As you say, perhaps it was all for the best."

That night Elizabeth prayed for Edgar and for her mother. He was not the type suited to heaven but as a good Christian she must wish him to go there with all her heart. And had she thought it over she would have said—in any case they are all changed first and some need to be changed more than others.

Mrs Hughes was easily persuaded to come to London. There was no other course left. She had no money of her own and did not want to have to go looking for work as a cleaner. She was sorry to have to leave her cronies who had stood by her during the sickness, death and funeral with many a cup of tea and harrowing tale of death and woe. She was also uneasy about being under the supervision of her two daughters. They might interfere with her. She would have to hide from them the little sum she had put by. They might stop her beer. Alone on the train she felt uprooted and melancholy until an elderly gentleman got into conversation with her and by his flattering attentions made her forget her troubles.

On Paddington station, sitting among her bundles sewn up with carpet thread and tied round with rope, waiting for her daughter to find her, she looked like some calm, patient peasant woman. She was still very handsome. Her snow-white hair and bright complexion showed to advantage in black. Her swollen feet and stoutness made her movements slow and weighty. She lowered herself carefully when she sat down and raised herself with effort, panting slightly. She looked dignified and easy to get on with. She was still one of those women whom shopkeepers favour and strangers notice.

Among the rush and noise of hurrying civilians and soldiers, shrill whistles and chuffing engines, although she was not deeply upset about Edgar's death, she let herself cry easily and noiselessly. The tears flowed down her pink cheeks as she watched Marguerite deal with the luggage, as she rode in the tram and as she entered her new home.

She found life in the boarding house to her liking. It was nice having so many men around the place, her daughters were never there and she could run things her own way. Every evening she could have her two or three glasses of beer in peace and if a lodger came in and chatted to her while she drank she was glad of the company. It was remarkable how quickly the kitchen looked like all her other kitchens, cluttered up, not exactly tidy but with a complex order. She placed her painted Chinese-looking tea caddy on the high ledge above the range, and near it a picture of Our Lady and a view of the sea near Dublin (where she had never been). On the dresser she hung two coloured calendars. The two photographs, one of

179

herself and one of Patrick, both looking set and stern as people did when they had to sit motionless for three minutes, hung on either side of the fire in tarnished gilt frames.

Women cronies she did not find for the moment although she talked and drank tea with the cleaner in the mornings. The greengrocer, the butcher, the baker and the milkman were soon her friends and, as in Cardiff, she whiled away many minutes talking to them about the war and life in general. She avoided visiting Marguerite at the hospital, although she always said she longed to. "It's my poor feet, dear." Knowing that her daughters would come only at weekends and for two hours at the most, she could be ready for them and tuck the beer bottles behind biscuit tins at the bottom of the cupboard. She took the weekly money from the lodgers and kept a fixed amount to cover her food. By mending their clothes and darning their socks, by occasionally cooking for them, she made a little more and she kept this extra by her without saying anything to Marguerite. Sometimes in the afternoons she felt a little lonely and then she slowly climbed the stairs to the first floor front (the man was always out in the daytime) and looked out at the people in the street below.

7

Marguerite had assumed that now her mother was restored to her she would be quite content. She did not see herself as restless at all and justified each wish for a change by saying that it would help her position or the position of the others, or oblige a patient or help someone else. She knew she had borne a burden, a burden which she thought of as her mother's second marriage. That burden was lifted now but she was weighed down by something unknown and she felt dissatisfied. She persuaded herself that her predicament was this: "Am I doing enough for the war? Anyone could take over my present job who has done the usual training. Should I not volunteer to go to the front, or at least to Paris? Is it not my duty?"

She spoke to the matron. "With my languages, French, Italian and—and others, I really ought to be drafted out there. I'm very happy here but I feel I could be of more use. There are not many nurses who speak languages."

The matron admired her enterprise, believed her to be motivated by the highest patriotism, felt too that a more usual type of assistant matron might be restful and said she would do all she could to help her. There was no difficulty. Nurses were needed in France. There was a responsible job waiting for someone in Paris. The transfer was soon arranged.

"I'm so glad. Thank you so much, matron," said Marguerite. "But there is just one thing on my mind. I must take my mother with me. She has just lost her husband—*not* my father—her second husband and I cannot leave her now. And she wants to help too, to do all she can. She would like to be a cook in a hospital or something like that. Although she's been accustomed to having servants and being waited on hand and foot, she is a wonderful cook. We all have to turn to these days and help ourselves!"

She secured a permit and passage for her mother. Only when she had it did she say anything. Mrs Hughes was not glad. She was afraid of war, of being near the terrible Germans and the sound of guns. She thought they might be drowned on the way out. "I don't know, dear. I must think it over."

"But there's no time. The passage is booked now."

"Well I wish you'd let me know before. If only you'd asked me."

"Mother I'm sure I mentioned it heaps of times. Probably you were not listening. You may never have such a splendid opportunity to travel. I've always wanted to take you abroad and show you the world."

"It's not like ordinary travel, with all the fighting and the torpedoes sinking the boats. After the war, now, I'd not say no to that."

"It's all arranged. You cannot mean to let me down. After the struggle I've had to get the permission. I almost had to go down on bended knees to people. It's a great privilege to be sent abroad. There are hundreds who'd give anything to be in your place. And where would you stay? Elizabeth's had instructions to dispose of the lease of the house. Then think what an amusing time you'll have out there, with all the boys to look after. And I'm hoping we'll see something of Michael if he has leave."

Mrs Hughes appealed to Elizabeth for help, but Elizabeth was occupied in resisting Marguerite's attempts to take her too. Also, she had never cared for the atmosphere of the boarding house and thought it a very good thing that they should pack it up. She also shared Marguerite's view that if their mother went abroad and spoke a foreign language her accent would be modified, she would use foreign words, and look more presentable. Perhaps, too, she shared Marguerite's fear that, left to herself, Mrs Hughes might marry again, and she did not want to have to be the one to guard against this.

"I think Marguerite is quite right," she said, "and I'm certain she would never dream of it if there were the slightest danger. It's a very short crossing across the channel. A very few hours."

And so it was that Mrs Hughes eventually found herself in Paris, living in a small furnished room near the Madeleine and going every day to cook for the troops. She missed not having a place of her own and at first she felt isolated by her lack of French. But soon she picked up enough to become friendly with people at work, women like herself, always dressed in black and mothers of families.

Marguerite was at the Hotel Astoria which was now a military hospital. She was absorbed in her new work. Here the cases were much more urgent. These were the really serious ones, almost fresh from the front line, and as soon as they were on the road to recovery they were moved somewhere else. Though outwardly calm and efficient everyone was tense and excited; and sisters and staff nurses were left more free to make decisions. In lowered voices they had constant quick consultations. And she liked the converted hotel with its long passage, lift, great dining rooms and drawing rooms as wards, bedrooms as smaller wards or nurses' room. She liked, too, the many different kinds of nursing uniform and military uniform, the sound of different languages, the presence of nursing nuns. News from the front was read with greater interest. The Germans had been near Paris once and there was always the dread that they would approach it again.

8

Thomas's pride was tender. It maddened him to think that Elizabeth had left Lisbon after making him come out there and installing him in the flat as though it would be a permanent arrangement. She had led him to believe that it was only a matter of time before he too would be teaching all the best families on the same footing of equality. The loss of Elizabeth's presence was painful. She had never spent a great deal of time alone with him, but he had seen her at breakfast every day and during other meals at weekends, and she had always seemed so concerned about his health and ambitions, so full of kind enquiries and affectionate sympathy. The flat had been so typical of her with flowers and touches. She had smoothed away the differences between the others. They had been together a great deal when they were small. Marguerite and Michael had been friends and he had believed that he and Elizabeth were friends. In his surly, silent way he had enjoyed watching her sewing things for her doll and running about the kitchen so trimly and when he was sent away and she went to live with Aunt Kenny he had missed her terribly. So that this parting was made all the worse by being a repetition of an earlier, less understood experience.

Now that she was gone he considered that he was the most important member of the family in Lisbon. He had come there before Kathleen and she taught only backward pupils. Duodenal ulcers made him fussy about food and subject to long stretches of sleeplessness at night. On mornings when he had to catch the train to Monte Estoril it would often be impossible to rouse him. Then when he did appear he was in a rage. To relieve his feelings he abused Kathleen.

"Why didn't you tell me it was Wednesday? Well if you did I didn't hear you. You're a perfect idiot, an absolute fool. You never think of a thing. All you ever bother about is yourself and the baby. And what would happen to you if I lost my job I'd like to know?"

He would never have spoken to Elizabeth like that and Miss Simpson could deal with him. But Kathleen made the mistake of being afraid. "Nitwit! Bitch!" he used to call her, often reducing her to tears.

When he was in a gay mood, rarely enough, there was still violence in him, and he might throw the baby high up into the air or pick her up so roughly and suddenly that Kathleen would stand by trembling. He had a way of demanding money, not as a gift but as a right. They were always hard up, for the lesson money was quickly absorbed by rent, food, Jacinta's wages and train fares.

"But I haven't any," Kathleen was always forced to reply.

"You blasted, selfish idiot. What do you do with your money? Where do you hide it? Where do you think I'm going to get my train fare? And if I can't get the train I'll lose the job. And whose bleeding fault is that?" This might be followed up by hurling a cup at her or throwing a chair. He was never without pain, a dragging ache beneath the ribs.

Fortunately he left to take a resident post in the country and Kathleen was left in peace. Shortly after he had gone, Miss Simpson moved to Oporto and Kathleen took a room in a neighbour's apartment. But this neighbour, half French and half English, a teacher of languages, also had to leave the town. She had grown very fond of little Lisa and was worried about Kathleen. "I've thought of a very nice place for you," she said. "I have a great friend, a mistress in the Ursuline convent at Saint-Jules in the South of France. I'm sure they would be glad of an English teacher there and I'll write off at once. They'll certainly let you keep the baby with you."

Kathleen and the baby went on a long journey, first to the Spanish frontier, from there to Irún, then on to Toulouse, and then, by the local train, to Saint-Jules. It seemed endless with all the changing and the luggage and the baby and Kathleen had too many preoccupations and fears to observe the changing scenes through which they passed. Arriving tired and anxious at the convent, she was told by the headmistress, "Is that the child? I'd understood she was much older. The very youngest we have here is six. There's no accommodation for a baby. She'll have to live somewhere else."

"But I've never parted from her, Madame." Kathleen did not know how to address the lady, knowing her to be a nun yet seeing her in secular dress. "She could sleep in my room. She'd be no trouble. She's very good."

It was useless to plead and weep. Mlle Tarnier was devoted to cats but did not care for small babies. She pretended she could not understand English well and made Kathleen repeat herself again and again. She watched the tears and emotion impassively and stated her terms. Kathleen might stay and live in if she wished but the baby must be placed somewhere else. The Saint Vincent de Paul nuns who kept an orphanage not far away would no doubt take her in.

Lisa, nearly three and very articulate in Portuguese which she had spoken all day with Jacinta, howled when she found herself separated from her mother and in a strange place where everyone spoke a language she could not understand. But in time she cried less after her mother's visits. The nuns made a great fuss of her, *"la petite anglaise",* and she soon knew the necessary words of French.

Monsieur le Curé patted her head and gave her *sucres d'orge*. Grandmère Thérèse (which was the name she gave to the nun who looked after her) was indulgent and spoiled her. Being much the youngest in the orphanage and considered a baby she was not put into the *tablier*, that regulation black overall with a yoke and pleats down the front which most boys and girls wear at school in France. She was made to look like a little doll. Also she was not a real orphan like the others and was therefore different. She grew fat, wayward and vigorous. As small children do, she loved the company of older children and imitated them, concentrating hard on using the words they used. Everyone laughed at her sayings and she played up to get notice. When she wet the bed and Grandmère Thérèse said she should be slapped, she said, "Oh no, it was the doll who did it. We must slap her." And after that her mother, the Curé and others who came to see her always asked, "And how is the naughty doll?"

Kathleen found Saint-Jules quite as picturesque as Lisbon. It was a small cathedral town, situated a little north of the Pyrenees. The streets were narrow, cobbled and irregular. The cathedral was famous for its carved pews, curiously alive with gargoyles and formal, curving leaves. A long, imposing flight of shallow steps led down from the Cathedral to the lower half of the town where the river ran, so that the Cathedral itself, on one side, seemed to be on a high platform and commanded an extensive view over housetops to the fields beyond. There was plenty of life. Farmers with heavily laden carts came regularly to sell their produce. A cavalry regiment lent a dashing air with its horses and uniforms. In winter the distant, snowy, glistening peaks could be seen from the convent windows. In summer the sky was blue and during walks she saw flowers and leaves cascading heavily over the high, golden stone walls which surrounded the gardens of most big houses, active with the buzzing of bees and the fluttering of bright butterflies. Then the most respected families, a few minor aristocrats, the mayor, the notary and the doctor, drove out in carriages.

After a year Mlle Tarnier left, leaving behind her thirteen cats. The new headmistress, Mlle Largne, was kind and adored small children. "Of course little Lisa must be with her mother. We can soon fix up something here."

Now that her baby was living with her Kathleen was perfectly happy. The Ursulines were kind and had explained the mystery of their dress. It was a Government decree about teaching orders;

during term time, in the presence of children they must wear secular dress; it was part of an attack on the Catholic church; the Government was in the hands of Freemasons. Not that the secular dress was at all like what other ladies wore. The nuns were dressed in an out-of-date style with deep neck-bands propped up with whalebone and covering them to the chin. They were always in black and wore large crucifixes on their breasts threaded on black silk. During the holidays they shut the convent and retired to a secluded life in the country where they wore their proper religious attire.

Kathleen worked hard to get the irregularities of English grammar into the heads of her pupils. Most of the girls were the daughters of farmers from the surrounding countryside, stocky in build, dark-eyed, brown-skinned, stolid without being phlegmatic, giving the appearance of smouldering self-control. They spoke with a marked Midi accent but Kathleen never noticed the difference between this and the thinner, Parisian tone of the teachers. With few exceptions they were not quick to learn, but they sat still during lessons and gave no trouble. They were very nice to Lisa who now became the school baby, a baby with forty mothers.

Kathleen was allowed to increase her income by giving private lessons to the ladies of Saint-Jules and cavalry officers. These new pupils had Lisa to tea and took her for drives. She was precocious and so envious of a girl four years older than herself that she taught herself to read. On her fourth birthday she was given a book of fairy tales by Mlle Largne. Written on the flyleaf was *"A bébé qui sait lire."*

Early in 1918 Mrs Hughes, fearing Big Bertha and the approach of the Germans, arrived in Saint-Jules. She begged Kathleen to let her have Lisa with her and the three moved into a small flat. It was in a narrow street above a grocer's shop and the smells of spice, coffee, dried beans and lentils filled the stairway. The flat was pervaded by the delicious aromas of fried onions, tomatoes, mushrooms and garlic, for Mrs Hughes had learnt to cook the French way. At first she paid what they had asked her in the market place but soon she got into the way of haggling as they all did and could beat anyone down. It was only her fair skin which distinguished her from the other women there and even so one might have thought her born and bred in the place. Missing her sons and uninterested in Kathleen she gave all her attention to Lisa, spoiling her as everyone else had spoiled her, letting her eat when she fancied at any time of day and letting her stay up late.

Marguerite corresponded regularly and passed on news of the others. Kathleen was still at the censorship and sent over her abbreviated sentences with many kind wishes to all and special messages for Lisa. Michael had been shell-shocked and was back in Cardiff. John was at the front and David was in India. Patrick's uncle was willing to hand over the boy at any time.

"I want him to join you there," Marguerite wrote to her mother. "If we do not get him now he will become a miner. I think I can wangle the passport through a friend of mine. You say there is a seminary in Saint-Jules. If only we could place him there for a year or so he might discover that he had a vocation."

A few months later not only Patrick, now fifteen, but also his brother Joseph, aged eleven, were in Saint-Jules as boarders with the Christian Brothers. The sudden change of environment had left them bewildered and although Patrick, at least, was glad to see his grandmother, the boys tended to be silent when they came to the flat or else giggled together.

Money was very short. Kathleen earned just enough for the flat, herself, her mother and Lisa. Now that the boarding house had gone, Marguerite had only her salary and that had been swallowed up by fares. The boys were ragged and their boots needed mending. Lisa, in a long blouse with a huge, square sailor collar and pleated skirt, with new ribbons in her hair, turned up her nose at the cousins.

"Are they orphans?" she asked, remembering the poor girls at the Saint Vincent de Paul place. If they had been she might have been sorry for them but as it was she wished they hadn't come. They were not presented to the best families as she was. They must be very stupid not to speak French at their age. One day when they were out walking in a crocodile they saw her drive past on the lap of a smart lady and she pretended she had not seen them.

9

Thomas was seriously ill, too ill to work. Living in the cheapest pension he could find, he wrote to Elizabeth. He had no money left and he owed two weeks' rent. She sent five pounds and a short letter:

So sorry to hear of illness. Sure will be better soon. Little patience and will find nice post. Write if need more and will help. If no improvement promise me see doctor. Far better stay there, more opportunities.

Lonely and wretched he found the money and letter intensely irritating and upsetting. He had gone off his food. Everything here made him sick because it was cooked in the coarsest, cheapest olive oil and had a thick, rancid taste. His pains never stopped. He was emaciated. He rarely slept more than two or three hours a night. He wanted to get back to England, to someone who would take care of him, and it seemed that Elizabeth did not want him there. He cursed himself for being dependent on his family and he was sure that they despised him if they ever thought about him at all. And this was quite wrong, quite unfair, for alone among the brothers he had made an effort, he had tried to better himself, and it was only through ill-health that he had failed.

Hoping for a lesson, for company perhaps, he forced himself to take the tram and look up two former pupils, two girls passed on to him by Elizabeth. He was kept waiting in the hall for a long time before they condescended to come down. They had often kept people waiting, including Elizabeth, but he was not to know this. And when at last they did appear, although they were friendly and apologised, he found them offhand and superior and he thought the apology a form of ridicule. They were sorry but they already had a teacher. He was sure this was untrue.

Not that there was a shortage of work. If he had advertised and gone the rounds he could have found something, he knew. But after that he did not try, and what was the use of having lessons to give when in all probability you would be too sick to give them? Brooding on his setback, imagining to himself how the girls must have laughed about him as soon as he left the house, he had no one on whom to vent his fury. Alone in his room, tired of his own company and the pain, he often flung a chair or a small table across the room, tore pages out of his books and scratched his hands and face. He swore at the servant girl when she tried to get in to clean the room. He had sworn at the landlady until he owed her money. Sometimes he barricaded himself in as though expecting them to force an entrance.

A short walk along the pavement with nowhere to go, no purpose but to try and make himself well by breathing fresh air, would leave him feeling exhausted and despondent. What had his life been? Orphanages, odd jobs in Cardiff, people nagging at him to get on and nothing to get on with, jobs provided by his sisters, second-hand suits provided by his sisters. They had tried to help him, the sisters had meant well. They were the only ones who had. He was angry with his mother for preferring Michael and the thought of Michael maddened him. What a selfish pig he had always been in that school! He remembered how everyone said Michael was so handsome and had such a good heart—that was because when any of the others hurt themselves and cried Michael started howling too, although he never lifted a finger to pick them up or help them. Michael had been his mother's darling, he had a pretty wife and children and Marguerite thought he was everything. Marguerite not only found jobs for him and gave him money, she loved him and treated him as an equal—as more than an equal. She had spent hours with him, he imagined, just talking to him and enjoying his company. When had Elizabeth ever spent any time talking to him, Thomas? And when, since they were grown up, had she treated him as anything like an equal?

His rages and gradual starvation produced an overwhelming physical weakness. His landlady found him in bed, unable to get up. A doctor was called in. He must be operated on soon. It was serious.

Now he wished someone was with him, anyone, even Kathleen. He was afraid of being alone during and after the operation. It was no use writing to Elizabeth. She would never come. Marguerite, whom he had not loved, came into his mind. She was a nurse and she would never resist an appeal. Pedantically, careful of grammar and handwriting, he wrote:

> "My dear sister,
> The doctor has informed me that it is necessary for me to undergo an operation which he considers to be serious. I do not wish any member of the family to be inconvenienced on my account for I have always endeavoured and striven to burden no one but myself with my sufferings. However at such a critical moment I believe my family would consider it wrong of me not to tell them of the impending operation. I know you will believe me when I assure you that were it not likely that the operation

might prove fatal I would never write like this. I fear my own ignorance of doctors and such matters and wish there were someone here on whose judgement and knowledge I could rely. The doctor mentioned adhesions and tuberculosis but unfortunately as a layman I am quite unable to understand. Perhaps you could think of some member of the family or trusted friend who could come out to me. I will not fix a date for the operation until I have heard from you and received your instructions.

If it be God's will that I should recover then let us hope my recovery may be lasting, but if it be His will that I should not, then I may go to a better place where there is no pain and suffering. I pray for you all daily and ask to be remembered in your prayers.

Your loving brother.

The war was near its end when the letter reached Marguerite. She had been spoken of as likely to get a decoration. The hope of this glory and recognition had almost become a certainty and she felt proud. Many tributes to her came from patients, colleagues and superiors. All sorts of men she had nursed had written her long letters and sometimes their wives and mothers had written too. The more she saw herself as nursing and helping her country, the less she thought about religion. Never departing from her faith in Catholicism she had missed Mass on Sundays many times without compunction. "In my position one has dispensation automatically," she reasoned, even though the Sunday morning in question was not spent at work, but strolling in the Luxembourg, writing letters, or chatting to a friend.

The letter upset her. Thomas had not been in her thoughts or prayers—it was a long time since she had prayed at night—and she had imagined that Elizabeth would be seeing to him. The part about God's will read like a cry of despair and reminded her of the way her father had spoken. She must certainly go to him. She must tell him not to delay the operation and promise to be with him within a week.

"I must have a week's leave," she said to the matron, and always unable to give the real reason, "my mother is desperately ill in Saint-Jules and I must go to her. Just until I can find someone who will look after her. She is all alone." Had she mentioned Lisbon and had she suggested longer than a week she might have been granted no leave at all or as much as she needed.

Borrowing some money she left for Lisbon two days after the letter arrived. At every stop she sent wires to other members of the family. She had another of her premonitions—Thomas would die.

She travelled third, on hard wooden seats, accepting thankfully the food and wine offered by fellow-travellers. Otherwise she would not have bothered to eat much. She listened to their stories, trying hard to seem attentive. Often she fell asleep, lulled by the rhythm of the wheels, waking with a start when the train stopped. During these dozes she dreamt always of disasters. Someone needed her and she was trying to get to them and something was stopping her, some locked door, some unknown, unending street with no turnings or people of whom she could ask the way. Premonitions, not only about Thomas but about the others, beset her. She felt that her mother needed her. She knew Michael was dying in a Cardiff hospital. She saw Elizabeth on a sick bed in London. She saw John, wounded and dying at the front. The two boys had run away from school and were lost somewhere without money. Each short dream ended with a pleading face or an outstretched hand or some heart-rending sentence. As she woke she could never quite remember what it was they had asked of her and who had asked it. She searched in her memory, as though to know exactly what had happened in the dream would tell her what was happening in reality.

She was not conceited, but now she knew more than ever that there was nothing she could not undertake, nothing she could not do, nothing she could not know, if only—if only what? There was some obstacle. She was sure she could see what was happening in other places and foretell the future. If she could only get into the right state of mind, make herself receptive to the picture, she could know anything. As her faith in her extraordinary powers came into her mind clearly as words, as a statement, so she forgot that she had had a premonition that Thomas would die. She now thought, "I will pull him through. Only I could do it." And as she approached Lisbon her confidence increased.

The humble pension and the poorly furnished room aroused no emotion either of pity or distaste. She no longer cared about signs of wealth and distinction although she often spoke as though they alone counted with her. In emergencies, Reilly's lived anywhere. When everything was settled it was different. She noticed neither the dirty sheets nor the rancid smell. She had not seen Thomas for a long time and he was ill. Therefore he was like a stranger and a patient as well as a brother and she forgot the war and the others and saw nothing but him. He looked grey and worn and unhappy. He was frightened.

"Well, Thomas," she said cheerfully, "fancy getting ill like this when my back was turned!" and then she knew that this line would not do. She looked more serious and took his hand. She asked him to speak about himself and listened in silence.

He had been thinking about his past life and his present plight for so long that the story came out in a rush with bitterness, hatred and abuse. His mother, Elizabeth, "that little idiotic bitch Kathleen, that blasted, selfish pig Michael!" had let him down and he never wanted to see any of them again. Surprised at the names he called them she betrayed no emotion and refrained from argument or defence.

"As soon as you are better you must come back to England with me," she said as though it were her dearest wish, and for the moment it was. "We'll take a house somewhere in London, in a good residential part where we can all be together. With your talents you are quite wasted out here. The climate may be very good but I quite agree that the food does not suit you and you want proper attention."

Intuitively she knew it would be unwise to refer to the excitements of her own life. She gave him to understand that all of them were having a very boring, miserable, uncomfortable time, but of course none of them were so badly off as he was. "Elizabeth kept talking about you. She wanted you to come to England but I was afraid the journey might upset you, because she had told me about you being sick. It was really all my fault. And mother was always wondering if you were all right and asking me if I would write and ask you to come to Paris. And now she keeps wanting to get you to Saint-Jules. But in a dull little place like that you'd be so bored and there would be so few opportunities. You have always been so delicate that naturally we were always worrying about you. But now everything will be all right. You must not be on your own again. Not that you cannot get on very well—you have done marvellously well here. Very few men would be given the responsibility of teaching novices. But with your delicate health you need special attention. We all think so."

He felt that the whole family was worrying about him and talking about him and he felt soothed. The next step was to relieve him from pain. She insisted on being given a sedative prescription by the doctor. She sat by Thomas as his stomach became numbed and he fell asleep. She promised that he would not be taken off to a Portuguese hospital and handed over to foreign nurses he did not trust. "I shall insist on the operation being done here. I shall nurse you. Leave it to me. You need have no worries."

The operation was not successful and the doctor was gloomy. "These foreign doctors know nothing," thought Marguerite. "Of course Thomas will get better." The doctor was baffled by her. She had told him she was no ordinary nurse, but a matron with long years of experience and a fine record of war nursing. She spoke to him in a mixture of French and Italian and he found it hard to understand what she was saying. She behaved towards him as though she, too, were a doctor and when contradicting him threatened to call in another opinion.

Her confidence was infectious and Thomas believed he was recovering. "It was a great success," she assured him. "I was surprised at how well it went off."

She was free with the sedatives and kept him out of pain. When he was awake and conscious she read passages to him from Boswell's *Life of Johnson*. It was a book she would never have glanced at of her own accord and she did not find it entertaining. The violence and rudeness of the Doctor's replies fascinated Thomas, who would have liked to be in a position to speak like that to the people who had wounded his pride. At each offensive repartee he laughed with a forced, histrionic laugh and cynical expression.

She stayed with him until he died. She saw him buried in a fine Catholic cemetery. With no companion but the landlady she attended the last Mass and followed the coffin. It worried her that there should be only two mourners and one of them half-unwilling. What a good thing she had come! If he had died alone who would have been present at the funeral?

She had long overstayed her leave and a letter from Paris forwarded from the address she had given in Saint-Jules told her that she was in some sort of disgrace and need not return for the war was over and the hospital was closing down. She never received her decoration.

10

From Lisbon, Marguerite went to Saint-Jules. Now that the war was over she would see her mother, her darling Patrick and his brother. Thomas's death had left her brooding and dry-eyed. In the flat, in the presence of her mother and Kathleen, she broke down and wept. She wanted to upset them, especially Kathleen who sat there so smug, so wrapped up in Lisa.

"Poor Thomas! It was heart-breaking. Kathie, you were the last to see him. Why did you not write and tell me he was so ill?"

"But Marguerite, he'd had the ulcers ever since Cardiff. I never thought I ought..."

"You never thought—you never think—you never will think."

For the first few days she would talk of nothing else. Again and again she described his suffering, the lonely funeral and his last words. These of course she invented but they were very real to her. "He spoke of you, mother. He smiled and looked so like father and he said, 'I know you will look after her and that is a great consolation to me.' If you had seen him, mother."

Mrs Hughes was touched at this tale of devotion from a son who had never sent her a line. She cried easily and gave Marguerite the satisfaction of seeing a steady flow of tears.

There was something terrible for Marguerite in the fact that one of them had died before the family was "on its feet". He had missed those future days when the Reilly's would live in the way that was their due. He would not be there to witness the fulfilment of her plans. She had assumed they would all survive till then and that after that death would take them one by one, in order of age. She kept shaking her head. "To think he should be the first to go. I had always hoped not to outlive any of the others."

Because Lisa was not in her orbit she was strict with her. "The child should be in bed. Kathie, you have let her become dreadfully spoilt. Why do you allow her to suck sweets all day?"

Then, quite suddenly, she changed. Lisa was her pet and she was paying as much attention to the child as the others did. She wanted her with her all the time. "I'm going out and I think Lisa should come too. She's been sitting in the house all day. It's not good for her." "Lisa can go to High Mass with me. You go on to the early one. She will enjoy the singing." "No, Lisa had better not go shopping with you, mother. It will tire her. She had better stay here with me."

And to Lisa her aunt's affection was all the more prized because she had at first been indifferent and severe. It was like a victory. And now she was not severe at all. On the contrary, she consulted her wishes, played with her and told her stories of Paris. She took her to the patisserie.

Marguerite could be very attractive to children because her inexhaustible energy matched theirs, and although she was bad at games which required concentration and a knowledge of rules, she was good when it came to hide-and-seek. Also she had a way of keeping things lively and at a high pitch. There was no mistaking that she was the most important person in the house and with her the most unexpected things happened. She kept changing her mind. There might be disappointments but there were also surprises. And it gave Lisa a feeling of great power to find that this aunt, so terrifying to Kathleen and Mrs Hughes, was under her thumb, would roar with laughter when she said, "What funny French you speak, Auntie. You've got it all wrong, Auntie, that's not the game we're playing at all." It was like being the favourite of a king.

Marguerite's determined efforts to attach Lisa to herself and to shake her affection for Kathleen were not conscious but that did not make them any the less effective. She never let up. Although she visited the boys frequently, urging them to become priests and work hard, they were of less importance to her now. Their futures must be secured but Lisa was to be the star turn. Soon she knew exactly what she wanted. Her mother and Lisa must be with her and that meant that they must leave Saint-Jules because she could not stay in this dead-and-alive place for ever and it was high time she began to make some money. The boys must stay here with the Christian brothers and Kathleen must stay too to keep an eye on them.

"You cannot leave here, Kathie dear," she said, "you have such an excellent job and wonderful connections. And this place seems to suit you. I've never seen her look so well, have you mother? You're quite a different person, and all your pupils are so devoted to you. Only yesterday Madame Bourgeain was saying of you..."

Kathleen was pleased at this praise and agreed that the place suited her very well.

"It's very nice for Lisa to know French," said Marguerite later, "but the child has a dreadful Midi accent. Have you not noticed it, *chérie?* The way she says *mamang* instead of *maman* and puts all the "e's" on the ends of words like *bonne* and *petite?* It's like a peasant. It's all right now but it will tell against her later. There is a very nice convent just outside Paris—the headmistress is a perfect dear and a great friend of mine—and she could go there for a little while before returning to England. There are one or two things I must clear up in Paris so I could take her. And mother will be there. I think it would break her heart to be separated from Lisa now."

Kathleen's eyes filled with tears. "Oh, don't take her away. I've never been parted from her. She's very happy here. Very soon she can be a proper boarder at the Ursulines and they're all so fond of her there."

"*Chérie* you must try not to be so selfish. Think of her future. If we bring her up in a little country place like this, what will she turn out like? You always think of yourself first. And she's so clever and bright. A child like that needs to have opportunities."

11

Kathleen was granted some reprieve. The flu epidemic detained them all in Saint-Jules for several months more. As a nurse, Marguerite felt she must stay to look after the victims. And although it was bad enough there with numbers of people dying daily, she was certain that it would be much worse in the big towns and that to go to Paris or London now would be very dangerous. Fortunately none of the family caught the infection, but schools closed down, pupils were sent home and Mrs Hughes, her two daughters and her three grandchildren had to stay in the one small flat. Everything was makeshift; the children slept in the sitting room on mattresses on the floor. Lisa hated it. The boys, who had taken a dislike to her stuck-up ways, teased her whenever they had the chance and broke her toys, and no one but Kathleen had time to listen to her complaints.

So that when the time came to leave Saint-Jules she was glad. At the railway station she suddenly felt frightened. The sight of her mother's unrestrained tears made her feel that some great disaster was happening and she sobbed loudly. She had heard arguments between her aunt and mother. She had heard her mother mumbling sadly about "hardness" and "domineering" and being "broken-hearted", and although she could not understand the English words,

196

the tone of voice and forlorn expression conveyed the emotions. She imagined that much plotting was going on inside the family and she knew that she was being taken away as part of the plot. The nuns and other people were always saying, *"Ta pauvre maman"* and this made her very sorry for her mother. It was depressing to be with someone you were sorry for. She became all the more fascinated by her aunt and yet afraid of her, for perhaps she was wicked like relations in fairy tales. In the train she continued to cry for her poor mother but her aunt and grandmother consoled her and people in the compartment petted her and she forgot. She remained at the convent in Vincennes long enough to eliminate the Midi accent. In the holidays she was hustled round Paris by her aunt sometimes, but usually her aunt was working and she was left for the day at the English Club. She slept in a room with her aunt and grandmother, she and her aunt in one bed, her grandmother in another. At the English Club she picked up a few more words of English and a lady sang a song which went to the tune of "Three Blind Mice."

> "Three nice girls, three nice girls,
> See how they run, see how they run
> They all ran after the same young man
> Who jumped into a furniture van
> And went all the way to Jappy Japan
> With three nice girls, three nice girls,
> One young man, poor young man.

This was the first English song she had heard and it made a profound impression on her, being so different in spirit from the songs she had danced to in a ring, *"Nous n'irons plus au bois"*, *"La Sainte Cathérine"*, *"Il était un avocat"*, and others. She assumed that it was meant to give you a picture of England, a strange country where people chased you in play and where you rode on a furniture van. She did not altogether like it. A little girl in the convent, who wanted to upset her during a quarrel, told her England was cold and rainy.

She had quite recovered from the loss of her mother, although she hoped she would come and see her and bring her presents. She had adapted herself to the convent and the young ladies at the English Club when she was told she would be going to England soon.

"No, Auntie, I don't want to go."

"But why not?"

She couldn't explain. Later she saw a coloured postcard of boy scouts camping and her spirits rose. "Do people live in tents in England?"

"Oh, yes," her aunt and grandmother assured her.

On landing, she looked for the tents. There was grass where they could be, as they were in the picture, but they were not there. Then they passed houses, just the same houses as in France. "Where are the tents?" she kept asking.

"Later, dear, later," said her grandmother.

That must mean that they would be in London. London would be all tents and there would be the dreaded but interesting furniture vans. The capital engulfed her with its greyness. The skies were grey, the pavements were grey and the houses were grey. The nice girls (she had thought of them like herself), the young man, the vans and the tents were all a myth or else she had been taken to the wrong place. For a time she thought her aunt had made some dreadful mistake.

12

Marguerite took over a large house in Pimlico in order to run it as a nurses' home for a matron friend of hers. It was a five-storeyed, late Victorian house, with pillars and a stone balcony jutting out over the door, the image of all the houses in the square in which it stood and all the houses in the streets around. It was dilapidated and the paintwork inside was a dark chocolate colour. The nurses would have no meals there but gas rings would be provided so that they could make themselves cups of tea.

"The big room on the first floor would make a beautiful drawing room," said Marguerite, "and Lisa can be out on the balcony all day. And the room underneath will be the dining room."

But all this was to be in the future. For the moment those large, high rooms were divided up into cubicles by green curtains. The rooms on the top floors were let to special nurses who wanted rooms to themselves and could afford to pay more. In the basement, Mrs Hughes, Marguerite and Lisa ate and slept and spent the greater part of the day.

Financially this arrangement was sound. You did not need a penny to start off with. A building society paid for the lease. The money coming from the nurses paid the mortgage on the lease in monthly instalments, allowed for living expenses and part of the fees at the seminary.

"I must get it all very nice first," said Marguerite. "When the place is all done up and running smoothly I shall go back to nursing and it will look after itself."

This life did not suit Marguerite. She had imagined that there would be very little to do and she found that there was always something to be seen to. Buying second-hand furniture, dealing with charwomen, keeping accounts kept her busy. After becoming the bosom friend of each nurse who came, she then grew indifferent to her. Finally there was not one lodger in the place she did not wish to avoid. She always came in and out by the area steps instead of the front door so as not to meet them. She was always saying to Lisa, "Oh, say I'm out." Details had always bored her and seeing to general upkeep and repairs got on her nerves. If a tap began to leak she let it go on leaking. If the windows did not shut properly she did not have them seen to. Several boards in the staircase were loose but she did nothing. She paid no attention to the many complaints.

She began to juggle with the money which came in. She bought a new suit for Patrick instead of paying bills as they fell due. Once or twice the gas and electricity were cut off. Mrs Hughes was becoming lazy and excused herself for not looking after things on the grounds of her "poor feet". She kept the kitchen warm, comfortable and like all the kitchens she had ever had. She cooked well for the three of them for she had grown very fond of her food, and she forgot about the rest of the house as long as she was allowed to.

The nurses complained to the matron and the matron had an interview with Marguerite. There was no drawing room and such a person could hardly be shown into the kitchen. Mrs Hughes' bed was there and it would not seem right to be the sort of family who slept in the kitchen. The conversation therefore had to take place in the draughty passage at the foot of the stairs. The matron, who had been led to believe by Marguerite's talk that the place was a paradise, was not favourably impressed and spoke with indignation. Marguerite could not stand being interfered with.

"I have never come across such a fussy lot of women in my life," she said to her mother afterwards while Lisa listened with interest.

"She seems to think her wretched nurses are children and we ought to spoon feed them. She's not at all grateful although we took this place on simply so that they could have somewhere to stay. And they all said they were so pleased and kept coming and talking to us. But that's how people are—all over you one moment and then going behind your back the next. I cannot stand being in a position where people can go along and complain behind your back. I said to her plainly, 'You can take them away if you're not satisfied. I'm very busy and have more important things to think about than all these little complaints. It makes no difference to me whether they go or stay. I've tried hard to help you out.' And wherever they go they will expect the earth."

The boarding house began to feel like a burden. She told herself that if only there had not been the boys and her mother and Lisa she would have given it up and gone back to nursing and thought of nothing else. Housework and shopping were not for her and she did what she called "concentrating on the administrative side" by fits and starts. Leisure was of no use to her because she did not care for reading and loathed going for walks. She enjoyed being with Lisa and spent the day playing with her. But in the end not even the child's company could compensate for this inactivity. She decided the time had come. "Mother," she said, much to Mrs Hughes' surprise. "Now that the house is quite settled and running smoothly I must go back to cases. Lisa can go to a boarding school. I've heard of a very nice convent. If I'm earning money I can pay the extra fees and besides, Kathie must pay more towards her now. You can easily run this place with a good daily. The nurses have nearly all gone and we'll get a very nice type of lodger who is no trouble."

Unfortunately ideal lodgers were not easy to come by. Any type of lodger was scarce and many of the rooms fell empty. She could not afford the loss of money with so many children to educate. She changed her attitude, put advertisements in the local tobacconists, was very pleasant to lodgers, boasted to them about the refined atmosphere of the place, collected one or two old ladies whom she did everything to impress. "Of course we are just beginning. But this will be the drawing room, when I've found just the right curtains, you know. And you'll be able to sit here whenever you like. And this will be the dining room. We'll have a very nice sideboard over there. And then we shall serve breakfasts in here." She became less casual about bills. Even after all this there was still an empty floor. She appealed to Elizabeth.

Elizabeth looked over the house and thought the top flat had possibilities. The disadvantages of having to climb so many flights of stairs were outweighed by the advantage of being so far away from the basement. She thought it over.

"I shall pay you a fair rent," she said. Depressed by the muddle in the basement she insisted. "It must be clearly understood that it is mine and mine only. I must have somewhere of my very own where I can have people. I don't want to seem hard *chérie*, but I cannot have all the family up here. It's only fair to me to keep it private if I pay you just what anyone else would."

Marguerite looked hurt and amazed. "But of course, *chérie*. Naturally. We would not dream of going up there or using it. I cannot think why you mention it. I cannot imagine what it is you fear."

13

Mauve was Elizabeth's favourite colour, a watery, pinky mauve with refined and attenuated associations. She would have a mauve room.

She had learnt something about furniture and already possessed a few nice pieces, some bought cheaply at sales, some given by lady friends who had to move after the war. A lightly-built, French writing desk, a glass-fronted china cabinet and an inlaid table she tried in different positions in the room until she was satisfied. The curtains and their bunchy pelmets were mauve shot with a metallic green. The divan was a paler mauve and so was the cushion which ran along the back like a giant sausage. Cushions in various shades of purple were placed at careful angles on the corded, shot-silk purple armchairs. On the walls she hung silhouette pictures in black frames, pictures of ladies in poke bonnets and crinolines with attendant men. Bit by bit she added objects which would give a Chinese look. First a black lacquered table with gold on it, then a small, painted cabinet containing fans and ivory carvings, and finally, on the writing desk, a huge ivory paper knife with a great multi-coloured silk tassel hanging from the end.

All this had to be done in her off-duty moments because she was now training at Guy's Hospital. The censorship and its high earnings had long ago closed down, she had been interested in voluntary nursing during the war and she hoped to make good money on private cases. She was now in her second year and living in hospital and she thought it a great extravagance to take on a flat. She could afford the rent if she dipped into her savings and she had always longed to begin a little home for herself. She felt she was doing Marguerite and her mother a great kindness by helping them out. Besides, it gave her somewhere to stow away the many articles she collected. Outwardly her bedroom looked tidy but each drawer was crammed full of oddments, such as the right hand of one pair of gloves, the left hand of another; one black stocking, one grey; small pieces of fur; brooches which had lost their pins; each thing waiting either for a new mate or some vital part to be brought back into use. She could never bear to throw anything away and when her clothes became out of date or torn in parts they were put away with the idea of being turned into something else as soon as she had the time. She was not hoarding for herself alone. She believed that these things might come in useful for Kathleen or Lisa one day. In hospital when she saw one of the nurses about to throw something away she would say, "Just a minute. Let me have a look at it. It might come in useful. If you don't mind I shall keep it."

Shortly after moving into her flat she gave a tea party there for some ladies who had worked with her during the war, ladies of good family. Dressed in mauve, with a long string of amber beads hanging to her waist, her hair draped about her oval face like an orderly bird's nest, she fussed sweetly, handed round tea in tiny cups, laughed and exclaimed at every remark her guests made. It was a great success.

She was soon very conscious that her flat was an oasis of gracious living in Marguerite's chaotic house. She was not unwilling to help her sister by saying a few charming words to the old ladies on the first two floors and creating a good impression. But she drew the line at sitting down in the kitchen. She was very polite about it, popping down for one moment when she came in to give her mother a peck and ask after her health and then saying she had a hundred things to do upstairs.

"When it's all absolutely ready," she said from time to time, "and that's a very big 'when', you must all pay a formal visit. We must have a family party."

Until that special day she discouraged them in every way from going up there. She locked her rooms and gave the keys to the cleaner, telling her not to part with them. She had duplicates cut for herself. For exceptional reasons Marguerite and Lisa did once or twice penetrate into the sitting room but no one was allowed into the fluffy sanctity of her bedroom. She was genuinely modest and had a horror of being seen at any stage of undress by anyone, including her female relations. Above her rose silk bed hung one of the ebony crucifixes, a rosary blessed by the Pope and a large picture of the Sacred Heart.

This setting was not only for her own satisfaction and the delight other chosen friends. It was to be the background in which Ribeira would find her. It was to make up to him for her lack of a family residence to which she could take him. She was training to be a nurse and she was resigned to a life of work, but the war and contact with Marguerite had increased her longing for security, for some permanent arrangement, and that had reconciled her to the idea of a good marriage. She did not actually plan it. Like Thomas, she thought of "God's will" as the deciding factor. But in case the proposal should come, there was the setting for it. Ribeira had written her the most ardent letters ever since she had left Lisbon. Her absence had increased his love and there was no doubt that he was considering marriage. Twice he had been on the point of coming to England to see her and now he was definitely arriving in a short time.

As the date approached she appealed to the others. "Marguerite, as you have no drawing room where one can show people in—and chérie when will you have one?—he must come straight upstairs to mine. The stair carpet is in very bad condition. It doesn't look at all nice. Now mother, when he comes, I want you to put on that very nice black silk dress you got in Paris. And don't wear an apron over it. There's no need to take him down to the kitchen. He can always go straight up to the flat, and so he need have no idea that you live in the basement. At the same time I must look properly chaperoned— those foreigners have such odd ideas—and so you must be up there too. You know you can look very nice if you want to."

Elizabeth was thirty-four now. There were a few streaks of grey in her black hair and her eyes looked tired. She had begun to use powder and a very little rouge. She had lost many back teeth and wore plates which did not show but which made her mouth move less freely, her smile was a little pinched, her lips were a little pursed when she spoke. In certain lights she was still a great beauty, in others she was faded. But she was not worried about her looks. Beauty was not associated in her mind with youth. Unlike Kathleen, she never scanned her face in the mirror with despair. She enjoyed sitting at her dressing table, among her little pots and bottles and ornaments. She was satisfied with the reflection. One could not look young for ever. It was her background which she thought might upset Ribeira, nothing else. In any case, much as she would like security, if marriage failed there were other things she could do. And marriage—well it was awful in a way.

14

Michael turned up in London. He arrived without warning one afternoon. He had answered no letters. The family had not known whether he was in Cardiff or not.

He had gone back to his old job of selling vegetables in Cardiff market. He had talked to his old friends as though he were sorry for himself. "With the wife leaving me like that and me shellshock, I've never been the same." But he was quite happy. He made no attempt to trace his wife or go and see his daughter and youngest son. He was glad to be a crock because it gave him an excuse for not working hard. Living in some poor lodgings near the market he had not felt lonely. In the daytime he chatted to the other men and sometimes in the evenings they went and had a drink together. His landlady was susceptible to his good-humoured, slow charm and looked after him well.

He didn't quite know why he came to London. Another fellow was going and he thought he might as well. Marguerite might give him some money and his mother certainly would if she had any. It took a bit of doing, packing up his few things, buying a ticket and getting into the train, but since the other fellow was with him it went quite smoothly.

His hair was grey at the back and snow white at the temples, but it was thick and springy and the round curls gave him the look of a classical sculpture. His blue eyes were pale and looked out weak and vague onto a blurred world. There was little time in the day when his head felt clear and he rarely thought. It was not that he drank a great deal, he couldn't afford it for one thing. But just one glass of beer would send him into a happy, soothed, fuddled state. He looked down at heel. His clothes were crumpled because he often did not bother to undress at night. His voice, after the army days, had a cockney note.

Propped up dreamily against the door post of the boarding house he asked the person who opened the door—it was one of the old ladies—"Miss Reilly at 'ome?"

"Who shall I say it is?" he was asked primly.

He had been well trained in Cardiff not to claim relationship unless he was told he could. He scratched his head and thought. "Say it's a man who wants to see 'er about something private."

Marguerite came up from below, gave him a startled look, thanked the old lady effusively for opening the door, watched her go back to her room and then approached him. "Come in, come in."

It was not until they were safely in the kitchen that she openly recognised him. Despite his mother's warm welcome and a nice cup of tea he felt uncomfortable. Marguerite looked a bit put out. He kept repeating, "Should 'ave let you know I was coming. Never was much of a letter writer."

Marguerite's feelings were mixed. Here was the brother she had begged to come to London but he looked different. She hadn't seen him for years. He had aged and become appallingly scruffy. He was like a tramp. What would the lodgers think if they knew he was her brother? At the same time she loved him and was sorry for him. It was wonderful to see him again. It moved her to see her mother's happiness. She was about to give herself up to welcoming affection when a sudden despair seized her. What would they do with him? What did he want? She was off to a case tomorrow. Lisa had been packed off and the boys were out of the way. Now here was someone else to be thought of. She walked up and down.

He wished she would leave off her pacing and sit down with them. He looked at her with anxious, watery eyes.

" 'Ow's the kids? Doing all right?"

"They're very well. Very well."

He thought there was nothing for it but to tell his story and so, slowly, he began. He had felt lonely, missed his kids, been hard up, wanted to see the family, had nowhere to go, wasn't feeling well. He repeated each misfortune several times and because his eyes were weak and bleary it seemed as though he was on the verge of tears. His mother looked sad and shook her head.

"Poor Mick. Poor Mick," she said and looked at him with tender concern.

Marguerite scarcely listened. "We'll find somewhere for you," she said, "but you cannot stay here. There's no room for you. Have you any work? What are you doing for money?"

"There's me pension, that's all. I must 'ave somewhere to stay a day or so. Then I could look round a bit."

Marguerite thought of other boarding house keepers she knew. No, she could not send him to any of them. It would create a bad impression. Her mother watched her anxiously.

"Poor Mick," said Mrs Hughes. "Sure, Marguerite, we could put him in Elizabeth's room tonight. She'll not be here for a day or two. She never comes twice in the same week. We've no need to tell her and if she doesn't know there'll be no harm done."

"No. Besides, it's locked."

"The woman's got the key. I'll get it off her. I'll say Elizabeth told me to. Or I could share a bed with you and we'll put him in the kitchen. Why not?"

Marguerite thought this over. Once he was in the kitchen he would never go. Elizabeth's flat would certainly look temporary, feel temporary and he'd know all right that it could be for the shortest time only. They could pack him off the next day. And they could hardly turn him out at once. Poor Michael. She allowed her mother to go for the key.

"Isn't it great seeing you again?" said Mrs Hughes when she returned. "Did you not think of bringing Maureen with you? She'll be a grown girl now! What's she like?"

He thought it better not to say he hadn't seen her once since he came back to Cardiff. "She's very well. She's still with her uncle. Both of them are. I can't look after them proper in my condition."

15

Ribeira arrived sooner than anyone had expected. The others had not been told the exact date of his arrival and Elizabeth expected him in the evening. When he came at two o'clock, straight off the train, hurrying to see the beloved who had been in his thoughts all these years, Elizabeth was at the hospital. Marguerite was at her case and Mrs Hughes opened the door. She was in an old, dirty dress, half-covered by a stained apron. She wore grey, split bedroom slippers. His English was difficult to follow but she quickly realised who he was. Flustered, she pretended she was the housekeeper.

Leaving him standing in the hall, she went downstairs, took off her aprons, changed into her hard shoes which she hated, cleaned her nails with a broken match stick, tidied her hair. When she came up again she admitted she was Elizabeth's mother. It would come out sooner or later. It was wisest to tell the truth. In any case he probably couldn't understand a word.

She plodded up the stairs ahead of him, presenting to him a great expanse of spreading back and a crescent of greying petticoat. She must take him to the sitting room on the top flat. That was what Elizabeth had said. One of the old ladies, hearing the noise, always in search of distraction from the immured uneventfulness of her own life, opened her door as they passed, stared at him with a wild, startled brightness, smiled and mumbled something. As luck would have it, his foot found the broken floorboard, he heard a sharp crack and nearly fell.

When they reached the top floor Mrs Hughes discovered that in her flurry she had left the key downstairs—she had not returned the keys to the cleaner. She now fell to worrying about how she would explain to Elizabeth that she had the key to let him in. Leaving Ribeira standing on the landing, slowly and painful she made the descent of the whole eight flights. She was too apprehensive of the long ascent to notice that the bedroom key was not hanging on the next cup hook to the sitting room key. When she reached the top floor she was no longer concerned about the visitor. Her legs and feet ached, she was short of breath and indignant at the length of the climb. She presented to him that look of purple agony which accompanies loss of wind. She pointed to her feet and, hoping he would understand French, gasped, *"Les pieds! Les pieds!"* Ribeira looked bewildered and courteous.

In the mauve room she pressed him to sit on one of the purple armchairs and lowered herself heavily onto the divan, making a deep depression on its smooth surface. What was she to say? How long was she to sit here? She had no idea. She panted, exhausted. Ribeira looked round the room as though waiting for something. Minutes passed.

There was worse to come. Michael, after a midday visit to the pub, having spent his last shilling, had come home to get some money out of his mother, had taken the key from the dresser while she was looking for her purse, had pretended he was going to leave the house and had softly gone upstairs for a nap. They had found a room for him near Victoria now and he was not supposed to be here, but he felt too sleepy to reach his lodgings.

The sound of voices in the next room woke him with a start. In a hazy way he felt alarmed. He knew that at all costs Elizabeth mustn't find him here. He knew that somehow he must get up, tidy the bed, get out very quietly, lock the door, replace the key and go off. The first thing was to reach the shelter of the kitchen and his mother.

He managed to get his legs off the bed, but as he sat there looking at the floor his head felt dizzy and the carpet seemed to undulate. He clutched at the table beside the bed, the dainty, round, one-legged table which held a number of objects and sent it to the floor with a loud crash. The noise cleared his head a little. He picked up the table, pulled up the pink bed cover and waited. He could hear footsteps coming towards the landing. Then he heard his mother's voice. He was safe.

On hearing the crash Mrs Hughes was alarmed. Who could be in there at this time of day? She at once thought of burglars because Elizabeth's fussiness had led her to believe that Elizabeth's possessions were extremely valuable. With a frightened look at Ribeira, glad to have a man by her, hoping he would deal with the intruder, loath to rise, she shouted, "Who's there?"

There was no answer for Michael had not heard. Reluctantly she rose, beckoned to Ribeira to follow her and went out onto the landing. She put her finger over her lips and bent down by the door to listen. There were unmistakeable sounds of movement. Bravely she shouted once more, "Who's there?" When the door opened and Michael appeared she was speechless.

What could she say? *"Un monsieur. Un resident,"* she explained at last while the two men stood by in silence. Then it occurred to her that if Ribeira knew this was Elizabeth's flat it would be quite wrong for him to think that a man had come out of her bedroom like that. "*Le frère,*" she said, "*mon fils,*" changing her mind. Having taken this course the only thing to do was return to the living room with the pair of them and wait.

The grey light which filtered through the net curtains was strong enough to hide nothing. Michael was tousled, dirty, unshaved, ragged and you could tell he had been drinking, you could smell it from a mile off. He hadn't a word to say and his head was fuddled. For the moment he looked half-witted as he smiled sheepishly.

Mrs Hughes pulled herself together. She began to speak in a mixture of French and English. She found Ribeira unhelpful and took a dislike to him. "*Le pauvre frère,*" she said, frowning. "*La guerre. Triste.*" She couldn't rebuke Michael in front of the stranger. When she signalled to him to go away he took no notice but just sat there blinking. She decided she would feel better with a cup of tea. After all, they might have to wait here for hours. And what were they waiting for? Was Ribeira expecting Elizabeth to arrive? Did she know he was there? If people didn't let you know their plans how could you do the right thing? She showed them out of the flat, locked the door with a heavy heart and took them down to the kitchen.

The kitchen had never looked more untidy. The bed was there, of course, unmistakeably a bed and piled with the linen from the rooms upstairs which she had meant to list for the laundry. She had had no time to clear away the lunch dishes and there was a smell of cooking. When she was on her own she sat in the dark but in honour of the guests she switched on the light, not that it made a great deal of difference. Owing to a sudden economy mania of Marguerite's the bulb was so weak that one could scarcely see to read and the dimness increased the air of poverty, although it hid a few faults. The two men sat down while she put on the kettle and cleared away. Tea consoled her and helped Michael to clear his head and decide to go.

When Elizabeth came in at four, shouted down the basement steps, "Mother, I must fly and get ready. I'm expecting him today," she was horrified to hear the answering shout, "He's here."

"Where?"

"Down here."

She hurried down to find him. Standing in the unflattering downward light, the deep hollows beneath her eyes and the drooping corners of her twitching mouth exaggerated, she greeted him in Portuguese and he rose and bowed.

Ribeira was not unchivalrous but his picture of Elizabeth had been dealt a serious blow and he could not help reacting. It was not only his unfortunate introduction to the family which upset him, it was even more the sight of her tired, thin face. Had he seen it change gradually over the last few years he might scarcely have noticed the process, but the image of her, glowing and round-cheeked as he had last seen her, had been with him the second before she entered. And her manner was different, much less gay, much more edgy and nervous.

Back in the mauve room, he listened to her excuses. She had not the same power of invention as her sister and disliked a downright lie. Besides, it was against her principles to blame the family to others. She confined herself to apologising for her own lateness, her misunderstanding about the time of the train. She said, with some truth, that Marguerite had rushed off to a case and her mother was not well. As she spoke she sat on the divan, moved to a chair, went over to light the fire. Surprisingly, some streak of pride and independence seized her and if he had uttered one word of criticism she would have turned on him.

But he was too well-bred to say or hint anything. He smiled and reassured. He had the air of a man paying a visit out of politeness. There was no passion in his dark eyes. He said he had had a very pleasant afternoon and was very glad to meet her mother, a charming lady. He was sorry her mother was not well. He made no mention of Michael. He took her to a smart restaurant that evening and behaved correctly.

He never set foot in the house again. During the fortnight which followed he produced a teddy bear which he had brought over for Lisa, for he had once seen the child at his cousin's house and everyone had told him that Elizabeth doted on her niece. He called for Elizabeth at the hospital in a taxi whenever she had a day or half-day off and bore her away to some place of entertainment. But he was not in love any more.

Elizabeth realised this and, with pride, made no attempt to turn the conversation to his letters and the subject of marriage. But the strain of the situation and the disappointment made her overwrought. He was staying at one of the best hotels, he was ordering suits in Savile Row, he was enormously rich and well-established. There was no doubting his advantages and the advantages which his wife would have. It was with relief she said goodbye, allowing him to keep up the pretence of hoping he would be allowed to go on writing to her.

She had not been home since the day of his arrival, and sitting in her mauve room, glancing at the china shepherdess in the cabinet, the shepherdess which all the ladies at her tea party had insisted was exactly like her, she wept. Worried about her, having heard her come in and surprised that she did not look in at the kitchen, Marguerite went up to the top flat with a cup of tea. She found her red-eyed and subdued.

"Here you are, *chérie*, take this." Marguerite assumed that Elizabeth had been very much in love and this increased her feeling of guilt. She did not like to ask if he had proposed. She imagined he had not. "Elizabeth, I never meant to let you down. I shall never forgive myself if..."

Elizabeth drank the tea and was silent.

"I hate to see you upset, *chérie*," continued Marguerite. "Look, I have an afternoon off tomorrow and I thought we might go and have tea with the Jamieson's, such delightful people and they would like to meet you. I've told them all about my beautiful sister."

"I have to be back at the hospital," said Elizabeth. "Marguerite, you've let me down. You gave me your promise that this kind of thing couldn't happen."

"I know, *chérie,* I know. But poor Michael! He had nowhere to go. As it was your own brother..."

To put the matter like this was intolerable. Elizabeth was angry. "That has nothing to do with it. You made a promise and you broke it. I can't trust you. You're thoroughly unreliable."

"Well if a man makes a fuss about your family you're well rid of him."

"Marguerite, keep to the point. Stop hedging. He made no fuss. That's not your affair. You're thoroughly unreliable, one will never be able to trust you. You always have an excuse. You're a past master at making excuses. But I'm finished with all this. I simply took the flat to help you but I don't need it. I'm hardly ever here. I'm going to store the furniture and when I've finished training I'll find somewhere of my own. You must find another lodger. I'm going as soon as I can arrange it."

A chance of marriage, of a good marriage, might never come again. Back in the hospital Elizabeth worked hard. She was a born surgical nurse. In the operation theatre she was steady and quick-witted. She did her dressings with a light hand. The sight of wounds and excrement were not pleasant, but it satisfied her temperament to turn something disgusting into something clean and hygienic, to cover over the horror with a clean, white bandage, to reduce the untidiness and suffering of the human body to a matter of forceps, clamps, retractors, chisels and scalpels, laid in neat rows and overhung by the smell of disinfectant. It satisfied her wish to be virtuous and do good. Besides, she was kind, all the Reilly girls were kind in their different ways.

<h1 style="text-align:center">16</h1>

When Kathleen arrived in England she found that her daughter had almost forgotten her. It seemed that Marguerite was now the mother while she was the aunt. It was holiday time and Lisa was at home, a taller, older, thinner, less vigorous Lisa.

"You can share a room with her," said Marguerite. "There's one on the third floor free at the moment. But if a lodger comes I shall have to think of something else."

Kathleen was greeted with no great cordiality. There were the perfunctory pecks from her mother and sister and, "Did you have a good journey? What was the crossing like?" but that passed quickly. While she was drinking her second cup of tea her account of life in France was cut short and she was asked about future plans. She had none. Marguerite refused to believe this and cross-examined her.

"I've been having tummy trouble," said Kathleen. "I mean to work as soon as I can but I need a rest first."

Marguerite took no notice of this. "I think she should train as a nurse. Do you not agree mother? I've been thinking that if the three of us were trained nurses we could run our own nursing home. There's a lot of money in it."

"I don't feel cut out to be a nurse," said Kathleen. "I'm very fond of teaching. I know it might be difficult to get something in a school because of not having my teacher's certificate. But I thought that perhaps I could give private lessons in Portuguese and French."

"No Kathie. I do not think that would be a wise plan. If you are so fond of teaching why did you come back? You were doing very well out there."

"Well, naturally I wanted to see Lisa." Kathleen's eyes clouded. "After all, I missed her. If you'd been in my place you would..."

"You could have had her there for the summer holidays."

"Yes, but out there, without a soul, you get lonely."

Marguerite looked on this as a slight to the two boys. Exasperated, she went back to the future. "It's not so easy to get pupils here. And really I cannot spare a room here where you could give lessons." She did not want her in the house. As a nurse she would be away in hospital for three years and then away on private cases. "And we need the money, Kathie. You cannot expect me to go on paying for Lisa's schooling and you surely do not want her to go to an elementary school."

"But I did send you money. I thought I was paying for her."

This irritated Marguerite, who boasted to herself and others that she alone was paying for the education of all the children. From that moment she treated Kathleen with scorn, as some wretched dependent who was trying to give herself airs. Regardless of whether Lisa was present or not she found fault with her.

"Kathie, why are you sitting about like this? You're making no attempt to find something."

"Because you put an advertisement in the papers for pupils you think you've done wonders."

"Kathie, when are you going along to the hospital for your papers?"

"Kathie, you cannot pick and choose what you want to do. You're not the idle rich though you fancy you are."

"No, Kathie, you cannot take Lisa out for a walk. She is coming with me to tea with some very nice people. Even if you do not care a pin what happens to her future, I do."

Lisa preferred to visit rich houses with her aunt. Sitting with her disconsolate mother she fretted. She was demonstrative and kissed her and told her she was all she had in the world. Aunt Marguerite never did that, her manner was dry and quick and though there was no tenderness there was a feeling of power in the way she spoke and never a demand for pity.

In desperation, dreading the end of the holidays when she would not have Lisa's presence to console her, Kathleen turned to

Elizabeth. She went to the hospital and had tea with her in her room. "Marguerite's so hard," she said. "What do you think I had better do?"

"Poor Kathie. You're not at all well, I can see. I quite realise how it is. Marguerite can be difficult, although mind you, we owe a lot to her. But I think this time perhaps she is right. You would be much happier out of the house and one can be quite happy in hospital. And in the holidays I'll help you to arrange to spend time with Lisa and you can see her in your off-duty time." Elizabeth kept to the rule of never running down a member of her family to anyone else at all. "I think Marguerite is trying to do her best for everyone, I believe she genuinely is, but sometimes the strain of it is too much for her. For your own sake, Kathie, I advise you to go in for nursing." She spoke as gently and sweetly to her as she spoke to patients when they were alarmed. She was persuasive.

Elizabeth's room was persuasive too. It was very small but it was comfortable and private. One would feel sheltered in such a place, out of the reach of badgering and bullying.

With the least possible delay, Kathleen began her training at Guy's. Elizabeth would be there and look after her, she thought. It was through Elizabeth that she had been taken on so easily. For six weeks she went to classes on anatomy, did a great deal of sweeping and dusting, learnt how to prepare invalid food and became acquainted with the routine of the wards, the regular timetable, the clock-like precision.

Elizabeth meant to be kind, believed that what she did was for Kathie's good, always spoke softly, but always reproached.

"A wrinkle in your stocking, dear. I only mention it for your sake."

"Your hair is untidy."

"Your cap is a little crooked."

"Your apron straps are twisted."

"These little things count, dear. They make all the difference. I hate having to mention them."

Fortunately Elizabeth was not in her ward and juniors and seniors rarely met, but one could not avoid encounters with her on the stairs and in the passages. And then sometimes Kathleen was lent to a ward for the day, and if that ward happened to be Elizabeth's the soft, gentle pricking never ceased.

Then one day Kathleen felt sick, dizzy and hot. She dragged herself out of bed, sat through breakfast unable to try a mouthful of the lumpy porridge and collapsed in the passage. She had a high temperature and her pulse was fast. It was a case of gastritis, anaemia and a touch of flu. For a month she lay ill and when that was over the matron told her she was too delicate for the work and advised her to continue her convalescence at home and keep to a diet.

"But Marguerite won't have me there," Kathleen said to Elizabeth, "and there's no rest in that place."

"Don't worry, *chérie*. I'll see to it."

Elizabeth had a talk to her mother. Mrs Hughes was mellower now and less intolerant of Kathleen. Because she doted on Lisa she wanted Lisa's mother to be well. She had witnessed many scenes of Marguerite's harshness and she felt sorry for her youngest daughter.

"Marguerite, we must let her stay here quietly for a week or two," she said. "She was always delicate, poor thing. It's not her fault. I'll look after her."

To Marguerite this illness was Kathleen's fault, just a part of her general lack of stamina. With no pity she observed her chalky face, her slow walk and uncertain movements. Reluctantly she agreed.

Lying in the dingy room in the sombre house, visited daily by her sharp-tongued sister, worrying about what she was to do, was like a nightmare to Kathleen and she made no progress. "Why should she go on at me about being ungrateful? Why does she say that if it were not for her, Lisa would be at a charity school? If she hadn't brought the child to England she would have been with me at the Ursulines and Marguerite could keep her precious money." She always meant to speak these thoughts to Marguerite but when the time came she said nothing. Several times her mother found her in tears. One evening she was in the deepest despair. Marguerite had had a letter from Patrick, announcing that he was on his way home and had no intention of becoming a priest. Kathleen had been blamed for this.

Kathleen was dressed and packing when her mother found her. "I must leave here. I can't stay here another day. I shall never get better. Please, mother, help me to get away somewhere. Anywhere. I don't mind where I go but I must get out of this house. I shan't get better until I do. I'll never get better here. Oh please mother help me."

"I'll tell you what we'll do," said Mrs Hughes kindly. "I've got four pounds put by. Don't tell Marguerite. You go down to Brighton. I know a woman who lets rooms down there. You go to her. And I'll ask Elizabeth to send you some money."

Kathleen was gone in half an hour. Her relief gave her strength for the journey and the late search for the house. The woman, an Irish crony of Mrs Hughes in the Cardiff days, remembered her as a child and looked after her. When she was better she walked down to the sea. Alone, she sat on the pebbly beach and watched the white-edged waves. She liked it here. It was peaceful. Whatever happened she must get well and never go back to the boarding house. But she couldn't live on the others for ever and they hadn't the money to keep her in any case. And she couldn't go back to France for that would mean never seeing Lisa. And she must earn enough to pay for Lisa. What on earth could she do?

17

Patrick was like his father, easy-going, pleasure-loving and lazy. He was also obstinate. He had never exactly agreed to become a priest but he allowed himself to drift into it because he could think of nothing better, it would be an easier life than that of his mining uncle and he didn't wish to oppose his aunt in so many words. He was religious and would remain so because no speculations were ever likely to shake his faith and the training of the Christian Brothers was thorough. A little bored, he lived through the years of incarceration and routine, seeing the world only on his daily walks with the others through the town, or on the way to the cathedral on Sunday. For the rest of the time he was surrounded by distempered walls in large rooms where the windows were so high that looking up through them you could see nothing but sky. He could speak French, of course, but his ways were not French, for he had arrived in Saint-Jules long after his most formative period. To his superiors he seemed docile and backward. After he had consistently failed his preliminary exam he was told he would never get through. He was advised to become a lay brother in some order if he felt he had a religious calling.

This did not appeal to him. He had seen himself, as far as he ever thought of the future, as some kind of parish priest, living in the world, probably in Cardiff. The thought of a monastic life scared him. Afraid that he might be forced into it if he remained, without a word to Joseph or any of his schoolfellows, he ran away. He followed the main road which led out of Saint-Jules to the east until he arrived at a solitary farm set in the open country. There he asked for work.

He soon realised he would never save enough to get home and wrote to his aunt for money. Farm work was hard, the hours were long, and his lack of imagination prevented him from worrying greatly about the reception he would have in England. Anything was better than being stuck in this country place. He wanted to be in a big city. He had burnt his boats at the Christian Brothers and they wouldn't take him back now even if his aunt wanted. During the journey he chatted, smoked and looked at the girls. He spent an afternoon in Paris between trains. Excited by the tales the other boys had told him of the brothels there, hoping that some girl would come up to him, he loafed along the wide streets. On the boat he strolled around the deck and spat into the sea. He felt very happy. He was in the world and he would stay in it.

Marguerite took the matter as high tragedy. Her face was at its most mobile and her gestures were wide. She wept, she wrung her hands, she embraced him with love, she reproached him and she begged him to tell her exactly what had led him to take such a step.

"What did you do without any money? I was so worried about you. I imagined you hungry, wandering about, not knowing where to go. When they wrote and told me you had just disappeared like that I was terrified. Why did you not tell me you wanted to leave?" She saw herself as an indulgent guardian who could be confided in.

When she learned that he had suffered no hardships, far from being relieved, she grew angry that she should have worried for nothing. Her tone grew sharper. Mrs Hughes looked on with sympathy and fear. Both women felt he had done something disgraceful, they had wondered about it together, something to do with girls.

"It was just that I couldn't get through the exams, Auntie, and they said I'd never get through. Brother Gabriel told me I wouldn't and he said I'd have to be a lay brother."

"Nonsense," said Marguerite, who persisted in thinking him clever. "Of course you could get through. What could he have meant by saying such a thing? Are you sure he did say it? Patrick, had he any reason for having a down on you and wanting you to go? Had you done anything wrong? Were you in any kind of disgrace?"

"No Auntie. I don't think he had a down on me." He reflected over this for some time and then went on slowly. "He never said he had."

"Tell me the truth. It's far better to be honest. Was there some kind of a row?"

Again he thought. "No, I don't think it was a row."

"What was not a row? Then there was something?"

"Just what I told you."

"But did they send for you? What did they say?"

"Well, yes, they did send for me. But that's what I told you about."

"No, you did not. What happened?"

"That was when Brother Gabriel said I'd never get through."

"Patrick, you're concealing something. He could never have said that unless there was something else. Did they want you to leave for some other reason?"

He couldn't make out what she meant. He could think of nothing. He thought perhaps they had wanted him to leave. The fact that he was the oldest boy there and should have been moved on long ago, if only he had passed the exam, had made them mention the subject of leaving. But he had never quite made out what it was all about.

Marguerite was certain that this exam story was trumped up, or else that he had deliberately not tried for the exam for some hidden motive. A boy with his brains! And even now he was trying to look stupid. He must be deliberately deceiving her. He was being dishonest and untruthful to her, who had done everything for him. If only he would make a clean breast of it and tell her everything, whatever it was, she would forgive him and perhaps sympathise.

They let him stay and sleep in the kitchen. Marguerite was on a case, a part-time case which left her evenings free. When she was at home she kept talking to him, trying hard to wrest his secret from him. She told her mother to see that he did not go out alone. She was afraid of something. She called in Michael to help her. "He might tell his own father—another man."

Nothing had shaken her so much since her mother's second marriage. At night she could not get to sleep for a long time but lay brooding over the situation. It was not only that he would never be a priest, though that was bad enough. There was something sinister. She went over everything he had said looking for clues and finding them, hundreds of them. She pieced together several stories, each worse than the last. When sleep finally came she was beset with nightmares.

She gave him chance after chance. "If you do not want to tell me, if you are too ashamed, just say that there was something, that you did something wrong. I only want to know that. Just give some idea. I've always been your friend." But he did nothing but repeat the story of the exams.

She watched him hard, beholding in him the depths of slyness. His eyes now looked extremely shifty to her, those wide-open, vague, blue eyes which had once been her delight and into which she had read such sterling qualities. His slouching walk, the way he kept his hands in his pockets were to her the symptoms of furtiveness. Her dislike of his mother and assumption that she was a thoroughly bad lot made her reason that he had been corrupted early and that all the time she had known him he had been pretending he was what she wished him to be. His look of bewilderment and anxiety betrayed to her his guilty conscience and a pose of stupidity. He was going to the bad. He was beyond recall.

She could never believe she was wrong. If the facts contradicted her assumptions then they were wrong or somebody was trying to mislead her. Once she had an idea in her head, nothing external to her could shake it, although she was capable of the most sudden switches of opinion when there was apparently no cause. The only thing for Patrick to do was to invent some crime, to own to some misdeed. Had he done so he would have found her censorious but appeased and again affectionate. But he was not to know this. She imagined some such scene of explanation and reconciliation many times and this increased her bitterness when she saw that it was not to be. And when she realised this she told herself he deserved no consideration, he had played her false, he had betrayed her trust. With a harshness she had reserved for Kathleen only until now, she ordered him out of the house.

"You must go somewhere else. I do not care where. I cannot keep you another day. "

"But I haven't anywhere to go, Auntie. I haven't any money."

"Do not ask me for money. I've done everything I can for you. Go to your father. Go to your uncle in Wales. Go to your mother if you can find her, or to her mother. I do not care what you do. You're dishonest and ungrateful and I want nothing more to do with you."

219

Persuaded that she meant it and that there was nothing he could do, he rose and went to the door of the dark kitchen. Mrs Hughes looked unhappy. "Marguerite, we must give him some money."

"Let him go to someone else for money. And how are we to believe he has none? I believe nothing he says."

Bewildered, he shambled up the basement steps. They heard the front door close behind him. Mrs Hughes sobbed. Marguerite, stony and enraged, stared at her in silence.

18

Kathleen went to see the matron at the Royal Sussex County. Fortunately the matron was considerate and they were short of nurses. Kathleen told her she had begun to train and had then fallen sick.

"You don't look at all strong," said the matron, "but I'll tell you what we'll do. We'll give you a month's trial."

The month's trial was extended. She had a start on the other probationers because she had learnt something at Guy's. She stayed.

The pay was nominal during training, so that when you had a day or afternoon off you could barely afford to buy a meal or go to the pictures. Sometimes when Kathleen had to pay for shoe repairs she could not afford to eat out. She dreaded going into the dining room to be greeted with, "You in, Treherne? Thought it was your day off," and to have to admit that she had no money. Most of the other nurses received pocket money from home. Rather than face these remarks, although they were not meant unkindly, she went hungry.

It was not easy for her to keep up with the timetable or to remember exactly what had to be done. Being left-handed and having to lay the tray for dressings for a right-handed nurse she had to think of everything back to front, like those awful problems of clocks in mirrors, and that took time and made it impossible to do these things automatically. The daily round left one with no pause between tasks, no second in which to collect one's wits and ask oneself what had been forgotten, so that at first she was haunted throughout the day by the dread of some vital omission. Then, because her sisters were nurses, because nursing was a successful part of their lives and she knew they thought her a fool, she was sure she could never be good at it and she magnified its difficulties. Making beds, dusting, giving round the bed pans and cleaning them up, tidying the sluice, cleaning the bathroom taps, washing patients and assisting at dressings seemed simple enough in themselves but she always assumed that when she did them she was leaving out something, there must be a catch in it somewhere.

Her pale worried face and her nervous movements soon made her the chief victim of the staff nurse and the sister. She looked as though she had done something wrong and when they spoke to her she watched them, humble and frightened. They were the sort of women who became the friends of Marguerite and Elizabeth. Her good-heartedness often got her into trouble. If a patient asked for a bed pan, no matter what time of day it was or what she was doing she would hurry to get it for them at once, where other nurses might say, "Not now, there's no time. You should have asked earlier. Now you must wait till the other nurses come back." The patients knowing that she would never refuse always turned to her, so that scarcely a day passed without several of these appeals and as a consequence she was always late. She was afraid of hurting patients who were very ill, and she imagined, quite wrongly, that those nurses who tackled them with speed and efficiency must be hard, so that she herself always took ages over a blanket bath, holding each limb as though it were made of china and washing it very slowly with a gentle, circular movement. As she was in the Medical Ward, many of her patients were serious, lingering, hopeless cases with diseases of the heart, the liver, spinal trouble, consumption; though they were occasionally sent home for a time they came back again.

In time she went the round of the wards, men's medical, women's surgical, children's and outpatients. She spent three months in each, sometimes on nights and sometimes on days. Wards she had visited only when taking a hypodermic to be checked by a second staff nurse, and which had had the enchantment of foreign ground, now became her own territory. Wards she had worked in before, she felt were familiar and hers, and when she looked in for any reason it gave her pleasure to see the beds and lockers just as she had known them.

Her superiors continued to find slight fault with her but she made friends among her equals. Left to herself, because she was unaggressive and affectionate, she had no difficulty in getting on with people. In Saint-Jules nuns and girls had liked her equally. As time went on and her confidence increased in the absence of her sisters she enjoyed herself. When the sea was warm she went swimming during her off-duty hours.

Thomas had often held forth about a sense of humour. In Saint-Jules one of the teachers had said that the English were remarkable for their sense of humour and Kathleen believed that she possessed it. "There's nothing like a good laugh," she said. "I always try to look on the funny side." She not only laughed at every joke she heard, simple or subtle, long or short, she also went in search of them. When nurses giggled in a group she approached them. "What was that one?" She bought comic papers. So that such happiness as there is to be found in "being tickled" and "laughing till the tears roll down your cheeks" regularly came her way.

The death of her husband and the interference of her sisters had arrested her. She no longer read anything which needed concentration. Knowledge no longer charmed her. In her leisure moments she liked to do things well within her grasp such as jigsaw puzzles, crosswords and games of patience. The friends she preferred were of a maternal disposition and with them she liked to appear childlike, touching and often made little slips in grammar and pronunciation in order to hear their laughter and corrections. But despite this wish to keep herself at a level where she must be protected she had moments of observation and insight which her sisters never had. She had a far clearer idea of what they were like than either had of her. She summed them up in two phrases. "Marguerite should have been a lady of the manor. Elizabeth should have been a nun."

She enjoyed her time with the outpatients best, and because she was so good there she was kept on longer than usual. There she was less hustled and the atmosphere was not so charged. The differences in rank between staff nurses, under-nurses and probationers were partly waived and everyone was jolly. There were constant jokes with the doctors and the row of waiting patients. These patients were mostly poor, came back time and time again and she got to know them. She found them grateful, helpful, entertaining and glad to confide their troubles to her. They looked on her as a very efficient and responsible person and this was new to her. Because she had been ill and poor too she understood them. She was at her best with them. Feeling important and at ease she laughed and said, "What, you here again? What is it this time? Same old story? Go on!" The nurses had names for the regulars. "Whiskers is here today. Old Slowcoach has turned up," and these nicknames would make the uninitiated probationers roar.

Unfortunately the eye specialist singled her out for approval and every eye case among the outpatients was handed over to her. She had a horror of eye diseases and even of healthy eyes and needed every ounce of control she possessed to wash ulcerated lids and put in drops while appearing calm and cheerful.

She saw Lisa very infrequently and only for a weekend at a time, always in the hated boarding house. During her second year she begged that Lisa might come down to Brighton during the fortnight she had off from the hospital. She found lodgings where they could be boarded for fifteen shillings each a week. For months she saved for this.

Lisa was all the more pleased to see her mother because it meant a visit to the seaside. She found her much happier, stronger and, what was most surprising of all, a splendid swimmer. To see her breasting the waves, going right out to sea so confidently, was impressive, especially when Lisa herself was terrified of water for the moment. Kathleen tried to teach her to swim and float and induced her to wade out waist deep. After afternoons on the beach they came back to high teas of crab, fresh white bread thickly buttered, damson jam, iced buns and tea. The wallpaper was covered in flowers and looked very interesting to Lisa. After tea the cloth was cleared away and replaced by a thick, red cloth on which they played cards, betting with matchsticks. Kathleen saw to it that Lisa won, for the child was a very bad loser.

The landlady told Kathleen that the crabs and cakes would be extra. There were endless pennies to be found to put into slot machines and buy ice creams. As there was no other source of money she took her watch to a pawn shop. "Now, you stay outside," she said to Lisa.

"Are you going to buy something for me?"

"No dear, not exactly."

"Then why can't I go in?"

"Not this time, dear. It's business and it's very dull."

"It doesn't look dull in the shop. I know I wouldn't find it dull."

Her mother had never thwarted her in anything and she felt puzzled. She looked through the rows of wedding rings and engagement rings laid out on cream velvet, the opened jewel cases with brooches on red satin, the apostle spoons, the silver serviette rings, attractive as a whole because they glittered and there were many of them, but with no particular object she fancied, nothing one could play with or turn into anything. Beyond them she saw her mother take off her wristwatch; a real gold wristwatch, she had been told, with a real gold wrist band which expanded cleverly when you put it on or took it off because there was elastic concealed beneath the oblong sections. After that she could not see what happened because her mother moved over and her back hid her hands. Walking home she wondered. At last she asked.

"Mummy, did you sell your watch?"

"No dear."

"Why did you give it to the man?"

Kathleen was unable to think of a good reason. Unwillingly she resorted to the truth. "He gave me some money for leaving it there a little while and then later I'll pay it back and he'll give me the watch."

Lisa grew anxious. "Are you sure he'll keep it? Suppose he gives it to someone else for money? Why did you want the money?"

Her mother changed the subject, pointing to a little boat on the sea.

"Are you very poor? Are we all very poor?" asked Lisa. This question had been on her mind for some time.

19

The greatest influence on Marguerite now was the behaviour of the people she met on cases. She preferred to be in the artistic world, and by that she did not mean men and women of genius starving in garrets or applauded by a restricted circle. No, she meant the most famous and highly-paid actors, song-writers, novelists and portrait painters. She nursed many "stage people" as she called them. Having been very popular with one case, an actor, she was thereafter recommended to his friends.

At these houses she heard much talk of being "bohemian", "having to rough it", "having to pig it". She did not observe consciously that frequently the tiniest departure from the normal procedure of these very well run households, such as not being

224

waited on at table because the maid had her half day off, was excused in this way. But the phrases took her fancy and she realised that by using them you not only explained away your present activities with a fine air of frankness but you also suggested the highest standards at other times of your life. She appropriated the phrases and found them useful. From then on her snobbishness took a new twist. To be erratic and irregular were the signs of belonging to the very upper reaches or to the artistic world. Too strict an adherence to regularity was very middle class. This solved any problem due to the difference between her ideals and temperament.

Actors and actresses pleased her better than anyone. Not only did they dress beautifully and floridly and live as ceremoniously as the best, they also talked with animation and never ceased to act. She understood this very well for she had no fancy for people being "natural" and she believed that anyone with spirit kept up a show. You owed it to society to keep yourself at a pitch of tension and exhilaration in company. It was all a fine conspiracy, it had always been, and people like poor Kathie who rambled on about being natural and sincere and "yourself", whatever that might mean, merely betrayed their lack of grasp. Art itself continued to mean nothing to her for its own sake; she had no ear for music, no eye for painting and no interest in reading. But she admired the life you led if you pursued the performing arts successfully. She loved to hear rapid talk of brilliance and talent and genius.

In these houses she now developed a new idea of herself and her family. She acted too, but not the part of a nurse.

"My father was very artistic," she said. "We were a very bohemian family, travelling from place to place, all over the Continent. I remember as a child being presented to all sorts of famous people. And how upset my mother was when I took up nursing! But I'm very fond of my work. You meet all sorts of types and it's so fascinating studying them."

She continued her act at home in the boarding house. Mrs Hughes was often unable to understand what her daughter meant but she was glad to find her so happy and voluble. The old ladies were also pleased when Marguerite entertained them with another excuse for not starting the drawing room and the dining room. "I know you must find me dreadfully bohemian, but that's what comes of belonging to an artistic family. We've always been the same. And I do so love beautiful things. I've seen one or two chairs and oddments

I liked but I'm waiting until I can find just what I want. I know you will understand although many people might not. And sometime, when I have a moment, I simply must tell you exactly how I mean it to be."

For the moment, the drawing room was let as a double room and so was the dining room. But everyone believed that this was very temporary. Any day, any minute, Marguerite might hit on the right furniture and all would be changed. The past had been perfect, the future would be too, but for the present one must rough it and pig it for many sound reasons.

So it was with a sense of being as impulsive and inexplicable as the best that she suddenly decided to spend a fortnight between cases in Germany. She would go and see a Passion Play in Bavaria. She would take a friend, Nurse Fairbanks, with her for company and audience. Her mind was made up one day and she began her travels the next, laughing at Miss Fairbanks' amazement and reluctance.

"No, Betty dear," she said charmingly, for she hoped to use Miss Fairbanks in a nursing home scheme, "you must not say it is too short notice. I shall be bitterly disappointed. I've always longed to take you abroad and you will so love it. We all make up our minds suddenly, you know, we're a very bohemian family."

Mrs Hughes and Lisa came to Victoria to see them off. The train was not crowded and Lisa could sit in the compartment next to her aunt until the minute hand pointed to ten. Mrs Hughes stayed on the platform. Marguerite, distracted by the happiness of seeing a new country and making a sudden journey, looked round beaming at everyone, kept jumping up from her seat, leaning out of the window, sitting down again, addressing remarks to strangers in the carriage and outlining to Miss Fairbanks, for the benefit of all present, the history of her travels.

"We're always dashing abroad. It is in our blood. My father and mother used to travel a great deal and we grew up very cosmopolitan. As for Lisa here, her first language was Portuguese." She turned to the child and say her melancholy expression. "It will be the first time she has ever been left behind."

The train gave a lurch, there was a hiss of escaping steam. It was time for Lisa to go. "For two pins I'd take her," said Marguerite. She thought rapidly, not one thought after another, but all together. Lisa was going to Brighton to her mother. Marguerite had not altogether cared for the success of the last trip to Brighton and the tales of

Kathleen's marvellous swimming and the high teas. She wanted the child to be with her as often as possible. Besides, it was good for her to travel. She would not grow up as humble and unvarnished as her mother. And then the child looked as though she would like to go and it was sad to disappoint her. On an impulse she put her head out of the window.

"Mother, I shall take Lisa."

"Oh no, Marguerite. She hasn't a ticket. And what would you do for clothes? Besides, Kathie's expecting her tomorrow."

That decided it. "I think she had better come with me."

"But what about the ticket? And Marguerite, all she's got is the clothes she's standing in."

These obstacles meant nothing to Marguerite. She feared neither railway guards nor the lack of necessities. "Do not fuss, mother."

She motioned to Lisa to stay where she was. As the train began to move she shouted, "Explain to the others. They will understand. Poor child, I could hardly leave her behind."

No thought for Kathleen's disappointment entered her mind, and if it had it would have caused her no worry. She put an arm round Lisa's shoulders and smiled down at her confidentially. "You knew you could trust me. That was what you were hoping, was it not?"

Until they reached Ostend, Marguerite was fairly composed although she had sudden bouts of inconsequent talk. But once on foreign soil a feeling that rules and regulations and timetables could now be discarded came over her and Miss Fairbanks and Lisa grew alarmed. In the first place she made them sit in a first class compartment and put up a great fight when the guard tried to make her pay a supplement before withdrawing to third. Whenever the train stopped she alighted at once to procure rolls and coffee, lingering in the refreshment room until the very last moment, jumping onto the train as it was leaving the platform, angry that it had hurried her and bearing away cups and saucers she should have returned. Several times, thinking her aunt had been left behind, Lisa began to cry. Five minutes later, Marguerite appeared in the passage, balancing cups and food. "I got on farther down. You should not worry."

In Brussels there was a pause of three quarters of an hour between trains. Marguerite decided she would go shopping and sightseeing. She took her time.

Miss Fairbanks and Lisa remained in the station with instructions to board the train as soon as it came in. They secured seats and chatted half-heartedly for a time. Then the worries began. Miss Fairbanks kept watching the hands of the clock and looking up and down the platform. Lisa bit the skin round her nails and kept asking, "Is she there yet? Can you see her?" As the train went off they lost all hope.

"Never mind, dear," Miss Fairbanks said consolingly. "She'll catch the next train. We'll wait for her in Cologne."

Five minutes passed, ten minutes passed. People walked down the passage and each time Lisa watched hopefully. A quarter of an hour had passed and it was clear Marguerite would never come. All traces of the town had been left behind and fields and trees rushed by. Lisa had little faith in a reunion in Cologne, for she might not be on the next train either or the station might be so crowded that they would miss her. This time she did not cry but sat in silence, her throat dry, her eyes fixed unseeing on the landscape.

Suddenly the door slid back and there was Marguerite, furious. "The door between the first class and the luggage van was locked," she declared as though it were a personal insult to her. "I had such difficulty in finding the man and then he had the coolness to say he would not open it. He was very unpleasant and I had to tip him. They expect tips for everything. And Betty dear, why did you choose seats so far forward?"

"But you told me to. You said the front was much less crowded."

"I'm sure I never said that." She sat down with a sigh. She felt that she always had to do the battling and people were always letting her down with their stupidity. She glared at her friend. Then seeing two strangers in the compartment who were watching her with interest, her expression changed. She smiled at them, pointed at Lisa. *"La petite. On a oublié sa valise!"*

Then, since there was an audience, in her best accent—just in case they knew English well enough to appreciate it—she said loudly to Mrs Fairbanks. "What a rush! You'll think us a very mad family indeed. But as I was saying we've always been very bohemian and cosmopolitan. You'll laugh when you see what I've got."

Producing a yard and a half of blue and white striped cotton, which looked very ordinary, she praised it. "This is just what I wanted. A beautiful piece of stuff. I had to try several shops before I found it." She laid it on the seat and began to cut, folding it over at

228

the top and making a rough hole for the neck. "But won't it be too short that way?" said Miss Fairbanks.

"No dear, of course not. And one wants plenty of fullness at the sides." She tried it against Lisa. "It may look short like that but I meant it to. I shall put a deep blue border all round the bottom. It will look very smart."

By the time they reached Oberammagau the dress was finished. Marguerite's talk half-persuaded Lisa that it was lovely, although the stiches showed and it was extraordinarily wide. But when she changed into it in the lavatory she found one side was higher than the other and it felt peculiar.

"There you are, you see," said Marguerite when she saw it on her. "It fits perfectly. It's meant to be wide like that. Children like plenty of freedom. And naturally I mean to make a belt for it so she can gather it in a bit. Does it feel comfortable? Yes, I knew it would." She gave a long, low laugh, the usual prelude to a confidence. "We're the kind of family who can turn our hands to anything, though I cannot think why, because we never thought we would have to work and were waited on hand and foot as children. I'm always running up little dresses for her. You see it takes me next to no time."

Miss Fairbanks, a middle-aged, good-natured, sensible woman, was beginning to wonder. When they reached their destination she noticed that Marguerite spoke to porters and people of whom she asked the way in French. This was surprising because she had told her she spoke fluent German. At last her curiosity was too strongly aroused to keep silent, "Why do you speak French to everyone, Marguerite?"

Marguerite gave her a look of suspicion and then laughed as though there was some joke. "Ah, you see, these people are Southern Germans, so near France that many of them speak French as well as German. And they prefer you to speak French to them. It's something to do with the war, you know."

"But this isn't near the French border. And they sound as though they're speaking German to each other."

"No, it's not very near the border, I know. But it is one of those provinces like Alsace Lorraine, always being fought over for centuries, sometimes on one side, sometimes on another, sometimes divided."

"Oh, really? But it sounded like German to me, though of course, I don't know."

"No, dear, naturally you cannot tell."

"But that man you asked didn't seem to know what you were saying!"

"Betty dear. I cannot understand why you keep on about it. The fact of the matter is that the people here, while understanding both French and German, speak a very peculiar dialect of their own, and the less educated ones, such as that man, cannot understand anything else. You cannot expect me to know every little dialect. To someone like you, who have never travelled before, it may seem strange."

From that time on Miss Fairbanks took everything Marguerite said with a pinch of salt. She was not the first to do so. But those people who saw through Marguerite did not necessarily cease to like and even to love her. Where her stories had once compelled their admiration they now held their interest as a kind of show. She was the sort of person who provided an endless topic of conversation to others. They would criticise her, laugh at her and, usually when the time came, find themselves doing just what she wanted them to do. When she had some scheme on hand the thickest of skins covered her; she saw nothing but the object in view and she heard nothing but the dictates of her will. At these times her face was her greatest asset, for those who were being exploited and bullied, especially if they had not known her long, would say to themselves as they watched the mobile mouth and frank deep grey eyes, "After all, she has a heart of gold."

And in many ways Miss Fairbanks became indebted to Marguerite. It was she who procured lodgings, although everywhere was full and she had not booked, by working on the feelings of the landlady. It was she who, when told there were absolutely no seats for the play, refused to take "no" for an answer.

"I booked them through the Catholic Travel Agency a very long time ago. This is most extraordinary. You must have made some mistake. Months ago. I am sure they have not tripped up."

The booking clerk fortunately spoke both French and English. "We have no record here."

"Do you think I would come all this way, without booking seats? I shall take the matter up with the Agency as soon as I return. I do not like creating a fuss but this is too much. My poor little niece has been looking forward to it for ages. She will never get over the disappointment. I cannot understand what has happened to the bookings."

Somehow three seats were found.

20

The more Elizabeth saw of Marguerite the more she decided to be on her own. On finishing training she rapidly became the favourite nurse of the agency to which she belonged. The best cases came her way. Every week she made at least four guineas plus her board and lodging. She bought second-hand furniture cheap and sold it to friends for more. She took out a mortgage with a building society and began a boarding house of her own. This was in a better street than the other and nearer to Victoria Station. There was a drawing room, a dining room, and a housekeeper lived in the basement and looked after the tenants.

A crimson stair carpet, watercolours in gilt frames and a polished table in the hall proclaimed that this was a superior place. Gilt mirrors, electric fittings which looked like candles on the walls, brocades, silks, Louis Quinze armchairs and fringed pelmets made the first impression of the drawing room more favourable. And though the brocades were faded, the gilt tarnished and the chairs uncomfortable on closer acquaintance, the faint shabbiness enhanced the feeling of class. These things might have been in the family for years. This was decidedly not the comfortable opulence of the *nouveau riche*. And Miss Elizabeth Reilly was like her place, faded like the brocade, pretty, with the air of another unspecified century, a lady, impoverished perhaps but of good family.

Rents were higher than at the other boarding house and meals were provided. Elizabeth was seldom there for the night. But when any trouble arose she came and dealt with it in person, handling lodgers with steely sweetness. She was driven to make money and scheme. She was more than resigned to spinsterhood. But the blue eyes seemed several shades paler under the heavy lids which now looked like creased thin paper and the fatigue which they displayed was not altogether physical. Some violence had been done to her feelings by her will. There had been some struggle which she had probably not realised and now those aesthetic reactions and

231

aspirations had been given a twist. Her face had not the dramatic tension of Marguerite's, but it was never in repose. Each perfect feature, each tired muscle, was no longer itself but a manifestation of her character, tight, watchful and fussy. With her eyes open she entered the cage of accounts, planned overdrafts, electricity and gas bills, mortgages and auction sales. There was little time in the day when she was not handling someone, her housekeeper, the furniture men, the bank manager, the patient or the doctor. So that her original charm was not turned on consciously as part of her business. She must be extra nice because the wages she paid were too small or the tip she was giving was sixpence instead of a shilling or the rent she was charging was high. Little sentences, little sighs and little smiles came from her as gratuities. Always she was on the alert.

When alone she did not idle. On odd bits of paper and the backs of envelopes she did sums with a rapid, sloping hand and beautifully formed figures. She mended, darned, took in, let out and remade. No dreams and fantasies beset her as they did her eldest sister, but she was at the mercy of her relentless nervous energy. Her only relaxation was prayer.

In church she drove the thought of work away when she was not actually praying that some scheme might come right. After communion the same feeling of refreshment automatically came. After confession the same feeling of a necessary duty performed and a soul free from stain. Sometimes, on some special occasion such as High Mass on Palm Sunday or the stirring Tenebrae, she experienced an overwhelming pleasure and consolation, emptying her head of verbal thoughts and shutting her eyes. It was like sleep with the lightest and gentlest of dreams, a release from herself. At other times prayer was similar to business, but effortless, a rapid run through the rosary, the gaining of indulgences as an insurance against a long spell in Purgatory, the set ejaculations. She did not deal directly with God and she did not make her own prayers. She outlined to one of His agents, a special protector or protectress of hers, what her prayer was for, to whose account it should be placed, and then proceeded to say the Our Father's, Hail Mary's and Glory Be's. Repeating the well-known words was restful and mechanical, bringing always the visual associations she had had since childhood; the kingdom of clouds and haloes, the earth like a globe with mountains and oceans, the daily bread as a white loaf with a rich brown crust, the trespassers in ancient Jewish dress in a sort of oasis with palm trees. These simple pictures came into her mind like lantern slides onto a screen, pushing away reckoning and care.

She nursed Sir Walter Snell at the Savoy. He was a large red-faced man with a taste for horses and women. He found her pretty and roared with laughter at her attempts to keep him away from the bottle. He liked to be treated as a naughty boy, in fact it was her use of the word naughty which first stirred in him a pleasurable sensation of his maleness and her femininity. He could see she was not very young but a good deal younger than himself. He discovered her one weakness, putting money on horses, and by encouraging her in this he had a delightful sense of corrupting. Interest in horses bound them together and he smiled and chaffed when she hurried out for the latest results unasked. He liked the Irish because he saw them as a nation of tweed-clad horse-breeders and dealers. Wagging a thick finger at her he said, "It's your Irish blood coming out," when he gave her a tip for the next race. He made bets with her; when she lost he refused payment; when she won he took the occasion of giving her a nice present. He had seen no other woman since his illness and it was inevitable that his hand should seek hers and hold it tight in a clammy heat. "You're a good-looking woman, you know."

Each time this happened she withdrew her bony, capable hand gently and shook her head at him as though he had been at the drink again. He was not the first patient to have tried this on and she took it in a very professional spirit. So handled, the situation was stabilised, Sir Walter assuming that he had not been really rebuffed, Elizabeth knowing she could deal with him. The little skirmishes became a ritual and between them they talked of horses and races and argued about the taste of medicine and the ill-effects of drink.

When he was better he insisted that he needed her during his convalescence and took her down to his house in the country. Here the nature of her work changed. She was no longer a nurse but a companion housekeeper. As his health improved he asked friends for the weekend. "Miss Reilly, I leave everything to you. You order the food and talk to the cook." His former housekeeper had gone and he found excuses for not getting another. "And Miss Reilly, you *must* come down to dinner with us. You can't leave me all alone, you know. Might have a relapse. And who'd be there to stop me drinking?"

She took her place at the head of the table in evening dress. She kept the conversation going when it flagged. There was no one present who was likely to question the interest of her little sentences for all were unused to women whose conversational rôle was a kind of first aid, the prevention of arguments and the smoothing over of differences and the leading away from anything in questionable taste. At the same time she did not feel liable to speculation what her relation to old Walter was. She was happiest when other women were present and to them, while the men were downstairs with the port, she kept confessing from time to time when there was an opening, "I shall only be here for a very short time. After all he is much better now and does not really need a nurse." She insisted to him that she must always be introduced as Nurse Reilly.

He had increased her wages, he made her presents and whenever she spoke of leaving he protested. "I'd be stranded. Look here, some people are coming down and I must have someone here to entertain them." When they were alone for dinner, facing each other across a polished table, made smaller by the removal of leaves, she was glad of the chaperoning presence of the servants. When they withdrew to the drawing room with its sporting prints and decanters and glass the skirmishing began, increasing as the decanter grew emptier. He had no worry about repeating himself. "Did I ever tell you, you were a good-looking woman? You need a man to look after you. Now don't be shy, I won't hurt you. Come over here. Aren't you going to be nice to me?"

She had one card she could always play when he seemed unmanageable. "I shall really have to go."

One evening he asked her to marry him. He saw her as a capable woman well suited to running his house and looking after him, desirable too for a short time, and sensible enough after that to let him have other women without making a fuss, not that he mentioned that particular part of the plans. He was certain too that her straitlaced ways were simply put on so as to get him to marry her and he looked forward to her pleased acceptance and a first embrace. Throughout dinner he smiled and smirked. As soon as they were alone he came to the point. As he spoke he came nearer and nearer and she could smell his breath and the cloth of his jacket. He placed his hand on her bare arm and suddenly pressed his soft, wet mouth against hers.

Never in her life had she been kissed before. She had been engaged twice in the Cardiff days and the fiancé had been allowed no more than to hold her hand. The horrid proximity of this coarse man, the smell of drink, the sound of heavy breathing, the moist pressure on her arm and above all the sudden kiss, were loathsome. She jumped back. No thought of the advantages of marrying him were in her mind. She shuddered, locked her hands together and looked at him with repulsion. Never had anyone dared. Never had she dreamt. Never, never, never. There was something she had set out to avoid, something she had not thought of consciously since she read those books in Madame de Chantabrie's library, something which was the blot and shame on the human race, something which explained to her fully the meaning of original sin, something from which she herself was singularly free, and it had suddenly approached her. She must remove herself at once from it, from the sight of his swollen cheeks, his boiled eyes, his loose full mouth, those two dreadful, shining lips which should never have touched hers.

She left the room without giving an answer. She had forgotten there was a question. Thank God she had never married. Thank God she had never made it lawful that such a thing should happen regularly—and worse. In her room, with a feeling of nausea, she prepared for bed. She was far too accustomed to activity to sit in a chair and think over what had happened. Fortunately removal from the scene of the crime made the feel of the incident grow fainter. The shock and loathing passed. She mastered them and hastily covered them over with her reason to lessen the pain. A man had attempted to kiss her. It was the first time that had happened and it would be the last.

21

Lisa was ill. A leaden apathy had seized her or rather had seized her surface layers for underneath dreads and fears had never been more vigorous. First she felt tired for a few days, so tired that she had to drive herself to get through the most ordinary things. Then she vomited and then a small red spot appeared on her wrist, growing day by day. Each time she remembered it, in class or in

235

chapel, she lifted up her cuff and saw it worse than she had thought, and her mind dwelt on sores and ulcers such as Job had been tried and plague spots and the black death. She would try to drive these thoughts away because when they came she felt her heart thumping and a kind of suffocation which she saw as one of the heavy grey clouds, which so often hung motionless outside the window, now filling her inside.

The spot, a ring of spots, was diagnosed as ringworm. As she heard this horrible name the cloud inside her thickened and grew darker. What did the "worm" part mean? Was it some living thing? Was it that dread disease of which King Herod had died, becoming all worms? It was infectious and the nuns decided to send her home. With no word of comfort, the dormitory nun, the dreaded and hateful Sister Aloysius, told her she was to be sent home at once. She thought they were probably expelling her. They had spoken of it so often. And though she hated this place she dreaded expulsion because it was supposed to leave a permanent blot on your name and no other school would ever take you after that and what could become of you if you could not go to school as other children did?

Sitting on the edge of the bed, afraid to ask questions, she watched Sister Aloysius putting her clothes in a suitcase, angrily, hurriedly. It seemed that the nun considered this awful affliction some sort of crime. Apparently it cast a bad reflection on her home. No child had ever had this sort of thing before. The type of child who got it was not the type they cared for here.

Because she was only nine they decided that someone should go with her to the bus and she was handed over to one of the lay sisters, one of the ones she had seen only in chapel before, because she had nothing to do with the school part of the building. Walking up the road to the bus stop, this nun said not a word. She had a heavy placid face and she did not look as though she were thinking about anything. She placed the suitcase in charge of the conductor and walked away. Lisa did not know whether to say goodbye or not. She thought it better to say nothing.

Waiting for the bus to start she looked at the ridges on the floor, noting the matchsticks and bus tickets wedged in, setting herself technical problems of how one would get them out in the quickest and neatest way if one had to. Technicalities and arithmetic were her greatest consolation and when things went wrong, as they always did lately, she would make her mind dwell on extraordinary, fantastic problems, such as how to throw a towel over a beam so that it would be looped over it twice. In the *Children's Encyclopaedia* she had seen a picture of the Australian boomerang and longed to learn its secrets. To be able to master your environment by skill and calculation was an idea to which she clung in a world of unreason. As the bus began the journey the throb of the engine brought back the wretched dread.

She knew she had failed. She was a dreadful failure and she believed it must be her own fault because she had failed to understand something. Plunged suddenly away from the delights of France and French food and attention and love and admiration into the greyness of England and watery boiled potatoes, with eyes in them and patches of black, and the loathing of the nuns, what appalled her most was the feeling that she could not cope with her environment. She was unpopular with everyone. Something about her was hateful. She was one of those people who would never be liked.

What in fact had happened was this: her French precocity and almost sophistication had made her seem strange and her aunt's success in paying reduced fees had made the nuns see her as some charity child. The French side manifested itself in various ways; she disliked games; she could not bear to lose—after all, in Saint-Jules all the girls had been livid when they lost–; she adored lessons and books, plaguing the class mistress to teach her long division of money, putting up her hand at every moment to ask a new question or give the right answer; she had always been first in class by a very wide margin; she had manifested a contempt for England and the English. After her first confession, walking back to the convent with Sister Martin, she had been told that her soul was now as white as snow and to illustrate this the nun said, "like a white flower" and pointed to some daisies on a scruffy patch of common beside them. Lisa took one look at them and said with distaste, "the flowers are always faded here," thinking of the flowers cascading profusely over the scented walled gardens near the Pyrenees.

But paying less fees than the others was her chief crime. To atone for that she should have been humble and grateful. But how was she to know? Her aunt's tales led her to believe that she came from the highest family and her father had been an engineer of great repute who threw great bridges over the mouth of the sea in Cardiff. So that when she put up her hand in class and the nun said, "Stop showing off" and all the girls laughed, she was amazed because no thought of showing off had been in her mind. And later when the nun said, "The airs and graces you give yourself! When you're only here out of charity, when you're paying less than anyone else!" she believed that this was a malicious lie.

She had put up a long fight. She had answered back, she had even thrown a pencil case at the nun. But in the end they had won by a series of terrible punishments. She had been locked in a cupboard, she had been whipped often, daily her knuckles had been rapped during music lessons, the nun coming down on them with a thin knitting needle every time she played a wrong note. She had been pulled from her desk by the ear and sent sprawling into a corner while all the others laughed. She had been kept behind from picnics. She had been put at the side table while the others had a birthday party. And all for offences which many others had committed without receiving more than a rebuke. And besides these punishments were the daily slights and snubs and deprivations which mounted up and up until scarcely an hour passed without a physical or mental attack.

By way of explanation the nuns spoke of a healthy naughtiness, a naughtiness which sprung from a good heart and high spirits and which, apparently, the greatest saints had displayed in their young days, and they contrasted this with her unhealthy, sneaking ways, because she never romped about and shouted, because she liked to spend her recreation reading a book, because she always looked as though she were thinking of something. The unfairness of this, for she had never sneaked or lied, goaded her into outbursts at first, but now she said nothing at all.

She had no allies among the girls. The idea that she was of a lower order than themselves had sunk in and it pleased them because they were fed up with her brightness in class. Her French, now almost vanished, had made them laugh and left a legend of her funny foreign ways. It had not improved matters when she said, "I can speak two languages. You can only speak one." Besides, like all children, they were conscious of the advantages of having a permanent scapegoat.

She had begun to tell her aunt and Marguerite had not listened, had not believed her. She had never told her mother because she saw her so rarely and her mother at these times was bent on giving her treats and she was bent on enjoying them. Besides, she did not think of her as someone who would fight for you. And in any case the convent was not all the world or all of time. There were the holidays in the boarding house or by the sea or abroad. Suddenly when things were past bearing they came to an end and you were somewhere else. And in the boarding house no one spoke of what had been happening while she was away or asked her how she had been getting on. They were very busy fitting new lodgers into rooms and moving others out. Now she told no one anything and she could no longer see the position clearly herself. She might have committed some appalling, nameless crime without knowing it perhaps. England was a very mysterious place, dull and half-lit, grey and ominous. France she did not remember well but it was certainly different.

The bus went through Stratford and Bow, along endless ugly roads, some with tramlines, some without. It passed a chemical factory which filled the air for a mile around with the stench of gasses and decay. As it seeped into the bus Lisa's dejection increased and she felt that she was soon to die. It was the only terrible punishment left, she had had all the others. She raised her cuff and saw the ring of spots and turned her eyes away. She looked so pale and full of trouble that the bus conductor smiled at her. This was the last straw. Other people had smiled at her and changed. He was smiling because he had not heard all about her, he had not yet learnt from the nuns the full measure of her awfulness and hatefulness. She could not return his smile but stared up at his face waiting for the expression to change as it must. A trifle put out by her unwavering concentration on his face he turned away whistling and swung himself up the stairs to the top deck. She knew then that he too had seen her for what she was.

She knew she appeared horrible but she did not feel wicked. She would not have minded feeling wicked because that was in one's hands. But this was like being ugly or having a nasty smell or something. She felt wronged but not guilty. It was her lack of a sense of guilt which had made the nuns dislike her more and assume they could not get at her. Night after night, no matter what they said, she had repeatedly dreamt she went to heaven and there was nothing surprising or unexpected to her in that. And even now, when she felt lower than she had ever been before, she knew that although she was going to die very soon as an expiation for something she had not done, she would go straight to heaven. But heaven was a dreary

239

place, in colour more like England than France, with nothing but clouds and playing harps and enjoying the presence of God. She knew this enjoyment could not be hers. And even though you couldn't enjoy it you must still go on and on for all eternity. She would like to stay in the world, not this part of it, for a long time, and then she would like to end.

"But if I *asked* God if I could stop. Supposing I didn't want to go on in heaven for ever, would he let me?" she had asked at catechism lesson and all had thought she was trying to show off as usual.

"You'll be very lucky if you get there," said the nun.

This was nonsense. She had done nothing, nothing specified against the commandments. She might have offended some crazy English worldly code but that had no bearing on the matter. God had a fine sense of justice and would certainly see things her way. She never confused God's judgement with the present prejudices of the nuns. As far as God was concerned all she hoped for was that she would be let off part of her everlasting reward.

When she arrived home after the long, long bus journey, the sky hung low over Pimlico and it looked as though it would remain like that indefinitely, in sullen refusal to shed its moisture and disperse. Walking down the square, avoiding the lines of the paving stones, for at this moment omens and observances were of great import, she kept pausing while she set down her heavy case. Leaving it outside the front door she walked softly down the area steps and looked through the kitchen window. The light was not on and it was very dark inside but probably her grandmother would be there. She tapped against the pane.

Mrs Hughes was surprised to see her, and more surprised to see her draw back when she tried to kiss her. "Well, darling? And what are you doing here at all?

"They told me to go, Grandma." Lisa was anxious not to spread her infection here (she would have quite liked to spread it at school).

"Why? What do you mean? Are you in trouble darling?"

"Yes, Grandma." She showed her the spot. "They said they couldn't have it in the school. It's ringworm, Grandma."

Mrs Hughes switched on the light to have a better look. "Oh, that's nothing. Just a little sore."

Lisa was not to be consoled so easily. Her grandmother would say anything to cheer her. "It's one of the infectious and contagious diseases."

240

There was a piece of apple tart over from lunch but she didn't fancy it. She could eat nothing. "I don't feel very well. I was sick the other day. Where's Auntie?"

"Out, darling."

"Will she be home today?"

"Yes, later on."

"Will she have a room for me or are you full up?" By that she meant that in her present condition she ought not to share a bed with her aunt in the basement.

Marguerite did not come in until after supper. She was angry that Lisa had returned so unexpectedly. She picked up the wrist roughly. "This is nothing. What did they mean by sending you home for this? Why didn't they write? Did they tell you anything about you going back?"

"No. I don't think they mean me to go back."

"I'll write to them and send you back tomorrow."

"But perhaps I'm expelled, Auntie."

"Nonsense. What for?"

"It's ringworm. I think they meant me to be expelled."

"Lisa, what do you mean? Have you done anything wrong?"

"Yes. They think I have."

"What?"

"Oh, a lot of things. I can't remember. I spoke in the dormitory last week. It was an act of disobedience. And now I've got ringworm." It seemed to her just as sensible to expel her for ringworm as anything else. And as she had not long to live it would not matter that the blot on her character would prevent her from going to other schools. She was far too unhappy to cry or complain. Neither her aunt's cross voice nor her grandmother's puzzled frown made any difference.

22

Some of Marguerite's cases lasted a month, some several months. Between them she stayed at "83", as they always called the first boarding house, after its street number. If the cases were in London she came home to "83" as much as possible. She was growing very lazy there. She hated any form of housework at all now and could scarcely bring herself to boil a kettle. She had in a doctor friend to look at her mother's legs, decided they were now better and made her mother work harder, cooking meals for favourite lodgers and cleaning out the ground floor rooms.

When Marguerite was forced to spend more than a couple of days in the house a feeling of weariness and depression came over her. She would lie in bed until eleven or twelve each morning, dulled, feeling that there was nothing to get up for; resenting the muddle of her bedroom, the half-filled suitcases on the floor, the lack of a proper wardrobe, the bits of furniture stored there; and brooding on the worse muddle in the kitchen, the muddle on the first floor, the second floor, up the stairs, everywhere. She blamed her mother and sometimes she blamed the cleaner. Elizabeth was the real culprit but she avoided blaming her. As Elizabeth's house was so fine she had a habit of dumping on Marguerite odd pieces of furniture, which she had bought in auction lots to secure better pieces. With a smile and a murmur of, "this will be exactly what you need for No. 7 or No. 8," she would graciously add, "and you need not pay me. We will call it a long loan." Very often Marguerite was not there when the dumpings took place.

To atone for this Elizabeth lent a pound or two when Marguerite was behind with the mortgage and feared bailiffs. They never quarrelled and they were in no way intimate. Their behaviour to each other had become excessively formal. They addressed each other as *chérie* and also *chère amie* and each encounter was a kind of miniature business conference. Elizabeth found Marguerite appallingly untidy and incompetent but she said no word of this to her sister or to herself.

Mrs Hughes did not like the new régime of hard work for herself and the lack of sympathy when she mentioned her feet. But in other ways Marguerite had become much more easy going. She watched her mother drink her beer quite happily. She was affable to the faithful cronies who came in for cups of tea. She was indifferent to the times of meals or anything else. Her energy was at a low ebb and she would sit for hours on the bed in the kitchen, while her mother worked, talking dreamily and vaguely.

Marguerite now had false teeth, but with a flair for appearance she had had her dentures made an exact replica of the teeth she had lost, with the same irregularities and the same big eye teeth, so that her mouth was still square and fanged when she smiled and all the characteristics were intact. She was marvellously well preserved. She looked older than her age up to thirty-five, but after that she scarcely changed. She looked experienced, mature and in no way girlish, but the coarse strong mottled skin was well moulded to the bones beneath, the square line of the jaw was as defined as ever, and lines and creases did not show up as clearly as they did on Elizabeth's soft clear complexion. There was not one grey hair on her brown head and the eyebrows were still dark. Her attitude to ageing varied from day to day. Sometimes she said she was thirty and sometimes she admitted she was over forty. In any case she felt she was different from other women and these things mattered little to a person like her. She believed that if she wanted to, with a touch of make-up and one thing and another, she could look as young as she liked. And there was no doubt that when she did take a bit of trouble no one could have guessed her age.

Most of the time in the house she did not bother about her appearance and when she lay idly in bed she removed her dentures, placing them under her pillow, so that when Lisa came in she was surprised at the face of a wicked old lady which she saw. "Turn away, dear," Marguerite would order, fishing under her pillow, and when Lisa next set eyes on her, the vision of age had disappeared. She kept Lisa busy running errands, often to the tobacconist—for Marguerite was now a chain smoker—or taking cups of tea up to the old ladies or going over to Elizabeth's house with notes. She hated to see anyone relaxing.

After one of these bouts of torpor in the home came news of a case in Oporto. She changed at once, rose early, combed her bobbed hair smartly, put on some powder with a skilled hand, a dark purplish powder which exactly matched her skin, and appeared in her one good suit. Her brain began to work and she made many plans.

"Mother, I shall take Lisa with me. She's still very run down and cannot go back to the convent till next term in any case. I shall leave her in Saint-Jules on my way out. Then Anthony—" (this was Michael's youngest boy) "—can go out there too to the seminary. Now I must arrange it all quickly."

Patrick was in Australia having migrated on a scheme which gave one a free passage and a guaranteed job. Joseph, who had left the seminary to become a waiter in Paris, was about to join him. She never spoke of either of them. Anthony, who was two years older than Lisa, had been placed in a boys' school near the relations in the north.

She left the greatest muddle behind her, her bed unmade, her older clothes all over the floor, lids of tins piled high with cigarette ends. She left the tidying to other people now, at the moment to her mother. On the journey her energy came back with its original force, and more. She talked with great animation. Lisa had never known her more charming.

In Paris she looked up old friends, showed them the child, spun stories of the family prosperity, spent money extravagantly in the big stores, money which should have paid off bills and money which had been borrowed, and laughed and smiled. The corners of her mouth turned up. The lower contours of her cheeks were like two semi-circles. She went late to bed and rose early and she never felt tired.

Having left Lisa with the Ursulines she journeyed on through Spain to Oporto, talking to her fellow travellers in a mixture of French and Italian, grieving over their worries, offering to do them services, opening and shutting windows from time to time, darting out into the corridor to make new contacts.

A car, complete with liveried chauffeur, met her at the station and drove her to an estate a short way out of the town. The house was set high on a slope above the Douro. Around it spread acres of gardens and vineyards with many whitewashed outbuildings where grapes were stored, sorted and pressed and where the great casks were made. One could see everything, owing to the nature of the slope, as though it were a picture painted before perspective had been mastered. A thin cloud covered the March sun and the light was soft and cast no shadows. There were no lines of brightness in the river below but an even, overall glaze. The still tidy landscape was welcoming and the lady of the house was standing on the porch ready to greet her.

"Nurse Reilly! You must be very tired. I can't tell you how glad I am to have *you* at last. Mother wrote so much about you."

There was a solemn pause after this because her mother, a former patient of Marguerite's, was now dead.

Mrs Etheridge took Marguerite by the hand and led her into the study. The walls were lined with well-bound books, dark polished boards were overlaid with small oriental rugs, a heavy centre table was surrounded by old Portuguese high-backed, carved chairs. In this sombre and studious setting, seated near the window on two more modern chairs, they found they had a great deal to talk about. They looked at each other, down onto the river, ahead over to the opposite slopes. Tea and sandwiches were placed on a small table by Marguerite's elbow.

She described the last weeks of the dead mother. "I was so fond of her. She was the sweetest person I ever nursed. I always put sugar in her tea and then she would look at me so nicely and say, 'But nurse, I don't take sugar!' And I can assure you, Mrs Etheridge–" (here she gave one of her straight looks which seemed to spring from the fullest of hearts) "—Yes, I really can assure you that she suffered nothing, no pain at all, and she had no idea she was going to die."

Mrs Etheridge's eyes were moist as she replied, "I am so glad."

Marguerite continued. "She was such a darling. Everyone loved her. Do you know you are very like her. The most extraordinary resemblance."

"It's odd you should say that. Most people thought we were very unlike."

"Nonsense! I should have known who you were in a second. You have just the same expression. I do not feel I am among strangers at all."

In no time Marguerite had taken on the aspect of an old cherished friend of the family. She asked for details about her present patient and as she listened her face unconsciously imitated the changing expressions of the speaker, her lips moving to form the same words. "How very sad for you," she said at last. "What a tragedy. I must do all I can to help you. We must spare him in every way we can."

The patient was Mrs Etheridge's brother, Alan Banks. Like Marguerite she was the eldest of a large family and she adored her brothers. Alan Banks was dying of cancer and he did not know it. The growth had attacked the bowel and the consequent diarrhoea was wasting him away. It had been diagnosed too late for operation.

"He's so weak," she said, "that he has to be looked after all the time. And naturally in his condition he has no control and there is constant cleaning. But there are two Portuguese men, male nurses, who will see to most of that. I want you to be spared that sort of work. You will be the responsible person to supervise the men and you must ask me for anything you need."

For the moment Marguerite scored her greatest success with Mrs Etheridge. This lady, predisposed to like her, now looked on her as her greatest friend. The patient, grey, cadaverous and gloomy, decided she would be very competent but had little hope of extracting from her the secret of his illness. The husband who was away on business much of the time played a secondary rôle in this house. If his wife liked the nurse then he must too.

Marguerite attended to her patient with the greatest devotion, but thanks to the male nurses much of her time was free. She was introduced to the regular visitors and she often accompanied Mrs Etheridge on visits. It happened that she took a genuine dislike to one of Mrs Etheridge's social rivals and she made a point of not concealing it.

Every evening she dressed, powdered and inserted pendant earrings into her pierced ears. After dinner she would hurry down the path which led from the house to the bungalow by the river where Alan Banks lay. When she returned she would sit by Mrs Etheridge and in a low voice give her report. No one in the family was allowed to mention the disease by name in the presence of servants or strangers in case it should get back to the patient, and every so often there would be a conspiracy to persuade him that the corner had been turned and he was well on the road to recovery. At these times Mrs Etheridge found Marguerite a more than able lieutenant.

Marguerite enjoyed herself. To be waited on and yet not to be idle, to mix with the best company, and to be abroad—it was just what she needed most. When her first cheque came in she found that her employer had added quite a fair sum as a present. With this she bought clothes; summer dresses, evening dresses, hats, gloves and shoes. She went regularly to the best hairdresser, she trimmed her eyebrows and she began to use lipstick.

Every evening there were aperitifs, wine with the meal of many courses and, naturally, the best port afterwards. At first, still horrified by the memory of the effects of drink on Edgar and poor Geoffrey Boyd, she refused. Then, just out of politeness she told herself, she sipped a little. She discovered that it had a marvellous effect when she was tired. Without noticing it she began to take more.

She should always have been like her mother, she would have been had she not determined to resemble her father in every way. But it was only a matter of time before many of her mother's traits came out in her. The first to appear had been an easy-going indifference to tidiness and routine. This had come early to her and late to her mother: for her father had been the soul of tidiness and precision. The second trait was a way of forgetting people, her nearest and dearest, when they were absent. Her mother had done this with many of her children. Marguerite, who had set out to think daily of every brother, nephew and niece, who believed that they were her whole life, now began to forget they existed. The third trait was a liking for drink. The fourth trait, which appeared when the drink habit had set in, was an awareness of men; a liking for male company and a wish to please them.

Her head was weak and it needed only a glass or two to lift her above worries and responsibilities. She became amiable to all present. Her eye dwelt lovingly on the silver dishes, the valuable glasses, the polished table, and the centre piece of flowers. Words poured from her easily and gaily. She felt triumphant. This was the life for her. She forgot she was a nurse. She forgot that in time her patient must die and she must return to the boarding house. She forgot the bills and lodgers. After dinner, after the visit to the bungalow, after the report, she listened to Mrs Etheridge playing the piano and during pauses she asked in a firm voice, "Please, that delightful thing from Faust you played last week. And that lovely little Italian thing from an opera—now what is its name?" And there was a touch of excitement in the polite attention she gave to the conversation of Mr Etheridge, his brother and his business friends.

And then it seemed to her a pity that the elation and heightening of sensations must come only once a day and she took a glass or two at lunch, although the nursing afternoon stretched before her and she must concentrate and have all her wits about her. A regular visitor, Mr Ford, manager of a large estate near by, found her very amusing. When he came to dinner she drank even more freely. He admired her face, believed her to be younger than she was and found her low voice, now made husky by smoking and a touch of bronchitis, the most attractive he had ever heard. He invited her over to look around his estate on her next free afternoon.

"Oh, do go, my dear," said Mrs Etheridge. "It will make a change for you."

As they walked round the estate he held her arm to aid her up precipitous paths and when the paths became flatter and smoother his hand remained on her elbow. She asked for details of the wine process. He insisted she should taste a sample or two. With an air of connoisseurship she shut her eyes and pronounced it delicious. "It has body," she said, "and yet no coarseness."

By the time the tasting was over she had had several glasses and he thought her most intelligent. He had an invalid wife living farther inland and he found himself hinting at the unhappiness of his marriage.

The landscape was moving before her eyes, sometimes the ground came near her and sometimes it seemed far away, now everything was clear, almost too clear, now it was blurred. She stumbled a little. His half-told story seemed the saddest thing she had ever heard. What a sufferer, what a martyr, and such a gentleman, so cultured and refined. She sighed loudly and she shook her head; she looked at his eyes, her own eyes bright with drink and sympathy.

Mrs Etheridge noticed nothing. In any case she disliked Mrs Ford and Marguerite could do no wrong. Not that there was any affair, but a great deal of emotion went into the friendship and kisses were exchanged. Marguerite had no romantic thoughts or speculations. In the morning when she awoke only her patient was in her mind. At lunch came a patch of muddled excitement about whatever arose in the course of conversation, in the evening a more prolonged exhilaration whether Ford was there or not. But she looked round at once to see if he had come and if he was there she watched his face, agreed with his opinions, backed him up strongly in the slightest argument. During the times they spent together she was absorbed in his personality and as his hand covered hers or his mouth touched her cheek she felt happy.

For many months Marguerite stayed here. In summer the sky grew bluer and the sun was strong. In the autumn the clouds came. In the winter Kathleen arrived as night nurse, for Banks was growing worse, and with her she brought Lisa who had cried and begged her not to leave her all alone away from the family again.

PART FOUR: FAILURE

1

Before Marguerite left for Oporto she had been negotiating for the lease of another large house in the neighbourhood of 83. During her absence the house fell vacant. Letters and telegrams passed between herself and Mrs Hughes and a building society with the result that this second house was taken over as a boarding house by the family. Mrs Hughes was not pleased. There were many journeys to be made between the two houses. Elizabeth, who was only too glad to be consulted, was constantly coming over to 83 to discuss business and many a glass of beer had to be popped into a cupboard and could only be drunk when it was much too flat. This new house was also referred to by its number, 52.

The paintwork at 52 was light cream. There were two bathrooms. It had been a boarding house before and all the doors bore brass numbers. A bus stopped within a few yards. Marguerite had written, "it is the sort of house that runs itself." But no house could run itself and until a sufficient number of lodgers could be found the housekeeper's wages must be paid out of 83. The new financial commitments worried Mrs Hughes. She had a gambling streak and might have enjoyed this ten years back but she was getting on now and wanted a rest. In spite of her easy-going disposition, in spite of her ability to enjoy herself in her own way, her life was suddenly filled with cares and worries and responsibilities which were all the worse because they were not really hers. The gentle tempo of her day was tampered with. There were callers at the door all through the mornings and afternoons and, cursing, she had to plod up the basement steps to interview a prospective lodger for the other house or a plumber or someone from the building society. And apart from all this there were plenty of things to be seen to at 83.

Each telegram which announced Elizabeth's arrival filled her with despair as she knew the questions and criticisms which her daughter would bring with her. "Mother, haven't the men seen to the stair carpet yet? But mother, darling, you've had a good two weeks. I know your legs are bad, mother, but you have only to be firm with

Mrs Potter (the housekeeper) and she will see to all that. You know I have told her to do nothing without orders from you."

If Elizabeth had a few minutes to spare after talk of the houses, talk during which she did sums on paper to make things simpler—as she believed—she would start on her poor mother's appearance or the state of the kitchen. Now that Marguerite was away she felt it her duty to keep her mother up to the mark. Sadly Mrs Hughes realised that she would have preferred Marguerite's erratic domineering to the consistent and polite badgering of her second daughter. And the trouble was that it was fatal to bring up "the legs" with Elizabeth or she would be lectured again. "Have you done those foot exercises I showed you? Do you soak them every night in that lotion I gave you? No? Well, mother, how can you hope to get them better? You really must persist. I had a patient who..." How much easier to bear was Marguerite's, "Oh, they'll be better soon. You must try not to think of them." She was certainly not going to spend the few idle hours which were hers in the evening patting, kneading and soaking her legs, nor was she going to take a bus ride to a distant hospital twice a week where she would have to wait for hours in the outpatients department before her turn came. She did not ask to have her legs cured. She asked to be allowed to organise her life around them.

Not that she put up with this talk easily. Often she answered Elizabeth sharply, calling her Lizzie into the bargain. "Stop that, Lizzie. You've told me before. Let's have a bit of peace, for goodness' sake." But this only made Elizabeth's faded face look sadder, sweeter and harder and she would answer with resignation and reproach, "I was only trying to help you mother, but as you seem not to want my help I shall say no more about it." Very quickly she would find something else to go on about.

All the same Mrs Hughes considered that she had two of the most devoted daughters that could be found. They kept her, they were concerned for her welfare and all this present hustle was part of a scheme to give her a comfortable old age. These considerations led her never to oppose their plans and she allowed her days to be filled with the many activities they imposed on her. She was on the go from eight o'clock in the morning until seven o'clock at night when she could begin to cook a tasty supper for herself. Every evening she had a chop or a piece of steak with some vegetables, and a pudding or pastry to follow. She was sure meat was good for her because she fancied it and on the strength of some discussion with the parish priest she decided that she had dispensation from fasting and abstinence and could have that nice bit of meat on Fridays.

She was such a pleasant-looking and friendly woman that Mrs Potter was soon devoted to her and conspired with her to keep certain things from Elizabeth and came over with a jug of beer for her in the evenings so that she might be spared the walk to the pub. But in spite of these comforts and a hearty appetite her health deteriorated. A cold led to pneumonia and she retired to bed.

When Elizabeth heard the news of her mother's illness, she hurried from the large country house where she was nursing to 83. "Mother, the doctor cannot see you down here," she said, looking round with disapproval at the kitchen, remembering how often she had told her mother she should not sleep there. "Mother, you must move to the first floor back. And mother, I've bought a new nightdress for you so that you will look nice and fresh when he comes. He is a specialist, the very best man and I want him to have a good impression of the place."

"It's warm in the kitchen," said Mrs Hughes. "It's the only warm room in the house. That back room is perishing."

"Yes, I understand that—but I'll try and have a larger gas fire put in as soon as possible. Now if you could get up and change while Mrs Potter gets the room ready for you. Mother, have you any better sheets?"

Mrs Hughes waved her hand in the direction of the linen cupboard. That evening she was presented with a tiny piece of steamed fish, which she hated, and a glass of hot milk for supper, and even so Elizabeth thought it was a heavy meal for anyone with a temperature. The following day she implored her daughter to return to her case. "Mrs Potter can see to me until we get a housekeeper for her. I can manage, dear. I hate to think of you losing your good case on my account. I can manage."

Although her condition grew worse she forbade Mrs Potter to write and tell Elizabeth so. She was glad of the rest but she longed to be out of this room. When her cronies came in to see her they looked blue with cold as they sat by the tiny gas fire, an economy of Marguerite's. She would never have a window open and for hours her commode remained unemptied so that the smell of the room became intolerable to all but herself, and even she was afflicted by headaches as a result of the stuffiness. Between naps and meals her time lay heavily on her hands when she was alone and she lay looking up at the ceiling trying to work out mortgages and insurance policies and wondering when the larger gas fire would come. The new housekeeper was a creature of Elizabeth's and she wondered how she could wangle that Mrs Potter came here and the other one went to 52. But after a time even that mattered less. She no longer pined for chops and beer. She felt ill, wretchedly, painfully ill. It was difficult to breathe, it was difficult to move and every part of her body ached. Elizabeth was sent for.

It was early January, the coldest time of the year. Outside, the snow lay on the ground, transforming the ugliness of the back yard, the roofs and window ledges of the houses around. Inside, the icy air came through the slightest gap around the door or down the partly blocked-up chimney. Elizabeth wrote:

"*Chérie,*

Have bad news. Mother worse. Condition critical so thought it best to let you know in case wish to return. Have left it as long as possible but know you would not wish me conceal anything. Serious pneumonia and strain on heart. Poor mother so brave.

Re. houses. Top floors, both rooms, let to nice type tenant. Mrs P. managing well but Nos. 4 and 5 without armchair or wash hand-stand. Also..."

In ten days, Marguerite was at 83 looking the picture of health and with a full purse. She agreed that her mother could not sleep in the kitchen but after the central heating in Oporto and the milder climate she admitted that the other rooms in the house were too cold. "We'll take her down to the south coast," she said to Elizabeth, as though she were made of money, "to some very nice hotel. They say it's much warmer there and the poor soul would be comfortable."

"Not to a hotel," said Mrs Hughes. "I wouldn't be happy in a hotel. And I don't fancy the journey."

Marguerite compromised. Mrs Hughes would stay in Brighton with her Irish friend. A car would be hired to take her down.

"Not yet, dear. If you could get a bigger gas fire or else have a proper coal fire in here that would do. It wouldn't cost half as much."

The doctor took her side and she remained where she was until the end of February. Under Marguerite's care she grew a little better. She appreciated her eldest daughter more than ever before.

Marguerite let her do as she pleased within reason, she often came and talked to her, she encouraged her to have people in and asked round the parish priest, and a former lodger with whom she had grown friendly. She had Lisa home for several weekends.

Lisa, who had travelled back with her aunt, had returned to the convent. Why, she would never be sure. Time and distance had softened her memories of the place. She had passed the important age line, for she was now ten, and could not be placed in Sister Aloysius's dormitory any longer. She would be with the big ones and what she remembered of their life seemed interesting and carefree. No big ones were ever hit, for one thing. Besides, she had been a success everywhere else, in Saint-Jules, in Oporto, in Paris, and this was a hoop she must jump. She must have one more try. Also she dreaded another new environment, happy or unhappy. She was beginning to need some sort of continuity. For these reasons and for others more obscure she had said, "May I go back to the same convent?" It was a mistaken decision but it was her own. No one had pressed her either way.

She loved her grandmother. When she was very young, on seeing a trio of anything, flowers, stones, trees or animals she had always said, *"La maman, la grandmère et la petite fille,"* where another child might have said, "Father, mother and little girl." Later the *maman* figure had weakened and been replaced by *tante*. Later still the figures in the group had seemed so different from the ones other children had that her attitude to her family grew uncertain and alarmed. She wanted to be the same as others. But just as her Frenchiness had queered her with the little ones, so now her nine months in Saint-Jules made her seem an oddity to the big ones, and as she was still paying reduced fees her troubles began again. But on one thing she had guessed right. They never hit the big ones. The physical terror was over.

During her weekends at home she sat on her grandmother's bed and chatted. She described to her episodes from the lives of Joan of Arc and Napoleon (no English figure had yet caught her fancy). She fetched things for her, acted as a spy for her and told her when Aunt Elizabeth was expected. She found nothing strange in her grandmother's wish to avoid Elizabeth and to be forewarned of her coming. She felt just the same about her. Aunt Elizabeth wore a sickly perfume, never said anything of interest and no one could be natural with her. And then there was the everlasting nagging and fuss:

"Lisa darling, that button is just about to fall. You're quite a big girl now and I gave you a work box for Christmas."

"Darling, I'm told you haven't been out of the house all day. Put on your outdoor things and go round the square. Were you going out in the same shoes? You know they would never let you do that at school. Go downstairs and put on your other ones."

"Now tell me, darling, what time did you go to bed last night? Have you kept your promise to me that you wouldn't read in bed? You gave me your word of honour. Now, darling, don't put on that expression. You want to grow up healthy and nice-looking, don't you?"

When her grandmother wanted to get up, Lisa would go and wait outside the door. From there, with a feeling of shame, she could hear the tinkle in the commode. Also, her grandmother was always spitting into an enamel basin and she could not bear to think of this. The smell of the room was horrid at first. In every other way her grandmother was a pleasant person to be with, indulgent and a good listener. She had never been an arresting figure in her life like Aunt Marguerite, but she represented comfort and security. She was always the same. Lisa found her very beautiful with her soft white hair and pink skin.

At the end of February Marguerite decided that her mother was well enough to travel and Lisa came home for no more weekends.

A car was hired and Mrs Hughes travelled down to Brighton with Marguerite beside her and Elizabeth on the small seat in front of her. As always the two daughters were purposive and formal together. Each spoke grandly to the chauffeur, each spoke with kindly condescension to the landlady, who remembered them as children.

Mrs Hughes had in fact been much better when the decision was taken but on the day of the journey she felt worse. The long drive was like a nightmare. She was conscious of draughts and aches. Her head was heavy and she felt sick. After the weeks in bed she could scarcely control her legs, and the walk along the passage to the front room was an ordeal despite the support they gave her. As soon as she arrived she undressed and went to bed. In bed the fresh sheets and pillow cases felt icy. The unfamiliar room made her eyes fill with tears. "I do feel bad, Maggie," she kept repeating, although words made her pant. "Don't tell Lizzie. Let her go off."

Sleep would not come. She was glad of Marguerite's company and held her hand and watched her eyes. She was glad too that Elizabeth had left for her case. The hard glare from the electric bulb hurt her eyes and she dreaded the dark. It was a plain, small, bare room with no bedside lamp. The curtains and bed cover were made of a thin cotton cretonne with a bold pattern in harsh colours; livid greens and orange reds. She liked her surroundings to be complex and rich. She did not think of taste—she never had—and neither did she criticise the room to herself, but the sight of it left her feeling unsheltered. Marguerite sat on the one armchair, a small wicker thing, painted blue and shading off into gold at the edges.

Sleep came at last and Marguerite tiptoed to the switch and turned off the light. Between short dozes in her chair she leaned forward to listen to her mother's breathing. When the first light filtered through the cotton curtains she looked at her face. By half-past nine premonitions had come. At ten she was asking for the nearest priest. She hurried to his house. Her mother must have the last sacraments.

Mrs Hughes recovered enough consciousness to say her confession and receive communion. She had few sins on her soul; a few faults of bad temper and lack of charity she mentioned; eating meat on Fridays and missing Sunday mass in the past she considered nothing, for she had told herself she had dispensation. She thought she would recover and, feeling as ill as she did, death had no terrors. Marguerite knelt at the foot of the bed and bent her face over the orange eiderdown. She was angry rather than resigned.

A few more years and the family would have been as she meant it to be, leading this splendid refined life. Her mother would be waited on hand and foot as she had been before, in her father's day. It was wrong that she should go now.

After the priest had gone she resumed her position at the head of the bed. Gently she shut her mother's eyes. At twelve she heard church bells and told herself that must be the Angelus. She repeated the words to herself. "The Angel of the Lord declared unto Mary and she conceived by the Holy Ghost." Her mother's name was Mary and she too had conceived. "Behold the handmaid of the Lord. Be it done unto me according to Thy word." Mary's reply might have been her mother's reply. How fond she had been of the Angelus! How often

255

when they were children they had all knelt down in the kitchen while she said those words! She saw her mother now as beautiful and refined, always beautiful and refined, widowed early and never recovering from the blow, as saintly as Patrick. The thought of Edgar was blotted out for good. In repose, with no struggle for breath, Mrs Hughes' face seemed to have lost all creases and lines. Her white hair, well brushed before the visit of the priest, remained tidily pulled up into a bun on top of her head. Her hands were folded over her breast.

"She has gone straight to heaven," Marguerite told herself.

The body had to be taken back to London and the funeral arranged. Marguerite spared no expense. Michael, Elizabeth and John attended the mass in Westminster Cathedral and followed the hearse. David was in India as a regular soldier. Kathleen was in Oporto. The two sisters bought new suits for the two brothers. Flowers were sent by the cronies, by the proprietors of the local pub and by the lodgers. Mrs Potter wept. "She was one of the nicest women I ever knew."

When all was over the family assembled in the kitchen of 83. Elizabeth, who was the practical one, made the tea. Her hand trembled and tears ran down her powdered cheeks. She looked grey and brittle and nervous. Of all present she experienced the greatest grief. Nervous and highly strung she was remorseless with herself. At this moment there could be no business to discuss, nothing to fuss about, and without these habitual props she found herself exposed to her own most secret fears and hatreds.

Marguerite might resent the untimely deaths of members of the family but her imagination soon filled with consoling stories and explanations, and she had always enjoyed drama. At great length she described the last moments to the others.

"Just as the Angelus was ringing, at that very moment she passed away. It was like a miracle and I knew then that she was going straight to heaven. And if you had seen her face you would have known too. She looked so happy and calm. And just before she died she turned to me and said..."

2

After her mother's death Marguerite installed Mrs Potter in the basement of 83. She herself went to live at 52 because it was new to her and the light paintwork took her fancy. It was certainly the more attractive house of the two inside, though the outside was almost identical, the same balcony jutting over pillars, the same effect of large slabs of stone with ridges between them, the same greyness and dirt. Soon she would have a housekeeper here too, she thought, and that would leave her free for cases.

The woman Elizabeth had found did not appeal to her and after a quarrel she was given notice. There followed a succession of maids and none stayed long. The work was hard and the longer Marguerite stayed in the house the more impossible she became. She needed someone to do the work and yet she hated anyone around. It was a vicious circle, because until she had trained somebody to take over she could not leave the house, and until she left the house she was too moody to keep anyone.

Depressed by the uneventfulness of life, she shut herself in the ground floor back most of the day. She had appropriated this fairly large room as her bedroom, determined to grade up from basement life at last. Here she lay in bed till late in the morning, rose reluctantly, pushed odd pots off the dressing table, produced papers from one of the drawers and sat there as though at her desk. When she thought it was getting on for lunch time she quietly went to the wardrobe and lifted from under a pile of clothes a bottle of red wine. She eased the cork out gently and poured a good measure into her tooth mug. Replacing the bottle she crossed the room, holding the mug, and sat on the side of her bed, looking out unseeing at the backs of the surrounding houses. She took her time.

Soon a happy glow came. After it came plans. One day she might decide to move round the furniture in the front room, which was now a dining room. Another day she might decide to move a lodger out of No. 6 and put him in No. 4. Anything might occur to her. For example, she thought the armchair in No. 7 would look lovely with a piece of green brocade over it. The maid could bring it down to her room and run and buy some brass-headed tacks. There was a piece of brocade in a drawer somewhere which had come in one of Elizabeth's lots.

She crunched two bright violet cachous, taken from a small box on which was a picture of an oriental lady. With sweet-smelling breath she shouted orders down to the basement.

"Get that armchair down from No. 7, will you? Leave what you're doing. This is urgent. I must have it now. And then run out to Leadman's for some tacks, like those I had last week. About three dozen."

The maid never knew what time of day she might be told to leave everything to go on some unexpected errand. Also she never understood why, whenever she was near Marguerite's door, Marguerite would pop out and order her away in a furious voice. Marguerite hated anyone being outside her door. She felt they were listening, spying on her, looking through the keyhole—though it was always blocked by the key—to see her go to her bottle.

Fearing a sudden visit from Elizabeth with more furniture which might involve her sister in seeing her room, she liked to dispose of bottles as she went along. Soon after a bottle was empty she would go downstairs, break it and put the pieces in the dustbin, moving the debris aside, so that each piece of glass would be completely covered. Each time she did this she had to get the maid upstairs first, on any pretext. Being unsystematic she never worked out at what time of day the girl would be bound to be upstairs and neither did she wait until her half-day off. No, she simply waited until the urge to break the bottle had become irresistible and then set about hustling.

After a week of this life most maids left. The more submissive kind stayed a little longer. None was tempted by the idea of staying on indefinitely as housekeeper after her period of apprenticeship.

The trouble with servants, thought Marguerite, was that they expected everything to be just so and they were curious. She had never thought of these drawbacks when she visualised the family waited on hand and foot. And even now when she dreamt of life in the future, with maids and all the rest of it, she assumed that then, naturally, their presence would not irk her in the least.

At tea time she had another drink followed by cachous and at supper time the same again. For long stretches she ate almost nothing. She could not bear having to sit down to a meal. At half-past one she went down to the kitchen, where a plateful of something lay ready for her—the maid had retired to somewhere else because Marguerite insisted that she liked to eat alone—and picking up the plate and a fork she walked round the room, eating a very little and throwing whatever she was bored with onto the fire. Her daily intake of the food provided would not have kept her going. Suddenly, in the afternoon or evening, and not every day, a desperate hunger seized her and she would powder her face, pat her hair, put on a hat at a becoming angle and rush to catch the bus to the delicatessen shop near Victoria. Here she would look round at the soused herrings, smoked salmon and liver sausage and buy anything she liked the look of, regardless of price. She would eat her purchases out of the paper, alone in her room, usually with no bread and always in her fingers. That done the craving would go and she would lose interest in eating for another long period.

She had lived pretty well ever since Bordeaux. At her cases the food was excellent and the cook was often foreign. She could not stand plain, English fare. In Oporto she had tasted every delicacy. For many months her meals had been of the choicest. Living in other people's houses, with everything provided, had left her unable to plan menus for herself. When the maid asked her what she wanted for lunch, she replied testily, "Oh, anything, anything." Even if she had possessed a good cook she would never have known what to ask for and it would have been a great bother thinking about it.

Fearing that they too might interfere with her in some way, Marguerite grew strange with the lodgers. Her door was just at the foot of the staircase and when she heard steps she could never resist opening the door to see who was coming in, who was going out, and to deter them from lingering. That made them feel *they* were being spied on. One young man who occasionally brought his fiancée there was driven wild by the idea that Marguerite suspected him of immorality.

None of them knew how she would behave. Sometimes when they came to her with a request she smiled benignly, drawled huskily, "Do step into the dining room and I'll attend to you at once. I have been meaning to have a chat with you. I like to know whether everyone is comfortable." As they listed their complaints, she displayed the most emphatic understanding and interest in her every movement. She would interrupt only to reassure, "Yes, I *do* see what you mean; I have the very thing; that is just what I meant to do myself; I'm so sorry, you can be sure it will never happen again." They would find themselves drawn to her once more—as they had been on the day they booked the room. These happy encounters were those which took place shortly after the wine.

At other times, after knocking repeatedly on her door, they would see her emerge, angry and distant. "What is it? This is not the time to come with complaints. I'm dreadfully busy doing accounts. No, no I cannot see to it now. You should speak to the maid." She would disappear behind the door and they would hear the key turn in the lock. This happened before she had had her nip.

When the quarterly bills fell due her need for drink increased. She had cleared the money out of the gas meters long before and it was all spent. Money from the lodgers had gone to pay off furniture bills and redecoration bills. There were always large sums she could not account for, because she forgot how much she spent on wine—a bottle of Médoc a day—how readily she paid ten to fifteen pounds for a dress or suit, how frequent were her purchases of expensive snacks, sometimes *foie gras* or caviar. She often lost a pound or two through carelessness. Any beggar or pedlar who came to the door received half a crown from her. When she felt sorry for a lodger she let him off the rent. One or two passing lodgers stole towels and crockery and these had to be replaced. She was the ideal landlady to swindle. Had she been systematic and careful she need never have been short, for as Kathleen put it, "Those houses would have been gold mines." Whatever her income had been she would have overspent and misspent. There was never a time when a bill came and she could write a cheque knowing it would be met. When final demands came, solicitors' letters, letters threatening to cut off light and heat, she worried terribly. For days she lived in great mental agony. She paced up and down her room and tore at her hair. She found it difficult to get to sleep. She had nightmares about bankruptcy courts and bailiffs.

After one drink she felt consoled and hopeful. In order to keep up her good spirits she took another. This left her tearful and angry. "I am sacrificing myself for the others. I have all the family on my back. I am carrying a burden no other person could. I am a martyr. And they are all ungrateful. There's not a drop of gratitude among them. The boys never write from Australia—never a word. I did everything for Patrick and he simply walked out on me." (That was her version of the story now). "Joseph was just the same. And I pay for Lisa's fees and clothes. I never stint her." (This was quite untrue for she had taken nearly every penny Kathleen earned, saying she needed it for Lisa). In some obscure way she believed she was paying for Elizabeth too, or else she argued, "If I had not taken her to Bordeaux she would never have got on. I helped her to start that house." She really believed she had given Elizabeth a hundred pounds. She could remember the scene. She could hear her own kind words as she handed over the cheque. But enough sense of reality remained with her to prevent her from writing to Elizabeth and asking her to pay the money back. "I shall never ask her for it back. I am not mean. When I give, I give."

If any decision she had taken appeared to be mistaken then the decision must have been forced upon her. She had never wanted to take on these houses. Every penny she made from them she had to give to someone else. She really believed that she was living near to starvation level in order to give Michael an occasional pound or buy a new gym-slip for Lisa.

One day a pretty, black-haired girl came to the door. She spoke with an Irish brogue. She was sixteen and her name was Eileen Murphy. "Could you let me have a room?" she asked. "I'd be wanting one very cheap. I've only three pounds on me."

Marguerite took a liking to her on the spot, as she often did to strangers, and showed her into the drawing room. She had taken her last nip only a quarter of an hour ago and the glow remained with her and made her friendly. "Have you only three pounds in the world?"

"Yes. I came over to England to go into service. But I didn't care for the lady I was to go to and I thought I'd have a look round."

"Poor you." This trick of referring to the person she was speaking to as "you" in a rather unexpected way had endeared her to many. "And tired you. You need a rest." She extracted from her her life story with details of brothers and sisters and schooling. She asked the maid to bring her a cup of tea. "Would you like a job here?"

Eileen looked at Miss Reilly, found her face attractive, felt sure that she would be considerate and easy-going. "I wouldn't mind."

Forgetting all she had said about needing a rest, Marguerite clinched it. "You can start tomorrow. The girl's only temporary."

Eileen was a treasure and she stayed. Coming from a farm in Wicklow, used to many wild members of her own family, she took Marguerite's moods in her stride. She had never been in service before and had no preconceived ideas about time and order. A boarding house was more enjoyable than a private family because she met different people and could flirt mildly with the men. She was sharp and soon realised that Marguerite drank. Far from worrying her, this discovery seemed a great joke and she had difficulty restraining her laughter when Marguerite smelt as though she had been eating violets. Smiling, she said at last, after Marguerite had been trying to get her out of the way, "Now don't you be worrying, Mrs Reilly. Give me the bottles and I'll see to them for you."

Marguerite was taken aback, began to protest, felt a sudden flush of anger and then laughed. She began by a giggle and then roared until the tears ran down her cheeks. "You're very cheeky, Eileen," she said, still laughing, letting out all the laughter she had suppressed until this moment. Overcome, they both sat down in the kitchen until the hysterics had abated. "Not a word about this," said Marguerite. "Nothing to Miss Elizabeth."

Eileen reorganised the house. She gladly took over responsibilities. "Let them all have bed and breakfast," she said. "Sure I can cook breakfast for them and you'll be making more money that way. And you're getting too little for No.7. It's a fine big room and you should put two beds there and have them sharing it. Two nice men there is what you want."

Listening to Marguerite's tales of the family—for they had many long talks together—she shook her head. "You're too good, Miss Reilly. 'Tis a great thing for a family when they have someone like you at the head. They're very lucky." She saw Marguerite as crippled with debts contracted by the others and drinking to drive away despair and worry. "Now you have a drink, Miss Reilly. It'll do you good." She even went and bought the wine for her sometimes.

Marguerite was the first friend she had made in England. Marguerite had taken her on with no references so that she could keep her three pounds intact. She was devoted to Marguerite. She had few illusions about her. She soon suspected that her own muddling was the cause of her troubles. She thought she dealt with the lodgers very badly. She was aware that many of her stories were exaggerated. But she remained convinced that Marguerite's faults were not only surface ones, but very temporary. She really believed that at any moment she would change for the better, becoming more methodical and truthful and cutting down the drink. She persuaded herself that she had a great deal of influence on Marguerite, and as far as the house was concerned she had. And always she told herself that underneath it all Marguerite had one of the finest and warmest of hearts. She put up with her imperiousness and criticism, things she would have stood from no one else for she had a proud and independent character. Marguerite, on her side, allowed back answers and frequent rebellion. In this way they could be described as understanding each other.

Marguerite handed over to her one or two dresses of which she had tired. She talked to her more freely than she did to anyone in her family. Sometimes, when she thought Eileen cheeky, she put on her best accent and treated her with *hauteur*. "You must not speak to me in that way. You must remember your place." When Elizabeth came, Eileen would be ordered to bring up tea on a tray and would be amazed at the *chéries* and *ma chères* which were exchanged, and find herself banished from the dining room by a nod. Miss Elizabeth treated her with condescension. "When she comes we all have to pull our socks up," she said to Marguerite and was answered by a frown.

3

Under Eileen, No. 52 prospered. She was therefore sent over to pull up 83 and Mrs Potter changed places with her. Mrs Potter's sailor husband came home and installed himself in the basement bringing three parrots and a marmoset. One of these parrots was presented to Lisa and she transferred it to the dining room. "I shall call it Polly," she said with pleasure. She loved to do things which seemed to her the norm. A donkey she would have called Ned; a large dog, Tray; a small dog, Fido. She believed that this made her the same as the other girls at school, little realising that children from the safe ranks of the middle classes go in for fancy names like Jeremiah when they have pets.

Her stay at 52 was cut short. Marguerite was interested in Anthony now and planning to have him over from France. She loved Lisa no longer. Part of her dislike for Kathleen she extended to Kathleen's child. Any criticism of the convent which she had chosen roused her to anger. When Lisa followed her round trying to tell her that she had been first in class and had a hundred per cent for maths, she told her to go away. "I'm busy now. Tell me later. Go and sit upstairs." With the child in the house, occasional drinks had to be taken with greater secrecy than ever. She sent her on long errands, she grumbled at her and finally forbade her to go downstairs and talk to the Potters. This was a dreadful blow. They were very jolly and had a gramophone with many records. Standing in the passage, not knowing where to go for a bit of company, Lisa wept. At first Marguerite took no notice and then as the sobs grew louder she lost her temper.

"Go out of the house," she said. "Go on. I cannot bear snivelling children. You know I cannot stand the sight of tears. At your age you should have more self-control." Perplexed, Lisa remained where she was and the sobs grew louder. Marguerite took her by the arm and dragged her to the front door. "When I say a thing I mean it. Go out of the house. Yes, right out, into the street, anywhere. You may come back when you have stopped crying and not before." She opened the door and pushed her out.

Lisa walked along the street and back again. She could not control her tears. Her grandmother had gone, her mother was away on a case and no one wanted her. When she returned home, her face blotchy but her eyes dry, she found her aunt's anger had abated. But they were ill at ease together and the next day she was told that her room was needed for a lodger and she must go over to 83.

"May I go and get my things?" she asked timidly.

"No, not now. I'll have them sent over later."

They were never sent. This was the beginning of a long series of moves from room to room and house to house during which she lost her favourite books, many pieces of a farm she was collecting and all her dolls. Marguerite either mislaid them or gave them to children staying in the house, allowing them to take them away with them because they said they had grown fond of them. There was nowhere in the world where Lisa could keep a possession in safety. She was allowed to take her parrot to 83 and Eileen looked after her well.

When Marguerite was on a case Lisa went over to see the Potters and the other two parrots and the marmoset. She divided her time between the basements of the two houses. When the house was full she slept with Eileen. This worried her a lot because no other girl at school ever slept with the maid. She began to realise that although her father had been a famous engineer there was some truth in what the nuns said and she was in many ways lower than the others.

Between cases, Kathleen returned to one or other of the houses, meekly handed over her cheque to Marguerite and watched her appropriate her best clothes—not that she had many. Although Marguerite did not want the company of either Lisa or Kathleen she did not want them to enjoy each other's company either. She thought up excuses for having one at one house and one at the other. She told barefaced lies about the number of lodgers. She forced Eileen and Mrs Potter to back her up by puzzling them with her long rigmaroles. "If the child sees too much of her mother she gets so dreadfully upset when poor Mrs Treherne has to go off on a case. She is very sensitive, too sensitive. They both are. And so, although it seems hard, we must do all we can to prevent them from spending too much time together. It will make them happier in the end."

This was said with so much feeling that although Mrs Potter and Eileen did not agree with her arguments, they knew that Marguerite was acting from the best of motives.

If Kathleen arranged to take Lisa to the pictures, Marguerite would find some way of putting it off at the last moment. Lisa was not sure who to blame. Her life was a series of disappointments and she felt that she had only to look forward to something for it not to happen. Sometimes she hated her aunt. Sometimes she was angry with her mother for being weak. She realised she must not be weak or she would go under. She began to protest and answer back. She was rude and bad-tempered with Marguerite. She often refused to run an errand for her, exulting in the fact that nothing could make her—no one could really force anyone to do anything. She was glad not to be in the same house. She trusted no one, not even Eileen. She lavished all her attention on Polly and spent hours by the cage in the kitchen of 83, teaching the bird to sing "It's a long way to Tipperary" and to say "Good Morning", "Hullo" and other simple phrases. She cleaned out the cage daily and chose the birdseed. She walked around with Polly perched on her shoulder. As a daring experiment she let her fly around in the back yard, relieved to find that she could not go far with clipped wings. When the time came to go back to school she wept at parting with her parrot. Her aunt was away, her mother was away and Eileen saw to the clothes and accompanied her on the long bus ride. Back in school she refused to write to Marguerite any more.

Now that she had two housekeepers, Marguerite was nursing again. She went to France with one patient, to Italy with another and to Devon with a third. After each case she returned refreshed. After a spell in the boarding house she grew morose and the drinking began.

Anthony came home for a short holiday. She devoted three weeks to entertaining him, three weeks during which she rose early, drank no more than a glass a day and made trips to the Tower of London, the Changing of the Guards, the museums, the parks and many theatres. He was delighted with the entertainment but he felt unsettled. Twice he was moved from one room to another. When there was someone in the dining room he did not know where to sit because his bedroom was right at the top of the house and lonely, and his aunt allowed no one in her room. Often he settled himself on the bottom step and stared down the passage at the two glass panes in the front door.

He asked about his brothers and sister and it was hinted to him that they had gone to the bad in some way. He asked after his father and Eileen took him along to the market near Victoria where Michael sold vegetables.

Michael was leading his own life. He never thought about his children and he corresponded with none of them. He had not written a letter of any kind for years and he never would again in his life. Every week he drew his pension. On most days he stood by his barrow and in fine weather he enjoyed it. His classical curls were now white, a yellowish white because they were never washed. His suit was so old that it was difficult to say what colour it had originally been. The dark funeral suit, twice pawned and twice retrieved, lay over the back of a chair in his room. He respected it as reserved for some special occasion—perhaps a wedding, perhaps a funeral, perhaps something he had not thought of.

There was an understanding that he should come and see Marguerite from time to time. The early maids had thought he was one of the many hawkers for whom Marguerite had a soft spot. Eileen was told everything. Mrs Potter knew because Mrs Hughes had talked to her. Lisa had no idea he was her uncle. Often she opened the door to see this man and ran to fetch her aunt. In her mind he was a tramp or pedlar who often came. He said, " 'Allo Lisa. Auntie in?" But the others might have said that too.

Bleary-eyed, beery, dreamy and unthinking, Michael continued his life. Every Sunday he went to mass. Often he carried on with a woman. He was lucky with women and ran into several who, besides being attracted to him, felt sorry for him and looked after him. It never cost him anything.

Anthony stood by anxious and chattering, looking up at his father's eyes, the bloodshot corners, the yellow whites, the pale blue iris. He waited for something, expected something. He continued to talk away, knowing that there was no point in it. Michael smiled down at him, uncomprehending. He had not thought of being a father for years and he could not begin now. It was just a lad by his side rattling on. Marguerite had said, "Tell him you want him to be a priest, Michael. Tell him he has a vocation." He obeyed her instructions. "I 'ope you'll become a priest, me boy. Yer aunt says yer going to be a priest. I 'ope you are."

Anthony had been uprooted from his uncle's home in South Wales, a home which Marguerite despised, but which in fact had many advantages and was part of a well-knit community. From there he had been sent abroad on his own, seeing no one but the stuck-up Lisa in Saint-Jules. When both their schools had been closed for the holidays they were both sent to a farm convent and were forced to play together. But Lisa told him he was stupid, laughed at his French and laughed at his English. Had Marguerite left him alone he would have been far happier. Having taken him she saw no need to give him a home. All the children she took over she soon rendered bewildered and insecure. Each reigned in her heart for a given time. Then came indifference. Then she told herself they were ungrateful and she had sacrificed herself again.

But for the moment Anthony could bask in his aunt's favour. He was affectionate and obedient. He had never been any trouble to anyone. He worked hard at his lessons and did not do badly at exams. His reasoning powers were above average but his memory was weak and he lacked self confidence. Three musical comedies a week, *"No, No, Nanette"*, *"The Desert Song"* and others, left him in a whirl. When you were with Marguerite she either took you from place to place, filling your head with a thousand impressions, too rapid to bear fruit, exhausting, incomplete, or else she left you to find your own amusement with no room to do it in and no possessions to do it with. This was the one holiday he enjoyed and, he thought, his aunt must be extraordinarily rich. This constant entertainment would most certainly be his at every visit. She promised to bring him home again soon. She promised to take him round the continent. In return he promised to be a priest. He was religious and she said it was a fine life and a great honour for the family to have a priest in it.

When she saw him off at Victoria she dried his tears with her handkerchief. He, a future priest, such a clever boy, was allowed to cry. His tears were touching and Lisa's were intolerable, although she was two years younger. Marguerite's own eyes watered. "You'll be home again soon," she said. "Now mind you write every week and work hard at your exams. And ask me for anything you want. I may have a case near there some time and then I shall come and see you. Goodbye, darling. Let me know if you are short of money."

4

With regular cases and full houses Marguerite was solvent. She continued to appropriate Kathleen's earnings and she never mentioned to her that a life insurance of £50 on Mrs Hughes should have been hers. She began to think of taking on a third house. John was a miner up north. He had no business to do such work. He was delicate. She really must get him down here, marry him to someone suitable and put him in charge of one of the houses. She had her eye on Eileen. That girl was a born business woman and would make an excellent wife. It was no use expecting the brothers to marry into society now. He really could not do better than Eileen. It was a miracle he was still single. She bombarded him with letters but for the moment he held out.

Through Eileen, who had many contacts in Catholic circles, Marguerite discovered a way to quick large profits. She undertook to give bed and breakfast to the pilgrims who passed through London on their way to Lourdes. Being near the station, her house was well placed. She stressed that she was a nurse, had no fear of sickness in the house and was prepared to take any kind of case. The lame, the blind, the crippled, the deaf, the dumb, the paralysed and the diseased came to her. She was paid so much per head and so much for taxis and other expenses.

The pilgrims came from one area on each occasion, from the north, from the west, from Wales, from Ireland and from Scotland, and each party stayed for one night. This night was like a nightmare. Fortunately Lisa was nearly always away, either at school or dumped in some orphanage or similar institution in France or England for the summer holidays.

Everything was turned upside down, everyone was displaced. The regular lodgers were unceremoniously made to share rooms with each other and given reduced terms for the occasion. Into each vacant room six or seven pilgrims were squeezed, some in proper beds, some in camp beds, some on mattresses on the floor, some— the children—on two armchairs. The stretcher cases remained just as they were on the floor. Many people slept in the dining room, on the landings, in the bathrooms, and in the passage. Every available space was used. Marguerite gave up her own room and either stayed up all night or dozed off in a chair. The kitchen downstairs was also filled with people.

The pilgrims were long suffering and grateful. Those with skin afflictions were only too glad to be taken in. They were a pathetic crowd, mostly poor, who had saved up throughout the year for this one final attempt to be cured. Marguerite picked her way through them, talking glibly and hearteningly of miracles. None that she knew of had yet been cured but she remembered for the benefit of newcomers many startling stories, and as she related them she so dramatised the scenes and visualised them so vividly that she became lost in her own inventions. Each story began, "The doctors had given up all hope..." Many believed her and their hope increased. She had been to Lourdes, for it was not far from Saint-Jules, and she described the basilica and the many crutches which hung there, crutches which would never be needed again because their owners could now walk.

She was not squeamish. She had no fear of a girl who had lupus and wore a dark veil over her face, but came close to her. Without horror she watched men, women and children toil up and down the stairs with jerky, twisted movements of the hip. Those with incurable diseases such as infantile paralysis seemed to her to have beautiful faces. She always described them later as, "With the most wonderful expression. If ever anyone deserved to be cured!" Lines of suffering and despair she did not see. And because they managed to joke and smile, as many sick people do, the idea of their courage brought tears to her eyes.

The pilgrims arrived in taxi loads and ambulances and for the evening the front door remained open. They were assembled in the dining room while Marguerite and Mrs Potter made rapid calculations. They were moved on and the next load dealt with. The last to arrive were tucked into odd corners. The healthy relations of the sick were imposed on and made to fetch and carry and left to find some floor space where they could roll themselves in a blanket.

In the morning all were awakened early and a sad procession made its way to the bathrooms and lavatories, shuffling, limping, being led by a friend in case of blindness or groping along the wall. Basins and jugfuls of hot water were carried round to the stretcher cases by Mrs Potter. The people in the passage were moved out of the way to make room for the breakfasts and they had to be herded into any available space for as long as twenty minutes, standing close together awaiting further orders. The house smelt of humanity and disinfectant. Crutches stood propped against the hall table.

Before their arrival, Marguerite would fortify herself in the usual way and place her bottle in one of the landing cupboards where she could get at it in the night. To stand up to the ordeal she had to change her nervous tension into a carefree excitement. Her head swam a little, her feet seemed to press onto a moving floor, faces were blurred and voices floated past her ears so that she could not quite catch the words. It was impossible to sit down and she could not stand unaided in comfort and therefore she was always searching for some support, the banisters, the table, a door handle or a chair. Moving from one support to another, with shining eyes and scented breath, she shouted orders, spoke words of welcome and comfort, fluttered her hands and never felt at a loss. She became something more than the landlady, she was an agent of the Church, a purveyor of miracles, a supervisory angel who left the actual ministering to others. When all were settled for the night and the hall was in darkness she would fumble in the direction of her bottle, sometimes squatting down beside recumbent forms to hear if they were asleep. Though fuddled about everything else, she retained a clear-witted cunning about the drink, remembering that no one must see her and manoeuvring stairs and corners skilfully. After a drink drowsiness might overtake her—although often she remained wakeful—and if it did she would realise hazily and with sorrow that she must not just lie down on the stairs as she would have liked, but make for some place and arrange herself in such a position that she could be discovered in the morning with no loss of respectability.

The mornings were the worst. With a throbbing headache pounding across her forehead and behind her puffy eyes, with weary limbs and all vitality fled, she had to make a superhuman effort. She longed for them to go so that she could retire to the privacy of her room and lie down. She could not face drink for the time being, and therefore she had to fall back on her own will. Because she managed to shake hands with each one as they departed, because she made sure that they were all away in time, she believed they owed her an enormous debt of gratitude. The mildest complaints—and complaints were extremely rare—left her indignant. "And the trouble I have gone to. No one else would have taken them in. I risk losing my regulars for their sake," she said, as though she were making no profit at all. It was she who was the sufferer and the martyr. It was they who were pampered and lucky.

Even in this soured state she was capable of many an impulsive, generous gesture. At these times she could afford it because her takings were enormous. She slipped five pounds into the hand of one poor girl as she left. She gave some clothes, not old clothes but her best, to a woman. And for this, oddly enough, she expected no thanks. It was for the comfort which she had failed to provide, for the hard beds and the rush and hustle that she expected them to be grateful. When the front door had closed behind the last pilgrim she would flop down onto the hall chair and press her hands against her hot brow. Then, almost loathing them, she saw that she had done a supreme act of charity. Then, more than ever, she was conscious of her virtue and her large heart. A few minutes later she would lie down fully dressed, remove her dentures and sink into a deep sleep.

Another set of occasional lodgers came into her life. These were her pets and her delight. Nothing was too good for them and no trouble was too great. They were priests, secular priests with parishes in different parts of the country. They had all trained together at the college in Lisbon, had known Elizabeth and Miss Simpson and now came up for reunions to London. Elizabeth, averse to tampering with her regulars, handed them over to her sister. Marguerite gladly agreed to have them whenever they liked. "I can always find something."

When the first reunion in her house was about to take place she decided to have a proper drawing room. The large first floor front with its French windows and stone balcony outside was chosen as the obvious place. Long brown velvet curtains were bought at a sale. Kathleen's piano was installed and remained always open and with a piece of music on the rest to suggest that someone had just been playing. A corner sofa and large armchairs were produced from somewhere and covered in a patterned chintz. The effect here was different from Elizabeth's. This drawing room was much less feminine; it contained a mixture of styles and it looked solid. Lodgers were told that the drawing room had come at last but soon found that they were discouraged from using it. The fire was never laid for them. Marguerite wanted the room reserved for the priests. It was to be entirely theirs during their stay. They would sit there laughing and talking, for they were jovial men. Like many good Catholics she adored the idea of jolly priests. Every quip, every use of slang which came from a man who had received Holy Orders seemed a hundred times more amusing than if it came from a lay person. It was a gesture of humanity, it was a declaration of tolerance.

For days before they came she visited the place, moving furniture, patting cushions and changing the music. On the day of their arrival she took especial care with her appearance and kept a hat on from the moment she had finished dressing until she went to bed. She had been on a case where the lady of the house always wore a hat at her own tea parties and this seemed the thing to do. Mrs Potter had gone to 83 and Eileen was now back at 52. She would be good with the priests. She would not mind being at their beck and call. She was Irish and religious and she would enjoy it.

With twinkling eyes and a wide fanged smile, Marguerite shook hands with each one as he arrived and showed him upstairs while Eileen followed with suitcases. She had not drunk a drop today but sat waiting for a knock at the door. When the knock came she had placed the welcoming and humorous look on her face long before she reached the door.

Father McLean, tall, plump and black-haired, arrived first. He installed himself in a chair by the fire and asked Eileen to run out for a bottle of whisky. This set him up further in Marguerite's estimation and she told the girl to lose no time in carrying out his orders. Later came Canon Gordon, Father O'Connor, Father Waterford, Father Simon and Father Anderson. They appropriated the drawing room and sent Eileen to buy beef sandwiches. "And more meat than bread or we'll skin yer."

When Marguerite, hovering at the foot of the stairs, keeping an ear open, heard from Eileen what they had said, she roared with laughter. "I bet it was Father McLean. He's such a sport. He's such a good sort. He'll have us all in fits of laughter." They exchanged knowing glances; they both saw priests in the same way.

Marguerite looked in to see if the visitors had everything they needed.

"Come in, Miss Reilly. Have a drink. Come on now. It'll do you no harm!" She could not refuse Father McLean's entreaties. Their presence gave her the excitement she had felt with the men in Oporto, but it was far more intense because these were men of God. Here were six vigorous, hearty, holy men. She sat down blinking, smiling, holding her glass with mock alarm, as though she had never had a drop before. The spirits acted quickly, a warm tingle spread from throat to stomach, the dark room looked as though it were flooded with sunlight. She roared at whatever they said, joke or no joke. She leant forward eagerly while Father Simon sang in his fine baritone. When the song was over she clapped enthusiastically and shouted, "Bravo" in a French accent. Then she took her leave of them and sailed down the stairs to her own room, there to dwell lovingly on the scene she had left.

In the morning they were called early and left to say their masses at the cathedral or the parish church. On their return they breakfasted and then remained quiet till lunch time while they said their offices and meditated. When they fancied lunch they had only to ask Eileen for whatever they wanted and they ate in the drawing room away from the common run of lodgers. In the evenings four of them, with Father McLean as ring-leader, went out in search of amusement, usually to a music hall. Marguerite accompanied them once to the Coliseum. Hitherto she had considered this type of entertainment "very ordinary". "I have always adored variety," she said, and when the others laughed at a comedian she did the same. Subtle jokes escaped her, she could make neither head nor tail of the patter, but tears of merriment ran down her cheeks. She was laughing at something, humour was as much a ritual as anything else.

The priests were glad to know of a good Catholic house where they would be left to themselves and therefore came to 52 not only for annual reunions but at any other time they had to be in the capital. The "Lisbon boys", as they were called, recommended 52 to other priests, knowing that Marguerite would always take in a priest at a moment's notice. Some were rich and some were poor; the poor were lodged at half price. She would not have minded running a houseful of priests at a loss. Regardless of what they paid she looked after them well. They all found her charming and golden hearted.

With them in her house her energy scarcely needed the further stimulus of drink, although she never spent long with them, knowing instinctively that the shorter her visits the more they were appreciated. It was an ideal arrangement, because although she loved fine company she also loved solitude and independence; here was the company in her house while she sat and thought of it in another room.

5

John arrived in London. Half his foot had been cut off by a runaway truck and he now had the alternative of a low paid surface job or falling in with Marguerite's plans for him. He thought he might as well have an idea of what they were. He was gaunt and limped and therefore she was put in mind of her father. It was strange that both should have injured their right leg. There was some significance in this, as in every coincidence, for her. Also she had known all along that it would happen. "When I wrote," she said, "I had a premonition that there would be an accident. I had a dream about it and it worried me. You know I'm psychic. I have second sight. There are people like that. One of my patients said she could tell I had it as soon as she set eyes on me. I think I get it from father. He had an uncanny way of knowing things in advance. If only you had come sooner!"

For the moment there were neither pilgrims nor priests—it was Marguerite's chief concern to keep these two groups apart in time— and there was even a spare room. She would treat John well and he must appear to be one of the respectable members of the family in Eileen's eyes; he must not seem like Michael. He was wearing the suit bought for his mother's funeral and he was presentable. She had supper in state with him in the dining room. Eileen brought up two plates of roast beef, Yorkshire pudding and potatoes, covered over with soup plates, and banged them down on the table with a saucy glance.

"She's such a treasure," said Marguerite, "and she's so pretty. And she comes of a family very like ours, a good Catholic family who've come down in the world. What a wife she will make someone!" Her approach was never subtle and if she had a scheme in her mind she

274

must out with it at once, regardless of whether the moment was suitable or not. "And she's a marvellous cook. A real home maker."

Several times he attempted to tell the tale of his accident but she interrupted him, insisting that he had told her already, that in any case her premonition had revealed to her all there was to know, and leading the subject back to Eileen. After the meal Eileen was asked up to join them in a cup of tea. Conversation might have flowed easily between John and Eileen and it would have furthered Marguerite's plans, but she could not bear sitting down and talking for long and she could not bear to see other people relaxing. She kept changing the subject, interrupting, sending Eileen downstairs for something, going off to her own room with the idea of having a nip, and then thinking better of it and sending John to have a look at the drawing room. By the end of the evening they were all worn out and nervous.

The next morning Marguerite rose early and went straight down to the kitchen. "Well, Eileen, and what do you think of my brother? He's the handsome one of the family we all say. And he's taken a great liking to you. He's such a nice character, very steady and reliable and it's a great pity he never married and settled down. Although, who knows, it may be the best for him in the long run. Perhaps we'll find a nice young wife for him and then I'd set him up in 83, yes, I'd hand over 83 to him and his wife. There's a lot of money in that house and with a good manager..."

Eileen, though sharp, did not see what Marguerite was driving at. In any case she was busy cooking the breakfasts and the loud hiss of frying bacon blotted out many of the words. It was unusual for her employer to appear here at this hour and like many efficient maids she preferred not to be spoken to while she worked against time.

"And when you've finished this lot of breakfasts," said Marguerite, "take something nice up to Mr John on a tray."

In the afternoon, after a nip, she had a bright idea. "Here's some money, John. You go off with Eileen to the pictures. It will do you good and I can mind the house."

She liked action to be rapid and she almost expected a proposal to take place in the cinema. When they returned and it was clear that nothing had happened she was ill-humoured. Did Eileen imagine that she had been given time off and a treat for nothing? Was the girl going to take this kind of thing for granted and become bold? Her expansiveness had gone and she was now the haughty lady of the

house. She mentioned that her room had not been dusted properly—
the last thing that she cared about—that the stair carpet was in a
shocking state and that she had had nothing but complaints from
the lodgers all the afternoon. When Eileen had been sent down to
the kitchen Marguerite started on John.

"Did you get any compensation? What did you do with it? Why
not take over a boarding house? You need very little to start it with.
You simply take over a mortgage from a building society. How much
have you got and where have you put it? Do you not think it would
be best to hand it over to me? What plans have you made? Mind
you, you would need some woman to run it for you, someone who
has had experience of boarding houses and knows how to handle
lodgers. If you could marry the right type you could do very well.
Have you ever thought of marrying, John?"

John listened and tried to answer when there was a pause. He had
nearly married a girl in the village but another man had taken her.
Then he had been courting a widow, nearer his own age, and the
slow courtship had been going on until he came to London. Perhaps
he should mention her. She would be a good manager and soon
learn how to run a boarding house. "There's a Mrs Earpe," he said.
"She lives near me and I was thinking of marrying her. I think she'd
be willing to come up here although her father and brothers are all
working there and she might not like to leave them."

Marguerite frowned. "Is she a Catholic?"

"No."

"John, you must marry a Catholic girl. And this Mrs, er... I forget
the name, she must be a widow. Has she any children?"

"Yes, two."

"John, how can you think of taking on two children like that?
Surely you want some nice young Catholic girl. Now I've been
thinking. You like Eileen, don't you?"

"Yes."

"I thought so. I could tell she was your type. I knew you would fall
in love with her and I know she is very taken with you, she told me
she thought you very handsome. I shall tell her tomorrow that you
have fallen in love with her. I shall help you over this because I can
see you're shy. You can leave it to me."

John raised his hand and opened his mouth in protest but
Marguerite ignored this and now started to outline the boarding
house business and get down to figures. He let her go on. Eileen was

certainly very pretty and it would certainly not be unpleasant to have her as a wife. Had she been in his village he might well have wanted to marry her. Besides it was Mrs Earpe, not he, who had started the courtship. But what he did not care for was the boarding house. He would have liked a home, a small private home and from what he had seen of 83, no one could call a boarding house that. Also he would be near his sister, under her thumb, and there would be no peace. He felt perplexed.

"Do you know, Eileen," said Marguerite at the next opportunity. "My brother has fallen in love with you. He told me so after you had been out together. He's very shy and you ought to give him some encouragement."

Eileen, though pretty, had a fear of not finding a husband, like many Irish girls. Back in Wicklow and Dublin many of the loveliest girls remained unmarried. At the moment she had led a middle-aged lodger with private means to the point of proposal; she did not love him but as she expressed it later, "any port in a storm." John was not a bad proposition and had Marguerite not tried to rush her Eileen might have taken him. For the moment she did not find the idea unattractive and when she next met him she blushed. On her next half-day she accompanied him to the cinema. Marguerite paid.

Now Marguerite believed that all was arranged. All that remained was to fix an early date for the wedding and decide whether they should take over 83 or start another house. She wrote to Elizabeth to inform her of her success. So confident was she that all was as she wanted it to be that she did not even question John. He must have proposed by now and Eileen must have accepted. In any case it did not matter; she, Marguerite, had done the proposing and she had done the accepting.

One evening Eileen came up giggling to see her. "What do you think, Miss Reilly. I've had a proposal."

Indulgently Marguerite smiled knowingly, "I knew it."

"Go on! You did not. Or was Horace saying something to you?"

"Horace? What Horace?"

"Mr Stebbing." Eileen was roaring her head off. "No. 5."

Marguerite's expression changed. Her brother's fiancée had no right to carry on with lodgers like this. She sat on the edge of the bed—they were in her room—and looked at the girl with fury. "You must stop this kind of thing. I hope you made it plain to him he had no right to do it."

Eileen tittered. "Well, Miss Reilly. He's not a bad man at all and I might do worse. He's been after me for some time. He's well off."

"Eileen, what are you thinking of? You are engaged to my brother."

" 'Tis the first I heard of it."

"What do you mean? You gave me your solemn word. You promised him. He's desperately in love with you. However, we'll say no more about it and he need not know about this." In her anger, forgetting that the girl had a temper too, Marguerite went too far. She looked at her contemptuously. "It's a very great honour for you to be marrying into our family and you ought to try and show your gratitude. After all you are only a servant and you owe everything to me. If I was anyone else I would have been against this marriage. Anyone else would have thought you were not good enough. But I am different. I know you have a good character. I am even prepared to set you up in a house of your own. After all, who are you that I..."

Eileen banged the door behind her and approached the bed. "Don't you talk to me like that. I wouldn't marry into your family if it was the last one in the world."

"Leave the room instantly. Leave the room. And when you've recovered yourself come back here and we'll discuss it properly."

After a moment's worry Marguerite dismissed the incident. Yet something told her she must act quickly. She hurried to a local solicitor and asked him to draw up a form transferring 83 to her brother. Having done that she returned home to find that Father McLean had arrived. John was moved out of his room and sent over to the other house. The fire in the drawing room was lit. She had a talk to the priest. "Eileen is going to marry my brother. It will be such a good thing for both of them and I'm going to set them up in a place of their own. Be sure and congratulate her when you next see her."

The congratulations were the last straw. Eileen went straight down and knocked on Marguerite's door. She was livid and she wanted an immediate explanation. "Why did you tell Father McLean I was going to marry John?"

"I've decided to think no more of what you said yesterday."

"But I'm not, Miss Reilly. I've no intention of it at all. Sure the poor man's never asked me and if he did now I wouldn't be taking him. I wouldn't be marrying him at all, it's you I'd be marrying and the Lord preserve me from that!"

After telling her many home truths Eileen went down to the kitchen, firmly resolved to pack her bags and go away, firmly resolved too to marry Mr Stebbing. At least he had no sisters to worry the life out of you. At least no one had made him want to marry her. He was a comfortable old thing and not the sort to go running after anyone else. He wanted a home and housekeeper. Well she didn't mind providing him with that.

Marguerite wept. Never had anyone spoken to her like that before, she thought. The girl was thoroughly impertinent and worse. She was wicked, downright wicked, to suggest letting down poor John. And yet this realisation of Eileen's wickedness did not make Marguerite any the less anxious to secure her. On the contrary, her blood was up and she must have her way. She went up to the drawing room. Here she spoke to the priest with the tones of sweet reason. Her low husky voice had never sounded more from the heart. The traces of tears of fury he mistook for tears of sisterly affection. Her poor brother! After pledging her word the girl was thinking of going off with one of the lodgers. "'You must speak to her, Father. Please help me out. I am so sorry to have to ask you but I know she will respect your word and I should be so grateful."

How could Father McLean do otherwise than believe her? What personal gain could she derive from such a marriage. It was, it must be the most disinterested wish to help her brother. In fact she would lose financially because she intended to give them 83. How could he read into her sad expressive face and into her gently husky words her ruthless desire to run the lives of all around her, her uncontrollable urge to play a God-like rôle? He had known her only as the ideal, golden-hearted landlady, tactful, obliging and considerate. He could see that it was with the greatest reluctance she had dragged him into this affair.

Fixing her eyes on the high curtain rail so that the large expanse of white below the iris gave her eyes the look of a martyr in classical paintings, she said, "When my brother told me he wanted to marry Eileen, naturally I thought for a moment her position not altogether... But then, I thought, anything for his happiness, and as long as she makes him a good wife, so far from putting obstacles in his way, I shall help them. You know, Father, we have always been such a devoted family. We share everything. I'm quite prepared to forgive her all this so long as she makes John happy."

Eileen was brought up to the drawing room and left alone with the priest. Marguerite hurried over to 83 to fetch John. During their brisk walk she told him what he must say. "Of course you must say she agreed to marry you. She did. It is no use you saying you never asked her. Of course you did. I did it for you. You love her, John, do you not? Yes, yes, I know you do. Did I not tell you only yesterday that all was arranged?"

In the drawing room they found Eileen in a rage. "You don't know Miss Reilly as I do," she protested. "It's a pack of lies. There's not a word of truth in it from beginning to end."

Marguerite with a look of infinite patience and tact, introduced her brother. "Now we must sit down quietly. Eileen dear, you sit down too and make yourself comfortable." How admirably did her smoothness and calm contrast with Eileen's outbursts. Looking at the girl straight in the eye, fearless because she now believed every word she said, Marguerite outlined the story once more. The marriage had been arranged and everyone had been satisfied; then a lodger had proposed and Eileen changed her mind; this was a terrible blow to John who would be heartbroken if he did not marry her; all she, Marguerite, wanted was her brother's happiness.

"Say you never proposed to me in your life," shouted Eileen. "Go on, show some courage."

John hung his head abashed. Had he told the truth, had he backed her up, Eileen would have married him. She would have won this round, made her point and vindicated herself in the eyes of the priest—and she had the deepest respect for priests. And having done that, grateful for John's support she would have married him—that is, if the man wanted her. But his cowardice decided her. If the fellow couldn't stand up to his sister now he never would, and what would life be like for his wife then?

Marguerite answered for him. "Poor John, he's very upset. Not only did he propose but he was accepted. And things had gone so far that my solicitor is drawing up papers to hand over 83. Now would I do that if no proposal had taken place, I ask you?"

Her victory was a moral one. Father McLean was on her side. But her tactics confirmed Eileen in her decision. She would get out of the house tonight. Marguerite accompanied her to the basement, walked into her bedroom and saw the half-packed suitcase. She was like someone possessed. Muttering, waving her hands, weeping, letting her cigarette burn away until it hurt her fingers, she persuaded the girl to enter her room, then darted out suddenly and locked her in. "I can see what you're up to," she shouted through the door. "You cannot get away so easily. You cannot break your promises so lightly. You cannot break my brother's heart."

She hurried to her own room and had a long drink. Her brother, who had been waiting in wretchedness in the dining room, knocked at her door and called to her. He must not come in here. She must have another drink and everyone must be out of the way. He must not go near the basement or he might try to rescue the girl whose shouts were growing louder all the time. "Go back to 83, John. Go along. I've a lot of work to do. Eileen is having an hysterical fit and we must all keep away from her. I know that. I'm a nurse and know what to do with people like that." She stayed with her ear against the door until his steps had receded along the passage and the front door shut behind him.

The next morning the lodgers came down to an unlaid table and no breakfast. Marguerite was in a deep sleep after the drink. Eileen had slept at last, had finished her packing, was now wide awake and ready to fight her way out into the street as soon as the door was opened. As soon as she knew the lodgers would be about she shouted with all her might. "I'm locked in. I can't get out." She heard people hurrying down to the basement. Some loyalty to Miss Reilly still remained. She did not want to disgrace her publicly and she knew she would be more likely to get her to open the door by reserving this as a threat. "Go and get Miss Reilly," she shouted. "Knock on her door and bring her down here. She may be able to find the key. It was an accident."

In view of the publicity Marguerite had to let her out. The lodgers would have sent for a locksmith. She told a long story of locking the door by accident, thinking the girl was out. There had been burglars down there once and they were afraid of a recurrence. Eileen backed her up in the story and even cooked the breakfasts. She left the house in good humour and with much affection still for her employer. Later she married Mr Stebbing.

John returned to his mining village, surface work and Mrs Earpe, whom he later married.

6

Marguerite fell in love. Her interest in men had come late, having to work its way through the many complex barriers which she had erected. Now that there were so few years left to her in which to feel a desirable woman, her sudden love was desperate.

A tall, fair man, at least sixteen years younger than herself, came to the house for a room. He was well spoken and well dressed; she saw the mark of a public school and perhaps one of the major universities. As she spoke to him in the dining room, she knew it was essential to impress him, she cursed herself for not being in her best clothes. He had no job for the moment but an allowance of three pounds a week from his family. This was small but nevertheless to be labelled "private means", magical words which conjured up a glorious background. Could he have board and lodging for less than that until he found something to do?

She was anxious to keep him. She felt sorry for him; such a gentleman, so honest about his position, so highly educated and yet in such straits. "Well, we'll see what we can do for you. Do not worry. I am not at all the usual sort of landlady and if you're hard up I would be willing to wait a little."

His cheeks were pink and his figure well padded but she saw in his round face the traces of many hardships nobly borne, perhaps hunger and humiliation. "You remind me very much of our family. We have very small private means now. You know what it is with taxation and death duties and one thing and another. There's nothing left of our estate. That's why I had to take on this house! By the way, I have forgotten to ask you your name? And who recommended you?"

"James Walker-Higham. Father Patterson of the cathedral."

Now her assumptions were confirmed; the double-barrelled name told a tale of breeding; Father Patterson of the cathedral indicated Catholicism of the highest order, for of all the priests there he was the most distinguished, the most closely connected with the great Catholic families of the country, the most eloquent preacher, the most likely to end up with a Cardinal's hat. Marguerite's accent grew ever richer. She held her head up and looked over her curving cheeks at the visitor. She pursed her lips, threw away her bedraggled cigarette end and held her hands together, very high, pressing them against the hollow at the base of her neck. "I cannot show you your room at the moment, but it will be ready by the afternoon. We are moving furniture about. I'm afraid I'm rather bohemian like that! Whenever I see a chair or something—you know I adore beautiful things—I feel I must get it and then I have to change everything round. You have come at a bad moment in a way. Next month I'm going to have the place done up. I do that regularly to keep everything fresh. The dinginess of many of the boarding houses round here is really appalling. *C'est terrible n'est pas?*"

He decided to stay and he found her interesting. There was a strong flavour about her and he was obviously going to be one of her pets. If he handled her properly he might get away with paying next to nothing. He was lazy and had long lived by his wits.

When all was settled and he had gone out to collect his luggage she sent for the maid. "Take Mr Seneki's things out of No. 2 and more them to the room behind. And I want you to do No. 2 out very thoroughly. Take the armchair out and bring down the..." Having completed her instructions, lengthy and complicated because she kept changing her mind, she now thought of herself. She would first of all have a bath. This was a very rare occurrence and usually, apart from her face and hands, she washed little. After the bath she covered herself liberally with talcum powder—a lodger had left a bottle of this behind some two years ago and she had kept it by her. She put on her best dress, her finest stockings and a hat. She made up carefully and well. She drank a very little wine and took her cachous.

She went up to the drawing room and looked around. Like the priests, Mr Walker-Higham must have use of this room. She set a match to the fire and put a new sheet of music out, a Portuguese fado which Kathleen liked and which came from Lisbon. That would show the family was travelled and cultivated. On the table by the window she laid a volume of *Gems from the Classics*, a massive collection of quotations and pictures, bound in green leather with gold letterings and edges. She opened it at random to suggest that serious reading had taken place. She dealt with dust by flicking her handkerchief.

When he returned she was ready for him and he was amazed at the change in her appearance. Excitement and the nip had brought colour to her cheeks and a sparkle to her eyes. She might have been in her middle thirties with her contours so intact and clear and she wore her clothes well. "I will show you up," she said, "the maid will bring up your luggage later." She paused at the first landing. "I must show you the drawing room. Please use it as much as you like. No one will disturb you there and the fire is always lit. If you like reading you will find plenty of books. And if you are musical there is the piano and quite a collection of music, all the classics and little things we brought back from our travels. My sister is a very fine pianist."

Having secured him as a lodger, having induced him to lounge all day in the drawing room, she now had to think up excuses for going there herself. "I've just popped in to get a book. Take no notice of me." "I've just come up to see if there was plenty of coal. I'm so sorry the bell does not work. We are going to have a new bell system installed but the men are so slow! You know how it is." He was at a loose end and glad of company and he would start a conversation, a fantastic conversation in which both showed off heartily. Minutes would fly, a quarter of an hour would pass, half an hour and Marguerite would forget everything she ought to be seeing to. Several times the phone rang and she was offered a case but she would not take it. Life in her own house was now too exciting.

The trouble was, thought Walker-Higham, that only breakfast was provided. If only he could find a way of having other meals for nothing. He was not long in finding a solution to this problem. "Miss Reilly, I do wish you'd let me take you out to lunch. I know of such a delightful place in Soho, just the sort of food anyone who has lived on the continent would like. You're too busy, you know. You should get out more. If you'll forgive me saying so, a person like you should see more of life." An earnest light shone in his greenish eyes.

The lunch cleaned him out and he made sure that she would notice this, blushing unhappily as he looked at the bill, looking preoccupied as they rode home on the bus. What a generous man, she thought, what a perfect gentleman. She really must do something in return. For the moment she had a balance at the bank and soon it would have the addition of Kathleen's cheque from her case and the takings from the pilgrims. She felt the time had come to live in the present. Now was the time to spend; she had had many years of struggle and she owed herself a treat. How well he understood this! How often he urged her to enjoy herself. "You have been a real martyr to your family!" he insisted, for she had spun the tale to him. "But you must not let them exploit you any more. I know it is none of my business but I would give anything to see you happy."

They lunched in Soho, they dined near Victoria and always she paid. Each time he protested just enough and each time her impulse to make a generous gesture could be relied on to sweep away his scruples. She rifled the gas meters, failed to pay bills and began an overdraft. She bought expensive clothes. After all she could not go out to these fashionable restaurants in any old thing. She bought sherry and spirits and together, in the drawing room, they drank. This was the culmination of her happiness. After drinking by herself in her bedroom for so long, she could now do so with a charming companion and the action could become a social action, a part of life which she shared with the best in the land. He filled up her glass time and time again and he questioned her about her finances, because her extravagance had made him extremely interested. There must be a lot of money in these houses, he thought, and she must also have quite large private means. In fact she was probably very wealthy indeed.

Drink made her ready to confide all but even less truthful than usual. She told him she had between four and five hundred a year and that she made about the same from the houses. Unfortunately a great deal of the money was spent on her brothers, sisters and their children. These nephews and nieces she multiplied and placed in the grandest Catholic schools. Her brothers were all professional men but they earned little. The sisters were nurses, of course they had meant to be doctors but the training was so expensive. She herself had almost qualified as a doctor but then nephews and nieces had appeared and she had had to start earning.

He did some sums in his head. He said, "You are too good. What you need is someone to protect you from your family." By the end of the evening he begged her to call him Jimmy and addressed her as Marguerite.

During the following weeks he made up his mind to marry her. He was not wholly calculating. Had she not been so rich he would never have dreamt of such a thing, but had she not appealed to him a very little he would not have dreamt of it either. He could not be said to love her but he liked her and found her amusing. The drinking was a bond and together, often tipsy, they both felt a sense of drifting adventurously through life, planning ways of making money in order to enjoy themselves. He had been manager of hotels and night clubs and he thought her unbusinesslike. If he had the running of this place, he could make a mint of money. It grieved him to see how badly she handled the maids and how often there was trouble with lodgers. Four rooms were vacant and this seemed to him a personal loss. He began to take over the management and she made no protest. "I shall interview the lodgers. I shall write you a very good advertisement," he said.

She had trouble with the maid and the girl gave notice. Marguerite herself could now be seen dusting banisters and cooking the breakfasts while a char did the heavier work. The lodgers found their bacon underdone or overdone, the eggs were burnt underneath, the toast was cut extraordinarily thick and irregular and was as black as pitch. Jimmy helped out, making a great display of his tender feelings. "My dear, you should not have to do these things. Here, let me," he said, taking the duster from her willing hand. "And tomorrow I'll be up at the crack of dawn and I'll show you how a breakfast should be."

His kindness brought tears to her eyes and she realised that he loved her in the purest and gentlest way. When he asked her for a loan of five pounds that afternoon she gladly gave it; it was the least she could do. It was an odd five pounds made up of thirty shillings in advance from one man, a pound from another, ten shillings from another and a collection of shillings and pennies from the meters. Rent, rates, lighting, heating, repairs, groceries remained unpaid. The first threatening letters came, the second and then the dreaded final third. Each post brought some hateful statement and one glance told what the typewritten envelope with the halfpenny stamp was likely to contain. At last her bank manager sent her a sharp reminder and suggested an interview. In the drawing room after two glasses of sherry her tongue was loosened and she told Jimmy something of her troubles. It was a mixture of naiveté and cunning. Always she remembered that she was supposed to have something like a thousand a year coming in, and yet she was in debt. Tangled, agitated, with a splitting headache—hangover and insomnia—she took her small steps up and down the room, shifting her weight from left foot to right foot so briskly that she looked like a mechanical toy, tipping over from one side to the other, a straight line from toe to crown. She had passed from tears to outrage at the ingratitude of her family. She now passed on to her contempt and loathing for the bank manager. "How dare the man write like that. How dare he. I shall simply take my account to another bank. We have dealt with him for years. He must be mad."

Fortunately for Marguerite, Kathleen arrived within the week. Marguerite was waiting for her and as soon as she opened the door began her tale of woe. She had done this trick to Kathleen so often and it had never failed. "Oh, Kathie. I'm so worried. I'm terribly worried. I do not know what I'm going to do this time. I really do not. There have been so many bills. I sent Lisa off two new gym slips and other things—and how expensive these things are, *chérie!* And then I had to have the roof repaired and now they're going to cut off the gas and electricity. The phone was cut off this morning. And if that happens what shall I do? The house is full, thank God, but they'll all go if the light goes. And then the fine on the mortgage is mounting up—every day it mounts—every day on that alone I'm losing ten shillings." This was gross exaggeration.

Kathleen was sorry for her. "Well, Marguerite, why did you get behind? I'm sorry."

"Look, Kathie. Be a brick. You're always a brick and I know you'll help me out. Have you got a cheque? Did they pay you?"

"But Marguerite, you've taken every cheque I've earned. As soon as I get into the house..."

"*Chérie,* I know. You've been a perfect dear. But I've kept an account of all that. And as soon as I'm on my feet I mean to pay you back. Besides, if anything should happen to me this house would go straight to you and so would 83. Everything I have would go to you. I'm doing all this for your sake and for Lisa. I want that child's future secured. She is so brilliant. But if this house closed down it would never go to her. Oh dear. I do so want to avoid that. It is not just for myself. Why, if I only thought of myself I should give up all this and do nothing but nursing."

Kathleen handed over her forty-two pounds, the wages of ten weeks at four guineas a week. She knew she had been a fool as soon as she endorsed it for her sister. In a flash Marguerite's tone changed. "Thank you, *chérie.* It was very sweet of you. Where are you going to stay? I'm afraid we're full up here. There's probably something at 83. And I'm so busy—so much to see to. You had better go over there to make sure there's something for you. Now hurry along." Marguerite neither offered her a cup of tea nor a cigarette. A thought struck her. "Did they not give you anything else?" Often after cases grateful patients added a small sum to the wages. In this case there had been ten pounds. Kathleen had observed the change of tone and the anxiety to hurry her away. Her sympathy had vanished. "No, they didn't," she said, and banged the front door behind her.

The forty-two pounds were not spent as they should have been. Marguerite paid three pounds off each bill with a promise of more and soon blew the rest on meals out and drink. When this was done she was forced to ask Jimmy for something. He gave her three pounds and went to look for a job. In spite of her crises over money the woman obviously had plenty and once married he would take charge and steady her. For the moment he was anxious to preserve the impression he had created of selfless devotion. Besides, now that the sister was hovering round, it would look better if he was working.

He found a job as manager of a night club by pulling strings. The age of cocktails and bright young things was well advanced and had reached down from the upper crust to underlying crusts. This club was a second-rate haunt and his duties began in the late evening and ended in the small hours of the following morning. He stood by the door and asked if people were members and made them sign a book. He hovered around the tables, sophisticated in his evening clothes and mirthless smile, paid to create the illusion that the clientele were the cream of the nightclub world. There were middle-aged men with young girls and there were young couples from the suburbs who attempted to look a great deal naughtier than they were or ever would be. Five pale-faced men played instruments in one corner while the couples rose and steered their way in the restricted space. It was unpleasant but too flavourless to be anything like an inferno. However, this spot fascinated Marguerite. It was a side of life she had not seen. She had nursed patients who betrayed through their fashionable blasé drawl an enthusiasm for these things, patients of good family. Several times a week she went there with Jimmy, sitting by herself at a table waiting for him to join her in his spare moments, filling in time by drinking. One could not say she liked it exactly; unobservant though she was she could not fail to sense the lack of *joie de vivre*, and jazz got on her nerves. But Jimmy's immaculate presence and the drinks made it worth while. To be separated from him for hours in the evenings was agony. She could not have too much of his company, she could not see his face too often. Afterwards they rolled home very tight, doing all the stock things like fumbling for the lock and swaying.

He proposed to her and she accepted. Then she made a speech about her duty to the family, an automatic speech, an echo of a past she had broken with. He disagreed with her and to make his point drew her onto his knee, kissed her hair and held her hand. There she sat as coy and blushing as a girl in her teens. She had forgotten her age, she had told him she was much younger than she was, and she did not doubt for a moment that he loved her for herself. She had had no practice at this sort of behaviour and felt strange. He could sense this and confined himself to displays of affection rather than passion. In any case that was what he felt. His infrequent kisses landed on her cheeks, brow, hair and hands. His fingers gave her hand a rhythmical patting. He was relieved when, trembling slightly, she withdrew herself from his knee and moved to another chair. She was shy with him now, and though longing for his gentlemanlike embraces never made the first move.

He rose late every morning and she personally took him up his breakfast on a tray. She supervised the preparations of this breakfast. The tray must have a fresh cloth each time, there must be two rashers of bacon and two eggs, the toast must be placed in a toast rack, the butter must be in little pats. While he ate, propped up with pillows, clad in a Paisley silk dressing gown—for somewhere he had acquired a very large and fine wardrobe—she looked at his ruffled fair hair and little moustache with the most besotted and doting expression. They called each other "darling".

All through the afternoon they sat together in the drawing room. Jimmy grew a little colder in manner as the days went by, but to make up for it he spoke constantly of the fine engagement ring he was planning to give her. This ring gave him an excuse for going out alone when life in the house was too much for him. All he had to do was say, "I'm going out for a stroll. No, you mustn't come with me this time," and she was sure he was going to hunt for the ring. When he returned without it she knew that it was only because he was fastidious and prepared to search until he found just the right thing. She never imagined that he had really been to a cinema.

He began to find excuses for taking her to the club less frequently; all the tables were booked for ten days ahead, he would be so busy that he would not be able to find a minute to talk to her, the owner might be there and would not like it. She missed him during his absences but she remained happy. The bills were still unpaid, demands continued to arrive but she took no notice. Soon she would be married to this handsome devoted man. Soon all her troubles would be over.

When she was alone she gave herself up to daydreams. The honeymoon would be in Venice with old palaces, gondolas and canals. She would ask her most distinguished patients to the wedding. It would be a very large affair at Westminster Cathedral. She would meet Jimmy's family at last and they would be pleased. There was apparently some trouble between him and his family, she could not quite make out what it was, but she would put it all right. She did not dwell openly to herself on the intimacies of marriage; they were like the concealed lighting which gave a glow to all her pictures.

Kathleen interrupted the loving couple one day. Jimmy was eating his lunch off a tray in the drawing room (now that he was engaged he had only to ask for what he wanted when he wanted). Marguerite was sitting on the arm of his chair. She rose instantly and glared at the intruder. "What is it, *chérie?*"

"Nothing. I just thought I'd like to play the piano. I hardly ever have the chance. I didn't know anyone was in here."

"Well, I'm afraid you can't play at the moment."

Jimmy looked lordly. "Introduce me, dear." The introductions were effected. Kathleen thought she had better sit down. She chose the chair nearest the door. Jimmy beheld one of the everlastingly sponging relations. He must show who was master. "I'm frightfully sorry," he said to Kathleen, "but smoking absolutely ruins my food. Do you mind putting out your cigarette?" She did as she was told. After a few minutes of awkward talk she slipped away.

She did not forget the insult and she was worried. Her sister seemed to be very friendly with the man. She had been sitting on his chair. She had a talk with Mrs Potter and learnt from her all that the last maid at 52 had told her. It seemed that Marguerite was thinking of marrying.

Kathleen was now thoroughly alarmed. She had believed that the houses were intended for Lisa. Acting on this assumption she had handed over nearly all her wages ever since she had started earning. She had discovered, too, that the fifty pounds left her by her mother had been taken by Marguerite and Marguerite had explained this away. "I invested it for you in the boarding houses. I knew you would like to feel you had a share in them." And now this man would take over everything and she and the child would be homeless and there would be nothing in her old age. The houses were not Marguerite's to give. And poor Marguerite herself would probably lose everything. He would make off as soon as he had got all he could out of her. A young man like that could only want to marry her for her money, could not possibly mean to live with her for long.

For once she did not confine herself to ineffective bitterness. She acted. From the seclusion of her back room in 83 she wrote to Elizabeth.

"Chérie. (Kathleen too had adopted this opening, a little half-heartedly). *Am very anxious about M. You know Walker-Higham in No. 2, M. is engaged to him. I don't think he's quite the right man for M. For one thing he's years younger, has no definite work, is doing something temporary in a night club, and I'm sure imagines M. is much wealthier than she actually is which boils down to the fact that he's marrying her for the money. He's very nice and suave and all that and M.'s absolutely head over heels, as she thinks, in love with him. I think personally it's just fascination.*

Could I meet you before you come and see M. and we can talk it all over. I'm sure she wouldn't be happy. I feel, I don't know why, that he's not genuinely in love with her, only for what she's got.

All news when I see you. Lisa will be home next week.
Love,
Kathleen.

By the time she had finished the letter, and this one was the most rapid she wrote in her life, Kathleen was feeling very sorry for Marguerite. She often felt sorry for her in spite of herself. She knew that this feeling was traded on but it continued. The letter was not sent in vain.

Elizabeth hurried down with two days' leave from her case. She dashed in a taxi to 83, had half an hour's consultation with Kathleen, said, "Let me deal with this," and walked from one house to the other with a brisk step and firm expression. She was let in by the maid. "Is my sister in the drawing room? Very well, I'll go straight up."

She opened the door and walked in. Walker-Higham, after a quick introduction, looked at her with insolent boredom. Her tone was like a rap over the knuckles. They had not told her they were engaged but she would let them know she knew. "So I hear you are my sister's fiancé. Naturally I was most surprised at the news and I must confess I am even more surprised now that I see you." She sat down and crossed her slim legs. She was as little afraid of strangers as Marguerite was, and she had had far more practice in dealing with difficult men. She looked at him straight and her eyes did not remove themselves from his until he had been compelled to look away. Her high controlled voice was dry and light and thin. "Well, congratulations, *chérie*. I should like to know your plans. You must understand, Mr Higham—" (the omission of Walker was a deliberate insult) "—I have to know because I have advanced my sister considerable sums—" (this was true enough) "—and I myself am rather short at this moment. Forgive me if I bore you with a business discussion."

During the discussion Elizabeth deliberately brought to light many facts. She spoke to her sister as though they were alone together. "As Mr Higham is your fiancé I know I can speak openly." It was revealed that there was a heavy mortgage on this house and on the other. Marguerite did not own them as she had alleged. There was no unearned income in the family, not the smallest amount, and there never had been. The brothers were not professional men. The nephews were not at the grandest schools. Marguerite, unused to considering the truth, was bewildered and appeared to hedge. She was not really hedging; she was trying to disentangle her fantasies. She spoke as though conscious of the truth for the first time, under pressure from Jimmy himself, because just as Elizabeth had expected, he was the most anxious to discover exactly what the financial position was.

When the discussion ended, Elizabeth sighed. "You know, *chérie*, I'm simply dying for a cup of tea." Marguerite therefore had to leave the room to look for the maid.

Elizabeth was left alone with Jimmy. She looked hard at him, with a mixture of amusement and contempt, forcing him to hear all the words she did not speak. I know your type. You know very well that I've got your measure. Well, now you know everything it's up to you to extricate yourself as you like. My only concern is that you should do so and I feel sure you will.

After the silence, she adopted the method of asking questions. Now her voice was weary and distant as though the whole thing was a great bore. "How long have you been in London? What exactly is your profession? Does your family live here? Has my sister met your family? What is this night club work? Is it interesting?"

To each fumbled reply she made the same comment. "Really!"

When Elizabeth had taken her leave, Marguerite went over to Jimmy's chair and stood looking down at the top of his head, wondering why he did not look up at her, wondering what he was thinking. He was unusually nervous, normally his hands and feet performed no functionless motion, but now his fingers scratched at the chintz and his toes beat against the carpet. He looked at her with a puzzled childish expression and it became him. She interpreted it. He was sorry for her. He was unhappy because she was in debt. He was considerate and generous. And she was the same towards him. The thought that he had been troubled on her account made her tears flow. She stroked his hair. She found his hand and held it. "I did not want you to be worried about my affairs," she said. "I have a great many worries but I did not want you to know. You've been so good to me and you have enough difficulties of your own."

In reply he cleared his throat and gave her hand a squeeze. He was sorry for the woman, he was good-natured and had no trace of vindictiveness but he was in a fix. He must find the right way of slipping out of this without a scene. He spent the evening lecturing her on how to run a business properly; it was the last good turn he could do her. She sat on the chair opposite him and listened with half an ear. She was glad to hear him speak like this. It showed he was interested in the place and looked on it as his. With him it would run very well. She poured out some sherry and a glimmer of gaiety came back to them both.

During the next day he managed to remove one of his suitcases from the house and left it at the luggage office in Victoria. The following day, as he was about to remove another, she met him at the foot of the stairs. He said he was taking suits to the cleaners. On the third night he took two big trunks to the night club with him. To make this seem normal and above board he took her with them in the taxi. He told her that he was reduced to selling his suits to members of the band. "I must raise some money to help you," he said. "In any case, I'm too fat for them now. You've been looking after me so well, that's why."

293

She smiled happily. "Poor you. I often wonder what you did for food before you came to me. You must have had some very hard times."

Several days later, with one small attaché case, he went out for a stroll (again she believed it was to look for a ring) and never returned. She waited in the drawing room for hours. She listened for the turn of the key in the front door. As each lodger returned she darted out thinking it might be Jimmy. Daylight waned and she sat half dozing by the fire. The sky turned to a dark blue and stars came out. The light from the swinging street lamp made the shadows go up and down, up and down, on the opposite wall. What was the time? He must come back in time to dress for his club. Or had he gone straight there? Perhaps he had a spare suit there. There had been so much talk of taking suits from one place to another. At eight o'clock she knew he would not come home that evening. She dragged herself up, switched on the light, drew the curtains and threw some more coal on the fire.

She drank three glasses of sherry straight off and went back to her chair. She worried a very little about Jimmy. Perhaps he had had an accident? No, he had probably been hunting through shops until they closed and then he had gone to a restaurant and then on to the club. He would go in a taxi. He would whistle for one, standing tall and well set up on the pavement, and then he would fling himself into the back seat, smiling, every inch a gentleman with his well-kept hands and double-breasted waistcoat. In the morning she would see him again and perhaps he would have the ring. He would be secretive about it and spring it as a surprise. He was like that, full of fun. He had slipped a framed photograph of himself behind a cushion and then told her that he thought she had dropped something there. How they had roared! She laughed now as she remembered it. During these past weeks she had grown softer and more dreamy. Her movements were slower. The boldness and lack of self-consciousness which had once been so characteristic of her had given way to a quiet shyness. Even with Elizabeth she had been yielding. Her square mouth looked moist, her skin looked smooth; some stirrings of sensuality had eased the tension of her limbs and now she could sit languidly for hours.

She would make Jimmy happy. He would have a very easy life here. She would make up to him for all the trials he had endured and everything she had would be his. She would take cases to make extra money so that he could live well, in the style which was his due.

In the morning when she took up his tray he was not there. The bed had not been slept in. There were no hair brushes and combs on the dressing table, no shaving things on the marble-topped washstand. As her hand touched the icy marble she felt a sudden apprehension. She opened the wardrobe, pulled out the drawers. There was nothing there. Slowly she went downstairs with the heavy tray and laid it on the kitchen table. She stood watching it, motionless and white-faced. She sat down on the hard wooden chair and looked out onto the area steps. She felt shut in, enclosed by the walls of this house, unable to rush out and search London. He must have had an accident, some dreadful accident. Perhaps he was lying in a hospital at this moment asking for her. She had not eaten for over fifteen hours and she felt disembodied.

She phoned the club and there was no answer. There would be no one there until the evening. She phoned several of the big London hospitals. She phoned Father Patterson but could not get on to him. At lunch time she nibbled a bit of dry bread and it choked her. She could not face proper food but she must put something inside herself. Worry was in every part of her, in her blood stream, in her head and in her heart. She lay down on the bed and tried to sleep. She did not want a drink, she would have hated one. She wanted only one thing, Jimmy's presence. She knew that without it she was not really alive. Each time the door opened, each time she heard footsteps she jumped off the bed and opened her door. Several lodgers and the maid saw her stare at them with large, blind-looking eyes, her mouth hanging open, uncomprehending, silent. A hundred visions of Jimmy, mangled, in a hospital bed, tormented her. If he was unconscious they would not know where to phone. Would he have his address on him? How would they know the name of his landlady?

In the evening, with a beating heart and trembling hand she phoned the club. The bell seemed to ring unanswered for ages. Her voice croaked through her dry mouth as she asked for him. He was not there. He had left the job the day before. They were sure. Quite sure. He had given notice a week before. They were absolutely sure. No, it would be no use going there. He was not there. He would not be coming back. He had not said where he was going. They knew nothing at all. She pleaded with the voice, trying to reach it though the mouthpiece which was now moist from her gasping irregular breathing. The voice was her last link with Jimmy. She confided to it. She was his landlady. He had not come home. He had disappeared. All his things were gone. The voice was sorry, it could not help her. It said he might have left London.

As she replaced the receiver she saw the truth. She knew that his hairbrushes would still be upstairs if he had met with an accident. She understood why suitcases and trunks had been taken away. The languor had gone for ever. Her limbs tightened and her face was set. She walked down the stairs like some regal character in a play, her chin jutting forward, her lips pressed together. She looked old, a very old lady with the glare of the badly shaded electric bulb in the hall shining full into her blinking eyes. She gained her room, locked her door and went straight to her cupboard.

A bottle and a half of Médoc awaited her. The half-bottle had a strange taste because it had been opened long ago, early on in the days of Jimmy, before she drank sherry in his company. But the taste was of no importance. She did not notice it. After one drink she wept quietly; after the second she became hysterical; after the third she felt sick, frenzied and in pain; after the fourth she fell onto the worn carpet, near the unlit gas fire, in a heavy coma which became a long dreamless sleep.

7

In order to deal with Higham, as she continued to call him, Elizabeth had had to leave the castle of the Duchess of –. When she returned to the side of her high-born, even royal, patient, she began to doubt the outcome of her words. Perhaps he had not grasped that Marguerite was poor. Perhaps, in spite of it, he still intended to marry her, run the house himself, make it pay and then make off with the money when a good sum had accumulated. No letter had come from London. She must go and see for herself what was happening.

While patting skin food into her patient's withered cheeks, for Elizabeth's easy duties included face massage, she asked for further leave. The Duchess would not hear of it. She was an elderly woman, bored with the solitude of her vast castle, fretful to find herself disabled by rheumatic joints, deaf when unaided by an ear trumpet. She had been a notability in her day, quick-witted, sharp-tongued, active and enterprising and now that she was the dimmest shadow of her former self she did not want the company of her equals; those of her own age would be equally tottering, those younger than herself might pity. With a paid companion you could do as you pleased, the relationship was uncomplicated. This nurse, who had first looked after her during a bout of rheumatism, was the ideal person to have by one; she was light-handed, well adapted to her new surroundings, useful at deputising with the servants, really indispensable. Since Elizabeth had come the old lady had found everything much smoother. The nurse appeared lively and charming because she always listened attentively and yet she was not one of these high-spirited noisy creatures. She handed one one's stick and trumpet with the greatest tact at the right moment. She did not try to call attention to her own personality, did not obtrude in any way, seemed to have no existence other than that which she was asked to have. It was tiresome and unexpected of her to ask for leave again.

"Why do you want to go?" asked the Duchess, with the sharp rusty voice of age.

"My little niece is home for the holidays and I like to see her just once each time she comes home. Just for a few days, your Grace."

"It can't be done. Not for the present."

"The poor child will be very disappointed. She was so looking forward to seeing me."

The Duchess disliked emotional appeals. She herself was no sentimentalist. "Later, perhaps. Not now."

Elizabeth, when professional, had a keen sense of her patient's reactions. She changed her line. "It is not just for the pleasure of seeing her. I am almost her guardian and have to see to her clothes and arrange for her to go to the seaside."

"Do it by letter."

"That would be unsatisfactory. Now that you are better and do not need a full-time nurse, perhaps Mrs Sandford..."

The Duchess did not want to lose her. "Well, let her come here then. Have her brought here."

"But she's with her mother."

"And why can't her mother see to her clothes?"

"I really must go to London."

"Let the mother come too. The house is big enough. You can put them in the east wing.

Elizabeth had not been fishing for such an invitation. In fact, Kathleen and Lisa might make a bad impression, unaccustomed as they were to this type of life. "That would be asking too much. Really, I would far rather not take advantage of such a generous offer. I would rather go and see them for a few days."

"Impossible. Let them come here."

And so it was that Lisa and her mother spent three weeks at this ancient and historic place. They journeyed up with mixed feelings. Lisa was excited by the journey but reluctant to spend any length of time under the same roof as her aunt. Kathleen looked forward to a bit of comfort but dreaded the embarrassment of meeting the great lady, knowing how tongue-tied she would be in her presence. If you were nursing a person like that yourself then you knew where you were and you could just do your duties, but if you were in the house out of charity then you did not know what to do with yourself. Each meeting with her sisters' patrons had been a failure, followed up by the old lament, "Why did you not speak up? Why did you look so awkward? Really, *chérie*," leaving her feeling like a silly child of ten, the black spot in the family. And then there were servants, terrifying with their critical eyes.

Elizabeth had decided that since she could not go to London, it would be better than nothing to have Kathleen here. From her she could learn every detail of Marguerite's latest history. It was more satisfactory than writing. She was waiting for them at the station in the least imposing of the many cars. In the presence of the chauffeur she embraced them and carried on a light conversation, but they could tell from her glances that once again they were not up to scratch. Her eyes took in every detail of wrinkled stockings, untidy hair, unpolished shoes and crumpled clothes. They knew that as soon as she had them alone the sweet plaintive carping would begin. They were not wrong.

They were taken to the side entrance, presented to the housekeeper, led to their wing and shown their bedroom. Here, with the door shut behind her, Elizabeth began. For a quarter of an hour they were made to feel how slack they were. Then she showed them into the library next door, where they would live in the day time and have their meals, while she herself ate with the Duchess. It was the bachelor's wing, dark and masculine. A heavy writing desk by the long window urged one on to write letters to brokers, turf accountants and head offices. The walls were lined with volumes not calculated to appeal to a child or a lover of light fiction; a history of the castle, a history of the locality, a history of the family, histories of other families connected by marriage and also of their castles and counties, books on pottery, lace, furniture, coins, castles, birds, guns, horses, sporting reminiscences, etc. Lisa looked hard for something which might interest her. The glass-fronted bookcases, though not actually locked, were tightly shut and seemed to say to her, "Private. Do not touch." As she walked round, peering at the titles, she heard her mother and aunt whispering together. They were afraid of being overheard by servants.

"Poor Marguerite. You should have seen her. She's nearly out of her mind. She locked herself in her room all day. Goodness knows what she does for food. I couldn't do anything for her. Fancy walking off like that, owing weeks and weeks of rent, too!" Kathleen did not realise that this was what Elizabeth had imagined would happen.

"Well, *chérie*, perhaps it's all for the best. Better to lose some rent than marry the man. I could see he was an adventurer as soon as I set eyes on him. Poor Marguerite." She was not sorry for her. She found the whole episode undignified. But as always, she would not criticise her to others.

When at last Elizabeth had to return to her employer, Kathleen and Lisa sat down, facing each other across the fireplace. They had a strong bond; they were allies against the aunts. They giggled and Lisa imitated Elizabeth. Then they heard footsteps outside, a servant again, and sat in silence. What were they supposed to do? Sit here, combed and washed, without raising their voices until dinner was brought in? What would they have for dinner?

That evening, as on every following evening—except Fridays— they were presented with a bird. It might be a grouse, a pheasant, a guinea fowl or something of which they did not know the name. It was brought in, brown and with its little legs pointing upwards, intact on a plain white dish. Their eyes lit up. A tiny portion of the breast was carved off for them at the side table, their plates were placed in front of them and the rest of the bird, legs, wings and other tasty bits untouched, was whisked away to the servants' quarters. It was very disappointing. Also, the maid who attended them was obviously rebelling against her present task. To her they were the nurse's relations, shabby, shy, always in the way, sitting there in silence while she laid the table, unlikely to leave any but the smallest tip.

On the next day they were afraid to venture out of their sombre wing until Elizabeth came along and ordered them out to enjoy the good air and lovely scenery, and then they walked furtively along the passage until they reached the side entrance and made at once for a place where they could not be observed from the house. Each time they passed a gardener, a cowman or one of the many people employed on the estate was an ordeal. Kathleen had no idea what to say and gave them a sad frightened smile; Lisa, in whom fear rapidly became fury, looked sullenly away.

Ahead of them loomed the occasion when they would be presented to her Grace. Elizabeth spoke of this as one of the happiest moments of their lives but they knew better. In time a few books came down for Lisa, books which belonged to the Duchess's now grown and married children. It seemed to her that her age had been grossly underestimated and she looked at the fairy tales and stories of kittens, puppies, horses and little children with disgust. Her childhood had contained nothing but a parrot and she could not be enthusiastic about the lives of other people's pets now. She liked long, heavy novels with crowded canvases and drama and history. Now she knew she would be bored.

Every morning was filled with one of the marvellous health-giving walks which Elizabeth advocated, every afternoon also. After supper, Lisa was packed off early to bed and her aunt came in afterwards, asked her if she had said her prayers, made sure she had no book with her and lowered the oil lamp. Lisa was afraid to tamper with the light after she had gone. The lack of electricity was infuriating. "Why doesn't the Duchess have electric light put in?" she asked.

"What's good enough for her Grace is good enough for you," said her aunt. Lisa thought this over and decided it was untrue. It was so typical of her aunts to think a thing like that. They were always measuring themselves by the people they nursed. She hated their patients, she hated the upper classes, she hated being taken to these houses where you could hardly breathe, she hated being taken out to tea and patronised. She wanted to belong to some part of society, any part, a poor part or a middling part, and not to be perched onto a fringe of it all the time, not to be the lowest person in the room, nor to be the one who had to mind herself, nor to be the one girl in the school who paid reduced fees.

At last came the fateful moment. Elizabeth was conducting the two of them round the portrait gallery, interesting to Lisa as a display of historical costume, when her Grace appeared. She advanced slowly towards them, her clever, birdlike face hanging forwards, her small keen eyes looking at each in turn. A kind of crumpling took place which was meant to be a smile and which revealed some blackish teeth. She extended a knobbly, ringed hand.

"I hope you're happy here."

Elizabeth glared at them. "Yes, thank you, your Grace," they said in unison with breaking voices.

"And tell me, my dear—" (this was to Lisa and it was kindly meant) "—which picture do you like the best?" The Duchess adjusted her ear trumpet to make certain of the answer.

"That one," said Lisa. Elizabeth looked furious. In the first place the child should not have pointed; in the second place she should not have chosen the one person in the gallery who was not a member of the family. The lady in the picture was a smiling Italian actress with full red lips and a striped green and white bodice, painted with a dashing, impressionist sort of technique. Lisa learned from her aunt's face that she had done wrong. It would look silly to change her mind or add anything further. She looked dogged.

The Duchess did not care one way or the other, having merely asked the question out of politeness. She was as anxious to get this meeting over as they were, knowing that there could be no profit in it for either side. However, she looked at the picture in question for a second. "Yes. She's very pretty."

In time they discovered there was a Duke too. He was usually away but now appeared for a few days. These days he devoted to every form of golf, clock golf, miniature golf and the usual sort. In cap and breeches, with bent back and grey beard, a bag of clubs slung over his shoulder, a favourite mongrel at his heels, he strode about the lawns. When he saw them in the distance he waved genially and they raised their hands timidly and discreetly in return. He gave word that the tennis court should be put at their disposal and had rackets sent to the east wing. Believing that every child must long to play golf he looked out some old light clubs and had them sent along too with a couple of balls. He also thought that Lisa and the mongrel would enjoy each other's company and when he had gone the dog was more or less transferred to her. She did in fact grow very fond of it and learned the delights of ordering an obedient and ducal animal to lie down and stand up, that gratifying exercise of small but unquestioned power.

Kathleen and Lisa might have enjoyed tennis and putting, might also have enjoyed the rolling parkland with its tall spreading trees had it not been for Elizabeth. Her admonitions and instructions turned every pleasure to dust, made relationships with other people impossible, whatever class they were. With her you could not just go out and play tennis, you must remember the servants and wear white. And when all was well and there was nothing to worry about, Elizabeth would take advantage of the appearance of satisfaction to drive her lesson home. "Isn't it kind of her Grace, Lisa? Aren't you a very lucky girl to be here? I hope you appreciate it."

Kathleen looked forward to going away. Lisa waged war obscurely to preserve her own standards and keep class out of it. When the Duchess sent down the Nativity Plays which her children had written long ago, she scanned the uninspired dialogue:

FIRST KING: We have seen a star.
SECOND KING: I am weary and can go no farther.
THIRD KING: We must follow the star.

Dukes or no dukes she could have done better at any age. And as for the illustrations! She did not mince matters with her aunt. "I found them dull."

She was shown the museum which the children had made. It was in a pretty round summer house in the garden but it contained little of interest. There were hundreds of bits of flint with labels stuck to them, the edges curling off, the ink faced to a strange brownish colour. There were pieces of potsherd, rows upon rows of them, such as you might have found in any garden. There were butterflies, their once bright wings now dusty and frail, birds' eggs of the less colourful sort and one rather exciting thing pickled in a jar, but no one could tell her the name or history of this. She envied none of it.

She was shown what had once been the nursery, a sunny upstairs room with armchairs covered in glazed chintz, a charming pattern with bunches of roses. Here, looking at the toy cupboards, still inhabited by veteran teddy bears, golliwogs and dolls, she felt unhappy. How cherished these children had been that their oldest possessions were still preserved. How sheltered they must have felt in here and how easily and delightfully each day must have taken its course until the festivities of birthdays and Christmas were reached, standing out like planets among the smaller stars. She wanted to leave the room and she knew she must forget it. After that the masculinity of her own wing felt more right. It was so unlike her that it could only be temporary and could create no illusions. She was a visitor for a short time who would never come again. She would always be someone living in a place which did not belong to her, for a very short time, to be moved on suddenly because a lodger had come or she must go over to the other house because the maid had left. Envy was the sourest and least productive of the emotions. It made her hate herself and paralysed her activities. She must put herself in places where nothing could evoke it.

8

Apathy alternated with grief. Marguerite sat hunched in a chair and stared at the net curtains fluttering in back windows, lay on her bed and stared at the ceiling. Energy returned only in the form of active unhappiness and then she rose and walked up and down in her stockinged feet, smoking one cigarette after another, stubbing them out anywhere and littering the floor with matches. Her eyelids were red and swollen with crying. Often her head ached and there were twinges of sharp pain in her chest. She seldom left her room and seldom unlocked her door. She never left the house.

She had hoped for a letter, a loving long explanatory letter, but the post brought only bills for her. She could not hope for a phone call because the phone had been cut off. The Jimmy days were near and remote; they seemed to have ended only yesterday and yet between then and now stretched a space of timeless sorrow. His photograph was still on the mantelpiece, smiling, sleek-haired like an advertisement—from Jimmy with all his love. She would not hide it in a drawer or throw it away and thereby cut herself off from him. She had no intention of disowning the episode. In spite of having seen the facts she pushed them out of her mind and resolved to see his behaviour as dictated by lofty and loving motives. She could find a hundred excuses for him. Had he suddenly walked in at the door she would not have uttered a single word of reproach.

She was left alone with her age, her dreadful age which was bringing her ever nearer to the change of life. She was left alone with her past and her future, for the present had no meaning, it was one of those patches of marking time until something happened, like sleeping for a long night between two days. Dreams of the family future were infrequent and weak, colourless after her dreams of a future with Jimmy. Dreams of her past, though also infrequent, were stronger and still contained glory.

She never looked through the front windows onto the street. Her world was limited to this ground floor back and the backyards beyond. She would not go out. The street was a glaring place where light beat down revealingly onto her as onto every other passer-by. Here she was hidden in a small space, in dimness and in silence. Perhaps she felt humiliated and afraid of meeting people, but more probably she wanted to keep out of the way of further disasters. She never thought about it. She had never sought an explanation of her actions; her compulsions were to her like the voice of reason.

The Médoc had long ago been finished and she would rather go without more than venture out. She did not crave drink often. A moment came one or twice a day when she hunted for an elusive bottle, telling herself she had seen one somewhere. Then she might emerge as far as the landing cupboard to look.

The char brought her cigarettes every day and cooked the breakfast. The maid had gone. Mrs Potter, long-suffering and devoted, had left 83 at last and moved to another part of London. There were five rooms empty at 83, four rooms empty here. There were piles of bills on the dressing-table desk. There was a big overdraft at the bank and the mortgage instalment was unpaid. So was the ground rent.

She could not console herself but now as ever she could have taken no consolation from others. Their sympathy and kindness would have irked her. Their presence would have been an intolerable strain. She never thought of people, not even those who might have been evoked by the few events of her daily life and the objects around her, lodgers and members of her family. The world consisted of herself, in this house, and Jimmy, far away. In the square miles between them there might have been no living soul for all the difference it made. When Lisa and Kathleen returned she spoke to them as though they were strangers. She was curiously mild and polite. She said very little and listened not at all. She did not mind whether they stayed here or at the other house. It was not simply that she could not be bothered to think about it, she *could* not think. Her mind could not see this problem any more than it could grasp the empty rooms or the threats of summonses. She spoke to her sister and niece with no expression of grief. To them she seemed no vaguer than she had been before and it seemed a good sign that she did not keep jumping from her chair and hurrying out of the room. They had also known her long moods of solitariness before. Kathleen imagined Marguerite must be all right; Lisa was thinking about other things.

They decided to stay at 83 where they could be on their own and do as they pleased. There some happy weeks were spent doing jigsaws, crossword puzzles, playing double patience and making trips to the cinema. They lived on fried eggs and cups of tea. They rose late and Lisa stayed up as long as she wanted. Kathleen went over to see Marguerite only twice and the visits lasted under ten minutes.

Marguerite recovered herself when Lisa was back at school and Kathleen away on a case. Her sudden cure was effected by the arrival of the bailiffs. The jolt brought her to life. It was the best thing that could have happened.

The thought of these dreaded men had often haunted her in the past for she held that they brought shame to any house whose threshold they crossed. And now they had come at last, two of them, one with a moustache and one clean shaven. This must be her lowest moment and all was finished. But really it was not so dreadful after all. Her mind began to work, ticking regularly like a clock wound up after months of disuse. Worry returned and with it came energy and will. Her pulse beat faster and her face grew expressive. She cared about something other than Jimmy, cared very much indeed. She was on her mettle, she was fighting. "Who sent you? Why was I not warned?"

"You must 'ave been, Mum."

"Nonsense. You cannot come in." She stood in the doorway, her arms flung out sideways so that they could not get past her without roughness. It was her first sight of the street for a long time but she was not looking at it. She had looked puffy and slack a second ago, now the skin of her face seemed to tighten until the big bones below could be discerned. Her eyes appeared less sunken in their sockets, the grey irises flecked with orange were no longer so obscured by the heavy brows.

"We 'ave to obey orders," said one of the men drily, producing a paper.

She allowed them in. Now there were serious immediate problems to be tackled. The lodgers must not know about the men and therefore the men must be placated and made to behave co-operatively. As soon as possible they must be got out of the house. The first thing to do was to change her tone. "Come in, come in. I do not envy your job. How about a cup a tea?"

The three of them had tea together in the dining room, tea prepared by Marguerite's own hands. As they drank she outlined to them her predicament. If the lodgers were to know that the bailiffs were in they might leave and then she would never be able to pay. So it would benefit the bailiffs' masters if the men kept to the drawing room, where she would give them a fire, and make themselves scarce. She would see that they were comfortable and in return she hoped they would be discreet.

In the evening she went to the wine store for the first time in weeks; for herself she bought some Médoc, for the bailiffs some beer. When the men were mellowed and grateful she made use of them. "I say, I wonder if you would help me out? There's a tap leaking downstairs." "I suppose you find it rather draughty. It's that window sash. If you could fix it tomorrow you'd be much more comfortable."

She was at her most charming with them, treating them as friends, equals, fellow conspirators. It was a long time since they had been spoken to like this. She found that bailiffs were very much the same as other people. When she approached them—as she approached all strangers—with the certainty that they would do what she asked and yet with the suggestion that they were being extremely obliging, she could bend them to her will. Taps were mended, the stair carpet was re-tacked, several windows were seen to.

The depths to which she had sunk while no longer appalling to her would be appalling to others, she knew, in particular to Elizabeth. With something like pleasure she sent her sister a wire. "Bailiffs in. Please wire thirty pounds. Letter following." And when the money arrived she felt exultant and paid the mortgage. She had achieved a great deal; she had extracted enough work from the men to cover their costs; she had wrung money from a stone—Elizabeth; she had suffered no hurt to her pride; she had kept the truth from the lodgers. She felt strong and full of self-esteem, confident that no one else would have pulled off these things. She knew she was indomitable and a woman of spirit and she believed that all these efforts had been for the sake of the family. For the brothers and sisters and nephews and nieces she had experienced the worst. Now the phrase, "If the worst comes to the worst" had a new and cheerful meaning. A letter of enquiry and reproach came from Elizabeth, and Marguerite scarcely glanced at it.

When the men had gone she settled the phone bill and rang up the agency which gave her cases. She would nurse again. She would go out and visit former patients; after all she still had her fine expensive clothes and she must make occasions to display them. She would go to the theatre. She would get out of the house. She would also place advertisements in the local paper, fill the empty rooms and procure a reliable servant.

She did all these things except find lodgers. Therefore she decided to sell the remainder of the lease of 83 and take four regular lodgers from there. It would halve her responsibilities to get rid of the house. She had never liked it and she told herself it was only for her mother's sake that she had taken it on, and also to help out the matron friend who had turned out so ungrateful.

Her newly restored energy and enterprise seemed to be in a vacuum. There was no one on whom to focus it. She had never been able to say she was doing something for herself, and in a sense that was true. There must be another member of the family involved, the one who was her *protégé* for the moment. She had worked her way through Michael, Elizabeth, John, Kathleen, Lisa, Patrick and Joseph and she never went back a second time to the same person. It must therefore be Anthony this time; he was deserving and there had been no break with him. Above all, he was the one who would be a priest. She had not thought of him for some time but now she had a pleasant dream in which he appeared and, taking this as a good omen, she wrote him a long letter—he was at the seminary in Lisbon—asking him to come home for the holidays and telling him of her plans to take him round the continent. His photograph faced Jimmy's on the mantelpiece; the puzzled childish eyes of the nephew looked into the light, self-assured eyes of the faithless fiancé.

She found she had changed since Jimmy's appearance. He had led her to believe that she would be in a high social position as his wife and she had most easily adapted herself to this idea. Now, in the houses of her patients, she was not content to be the nurse. A life based on the patronage of the rich was intolerable to her. It was she, Marguerite, who should be the employer. She could have nursed if it had been taken as a great favour, and one or two patients were forced into expressing their obligation. But to be in a house which was not her house, surrounded by servants who were not her servants, given orders because she was paid, was not the life for her. At the same time, when the illness was severe and the suffering acute she displayed all the devotion and sympathy which had characterised her in the old days. Her pride did not stop the many impulses of warmth and generosity, if anything it drove her into them because she knew that what happened to her heart was her own affair and not a matter of payment and dependency.

Having rung up former patients who asked her to tea or dinner, she appeared beautifully dressed, imagining that she would enjoy herself. She sailed into the room with her erect, but now dated, carriage, fully expecting recognition. But after a few minutes she found that she could not listen to the talk, she could not bear the fact that they were richer and higher in the social scale. It was now impossible for her to play a secondary rôle. *She* must be the controlling spirit, *she* must direct the conversation and *she* must do the acts of condescension. She had the character of a dowager and not a hundredth part of the income necessary. She had never at any time considered herself inferior to her patients and now she realised that they did not really treat her as an equal. In any case she would not have been satisfied with that, she must be their superior. Not that she wanted flattery or respect. These she received and they left her unmoved. "Nurse Reilly is so wonderful. One of the most remarkable women I know..." would be said to her face when someone was presenting her to a friend. No, she wanted to control these people in some way, to interfere with them and to alter the course of their lives.

For these reasons Anthony was now the only person left to her and for these reasons she quickly lost her interest in paying visits. She returned to 52 and wore her best clothes for her own amusement when the fancy took her. Here she was a queen in her own domain. It did not matter what the domain was so long as it was hers.

9

When Anthony returned to England there were four of the "Lisbon boys" in the house. He too was a Lisbon boy and they hailed him as one of themselves, asking him questions about the old seminary—"Is Pickton still there? He must be getting doddery!"— and reminiscing for his benefit about their former escapades. Two of these priests were something of a legend in the school and he had heard many tales of them, so that to find himself with them in this way was delightful.

Marguerite had taken him up to the drawing room at the first opportunity. To her eyes he was manly and self confident. In fact he was as bewildered and shy as ever. Besides, there was something on his mind. The greetings and laughter of the priests, though exciting, only increased his uneasiness. They were under an illusion and so was his aunt. They all thought he was going to be a priest but he knew he had no vocation. Through the influence of Father McLean the greater part of Anthony's fees had been provided for by the Church, naturally on the understanding that he was to be a priest. On this understanding too Marguerite had bought him clothes, had sent him pocket money and was now making much of him. He had long dreaded the moment when he would have to tell the truth and everything that was happening now was going to make it a hundred times more difficult. He did not want to lose the favour of these fine, large, cheerful men. He loved his aunt and did not want to upset her. She was his family. Like Lisa before him he had found Marguerite a substitute for mother and father. She had been gay with him and entertained him. It had been impossible to resist the onslaught of her determined devotion and it would be terrible if it were not always there. For himself as for Lisa—in spite of herself—the word "Auntie" had a particular meaning; it evoked not a relation who occasionally entered one's life, but the guardian and the protector. "Auntie" in the more usual sense applied to Elizabeth.

Anthony had prayed, searched his conscience and meditated. He had discussed the idea of a vocation with his fellow students and it seemed to him that their feelings were different from his. It was not that he was worldly or yet interested in women, it was just that the sense of vocation was absent. He was like someone who had waited for an apparition which he now knew would never come, and it seemed to him very wrong to take Holy Orders without the apparition. Some confirmation of his mission would surely have come from heaven. He was very religious and had no doctrinal worries. The teaching of the Catholic Church seemed to him foolproof in every way and he found it hard to believe that there were so many intelligent heretics and atheists in the world.

The priests took him to the Coliseum and Marguerite took him to the theatre and the shops. He was growing up but underdeveloped in the chest and shoulders and he stammered. She never corrected or criticised him. His diffidence she called refinement and naturally she thought he resembled her father. She had decided to take him to Germany, up the Rhine and perhaps on to Berlin. She could not afford the trip but that did not matter. She would find the money somehow. If the worst came to the worst, Elizabeth could be relied on to react to bailiffs and the threat of shame. She outlined her plans to him.

This was too much for Anthony. He longed to go but he felt he could not accept the treat on false pretences. He must speak before the tickets were bought. He must be brave and get it out before another day passed. In the morning he tried but his mouth felt dry and he could not think of the right words. In the afternoon he was taken off to a matinee. In the evening he knew it was now or never.

"There's something I'd like to tell you, Auntie."

"Yes, dear?" Marguerite was listening with half an ear; the presence of her favourite meant something to her but his words were of no importance.

"It's about being a priest."

"Yes?"

"There isn't anything you'd rather I did, is there?"

"No. Was that the door bell or the phone? Just pop out and see."

It was neither. When he returned he had to begin the introduction all over again. He had not foreseen the difficulty of getting her attention. He remained standing this time and folded his arms. "I was wondering what you thought about my being a priest?"

"Yes, yes?"

She was still not listening. It was no use expecting little questions from her which would lead to his frank answers. He must make a statement. "Auntie, I haven't a vocation," he whispered. Receiving no answer he repeated it after clearing his throat.

"Of course you have, Anthony. What makes you think that?"

"I know I haven't. I've been thinking about it and I know. I thought if there was anything else I could do..."

She waved her hand. All this was nonsense. She knew more about vocations than he did. "Yes, you have. Do not worry yourself, dear. Many people have doubts like that. Many priests have told me that they often felt uncertain during their last years."

"But I don't feel uncertain. I do all the time. I mean, I feel certain all the time I have no vocation."

"They did too, dear. You should not worry. I know you will be very happy as a priest. I knew from the first that you were the one with the real vocation. I always thought Patrick and Joseph had none. That was why I was upset when they were not frank with me. They were very ungrateful, the pair of them. I was heart-broken."

"Auntie, really I don't think I should take Holy Orders."

She did not seem at all upset. "We'll see. We'll see. You must have a long talk with Father McLean." That would do it, she knew. She did not want to discuss the subject further.

He had expected anything but this refusal to treat his problem seriously. He had steeled himself against her anger and grief. For the moment there was nothing more he could do. Perhaps the priest would understand.

On the following afternoon he had a *tête-à-tête* with Father McLean in the drawing room. "And what's this I've been hearing about you, my boy?"

"Father, I feel I've no vocation."

The priest's face looked solemn, as far as the rounded ruddy features allowed it. The fat forehead wrinkled and the black brows descended over the eyes. "Are you sure? What makes you think that?"

Anthony described his soul's history over the last year. He spoke of his prayers and search for enlightenment. He forgot his fears, lost in his determination to get the thing clear. A vocation was a mysterious thing and he hoped that this ordained man might reveal to him exactly what it was, might even give a definition. He stressed that he had no religious doubts, that he had no dislike of celibacy, that he had really intended to devote himself to God. "If I had a vocation I'd know, wouldn't I? Not everyone who wants to have one can have it."

Father McLean was an honest man and believed what Anthony said. He believed in vocations for he had heard the call himself. He shook his head and thought hard. He could give no definition and he could shed no light on the subject. This sort of thing had happened before and would again. He saw it in a broad perspective, a certain percentage were called and others were not. It was hard on those who wanted to be and were not. But as long as the boy remained a good practising Catholic there was no great tragedy.

"Would you speak to my aunt about it?" said Anthony. "She would understand if you explained it to her."

Marguerite listened to the priest respectfully but with growing irritation. She did not care for speculation. You could make yourself do anything, you could persuade yourself of anything and Anthony should have done so. "But Father, can you not persuade him that he has a vocation? I'm sure he has really."

"No, Miss Reilly. Only he can know that."

She did not buy the tickets for Germany. As long as the priests were in the house she managed to control her feelings. Anthony was very gentle and she could deal with him more firmly on her own. Meanwhile she noticed his stammer and awkwardness and she sent him out to visit London on his own, disinclined for much of his company. There was something less cordial in her manner towards the "Lisbon boys" but they were not the sort to notice it. She foresaw a battle followed by a victory and the prospect was tedious to one who liked to settle things once and for all without delay.

The storm broke on the day after the priests had left the home. "You must make up your mind to go back to Lisbon for at least another two terms," she said to Anthony. "All the arrangements are made."

"I can't, Auntie. Not if I'm not going to be a..."

"But you are. Of course you are. Father McLean told me in private that you'd get over all this in no time. *He* knows you will. He it was who told me to send you back."

"But he himself told me..."

"I'm tired of all this talk. I know perfectly well what Father thought. He would not say one thing to me and another to you. He told me distinctly that you had a vocation. And really, Anthony, I am not asking you to decide about that. All I want you to do is to go back to Lisbon and then you will have plenty of time." She would write to the Father Superior, she thought, and ask him to work on the boy. "All I want you to say is that you will go back next term. I must write off about it as soon as possible. And soon as you've decided we can go to Germany—there's very little time left."

"I... I won't go back to Lisbon. Auntie... I..."

"You have upset me very much with all this bother. I cannot think what it is all about. I have been very patient but if this nonsense goes on you will have to go and stay somewhere else. Now make up your mind."

"I have made up my mind. I won't go back to Lisbon."

At this Marguerite burst into tears of anger and sorrow. She walked to a chair and sat down with her face in her hands. Why was it that people would not do as she wanted when she had been very docile as a child and had always done what her mother and father asked. This generation was going very wrong; they were all stubborn and ungrateful and it was baffling. "I've had nothing but ingratitude from the lot of you," she said in a tragic voice. "After all my sacrifices you've turned on me one after another. I thought you were different from your brothers and I made more sacrifices for you than for any of them. You cannot know what it cost me to keep you in a good school and then to find somewhere for you to stay in the holidays. I've had to do without so many things for your sake in order to provide the money for your education. There was no need for me to look after all my nephews and nieces as I did. No other aunt would have done it. But I wanted to give you a chance in life and I knew that if I did not take you away from poverty and ignorance no one else would. I did everything for you. I put you first and never thought of my own comfort."

Anthony felt very upset by the sight of her tears. "I'm sorry, Auntie," he said, "I'll try and pay you back. I'm not ungrateful." Far from feeling ungrateful he would have given anything to be able to hand her back some money. He did not doubt that she had made sacrifices and he knew he owed everything to her. But this could not alter the fact that he had no vocation; it had nothing to do with it. Stammering, he tried to explain this, put his arms around her, but even with her favourites Marguerite did not encourage or require displays of affection. He stood still and stared at her. Lorries rumbled past the window, the clock ticked, mournful in its precision; he had never felt so unhappy as during this brief silence.

Drying her eyes she thought over his words. "Vocation," she said at length with scorn. "What is all this fuss about? I cannot think what you mean by a vocation. It is simply a wish to be a priest and you have told me time and time again that that was what you wanted. I have spoken to many priests, great friends of mine, now Provosts and Monsignors and even Cardinals and I know all about it. They have often discussed the subject with me. It is simply that you want to be a priest. They did not make all this fuss and bother. After all, nursing is a vocation and I know about that."

He was moved but resolute. Nursing seemed to him very different from the priesthood, and although he did not doubt for a moment that she had had these conversations with Cardinals, he felt she might have misunderstood them in the same way as she was misunderstanding him. He did not know whether she was clever or not, if she was able to grasp other people's ideas. That same question had often been in Lisa's mind too; her aunt could think up many daring schemes and often carry them out, she was never at a loss, but she also never really understood what was said to her. Was it a failure of intelligence or a matter of temperament, indifference to the workings of other people's minds? He did not know whether Marguerite was really discussing the subject or not; after years of training in logic and theology, although not brilliant, he had acquired the habit of considering a subject carefully and by itself. He decided not to go into the question again. Gently, almost in a whisper, he repeated, "I've decided not to go back."

For the rest of the day Marguerite remained in her own room. She had a small nip, meaning to think things over, but she achieved nothing beyond blank depression. The next day she talked at great length, pointing out to Anthony the disadvantages of his present position. He was at an age when he should be earning now and he had no training for any job. He had had his specialised education for the priesthood and he was throwing it all away. What would become of him? How would he earn his living? Jobs were hard enough to come by these days even for people with experience and training. Did he imagine she was going to support his idleness? Where did he think the money was going to come from? If he did not intend to go back to Lisbon then he must look for something at once. She had made enough sacrifices.

Because Father McLean had taken his side and also because she had a faint hope left, Marguerite did not deal with him harshly. There were scenes and she went so far as to say, "You should go down on your bended knees and thank God that you hardly knew your mother!" But she did not turn him out of the house, and between the storms she still retained much affection for him.

Sometimes she thought that the fruitless search for a job would drive him back to Lisbon. Every day he went off early to look for work in answer to advertisements. Every evening he returned tired, hungry and despondent after a further realisation of the struggle for existence. He did her bidding patiently, helping in the house when he was there, even cleaning out the bedrooms when they were short-handed. He was moved to a camp bed in the kitchen and this meant going to bed late and being up early before the breakfasts had to be cooked. There never seemed to be anything to eat but bread and cheese. When the Lisbon term had begun and his decision was therefore irretrievable, Marguerite took the position seriously. She phoned friends and patients and asked them if they knew of anything. She put advertisements in the local tobacconist asking for pupils. But the slump was on and no one wanted the luxury of a tutor or lessons in foreign languages.

Gradually the standards lowered. At first only a respectable black-coated occupation would do but no one wanted an inexperienced, untrained clerk when they were busy sacking their staffs. Then selling Hoovers from door to door was thought suitable. "After all," Marguerite said, "some of the men who come here like that have very nice accents," and for a week Anthony did this on a commission basis, only to find he had made no more than five shillings. Then the job of office boy was not to be sniffed at for it was the first step to being a clerk and he could work his way up, but no one wanted an office boy. Then she even allowed a trade, believing that his good education would more than compensate for lack of apprenticeship and that any builder would be only too glad to employ the boy. But manual work was hard to come by and the Labour Exchange could offer him nothing. Like the bills and the shortage of lodgers, Anthony's future was a nightmare.

Finally it was Michael who found employment for him in the vegetable market. "Take it," said Marguerite, "you cannot pick and choose. It's all experience and soon you will be able to be an assistant in a very nice shop." It never occurred to her that by her

315

previous actions she had led him to believe she was made of money; she did not sympathise with his present unhappiness and worry. You gave people chances and then it was up to them. She had fended for herself ever since she was sixteen and those who could not do the same were spineless and stupid. The increased unemployment and difficulties of society had passed her by, and she had no idea why the house was not as full as before, attributing it sometimes to the inefficiency of the maid and sometimes to the fussiness of the younger generation.

Anthony grew pale and thin. The little self confidence he had ever possessed was gone. Daily contact with his father had deepened his depression. With a limited intelligence and lack of enterprise he could look forward to nothing but years of dull, low paid, hard work during the week and lonely uncomfortable leisure. Marguerite rarely spoke to him unless she wanted him to run an errand or do something in the house. "I did all I could for you," she said, "and you only have yourself to blame."

PART FIVE: DECLINE AND ABDICATION

1

In time Anthony left the house, moved out to his father's lodgings. Marguerite saw him go without emotion, asked him to keep in touch with her and gave him money. She wished him well but she felt cold, alone and with no one to care for. There would be no more pilgrimages this year and the priests would not return for many months. Nursing had slumped and good cases were hard to come by. The only bright spot in the present situation was that it was easy to get a maid and keep her. Everyone wanted work.

It was as though she heard the ominous tolling of a deep-toned bell. Her middle age was moving on and she was ill and lonely. Bronchitis made her breathing difficult and she must give her mind to dragging the air through into her lungs past the obstacles and letting it out again with a push. She coughed a lot, a thick clotted smoker's cough. She could not get out of these four walls with the paint peeling off outside and paper splitting inside, dusty and stained, untouched by her former frequent plans to clean and brighten. There had never been enough money for it, the builders had not been good enough, the moment had never seemed right. She was held here as though by a spell. Malevolent magic had cast over her this ignoble and undeserved fate and she must keep it to herself. Why? For family reasons, for reasons connected with her father, for the simpler reason that there was not a soul in the world who could help her.

Slowly her drinking increased. Days passed in which cunning about bottles followed fitful sleep filled with many vivid short dreams so that she could never be sure whether some extraordinary occurrence had just taken place in this room or not, whether really a lot of people had been talking and doing dramatic things or whether it was an illusion. And if it were an illusion, had it been waking or sleeping? When restlessness came she walked to the end of the passage and back, or up the stairs to the drawing room where she sat stiffly on a chair by the unlit fire. There was no motive for this, no purpose, nothing but a heavy sense of bewildered searching. She had been pushed up a cul-de-sac, unable to turn back and go out the way she came and she was being stifled. There was no money with which to go abroad and make a break with her present self.

The only thing to which she gave her mind was the avoidance of her family. With something of the old scheming she wrote Elizabeth long letters explaining why it would be inadvisable to come and see her: "I shall be on a case and I am very rarely in. It would be a great pity for you to make the long journey in vain and really there is nothing to discuss for the moment..."

She also begged her to find somewhere for Lisa to stay in the holidays.

"There is no room here and it is no life for a child. She needs good country air and if you could find some nice family abroad where she could go *au pair* in return for English..."

More than anything in the world Marguerite loathed visits from Elizabeth and they could not be avoided indefinitely. Elizabeth might appear at any moment, mentally as fresh as a daisy, her head full of facts and figures, concrete and precise questions coming from her tight, cautiously reddened mouth. And the first warning of her, either confronted by her neat presence at the door, or hearing from the maid, "Miss Elizabeth is here," Marguerite must dart into her room, splash cold water on her hot head and crunch cachous at a great rate before emerging for a conference in the dining room. And how difficult for her it was to know what Elizabeth was driving at, and to avoid the look of her steely reproach in the faded blue eyes. Marguerite lied and lied—anything to send her away.

"The rooms are all full, *chérie.*"

"Yes, I've paid every bill. Everything is seen to."

"No, I cannot find the receipts at the moment. I'll post them on to you. I'll have a good hunt today and you shall have them the day after tomorrow."

"Of course I mean to pay back the money. I quite understand you need it. You shall have it next week at the latest but I have no cheques left in my book at the moment."

"Of course the lodgers are suitable, *chérie.* What makes you ask such a question? A very nice type of person—very refined."

Elizabeth suspected that Marguerite drank but never risked a frontal attack, retaining a respect for her sister and unsure what she would be up against. She suspected too that the quality of the lodgers had deteriorated, her misgivings aroused about the occupation of two young ladies she had met in the passage. She was certain that debts were mounting. After fruitless talks she decided to come to the house one day while Marguerite was away and see what she could discover for herself. Marguerite was quick to guess this and it became her strongest reason for not returning to nursing.

Elizabeth's visits increased and were unannounced by letter or wire. Marguerite dropped formality and adopted the tactics of interrupting the conference by leaving the room. She suddenly rose from her chair with, "That's the phone" or "I left the kettle downstairs" and hurried out. Then, with no intention of returning, she stayed in the kitchen, keeping her ears open, looking forward to the moment when footsteps hurried along the passage and the front door banged as Elizabeth flew off to catch a train or keep one of her many appointments. And when Elizabeth grew persistent and followed her down with an angry, "I wondered where you'd got to," Marguerite made no attempt to apologise.

"*On ne peut pas parler devant la bonne*," said Elizabeth.

"*Dommage*," said Marguerite, not budging. "*J'ai tant á faire ici.*"

To Elizabeth, each visit was a disappointment and source of future worry and prayer. She could get no sense out of Marguerite. There was no way of appealing to her or frightening her. Kathleen was brought into the situation as Elizabeth's ally, and between cases—always night duty now—she spent a few days at the house and tried to discover what was going on. Marguerite did not mind this so much; she could deal with her and reduce her to tears by one harsh word; she could behave as though she did not exist.

"I've done everything for my sisters," thought Marguerite during her lucid moments. "And now they come bothering me with their worries and asking me questions and treating me as though I owed them an explanation of my every action. What right have they?" She forgot how much they had lent her. Whatever they lent or gave now could never repay all she had done for them. She would answer nothing. She would find a way of avoiding them altogether.

Now that there were many empty rooms upstairs she had a wide choice of refuge and they could not follow her up and track her down because they would not know which rooms were empty and which were not. Afraid of their visits she led a nomadic life within the house, sleeping sometimes in one room, sometimes in another, always between blankets to avoid the trouble of making a bed. She travelled light and left no traces, only the bottle in her hand. The maid, who stayed for fear of unemployment, thought her mistress nearly insane, but she was careful to say nothing to the sisters when they came. She had been warned that if she did she must go. She said stolidly that Miss Reilly was out when she knew her to be in the house.

Having discovered this way of evading pursuit, Marguerite could drink when and as much as she wanted. Her drinking varied; some days she contented herself with small nips and looked through her bills and receipts in an attempt to come to grips with her affairs and show the others she could run a business without any help from them; on other days, disheartened by the result of her researches, she emptied several bottles of Médoc, lost touch with actuality and lived a varied, eventful life in her dozes. Her head never grew stronger because her stomach never grew fuller and a small amount of wine produced an effect. She was sorry with drink, fighting and raging with drink, ready to take on all comers and give as good as she got, sick with drink, merely stimulated with drink or flat out with drink. But she was never a dipsomaniac; it was not the drink she craved, it was an absence from herself here. A change of environment or a piece of luck and it might all have stopped.

During the fits of stimulation she indulged in fantasies, somewhat heightened versions of her former ones. One day when she was sitting in the drawing room watching the maid dust the piano she burst out, "To think that not so long ago I used to press the bell—yes, all the bells worked beautifully then—and a footman with a powdered wig came in with my tea on a silver tray. Of course this was not a boarding house then and we entertained a great deal. I was engaged to a young Lord, I might have been a Duchess now, but I had to give him up for the sake of the family. He was heartbroken. We had crimson carpets everywhere, all up the stairs to the very top of the house, and oriental rugs and priceless furniture. But I had to sell all that for the sake of my family." These times were her happiest in the house for she lost herself in the scenes she described.

Her other happy moments occurred outside the house on Sundays and Holidays of Obligation. Every Sunday she went to high mass at the cathedral, dressed in her best clothes, carrying the prayer book given to her long ago by her father. She was present at mass but she could not be said to have heard it because she either went through the rosary several times, oblivious of what was going on at the high altar but conditioned to kneel and sit at the right moments, or else she let her thoughts wander. On her way out, no matter how hard up she was, she dropped five sixpences into the slot of the poor box and bought a booklet or two by the door, lingering there for some minutes in the vague hope of meeting someone—she did not know who and could have thought of no one it might be. On feast days she went to early mass at the local church and received communion, again in her best clothes, having made a dash to hear confession the night before. But confession was to her merely an act of piety; such as she did not sin and require absolution.

At the local church she cut a figure, promising the admiring nuns wonderful things for their jumble sales and listening with moist eyes while the priest told her of cases of hardship in the district. There was a large passageway between the inner door of the small church and the door giving onto the street. It was here she stood on the roughly paved hard floor and spoke to nuns and priest in a lowered voice to the wheezy accompaniment of the small organ. It was a hushed but animated place through which members of the congregation kept passing, some controlling children who could run free when the main door was reached, some with downcast heads and collected thoughts. At the end, where the light from the street had turned to deep shadow, began the nuns' quarters. She had lingered in the porches and on the steps of many churches; sometimes lit by a bright sun in the blue sky of a Catholic country where the exuberant crowd could take its religion as much for granted as its nationality, sometimes in England and Wales, where Protestantism had laid its chill grey hand on the daily lives of the Papist minority so that all but a few Irish who had lately immigrated seemed exactly like the heretics for whose conversion they prayed. Always she had enjoyed it because it was the one thing in her life whose continuity had not been broken.

"Here is something for your poor, Father," Marguerite liked to say, producing ten shillings from her bag, sometimes all in shillings because it had just come from the meters.

She was looked on as a pillar of the church and the soul of charity. At these times, having abstained from the bottle for many hours, she saw her rôle and her audience with clarity. Refreshed by her own virtue and the smells and sounds of religion she walked home happily through the grey uniform streets. Once the door had closed behind her the episode and the emotions it evoked were finished.

She was thinner. The clothes bought for Jimmy's benefit now hung loosely around her. Short skirts, in fashion for many years, revealed the bandiness of her legs and the curve grew more marked as she trod down the outsides of her heels. In the days of bustles she had thrown forward her chest and thrust out her behind; now the chest was tightly compressed in a bust bodice but the behind remained prominent and gave her the look of a trotting pony as she walked with small firm steps. The average height of women had increased and she looked very small despite her belief in her fine height. Her figure told a tale of changing fashions in dress and posture but her face was her own; not the ideal of beauty of any century, but fitting an epoch when women had the vote and careers. It was still plump and square. Age had given it a rugged rather than a lined look and there was not a grey hair in her head.

Summonses and bailiffs appeared again. Marguerite demanded help of her sisters and received it, but this time Elizabeth was out to bargain. If Marguerite expected her to hand over money every time she was in a fix then she, Elizabeth, had a right to know every detail of the financial position and also to interfere in the management of 52. Marguerite would not agree to this because she knew that once the management of 52 was altered, her position as head of the family would be gone; they would make it a kind of partnership with herself as a sleeping partner and they would have the right to come here whenever they wanted and stay for weeks and bring in their own maid or housekeeper who would spy on her.

Her interview with Elizabeth was stormy. First she wept over her misfortunes and allotted blame to all but herself, then she dried her eyes, gave warm thanks, promised to take any advice given, said she longed to see more of Elizabeth (had always wanted to, but...) and included Kathleen in her thanks. "You have been such bricks. You are such dears. I do not know what I should have done without you," then veered round and raged against ingratitude and interference. Finally they reached a deadlock.

"It's like pouring money down a drain, *chérie*," said Elizabeth.

"I shall never ask you for another penny," said Marguerite.

"*Chérie*, do be reasonable. There's no need to get angry. But you can hardly expect me to pay time and time again without having some say in..."

"I expect nothing of you at all."

The next time a crisis came Marguerite resorted to a money lender. They had driven her to this and theirs was the blame. She saw an advertisement in the papers which offered easy terms

322

without guarantee. Furtively she boarded the bus for Maida Vale, anxiously she pressed the bell of a semi-detached villa. She found herself in a front room, sitting on the largest piece of a three-piece suite, spinning a tale to a small grey-haired man. He was ingratiating and insolent, implying that he neither believed her nor wanted to hear about hardships. He wrote her name and address in a ledger and handed over fifty pounds. He wanted some proof of her identity and made her produce an envelope addressed to herself. She reached home tired and upset, for the first time feeling she had done wrong and would have to pay the price. The next day she sold or pawned her best clothes and the silver frame round Jimmy's picture. She would put the proceeds away in a money box so that when the interest fell due...

2

Elizabeth did well for herself and reached her goal. A woman patient grew so fond that she offered Elizabeth a substantial yearly income for life in return for her company. The woman, Lady Watson, a pious Catholic spinster of irreproachable connections, lived in a small country house, kept two maids, a cook and a gardener. She considered her chosen companion to be wonderfully pretty, charming, witty and sweet-natured. She dreaded a lonely old age and also thought that if Elizabeth would run the house she herself would be left free to play golf and look after the birds in her aviary.

The family were told the good news.

Lisa said, "Goodness! Fancy anyone *paying* Aunt Elizabeth to live with them!"

Kathleen thought, "She has given up all independence. I could not bear such a life."

Marguerite thought, "It's very lucky for her but then her patients have always been fond of her. I've never shone like she does."

Now began the country life for the second Miss Reilly. Every morning a maid in cap and apron gently drew back the bedroom curtains to let in the light and the twittering of birds. By the bed stood a white daisy-sprigged teapot, cup and saucer and sugar basin on a freshly laundered, embroidered cloth.

"Thank you," said Elizabeth brightly, for sleep never lingered with her but fled in a second. Wearing a mauve hairnet, her thin face glistening with cold cream, she sat up and donned a fluffy bed-jacket. As she sipped the hot tea she could see the built-in cupboards; the carpeted floor; the curtained dressing table with the silver hair brushes; the china shepherds and shepherdesses reclining, standing, capering with love, with flower baskets or with pipes, all along the window sill; the watery, misty water-colours on the walls; the swollen, shining, rosy cushion on the period armchair.

After modest dressing, she appeared at breakfast in a tweed suit with the most discreet of checks; thick, serviceable brogues of a very good make; and sensible lisle stockings. In her ears sat two squat silver-mounted artificial pearls. She was made up carefully and her face suggested constant beauty treatments which had not yet yielded the expected results. She poured out for her friend and chatted gaily.

"I do hope Charlie (one of the birds) stops moulting soon. My dear, if he goes on at this rate he'll look like a tiny vulture."

"Hasn't the beak for it, Liz."

"Not *yet*."

They laughed, Elizabeth in a thin tinkle, Lady Watson in a rich contralto which rumbled up from below a full bosom. After bird talk came comments on news in the papers—*not* political news—and then golf talk. All the while Elizabeth simulated the greatest interest so unremittingly that she may have thought she felt it. She had learnt much about birds by now and yet not enough to lose her charm as an ignoramus. She knew the difference between niblick and mashie, between bunkers and tees; she knew the significance of a low handicap. She could rattle on about the personalities at the club, careful never to be malicious about the upper crust, allowing a note of humorous contempt when it came to the traders and parvenues. She endeared herself to her benefactress by suggesting that although golf and birds were fascinating yet it was original and eccentric to pursue them so hard. Instinctively she had a flair for flattery; without knowing why she could tell whether the person she was with liked the frontal compliment such as, "You are so clever," or the concealed one, "My dear, you can't even make a cup of tea." She knew whether people wanted praise of themselves only, or their class only, or their way of life only, or all three.

As often happens when little emotion is daily expended, the talk would have led one to believe that feelings ran high. "Charlotte," said

Elizabeth, "I simply dread what'll happen when you come home after Mrs Taylor beats you. What shall we do with you?"

Charlotte, the mildest and most good-humoured of souls, liked to think she was dragon from time to time. "Ah. No soothing down for me this time, I can tell you."

Elizabeth sighed. "Oh dear. I know."

After breakfast Charlotte set out for her game, trudging to the garage with turned-out toes, a partridge feather tucked into the ribbon on her hat, pausing *en route* for a talk with the birds in what she believed to be their own language. "Tweet-tweet, cheep-cheep." Had she been an animal, Lady Watson would have been a magnificent black seal. Never was that more clear than when she cocked her head on one side and jutted forward her pursed lips for the reassurance of her feathered friends.

Elizabeth waved a hearty good-bye from the dining room window and then stepped firmly to the kitchen. Here she gave sweet clear orders and perhaps discussed a recipe. A word with the gardener, a word with a maid, phone calls to friends and tradesmen and letters occupied her next hour. Then she re-arranged flowers, changed the water, glanced at announcements of auction sales and bargains, paid a ritual visit to the birds, chirruped at them and did a little gardening. She knew how important it was to have a hobby in this circle and how devoted to it you must appear to be. Gardening would do for her; with a gardener to do the real work she would only have to tie back wayward shoots, snip off heads and tackle the weak-rooted weeds. In any case she had always loved flowers so long as they were not too bright—what is more refined than a pale flower? When neighbours came to tea she had something to talk about, better still to question them about. She won their hearts with arch modesty. "I simply adore it but I'm hopelessly amateurish. Really I can hardly tell the difference between a dandelion and a buttercup, so please don't ask me anything. Now you're the expert and I warn you I'm going to pick your brains."

She was not happy. Such pleasure as she derived from her chosen surrounding was moral rather than sensual. The dainty rooms, the well-served meals, the flowerbeds and shaped hedges were symbols only. Her nervous energy had little to do. The small scheming of whether to ask so-and-so to tea with so-and-so and how to refuse an invitation tactfully used up about one twentieth of her capacities. Pleasing her friend used up none because it had become second nature with her to play this game. Without having to think about it she had swiftly left out the "l" in "golf", pronounced "girl" as "gal", broadened her vowels and dropped a few "g's".

Relaxation was not for her now. Had she gone straight into this life from Bordeaux, or even after St Joseph's, she might have enjoyed it. As it was, she felt time was passing, there were things to be done and she was not doing them. She had sold the lease and furniture of her boarding house and the break with business worries was like the loss of a limb. She had been paid a good price and she had money of her own. She had all the clothes she needed, she had the status she had sought, for no one dreamt she was a paid companion and all accepted her as Lady Watson's very dear and very equal friend. The Cardiff days might never have existed. They did not return to her even in a nightmare form because her heart had never been involved there. But they had left her with the feeling that she must battle. And what battle was there to wage now that bloodless victory was hers?

At lunch she beheld a table, polished to mirror-like perfection, reflecting lace mats, Crown Derby china, heirloom silver, cut glass tumblers, damask napkins and her own central flower piece. She heard the squeak of the maid's shoes and the girl's humble breathing as she bent down with an offering of plain, boiled, parsley-garnished vegetables. Elizabeth was full of Christian charity but she assumed the girl was of a different order of beings. In fact her assumptions were just the same as those of Lady Watson. But Lady Watson had imbibed them, as it were, from the bottle held out to her by her nanny.

During lunch Elizabeth listened and talked coyly, archly, cajolingly, firmly or sensibly according to the subject.

Afterwards she gardened if it was fine, did mending and sewing if it was wet. At tea time visitors might come or she and her friend might go out. In either case she knew what she must say and how she must look. She lived her life as a profession.

Before dinner came the bath into which she sprinkled a few drops of expensive bath essence, a chaste non-seductive perfume, lavender or verbena. Like herself, Lady Watson had kept clear of men.

In the drawing room the two well-washed women sat, bare-armed, decked with cautious jewellery; a few colourless stones in a plain setting, a badge rather than an embellishment. They were powdered and groomed. Each had her hair parted on the side with a wave over one temple and a shingle at the back. Each had beside her a beaded evening bag containing chiffon handkerchief and powder compact. Each wore fine silk stockings and gold or silver shoes. They filled in time by reading. They could choose from the works of Belloc, Chesterton and other Catholic writers, the last two hundred books of the month, the many novels purchased on the recommendation of the girl at Smith's, the leather-bound volumes inherited by Lady Watson, or the instructive books on birds.

"Quite a nice story, dear."

"A little sad."

"Very improbable."

"One of these horror things."

At dinner time more silver was laid out, wine glasses gave promise though neither touched a drop of alcohol unless they had colds, soup preceded other courses and the maid's apron strings were frilled. Hobbies, friends, weather and the Church provided food for conversation. Politics were not discussed. Candles flattered the faded faces and lent brilliance and vivacity to the tired eyes by placing a miniature flame in each pupil, creating the illusion—for whose benefit?—that here were two lovely women, one massive and exuberant, the other exquisite and frail, repositories of gracious living, justifications of the present income distribution. Lady Watson was the happier of the two because most of this stretched back to her childhood and she loved her friend.

"I must go and tell cook how we enjoyed it," Elizabeth said at the end.

She thought it essential to give a word of praise to the servants daily. At other people's houses, if she knew the household well, she made a personal visit of thanks to the kitchen. She believed that graciousness made servants "adore" people.

After the final meal came patience and sewing, then early to bed with a good book, to be read by a rose-shaded lamp before prayers. But after prayers, sleep did not come easily to Elizabeth. Even as she tucked the grey waves under the hairnet and patted on the cream the pursuing thoughts had begun.

Might buy rest of Marguerite's lease, install good housekeeper, woman *I* can trust, put partition through back rooms, make kitchenettes and bathrooms on every floor, cut out breakfasts, let as flats. Better type. Longer notice. Monthly at least. Might buy that antique mirror and put in 52 for moment. Going for very little.

Could sell it for more. That other sale? Might go. Could put odd pieces here for moment. Which horse to back? How much? Both ways. Could cut old dressing gown at waist, make sleeves fuller with skirt material, not worn there, pretty bed-jacket. Silk bought at church bazaar nice trimming. Remember write Kathleen, tell her Marguerite probably *not* bought new shoes for Lisa. Must ask Lisa here next week for holidays. So sullen now and religion is slipping. Nothing like really nice Catholic home. If 52 flats then K. and L. could have real home together at top and M. abroad somewhere for a time. L. very impertinent last meeting, no manners, nuns displeased. Send her letter and apples. No acknowledgement of last. Mention this.

Kathleen was the first to pay a visit. She arrived, as arranged, in tweed suit and stout shoes, a never-before-worn evening dress in her suitcase.

"Did you pack your bag tidily, *chérie*? Is your nightie all right? Remember the servants always do the unpacking here and they judge one by these things. It looks bad for *me* if... What is what, dear? Ah, yes, I see what you mean." It was a long piece of silk with an ivory handle, running down the wall above the bed. "A bell, *chérie*. On no account pull it. Never ring."

Lady Watson was resigned to meeting the relations once in a way. It was explained that her golf and birds would leave her little time for them. At meals she was the only person at ease. Under the table Kathleen felt a sharp kick on her ankle. The maid had asked whether she would like anything to drink. She must say no.

In her humble way Kathleen pleased. She effaced herself, becoming like a shadow on an armchair, an illusion at the table. In the solitude of her bedroom her personality returned to her body; feeling a devil she fished a cigarette case from her sponge bag, took out a cigarette, lit it, opened the window wide and puffed the smoke into the night air, rubbed the stub on the stone beneath the creeper and popped it back into the cigarette case.

Marguerite was invited. It must be done, Elizabeth had decided, after many an hour of internal argument. After all she had never yet failed to rise to an occasion. But Marguerite mentally declined the invitation and never sent a reply. It looked bad. When Lady Watson asked if she might be expected, Elizabeth's white conscience was specked with a lie. "She may be abroad. She may not have had the letter. I think we'd better not expect her."

Lisa had no choice. She spent a week there, was told about tidy packing and the bell, was urged to display an interest in birds, country life and gardening.

"Do thank Lady Watson very nicely. It was sweet of her to have you. If she took a liking to you she could do a lot for you. But you must make an effort. Do say how much you admire the house and garden and the lovely view from here, and how glad you are to have a week in the country and how tremendously you've been looking forward to it. And be very tactful with Bessie."

"As you know everything I'm to say, you might as well say it for me."

"*Chérie*," a flush rose to Elizabeth's cheeks. "What a very rude thing to say. You're so insolent these days. One tires to give you a happy holiday. One does all one can to give you every chance. I'm very disappointed in you. Now try and look pleasant, brush your hair—how long have you had that dreadful fringe?—and come downstairs. You have only to be natural and nice."

"Natural? It didn't sound like that."

During tea the words she must say choked Lisa. How heavenly it would be to say frightful words like "damn" and "bloody" and upset everyone. Unconvincingly, like a litany, she voiced her praises.

"What a lovely house! What a beautiful garden! What a lovely aviary!"

She felt she had abased herself by this amount of sucking up and atoned for it by morose silence.

After dinner she was packed off to the kitchen to tell cook how much she enjoyed the pudding. Elizabeth tried to make her picture herself as a happy little girl, artlessly expressing her thanks in a winning way. Lisa could picture it all too well! She was damned if she would. "Thank you for the nice pudding," was not at all artless and not at all childlike.

3

Lisa had changed schools after matriculation and was now a boarder in a London convent. She needed a Larousse; she was sure she had seen one in the drawing room; she was given permission to go home one Saturday afternoon and find it.

She knocked at the door of 52. There was no answer. She knocked again, still gently and just once. Then, brushing aside all she had been told about waiting a full three minutes between each knock, she grasped the knocker and kept up a continuous hard banging. There was no result. She looked through the letter box but that revealed nothing but an empty hall floor. She went down the area steps and banged on the kitchen window, trying hard to see inside but always interposing her own reflection. She climbed up again and attacked the door with desperation. Steps sounded, and one of the young ladies, suspected by Elizabeth, opened.

"Is my aunt in?"

"No, I don't think so, dearie."

"Oh. Thank you very much for letting me in." She liked the two young ladies; they gave her chocolates and talked about clothes; they wore a lot of lipstick and young men in sports cars came to take them out.

She had the house to herself but this gave her no satisfaction. She would have liked someone to welcome her—her aunt. Always she hoped that next time she came home her aunt would be really glad to see her and make a fuss of her. Slowly she climbed the dark staircase to the drawing room, noting, without taking it in, that the door to her aunt's room was ajar. The bookshelves were dusty; the Larousse was not to be seen. Perhaps she had imagined it. Perhaps it was somewhere else. Perhaps a lodger had walked off with it, as they so often did with things her aunt promised would be kept for her. She looked out of the French windows and saw the smuts stirring in the wind on the balcony.

Then she remembered the open door. She had never been alone in her aunt's room. It would be interesting to have a look around—and if anyone discovered her there she could say she was hunting for the book.

Quietly and slowly she went downstairs, because there was something about 52 which hushed one's voice and restrained one's movements. Quietly she pushed the door. It resisted; there was something behind, something which did not make a noise when the door pressed against it. She squeezed through and looked. There was her aunt lying flat on the floor at the foot of the bed, her eyes shut. Frightened, Lisa shouted "Auntie" and drew away. Was she in a faint? Had she had an accident? Or was she... dead?

No, she was breathing. Her chest and stomach rose and fell like the Sleeping Beauty's at Madame Tussauds. She was in deep shadow because the bulk of the bed cut off the poor light from the window. Lisa switched on the light and bent down, her heart pounding, her mouth trembling, her eyes losing focus and doubling the outline of the square face by her side. Aunt Marguerite must be dreadfully ill— she must have fainted suddenly. Perhaps she had hurt herself.

Lisa began to cry. At this moment she loved her aunt and more than that she felt a sense of dreadful tragedy to see this figure, who had always represented strength and vitality to her, now prostrate and helpless and with no one to know about it. Perhaps all the time she had been shut up in here by herself she had really been very ill and wanted to hide it from everyone. It would be like her; she was brave and independent. She would never admit to weakness.

For a long time Lisa had supposed her aunt must have some secret and now she felt she knew it all and, as often before, dramatised her. Above all her aunt must not die, must not be taken ill alone like this, must not pass away in ignominious obscurity. She, Lisa, would take care of her, would tell her she had guessed all, would show that she was not ungrateful (for Marguerite had often told her she was), would gain her confidence and would once again be the favourite. She had always reacted strongly to her aunt, and even when she hated her it was a form of frustrated love. From her aunt had sprung her moments of greatest humiliation and loneliness, and from her aunt, long ago, came reassurance and comfort. She could not help admiring her, her lofty manner, her refusal to suck up to anyone (how different from Elizabeth!), her look of unexplained intensity, her stories which were obviously untrue, her strong face, her moods. Like others, she felt certain that Marguerite might love her again suddenly at any moment, was really full of affection for her and only concealed it because... because? Of course, she knew now, it was because she was really so ill. Marguerite must have made a tremendous sacrifice. Knowing she had some incurable disease she had decided to push Lisa away from her in order to spare her feelings in the long run. It was perfectly clear. Lisa's tears came faster.

And what was this disease? Probably one of those which were fatal, consumption or cancer, and which people always tried to hide from others. Probably Marguerite had not long to live and the doctors had told her so. Wiping away the tears she clumsily let her hand drop onto Marguerite's chest. Marguerite's eyelids fluttered and parted. Her voice, thick and far away, muttered, "Who is it? What do you want?"

"It's Lisa, Auntie."

"Who is it?"

"Lisa."

"Who is it?"

"Lisa."

"Who?"

She shouted. "Me, Auntie. Lisa. I came home for a book, that's why I'm here. It's only me."

Marguerite was either taking nothing in or pretending. In a second Lisa's sad love turned to fury. In the situation she had visualised, her aunt would have been glad to see her above all others, would have recognised her if no one else, would not have kept repeating the question in this idiotic manner. She rose to her feet.

Her aunt's breath smelt of drink and, had Lisa looked, she would have found the half-filled tumbler by the bed. But drink was not in her mind and therefore she did not put two and two together. Yet, now the imaginary drama had vanished, she was filled with nausea for other reasons. The bed with its grimy sheets was unmade, the carpet was stained, the windows had not been cleaned for months and the rain had driven the dirt into long uneven smears, flies buzzed around the bulb, the huge basin on the washstand was full of grey, thickly-scummed water, the cracked jug was covered in black marks where water had made dirt adhesive, there was a smell of dusty carpet, cigarettes and sweat, and worst of all there was a glimpse of an unemptied chamber pot. The litter everywhere was indescribable. There was no single object which could be called clean or bare. And with the mass of unnecessary furniture one could hardly move. It was like a derelict junk shop.

Marguerite kept repeating her question, sometimes with open eyes, sometimes with shut. Then she changed. Raising her head a little from the shoulders so that the chin doubled and trebled and the mouth fell open, she stared into the light. "Who's on the stairs? Who's in our room?" This meant the drawing room. "Who's downstairs? Who's in our room?"

"No one. I've just been up."

This made no difference, Marguerite's question had been asked not of Lisa but of someone who had recently figured in her dream;

only the dream person's reply would have counted. "Who's in our room? Who's in our room?"

"Well if you like I'll go up and see again. Shall I?"

"Who's in our room?"

Anything to put her aunt's mind at rest and anything as a first step to altering the present situation. Conscientiously, Lisa went up and had a good look. Of course there was no one there.

"There's no one, Auntie. No one at all. Who did you think was there?"

Marguerite's question grew more urgent. She was not repeating it mechanically, she *must* know. In her dream something mysterious and terrible had been taking place in the house and she knew it to be full of people. Moneylenders, bailiffs and two queer lodgers who were really spies from the creditors in disguise had been walking about and gone off up there for a conference against her. "Who's in our room?"

"No one, Auntie. No one. If you heard steps up there it must have been me. I went to get a book. But that was all. There wasn't anyone else. I shouldn't think there's been anyone there for ages."

Marguerite's faith in the dream began to weaken and the fact of Lisa's presence dawned on her. "Is that you, Lisa? Would you run upstairs, *chérie*, and see who's in our room?"

"But I've just been. There wasn't anyone."

"You have not. Why are you always so lazy? Run upstairs and see."

Now Lisa thought her aunt was out of her mind. To humour her she made the journey once more. "No one. I told you there wasn't."

Marguerite rose on her elbow. She moaned; in falling something had been badly bruised and her position gave her cramp. Her head was aching and the cough which was forced out of her seemed to cleave her skull in two. Along the nerve tracks rushed the sharp pain and she screamed.

Lisa went white. "Are you all right? Can I get you anything? A glass of water?" In books it was always a glass of water. She bent over her. "Shall I help you to get up? Do you feel bad? Shall I go and get someone?"

To Marguerite these questions were like the buzzing of some irritating insect. "No," she said angrily. "Do as you're told. Go and see who's in our room."

Slowly, Lisa made the ascent. In the drawing room she sat down on the corner sofa and wondered what she must do. Her tears had ceased but she was far unhappier than when she had cried. There was something appalling about this situation, which could not be dramatised, which could not be interpreted, which was itself and nothing but itself. Her aunt was lying on the floor in great pain and full of silly thoughts. If only one could press a button and find that a djinn had made the bed, emptied the slops, cleared away most of the furniture, undressed the aunt, relieved her pain and popped her back into the bed and drawn the curtains. But things did not happen like that. Lisa must do the djinn's work and it was a dreary task.

When something had to be done, Kathleen's mind went fuzzy. Lisa's mind, while remaining clear, paralysed her activities by a hundred possible plans. She would tackle the job this way. No, it would be better that way. No, the best thing was to do the thing thoroughly, go right downstairs, get brooms, dustpan and pail, put her aunt in the dining room and come back for her when all was done. She felt she had done it all and was exhausted, like a dream just before waking in the convent which tells you have dressed, heard mass, made your bed and breakfasted—and then you find you have it all to do. For many minutes she sat idle.

Why did she think she must set things to rights? She did not ask herself that. She did not even hope that the maid would come in and help her, did not consider asking the young lady upstairs for help. At some level of consciousness she knew that no one else ought to find Marguerite like this, guessed that there might be a bad implication possible, could not help her loyalty.

In the bedroom she found Marguerite still on the floor but sitting up. She had been scratching her hair and rubbing her face with a dirty hand so that she looked horrifying and pathetic.

"Auntie, would you like to go to bed? Shall I tidy the room and make the bed? Do you think you could get up and undress by yourself?" The thought of undressing her aunt was revolting. "Auntie, are you very ill? Do you often get like this? Do you know what's the matter with you? Please tell me. Please."

Marguerite's answers seemed highly irrelevant. "I've had nothing but ingratitude from all of them and then they come here ordering me about and asking questions. They send their spies here—even the children—and never stop asking questions."

Marguerite's head was spinning round and round. She was somewhere in the house but which room was it? Viewed from behind the bed rail, misty, never still, it looked unfamiliar. When was it—a short while ago—a long time ago—there had been a lot of people with her and they had all gone to some other room and now they must have sent Lisa down to question her. "You go back to the others. Go and join them and do not say a word about me. Do not tell them where I am. I do not wish to see any of them. I'm sick of the way they come here badgering me."

"There's no one upstairs. There's only me in the house and one of the lodgers." Lisa suddenly remembered that people could be delirious during illness and might say anything and might not know where they were, who they were or who you were. If that was the case she must expect no cooperation but rely entirely on her own strength to get her aunt to bed. She squatted down on the floor and manoeuvred an arm round Marguerite's waist. Time was moving on and she must be back at the convent in time for the rosary. Her arms were weak and Marguerite was heavy. She tugged. She would not bother to undress her or tidy the room. She would put her on the bed just as she was and cover her over with a blanket. Then she would shut the door and hope for the best.

"Oh, Auntie, please help me," she panted. "Please get up. If you could only get just as far as the bed, then you could lie down and have a sleep. You might feel better after a good sleep. Do you know what's the matter with you? Are you ill? I do wish you'd tell me."

After a struggle and a silence Lisa despaired. Then suddenly with a heave and a jerk Marguerite was on her feet, swaying, her palms pressed against her temples, her fingers raking through the edges of her hair. "What do you want, dear? You should knock before coming in. What is it? I'm very busy."

"I came home to look for..." Lisa burst into tears.

"Why are you always snivelling, dear? It's a very bad habit. Tell me what you want. I've very little time." The voice was less thick and the accent was growing more lordly. Lisa was in her sanctum and must be got out. "Would you go and get me an envelope out of the drawer in the desk? A very urgent letter. Thank you."

When Lisa returned the door was locked. No answer came from her knock. No sound came from within. She called and rattled the handle of the door. She put the envelope in the pocket of her navy blue school coat. The best thing was to go away.

As she reached the front door she felt she was hatless. The hat was in her aunt's room. How could she go back without it? How could she explain? "I only want my hat," she shouted. "Please let me in. I must have my hat. Auntie, are you all right? Could I have my hat?"

She must say she lost it. At this convent the nuns were nice and would not be very cross. Her eyes felt hot and the sudden gulps which follow tears sprang from her throat like hiccoughs. Oh, what would happen to Aunt Marguerite? Had she lain down and gone to sleep on the bed? Had she dropped back onto the floor? Was she dying in there and when, finally, the door was broken down, would people find her there, still and cold? Should she warn anyone? Should she say anything? They said that if you had character you rose to any emergency. But then an emergency should be clear and not a puzzle. And if the person in the emergency wanted no one? Then to go away and be silent must be best.

4

It was during the following holiday that Lisa learnt the truth. Returning to school with many unanswered questions and many dreads she had even believed that she would never see her aunt alive again. Waiting daily for telegrams or black-bordered letters she often anticipated her reactions. But when she returned home her aunt, though seldom to be seen and in not very good health, was up and about and in better spirits than usual.

When Kathleen returned home from a case, she found that in return for a small sum Marguerite made herself singularly pleasant. Kathleen and Lisa were given a room each, were allowed to use the drawing room as much as they liked and, when they met Marguerite, given vague but friendly smiles. All three were at peace, with no cloud on the horizon but a possible visit from Elizabeth or, worse still, another gracious invitation.

One afternoon when Lisa and Kathleen were about to leave the house they ran into Marguerite near the front door. "We're just off to the pictures," said Kathleen, who always thought her actions required explanation and justification. "You see we so rarely have any time together and I thought it would be a treat for Lisa and it's months since I went myself and after all you need something like that once in a way."

"Of course, of course," said Marguerite, smiling. Her present gentle smile never seemed to leave her lips. "How nice. I think I'll come with you. It's so long since we had an outing together." She went to her room to get ready and reinforce the sweetness of her breath.

She was swaying a little and Kathleen's forehead grew so furrowed with anxiety that the arched eyebrows disappeared under her helmet-like hat. Lisa noted only the strong smell of violets but this she had long attributed to the powder her aunt wore because the purplish colour suggested the smell. In order of age they went out of the door, then with Marguerite in the middle they walked to the bus stop.

As they boarded the bus Marguerite nearly lost her foothold and clung to the bar. Inside her politeness to all was effusive. "Excuse me. So sorry. Did I inconvenience you? Now, Lisa *chérie*, you sit with your mother, you and *maman* so rarely have any time together." Her words came out a little blurred in the consonants, a little foreign in effect. Her smile was now a wide grin.

The fresh air had made her head full of bubbles and altered the shape and texture of familiar objects. Having nodded and smiled at every passenger in sight, she felt no one would be hurt if she now looked out of the window. She turned her flickering eyes towards the street but the light was harsh and the sense of movement too much for her. She felt she might faint. Cautiously she concentrated on the back of the seat in front of her and let her eyelids drop gently. Her head nodded and dropped forward.

"Auntie doesn't seem to know this is our bus stop," said Lisa.

Kathleen prodded her sister. "Here we are, *chérie*. This is where we get off."

"Where? What do you want? Where is it?"

Kathleen looked around anxiously to make sure none of the passengers might know her. "Come along, *chérie*. Here we are."

On her feet, with a large street to cross and noisy traffic speeding to south and north, Marguerite felt that someone was trying to make her swim a fast flowing stream filled with giant fish. This was probably another dream and it would be wisest to stay where she was and take no notice.

"Oh, come on, Auntie," said Lisa.

"Look, *chérie*, we can get across now," said Kathleen.

"There's no traffic coming this way now," said Lisa.

"I'll take your arm," said Kathleen.

Marguerite smiled at them and struggled to get out of their grasp. "Leave me alone, dear. Do not make this fuss. What is it?"

The traffic had begun to move again when consciousness of her position came and suddenly she darted across the road, regardless of motor horns and grinding brakes. Somehow she reached the other side intact.

"You should have crossed when I did," she said to the others when they joined her. "You have to do these things firmly. Motorists hate pedestrians who keep starting out and then darting back. I know because I used to drive a great deal myself."

Naturally she had very little money on her and Kathleen had to pay for the seats. There had been some talk of this being Marguerite's treat and she murmured something now about paying it all back later and giving many more treats as well. Standing in the carpeted foyer among palms and hydrangeas she saw some well-dressed people and, beckoning to Lisa, spoke to her in a loud voice. "It is very odd that I should be in a cinema. I do not altogether approve of it. I adore the theatre. The real acting is there. And opera too I love. In Paris, every week I went to the *Opéra* and the *Comédie Française*. In Italy, in Portugal, in Germany... some day, *chérie* Lisa, I shall take you there." The well-dressed people had moved on. The time had come to go up to the circle and take her seat.

Something about the shallow, carpeted, rounded steps took Marguerite's fancy. She felt very, very tired and they looked inviting. Besides, she wanted to get in touch with the passers-by, all of whom now seemed to her high-born, cultivated and interesting. For a brief time she would have liked to have become the best friend of each one, to hear their confidences and to tell them her tales. It was not only drink, it was also the long incarceration in 52 that sent excitement to her head. She sat down on the side of one of the delightful steps, smiled at everyone, and looked at their faces with appealing love and friendship.

"Why is Auntie sitting down?" said Lisa. "Is she ill? What's the matter with her?"

Kathleen looked grave. "She isn't quite herself. She may have had a little too much."

"A little too much what?"

It pained Kathleen to bring it out, the more so because the child, normally sharp and sophisticated, now seemed very innocent. At any other moment she would have lookedfor a circumlocution but time was passing, this was a public place and people were staring. "Drink," she whispered.

Lisa was surprised and then shocked. So this was a drunken scene. This sitting down on the stairs like that was drunkenness. Her aunt's secret illness, her odd behaviour, her every eccentricity were explained away by this one horrid, sordid fact. All that ridiculous talk about Paris, too! She wished the earth would swallow her up, or rather, swallow up her aunt and leave her free to enjoy the picture. "What shall we do?"

They stood, one beside and one below Marguerite, blotting her out from the sight of the bewildered usherette, blocking Marguerite's view of the people. This was just want she wanted least. "Do get out of the way. I can see nothing. Why are you standing there?"

"*Chérie*, you must get up. Do pull yourself together. There are only a few more stairs and then you can be in a nice comfortable seat."

"Is the lady ill?" asked the usherette.

Kathleen fumbled. Lisa was quick. "Yes. She feels a little faint. She'll be all right in a moment. The best thing is to let her stay here for a minute. I hope we're not blocking the way."

Marguerite had put down her bag and had her head in her hands, her hat pushed back. Quietly and out of tune she hummed a favourite chorus from a musical comedy. Here was a fine occasion, she could not quite remember what, and she would be very happy if only her family would not make a point of standing in her way. Why were they always interfering with her? Why did she so patiently put up with it? She bore them no ill will, she loved all the world, but if only she could see. They were trying to get her out of her seat, too. Why? "I'm all right here," she said, "perfectly all right, *chérie*. If only you'd stand to one side and let me see. Why do you not find seats too?"

Lisa had had enough. She gave a rough tug at the elbow. "Come on, Auntie. Everyone's staring at you. This isn't the cinema. You're sitting on the stairs."

Between them, using force, they half-carried her to a seat. Lisa, outraged, would not sit next to her. "How long has this been going on?" she asked her mother, and her voice sounded strangely like

Elizabeth's. "Something should be done about it. I shan't be able to enjoy anything now."

In this dark place, with the blare of music heralding the impending talkie, with the sudden flashes of directors' and producers' names, travelling up, fading out like illuminated advertisements in Piccadilly, Marguerite felt that she had been taken out of the real theatre and put into a corridor giving onto the street. She looked around, twisting and turning her head. She stood up, sat down, stood again, protested loudly. "*Chérie*, why are we here? What is all the noise?"

"Shh," came from behind her. Her blood was up. "Shh," she returned with interest. "Shh." She had a brainwave. This was the interval. Splendid. She felt desperately hungry. How long was it since she had eaten? She fancied something very nice. Perhaps there was a little delicatessen shop near by.

"Where are you going?" asked Kathleen.

"Do not fuss, dear. You wait here."

"Let her go," said Lisa.

They heard her stumble away, over feet, past knees and into the aisle.

"I hope she's all right," said Kathleen. "I'm so worried in case she gets run over or something."

"Let her get run over."

For a time their sorrows were forgotten in the film. Then came a moment when a blonde was realising that after all her husband was the one she loved. In a series of close-ups, the knowledge dawned in her five-inch eyes and the music, heavily orchestrated, with a repeated phrase of descending chromatics of Wagnerian origin, brought home to the audience the suffocating implications of the blonde's emotions. But to Lisa, also susceptible to chromatics, it brought home her own plight. She would have given anything to change places with the blonde, to have eyelashes like spokes and nothing on her mind but the choice between two men. She was becoming more and more heartless. If only her aunt were run over—and Elizabeth too and if only her mother would go away abroad somewhere and if only 52 were burnt down then there would be an end to it and she would be on her own, able to start freshly from nothing. She would concentrate on acquiring some wealthy man and getting away from the past. She didn't care what became of the rest of the family. They were not really her family. She had no physical resemblance to any of them. She was a Treherne and not a Reilly. If she had to choose between two men she would choose the richer, and quickly too.

Marguerite returned to her seat. She had had an interesting excursion. In Lyons Corner House there had been little bits of anchovy, little bits of *pâté*, little bits of olive, covered in gelatine on tiny biscuits. There had been a pretty friendly girl, really much too refined for the job, and they had chatted. Marguerite's warm grey eyes had extracted a sad story; the girl was supporting a sick and widowed mother. "If you ever need any help," Marguerite assured her, "just phone me up and let me know," and she wrote down her number. Then, in the cinema, she had talked to the usherette who believed her to be sick and the girl, again very refined and with the most cultured voice, had helped her to find her seat. The world was full of kind, sad people and nice girls who did a lot for their families. She would like to help them all and see more of them. She could tell them about running a boarding house—they would need no capital. A nice building society... Still fumbling in her paper bag she fell asleep.

After the film they had to wake her. She was sober, refreshed but not forgetful. "Just a minute," she said with a clear voice and sensible expression. "I must find that nice girl who was so helpful. Such a charming girl and so kind. If it had not been for her I should never have found you. Why did you take seats in an awkward place like that?"

She held out a hand to pull Lisa in her direction. Lisa jumped back as though she were touched by a leper. She spoke with hatred and contempt and her heart was like a stone. "We can't wait for you. I must go home now. Come on."

"I must have a word to the girl. I should like to leave her my address. The poor soul. Some day I may be able to help her."

Why, thought Lisa? What right had her aunt, who had failed *her*, to go taking on other protégées? Seeing that Marguerite took no notice of her protest but went off by herself, knowing that they would have to wait for her, Lisa turned to her mother. "I loathe Aunt Marguerite," she said. "I absolutely loathe her."

5

As though to bear out Lisa's worst fears Marguerite disintegrated visibly before her eyes for the rest of the holidays. Kathleen had to go to a case and Lisa was left by herself. She found that she had endless time and no company. She joined the public library, collected books on her ordinary ticket and student's ticket and retired to her upstairs bedroom to read and read and read.

The room was dark and shabby, the former refuge of a humble clerical worker who had placed his penny in the meter every evening and eaten a modest supper of sandwiches and cups of tea. Lisa made no attempt to make it brighter or more comfortable, although she could have moved in furniture from any of the empty rooms had she wished. But there was no point in it. Once she had struggled to make a room look nice; she had bought pots of paint from Woolworth's, she had made curtains and a bedspread... and then a lodger came. The wish to beautify her environment had not gone but lay buried and crushed.

She too wanted to see no one, wanted to be left alone. She hurried into past centuries, there to relax with the characters of Richardson and Fanny Burney, gentle personages in still, water-coloured landscapes. Their every difference from herself made her cherish them the more. She could only do with very long novels, ones in which she was immersed for a long time so that she could live in them, ones in three volumes with lavish detail. And they must not be about the present.

When she wanted something hot she had to cook it for herself. Usually, with such money as she could extract from her aunt, she bought dried apricots, nuts and dates and lived on these, stretched out on her bed with a book. The lodgers too kept to their rooms. This was a house of solitaries and recluses. The phone seldom rang. The front door seldom opened. The only moments of animation were when one of the flighty young ladies hurried downstairs to speed away from the dimness to the bright lights of the West End. Noises from the street came up to the windows as though to emphasise the inactivity within. Morning turned into afternoon and evening, unpunctuated by meal times. Time was out of their hands. None of the clocks were in action, for who would wind them? The bath geyser was not working. Dust had settled over everything. Whatever one's fingers touched left them black. 52 had cast a bad spell over all who must live there, paralysing young and old alike and sapping their hopes.

Outside the sky was often grey and then it was a comfort to think of possible rain because many others in the city must stay indoors and fall back on their own resources. But when the sun shone brightly it seemed a challenge one could not accept. Everyone, thought Lisa, except her aunt and herself and the sadder lodgers of the district—the aged, the infirm, the poor—would be going out making the most of it. She might venture down to the embankment to see the Thames glisten, but in order to get there she must pass rows and rows of sombre houses like 52, all boarding houses, filled with windows, behind each of which a pair of lonely eyes would probably be peering through lace or net curtains.

Often Lisa felt she would burst with melancholia, especially at dusk when the swinging street lamps projected the swaying shadows and led one to think of death. One evening in the drawing room by the unlaid fire she opened an old trinket box of her grandmother's and onto the dusty carpet fell a tiny ivory skull. This brought death closer, perhaps tomorrow, perhaps tonight in her sleep. What would she die of?

Her daily encounters with her aunt left her heart ever more chilled. What was becoming of Marguerite? She looked battered. When she mislaid her dentures she seemed like a sad old witch whose spells had recoiled on herself. One must not start being sorry for her or there would be no end to it. It would be like taking poison from her. One must blot her out from one's thoughts.

The fact was that Marguerite had reached her lowest point. She was ill and her body was scattered with areas of numbness and pain. She could not move from room to room any more to give Elizabeth the slip but stayed on the ground floor. Often she lost control of her actions and collided with things and the daily accidents left her bruised and scarred. There was a gash on her forehead terrible to see. Her arms, when the sleeves were rolled up to the elbow, showed deep scratches and yellow bruises. Her bandy legs seemed scarcely able to support her and through the stockings came glimpses of further scars. She scratched her head so hard and so often that bright scarlet scabs showed in the partings and flakes lay on her shoulders.

She would have liked a little kindness from Lisa, practical kindness which would involve running errands. The girl's clipped sentences and scorn were meant to be noticed and Marguerite, sunk in a black dream though she was, could not fail to observe them. Lisa was treating her like a delinquent child or an idiot. Lisa was avoiding her. Lisa was flatly and coldly refusing to oblige in any way. One small request and Lisa's face hardened and she said something to wound. When Marguerite called to her up the stairs no answer came. Between them stretched many flights, full of loose boards and other perils and Marguerite could not undertake the ascent. One evening when breathing was hard she heard her come in and walk quickly past the door. "Lisa," she called, "come here."

"Very well. What do you want?"

"I feel very bad dear. It's my chest. I wondered if you'd stay down here and mind the door and the phone. I wondered if you'd go to the chemist."

"The chemist must be shut by now. And who's going to ring up or come to the door? No one ever does."

Lisa turned her eyes away from the agonised face. Her aunt could breathe properly if she wanted to. This was all put on. Once she had come home and suffered for her and it had really been all drink. Never again. Never. And all this was drink too—and smoking. With a chest like that she should give up smoking and then she could breathe easily enough. Every gasp, every rasping attempt to clear her throat seemed intolerable, like an unending passage of misery in a badly cut film.

In spite of herself, Lisa looked at the bruises and the gash and the twisted features and she hated her aunt for every one of them. Marguerite was doing this to get at her. Her whole aim in life had been to get her down, to isolate her, to render her unfit for the world of proper families and lit fires and ordinary conversation.

"Lisa, you're most ungrateful."

"Don't talk to me about gratitude. I'm paying for myself with scholarships now. As soon as I can I'll earn my own living."

On Sunday Marguerite asked her about mass.

"I'm not going," said Lisa.

"Did you go to an early one?"

"No, and I'm not going."

"But *chérie*..."

"I know. I don't believe in it." She had no fear of her aunt left, no respect either now that she knew she drank. On previous holidays, partly to humour and partly to avoid explanations, she had accompanied Marguerite to church or else pretended she had been to early mass. Now it was almost a pleasure to see her so upset. She watched her aunt's back retreating towards the front door, go up in her best clothes, a black fox thrown round her neck back to front so that the beady malicious eyes glinted above the shoulder blade. She's off to fortify herself in the house of God, thought Lisa, and she could have laughed to think that all through mass the fox-adorned lady would be worrying about her niece's soul.

Marguerite could hardly believe her ears. Lisa had not been her favourite for a long time and would never have been again in any case. But until now, no member of the family had left the Church, not even Patrick and Joseph.

"Tell the nuns if you like," said Lisa before she went back to school. "But if they expel me, how will I get my next scholarship?"

Marguerite was at a loss. None of them had ever spoken to her like that. Never before had such cold hatred been displayed. And somehow the girl was hinting that it was her aunt's behaviour which had made her lose her religion. This was worse than the debts, worse than Anthony. This was an additional nightmare to haunt day as well as night, to strengthen the feeling of being up against too heavy odds, to lead to wine and then turn the wine to gall. Should she write to Elizabeth? Her pride said no. Besides, Elizabeth would keep coming here to talk about it and there would be no peace. In any case the girl loathed Elizabeth and would take nothing from her. Should she speak to Kathleen? Kathleen probably knew about it and could do nothing; she had always treated her daughter like a queen and deferred to her and Lisa would take no notice of what she said. She could not write to the nuns for the reason Lisa had so mockingly stated.

What made it worse was that Lisa was the only successful one. She carried off every prize, sailed through each exam with flying colours, excelled at every subject, was marked out as the only girl who would be certain to get a scholarship for a University. But what did it profit a man if he gained the whole world? Yet for the sake of the family she must be urged to gain the world. It was no use arguing with her. She would discuss nothing.

Religion was simple to Marguerite. She might be erratic about the observances but that merely emphasised the security of her faith. She was not mystical, and thought less about heaven and the mysteries than Elizabeth did. But it was her one form of social integration, it was the only thread which still connected her with millions of others. She trusted God and she loved the Virgin, she liked the feel of the wooden rosary beads like talismans between her fingers; she liked the small white plaster statues in the shop by the cathedral. These things were familiar and of good omen rather than connected with doctrine. To take something for granted is to put it beyond one's thoughts and when others seem to analyse and speculate it makes no sense. They appear to have lost their bearings through the mechanical irrelevant workings of the mind. So Lisa appeared to Marguerite but in her case the loss of bearings had led to an abyss.

This blow led back to the bottle. Each day brought a new physical wound. Something was happening to Marguerite's eyesight but she still boasted to herself that she alone among the sisters would never need glasses, just as she had no grey hairs. She could not judge the distances between herself and objects. When she read, and she read only letters and bills, she cursed the bad writing or the faint impression of the typewriter. Her eyes looked deeper and deeper, peering out from the middle of her head. Their brightness was dimmed by shadow and the enlarged pupils made them look darker. They felt full of grit and fallen eyelashes. She kept rubbing them, the tension in her mind making the knuckles rub harder than she meant them to, so that the eyelids were red and swollen and the eyes were bloodshot. The sides of her large, well-shaped nose had grown fleshy and they too were sometimes scarred.

Everything had become enormously difficult. Things one never had to think about before, such as seeing, breathing and walking along the passage to the lavatory or front door, required thought and effort. After a drop of wine she grew confident and undertook these small journeys rashly. It was then the collisions and falls occurred. Never before had furniture been so perilous. The iron end of the bed, the square edge of the chair and the jutting hall table were menaces.

6

Lisa was proud to be at Oxford. Now at last, she thought, she was to meet the part of society which counted, the learned, the brilliant and the talented. They came from famous schools and cultured homes. They spoke of the arts with airy familiarity, they had read, had seen, had heard and, above all, they talked. There was talk about ancient civilisations and archaeology—this was new to Lisa. There was talk about politics and eminent men—this was new, too. And they had little phrases and clichés which suggested much cosy humour at home and which she sometimes mistook for spontaneous wit, such as the description of ordinary cheese as "mouse-trap". She listened and marvelled, she spoke either hesitantly or in a great rush, hoping she would make some kind of mark, wondering whether she would ever have the gift of making people listen to her.

The drive for scholarships had left her exhausted and the idea of education would be for ever associated with struggle and hurry. But the corner was turned now—she was not to end up as a typist at two pounds ten a week, neither was she to end as a governess or English teacher.

She was very short of money. Scholarships amounted to two hundred pounds a year. Fees came to one hundred and fifty. That left her fifty pounds on which to live in the vacations, buy clothes and the necessary books. A sudden demand for a few pounds for an examination fee cleaned her out. She had to limit her smoking and keep to Woodbines. She worried about the dinginess of her wardrobe: two suits handed on from Elizabeth, old-looking and ill-fitting, two dresses bought at the guinea shop, one coat and three jumpers. She worked out budgets and always it turned out that the maximum she could allow for clothes was five pounds a year.

Life in college was luxurious to her. In the first place you had a room to yourself which you *kept* as long as you wanted to. There was absolutely no question of being turned out at a moment's notice and seeing it taken over by a lodger while you were told to shake down on a camp bed in the dining room, the kitchen or even the passage. Such possessions as you had were quite safe. There they were, in your own private cupboard. When you went away your cupboards were not all turned out and the contents mislaid or given away to other people. There were numerous bathrooms with large clean baths and shining taps from which the steaming water came rushing fast. How unlike the thin trickle from a geyser which nearly exploded when you lit it, which needed three pennies in the meter to produce a small, tepid bath, and anyway no one in the house had any pennies and you had to dash out to the tobacconist's to get change. Then in college there were airing rooms and ironing rooms with electric irons. Lisa thought she would be neat and highly organised. But 52 had left its mark on her, she had been too long without wardrobes to use them efficiently and her clothes were left over chairs. She had been too long without a proper bathroom to take baths as a matter of course, and either went without for days or else had two the same day, lying dreamily in the water, emerging with a pounding heart.

She was in her room a great deal of the time at first because she had not got to know many people. She sat in her armchair and looked at the fire without a thought in her head but the image of the flames and the glowing coals beneath. She was used to solitude where the eye had nothing to watch. Now that there was the movement and colour of the fire she felt quite busy. Her room remained very bare because she could not afford to buy extra furniture. In any case Elizabeth's dumpings had made her sick and tired of rooms which looked like an unprosperous junk shop, and she prized the large expanse of floor.

It was good to have regular meals in comfort. It was comforting to have the day clearly divided into morning, afternoon and evening, to know the value of an hour, a quarter of an hour, and five minutes, to appreciate the difference between two o'clock and three o'clock. Bells rang out and told you where you were, exciting the ear because the intervals of the chimes were not attuned to the ordinary scale, not covered by a knowledge of tones and semi-tones. You could not hum it right.

Each day began with a fine knowledge of time. You were called and you remembered there were "rollers" to sign. You did not have to put twopence in the meter and hunt for a rusty frying pan and broken saucepan. No, you went down to breakfast and in the hatches you found plates of eggs and bacon, or kippers or kedgeree. On the tables were racks of toast, rounds of butter and great urns of tea, coffee and hot milk. Everyone was moving about, fetching what they needed. This was the beginning of the day, a prelude to so many hours of active life. The Principal had spoken to the freshers about the "life of the mind", she had said that was what they were here for, and the phrase was always evoked for Lisa at breakfast time. Any new phrase of this kind which came her way, no matter how trite, set her wondering. "Is there anything in it? Would it explain a lot of things?"

The thought of leaving this haven after three years made her panic. To return to the boarding house for vacations was bad enough but to return to it for good was unthinkable. At the same time there would be no point in going away from it to end up in other lodgings. It was a home she wanted. Every young man who spoke to her and asked her out she looked on as someone who might provide her with a secure future. The place was swarming with well-spoken, eligible young men. She did everything to captivate them, flirting in a heavy, anxious way. A letter in her pigeon hole from the rawest and pimpliest of dim undergraduates gave her a feeling of pleasure and excitement. It was a little crumb of love. It might lead to something.

Her colouring was poor, mousy hair and pale cheeks, but her features were regular and her figure looked well enough. With a fluffy perm and plenty of make-up she could more than get by in a place where the women tended to be plain and were heavily outnumbered by the men. Also she had the kind of drive and concentration on the other sex which leads to success. Those who were attracted by her thought her very pretty, those who were not found her ordinary looking.

Each new invitation seemed a miracle. When one of the male personalities of the place took an interest in her she was beside herself with exhilaration. Sitting in the "George", observing the nonchalance with which he paid the huge bill and nodded to other celebrities, she prayed that this might not be the last time he would take her out. She worked hard to keep the conversation going and this did not come easily to her because she had no flow of small talk. There had been none at home. No one had ever made an observation lightly. Marguerite had spun tales or spoken of debts. Elizabeth had picked holes in appearance and manners. Kathleen had related the plots of films and novels. When the celebrity murmured "I love you", Lisa breathed more freely. "I will be all right." She needed no pressing to become engaged to him. She became engaged to several people, one after another, sometimes two at once. She could not bear to let anyone go.

At the same time she was careful not to appear flighty to the college authorities. She handed in her weekly essay in good time. She attended all the lectures she was supposed to and she worked hard. To be sent down for being fast, as some girls had been, would be the end of the world. And if marriage failed—she was taking no chances—she would try hard to be a don. What paradise a don's life would be! One would be settled in this sheltered spot for good. There would be the endless hot baths, the private rooms, the food prepared for you, the central heating and the carpeted common rooms where you and your colleagues talked so cleverly and easily. It would be better than marriage really but it would be harder work to get it.

In the convent she had read Thomas Aquinas, Morley's *Life of Gladstone* and the works of Bulwer Lytton. At home she had read earlier classics. In Spain she had read nothing but French and Spanish. Now for the first time she was introduced to modern English literature. Life as depicted in the works of Henry James, Virginia Woolf and their imitators seemed to her to be the thing to aim at. It was so mild, so wonderfully mild and slack. There was very little wear and tear and pressure, but you commented and commented, you thought and thought, you savoured every little thing to the full. Of course there were misfortunes, but they were of a high and mysterious order, misunderstandings with people, peculiar misunderstandings which were difficult to grasp and express, and you suffered exquisitely while the servants drew the curtains, put some more coal on the fire, or brought in the toasted tea cake in covered dishes. She felt she could do with that kind of unhappiness.

And then there were bits of "nature" in such books, aspects of nature that Lisa had never considered before. You stood by the window during a period of suffering and you noticed the long shadows on the lawn—like groping fingers? She loved those scenes where the trickle of action was held up while you were told "a twig snapped" or "a leaf fluttered down", as though the characters who had been behaving so soberly and decorously in the drawing room or on the terrace were now revealed in their true colours, as sensitive as wild animals, their fine ears pricked up for every little sound, their quick eyes darting to right and to left, missing nothing. As a lady don she could do plenty of that. How terrible it was to think that in the square outside the boarding house, year in and year out, twigs had snapped, leaf after leaf had fluttered down, and not one of the family had ever noticed it.

7

Marguerite went to San Sebastián. She said it was to chaperone Lisa but really it was because she was finished for the moment. She no longer had 52 or any roof over her head in England. With the loss of her home had come the loss of all income. She had made a last gamble and it had failed.

"These days people want flats," she had said, echoing Elizabeth's words too late. "They like to be able to cook themselves a meal when they get back from work and avoid the expense of a restaurant."

So builders had come. Plywood partitions were erected across the large rooms, bisecting roses and cornices, making four rooms of two, one window to each front room, half a window to each back room. The foreman had won her confidence—his accent verged on the refined—and she had placed herself in his hands. Her taste was for something large, grandiose and rich but he persuaded her that these smaller rooms must have a plain paper bordered with a small frieze. She also liked full sombre colours but he explained that these would make the rooms look dark. Buff paper went on to all the walls of the mangled top floors, not plain at all, for by plain the man meant speckled. The niggling frieze was in shrill greens and oranges. Marguerite believed this to be the latest style and called it "modern" because it had a cubist look. The total effect was cold and skimpy, unsuited to the solid, oppressive dignity of the Victorian house, fighting with the memories of bonneted servants in the basement and carriages outside the pillared door.

There had been some misunderstanding about payment. Marguerite had hoped Elizabeth would pay since she was so keen on flats. But the bill had come to her and though she lamented, "But chérie, it was on your advice, I would never have done it otherwise," it was of no avail. The sisters had learnt about the moneylenders and this had hardened them.

It took a long time to complete the work and for months she was able to live in hopes. Once there were flats upstairs they would easily let and money would pour in.

With men in the passages and on the stairs, pots of paint on the landings and long ladders propped against the walls near her room, there was no more solitude. She was driven out. Sometimes she went to the local church to pray for good tenants and for Lisa, or just to sit on a bench and look at the altar. Sometimes she went by herself to the cinema and emerged with a headache.

But luck had been against her and the flats would not let, not even at the price to which she finally lowered them. For a year she struggled and clung on, alone in term time, in the holidays with Lisa (now left to pursue her reading in a room half the size of the one she had had before). At last she found a man who would take over the house as it stood for three years. That meant she would not continue to lose money and what he paid her could go towards debts.

It was the long vacation and Lisa had a passion for the south, founded on memories of Saint-Jules. She would go abroad and give English lessons as her mother and aunt had done before her. A month after her departure, Marguerite joined her. "You need someone to look after you," said Marguerite. She was too proud and too mistrustful of her niece to tell her the truth.

In San Sebastián, with Lisa living at the other end of the town as governess to two children, Marguerite took the cheapest room she could find. It was a long, very narrow room so that the end furthest away from the window was in deep shadow. The obscurity suited her and in the dark part she sat or slept. She found work as part chaperone, part English teacher to three girls of good family and for four hours a day accompanied them on walks or sat and talked to them in English while they sewed. She was back where she had started, but in Bordeaux she had been young with everything before her, whereas now... Even she could not fail to sense the failure and wasted effort and although she attributed it to the ingratitude of each member of the family in turn this did not console her.

She was unhappy. Her pride was daily hurt by having to pander to her employers, and pander she must to have enough to live on. Lisa rarely came to see her and when she did spent her time rubbing salt into the wounds. No one ever wrote to her except Elizabeth and those letters would have been better lost in the ocean *en route*. She was a rootless wanderer, unwanted, unappreciated.

She could not learn the language. It was too like Italian and therefore her Italian got in the way and she said "ch" for "c" and used words which had remained in Italy but lapsed in Spain since the days of Vulgar Latin. Often too she used French. All the bits of foreign languages she had spoken became welded together in her head as one foreign language. She was surprised and upset when people did not understand what she said. She rebelled against Lisa's criticism of her accent and her attempts to explain, philologically, the differences between various Latin languages. "Very interesting, dear," she said, "but I know all that."

She had expected the continent to welcome her with new friends, a blue sky and good food, regardless of her income. But it rained and rained and the meals provided by her landlady were ruined by the taste of coarse oil. The only comfort was that the local wine was fantastically cheap, far cheaper than cigarettes. She could have found a job as Lisa had, living in with a wealthy family and then the food would have been delicious. But her pride would not hear of it. It would complete the reversion to Bordeaux. If she had earned nothing else she had earned the right to be on her own for part of the day.

During one afternoon off Lisa went to her aunt's lodging and found her asleep with a bottle of wine near her. She left a note to say she had been and went away. On her following free afternoon she hurried back. How dreadful it was to have the responsibility of this aunt! And Marguerite was supposed to be here to look after her! What would happen if her pupils discovered this? She found Marguerite at home and sober.

"Auntie," she said with fury. "I've never said anything about it before," (this was true, the subject was distasteful) "but really you must stop drinking. You were blind drunk last time I came."

"I was just having a nap, dear."

"Nonsense. How much do you drink? Can't you see that your pupils are bound to notice sooner or later and then where will you be?"

"I do not know what you mean." Marguerite flushed.

"Don't hedge. You know perfectly well. I've known for ages. I dare say all your life you've been like this. You might consider me—you never consider anyone but yourself. Why don't you go back to England and leave me in peace?"

The sudden attack found Marguerite weak. She waved her hands, "I cannot."

"Why not?" Lisa's tone was becoming more and more like Elizabeth's.

"52 belongs to someone else now."

"How? Who?"

"Well, I let it to a man."

"The whole of it?"

"Yes."

"But why? I thought it was all going to be let as flats."

"It did not let, dear." The thought of that history made her feel tired. It was all very well for this girl who, thanks to her, had never had to struggle, who had had the best of educations. "I never told you, dear. For years I've struggled to keep you all going. There were the boys and then there was you and..."

Lisa flew into a rage. Speechless she went to the cupboard, found a half-empty bottle and held it up. "Whenever one begins a discussion with you it ends with what you've done for all of us. Look at this. And then you say you don't drink."

She could not see Marguerite's face in the dimness. She waited for a reply. "Look at it, Auntie. Why can't you be honest." Still holding the bottle she switched on the light.

Marguerite was thinking about other things. She was very tired. All the morning she had been on her feet, her corns aching and her back playing up. Above all she would have liked a quiet nap. Her face was a picture of sorrow.

Thinking she had made her feel shame at last, Lisa softened and laid the bottle down. "Are you getting any money from the house?"

"No, it's paying off debts. There are so many debts."

"What sort of debts?"

"Oh, the builders and others."

"And what are you living on?"

"What I earn."

"But that can't be enough." Seeing where this might lead her Lisa was silent. The decent thing would be to hand over some of her own small wages. But why should she? What right had they to saddle her with this liability? She must remain indifferent. She must be as she had been before she knew.

However, the thought of her aunt's plight remained with her. She tried to forget it but the sorrowful face kept coming into her mind. On her next visit reluctantly she produced ten pesetas. "Promise me you will not spend it on drink. If you lose your job I can't support you."

She had underrated Marguerite. In the first place Marguerite was never very drunk these days. In the second place her will was as strong as ever and she could rise to an occasion if it was absolutely necessary. How many times had she not gone to her pupils, her head swimming, her thoughts muddled, and put up a magnificent act as a straight-backed, steady, reliable English teacher? With the aid of cachous they need never know. As she trotted along beside them on their walks, smiling, as she spoke rapid English and urged them to reply in the same language, they could not possibly have guessed that she saw them double and coming and going, now looming towards her, now receding into the distance. They could not know what it cost her to walk to her chair and sit in a dignified position. She had complete confidence in herself in this matter. She had never lost a job yet and she never would. Her pupils admired and respected her, just as her patients had done. They knew she was a cut above the other English teachers with their cockney accents or Irish brogues. They could gather from her hints and bearing that she came of exalted stock.

She pushed back the ten pesetas, much as she hoped they would be offered again on better terms. "No, dear. Keep them. I can manage. If you are going to start lecturing me like all the others I would rather do without them."

Surely it had been Marguerite who had done the lecturing. "Who on earth lectures you?"

"All of them. Elizabeth in particular."

At this name, sympathy filled Lisa. Had Marguerite too been subjected to the nagging and the carping? "I'm sorry, Auntie. I never realised what a time you had. I never knew about the house." She pushed back the ten pesetas. "Please take this, Auntie. I don't mind if you use it for drink. You've done so much for me." What possessed her to say that when all along she had been fighting gratitude? She felt she could not bear to leave her on this emotional note, they must spend half an hour together somewhere impersonal. The conversation which had taken place must be quickly covered over. "Look, let's go out to tea somewhere."

Over chocolate and cakes and sugared water they talked. Lisa described her brushes with her employer and Marguerite sympathised. "You cannot call your soul your own," she said; that expression was a favourite of hers. "There is nothing like independence, Lisa. Poor Elizabeth! I would not be in her place for worlds!"

After sympathy, Marguerite sensed that now was the time to spin the sad tale. She spoke of the house and Elizabeth's nagging, she spoke of her long struggle to better the family, which had such high origins and then had fallen on evil days with the death of her father. And she told all this very well. She was eloquent without being embarrassing. The presence of strangers at other tables made her hold herself splendidly and keep her head high. Her smart hat and the soft lighting flattered her.

355

Lisa's compassion cost her month's wages. But it was worth it for the moment. She could at last feel that she was her aunt's ally and that she alone understood her. By becoming reconciled to her aunt she was reconciled to her ancestors and this was necessary for self esteem. They made it up.

Marguerite had never bored her; too much emotion, pleasant and unpleasant, had been bound up in her person. What style her aunt had! What a person she was! She was not a shadow like Kathleen. She was not an appendage of the upper classes like Elizabeth. She lived in her own world, she was absolutely on her own, dependent on no one for anything but money—and what did money matter?

All this was useful to Marguerite and she was glad of the change of heart in Lisa. But she did not feel victorious. She had not sought to regain her affection or her respect and she had no craving for her company. But of course this might lead her back to the Church in time. Perhaps her prayers were about to be answered.

8

Marguerite was back at 52. The man who had taken over the lease had gone bankrupt and she was forced to leave Spain. But things were better now; the slump was past; every room and every flat was let. For Lisa there arose the question of bringing home the young man or young men of the moment.

"If I keep saying, 'No, don't call for me there. I'll meet you out,' it looks so strange," said Lisa.

Marguerite set her face against it. Had the girl no imagination? Was she incapable of dreaming up a convincing reason for such a small thing? "Meet him out, dear. Meet him out. There's nowhere to show him. I've got someone in the front room. We do not want to let you down. After all, your college friends would not understand."

"But Auntie, he knows I'm not rich. I haven't pretended anything."

Marguerite looked on this sort of honesty as cowardice, a lack of spirit, an inability to bluff it out, an inheritance of Kathleen's humble ways. She didn't want these young people coming in and out, criticising her domain. She would have to appear and talk to them. She would never know when she could take a sip in safety.

If the young man were a fiancé, Lisa would persist. "But he naturally expects to see my family. Only once, you know." She was ashamed of her family and she wanted to fight her shame. To her, loyalty meant honesty and she could not realise that to Marguerite loyalty to her family meant the very opposite. Her aunt was not helping her at all.

"You seemed determined to make me a snob," said Lisa sententiously.

Marguerite was bewildered by this statement. It made no sense to her. She did not enjoy having Lisa here because it interfered with her privacy and drinking (now very much cut down). At the same time she must further her interests. If a young man phoned and Marguerite was the one to lift the receiver she put on her most lah-di-dah accent. In a rich husky voice she drawled, "Who is that? Ah yes. I have heard a great deal about you. Just one moment. I believe she is in. Do you mind waiting while I go and see? Thank you so much."

Once, in spite of everything, a young man did come to the house to collect Lisa and Marguerite saw to it that he only stayed a minute. He was well dressed, spoke with the Oxford drawl she so admired and his car was standing outside as a further statement of his income group. She showed him into the narrow hall majestically, extended a hand, explained without hesitation and with a charming smile and straight look, "Such a pity you call at this moment. I'm afraid I must keep you waiting here. Some friends of ours are having a little gathering in the drawing room. They are staying with us for the week and I know it would not be at all entertaining for you to have to meet them all and talk to them. It is always so difficult to get away. They would seem quite old fogies to young people. And I'm sure you're in a hurry to fly off." The drawing room at the time had four beds in it and was occupied by an Italian waiter and his large family.

Lisa was amazed by her aunt's attitude to her. Why did she care so little for her company? Why was she not anxious for her to make a good match? Marguerite never questioned her about any young man or his intentions, never bothered whether she came in late or not, did not care how much she went out or where she went. After all this talk of getting on in the world, why did she hurry away on some flimsy pretext whenever Lisa began to tell her how she had done last term? Surely they had made it up in Spain and become friends.

Even at this age Lisa would have been glad of her aunt's love. When occasionally she came home to be greeted by Marguerite's "How's you?", that expression she had most enjoyed as a child because it was very personal and bad grammar, she felt warmed and hopeful. But there was nothing there. Her day in Marguerite's heart was past. She might be the star turn of the family, her aunt might boast about her to the lodgers and even to the milkman, but the love went elsewhere.

There seemed no excuse for it. Her aunt was sober and, now that the most pressing debts were paid, sufficiently free from anxiety, one would have thought, to open out and talk. By contrast with Oxford, where people sought each other out and talked and talked and talked, Marguerite's silence and elusiveness were all the more slighting.

9

At the end of Lisa's second year, Marguerite found a new outlet for her powers of affection, long dormant.

David was living in Dublin with a wife and two children. Discharged after completion of long service in India, untrained for skilled work and with his wife expecting another baby, he appealed to his sister. Marguerite was delighted. Another brother, one who had never been properly taken under her wing, now needed her. And there were the children. She asked him to send photographs. With their pictures in front of her, she smiled from ear to ear and made the ridiculous face she always made to babies.

"They are pets," she wrote to Elizabeth, "and the wife looks a dainty, charming person. I would give anything to have them in London. If you will pay half the premium we can set them up in their own boarding house."

Their imminent arrival promised a new lease of life to her. She knew when their train would be in. Repeatedly she worked out the time they would appear on the doorstep. She hovered expectantly in the passage. She opened the door and looked down the street, searching the grey pavements for four figures, two big and two little. When they came at last she was so happy that she could scarcely speak. She kissed her brother, she kissed his wife, she picked up each of the children in turn and hugged them.

"I've never seen such lovely children. What a fine boy William is, much taller than I thought, and what intelligent eyes! Patricia's just like Elizabeth—she'll be a beauty and quite a little madam."

As long as they were in the house with her she was up and dressed early to see that they had everything they needed. She spent hours playing with them and watching them. Of all the children she had ever loved these were her most lasting darlings. The others might have been her sons and daughters and therefore there had been the conflict of successive generations and the idea of using them as instruments of her ambition, but these were like grandchildren in age and therefore she had all the indulgence and tolerance of a grandmother. She did not want them to raise the family fortunes, no, they were the ones who were to benefit from the efforts of the others.

When the next child was due, David and Mary were in their own house in Curtis Street. They lived in the basement and on the first floor. The other floors were let as single rooms. The child, a girl, was called Margaret after her aunt. As soon as Mary came out of hospital Marguerite went over to her every day. "You must breast feed her," she said. "There's nothing like mother's milk." She particularly liked babies when they were red and crumpled, she was sensitive to their wishes and passions and she was on their side. She felt at home with nappies steaming in front of the kitchen fire, cups of tea on the table and children running around.

For the first time in her life she had a full social life which she enjoyed. And how different it was from the social life she had planned! Here were no high-class friends waited on by servants and here was no high-sounding talk of the stage, travel and the arts. On the contrary, the only word to describe it was homely.

So that Mary should have plenty of friends and not regret leaving Dublin, Marguerite introduced her to people at the local church, accompanied her to the weekly whist drives and encouraged her to find cronies. Mary lost no time in doing this. Like most Dubliners her idea of happiness was to keep open house for her women friends and sit in the kitchen gossiping easily while the kettle sang and the children clung to legs of chairs and people. The cronies were for the most part cleaners or in service—for Mary herself had been a maid—without pretensions and without airs.

It was a further stage in the process by which Marguerite was getting more like her mother and less like her father. She was at ease with these people; she was one of them and yet they looked on her as something special. She responded to their praise of the children and the presents they brought them. Here everyone was impulsive and generous like herself. In this society you could feel as free as in solitude; no one expected anything, no one made demands. The unity of religion, love of children and cups of tea was enough.

Besides, she could interfere to her heart's content. They all did. Anyone of them might say, "Mary, do you mean to tell me you're letting the child eat all those sweets?" and Mary would reply with good humour, "Sure and why not? What harm will it do him?" This would lead to shaking of heads, dismal anecdotes of rotting teeth and fatal colic, and no one would worry.

Mary thought the world of Marguerite. "Sure and there's no one like her. She's a heart of gold." She never quarrelled with her because she was far too good-natured. She always agreed with Marguerite, always expressed gratitude for her advice and when Marguerite had left the house she forgot the advice and did as she pleased.

Now that Marguerite's heart had opened again it responded to more and more people. She interested herself in parish affairs. She had a stall at every bazaar. In her best clothes she did an impressive act as a saleswoman, sticking out for the labelled price and then, if the customer was poor—and they nearly all were, for few Catholic Irish prosper in this country—she would let them have what they wanted for next to nothing and make good the difference from her own pocket. She attended whist drives, the despair of her partners, the delight of the organiser. She was soon well known and many came to her with tales of woe.

She took on the troubles of others gladly. They moved her to tears and to action. She could not bear to disappoint anyone—except of course Elizabeth, Kathleen and Lisa—and yet she could not forbear to raise their hopes so high that disappointment was bound to follow. Three vacuum cleaner men came to the house regularly because she was never able to tell them she did not want a vacuum cleaner. She found work for members of the congregation and their relations. To make work, she kept having the stair carpet moved up or down. It was threadbare in patches and almost every week some man whom she wanted to help chopped out another bad patch and tacked a better bit over it. Other men tinkered with the door handles and window sashes. Others strengthened the plywood partitions which were always coming to grief. There was always the sound of hammering in the afternoons. While the workman of the moment was in the house Marguerite stood by and watched him, talking, caring little whether this led him to stand idle or not. She enquired after the health of wives, children, nephews, nieces, brothers and sisters. She promised to look out odds and ends which might help, she gave him food to take with him and made him cups of tea.

She resorted to alcohol only when someone came from the other world—the world of successful people—in the shape of prospective lodgers and Lisa's friends. To deal with them was an effort and she must stimulate herself. They carried with them no aura of struggle, no suggestions of hardship. They expected one to make conversation; words rattled out of them, every one of which denoted class and leisure. She would not take this lying down but must rattle back too, in the accent of a stage duchess. And when the conversation was over she was exhausted and bewildered. She liked to claim acquaintance with such people in the past and she still thought she might mix with them on equal terms in the future, but for the present she wished they would keep away. Her heart was thoroughly democratic—always had been—but a small part of her mind persevered with dreams of grandeur. Her heart had won and she had found her right place. She, too, had cronies.

Who were these cronies? First came David and Mary, their circle and the church circle. David was now a bus conductor and Marguerite never once minded this or urged him to better himself. "The great thing is, he's happy," she said and it sounded very like her mother. He was thin, desiccated after his service in the East, simple, puzzled, a model husband, a devout Catholic, a fond father. He loved Patricia best and would often sit her on his knee and stare at her like one who can scarcely believe his luck. He felt a little awkward with all the talkative women round the table. Silent and collarless he smiled sociably at no one in particular when there was a burst of laughter. His chiselled features and fine eyes always seemed to wear an expression for which they had not been destined. Gone were the days when he had put natives in their place and knew himself to be one of the master race. He had never been particularly cruel, for he was the mildest of souls, but he had done as others did, unquestioningly. On his days off, Marguerite went over to enjoy his company.

Less loved than David, but now completely acceptable, was Michael. His hair was still thick and curly, his eyes more watery and vague than ever. He was a barman now and the job suited him to perfection. He dropped into 52 regularly, openly as Marguerite's brother, the relationship admitted to all the lodgers. Conversation did not exactly flow between his sister and himself but they understood each other, they extracted some satisfaction from sitting together over tea. She never nagged him and she sheltered him from Elizabeth, warning him of her arrival, intercepting him at the front door if she was already there. After a happy silence he would rise slowly. "That's all the news. Well, I must be going. Nice seeing yer."

On most mornings an elderly Russian musician came to practise on the piano. He had been professor of music at the St Petersburg Conservatory (both he and Marguerite called it *Conservatoire*) before the revolution. After long years of penurious exile his own piano had had to be sold, he had no more pupils and his fingers were stiff. He believed that this stiffness was due to lack of practice rather than age. To the end he hoped he would loosen them again. His thick hair, which would have been white if it had not been yellow with dirt, fell to his shoulders in a long straight-edged bob, fanning out below the permanent indentation caused by his hat. It was an old top hat, the lining encrusted with grease. With his bristling eyebrows, bent shoulders and liquid accent he had a grand air. After paying his respects to Miss Reilly in a mixture of French and English, he climbed the stairs, firmly gripping the banister, to the drawing room. (Now that he had come into her life, Marguerite kept the drawing room clear of lodgers). There he took off his ancient velvet-collared overcoat, placed his top hat upside down on the piano, lowered himself on the piano stool and began. He never played pieces; that would come when the fingers, as knotted-looking as old twigs, loosened. A few scales were attempted, of many octaves, starting from the rumbling bottom of the keyboard and pursuing an uncertain course to the woodenly tinkling top. The came exercises; trills, chords, arpeggios and above all shakes. He would settle on his favourite interval and go at it, da-da, da-da, da-da... changing fingers every now and then.

He muttered to himself. He reprimanded himself as though he were dealing with a backward pupil. He pounded and he thumped. Every imperfect note of the piano, and there were many, was brought to light. Frequently lodgers complained of the noise and said that they would not have minded if he ever played a tune. Marguerite told them the story of exile and used the magic words of Professor and *Conservatoire*. After an hour or more he rose, descended, paid his respects to Miss Reilly once more and shambled away to humble lodgings. His wife had died some years before. Marguerite, afraid he was starving, told the daily woman to take him up a tray whenever he came. She never forgot to ask him how he had got on.

He would shake his head, hold out his gnarled hands and say, "Ees these... *Mais ça va mieux.*" They behaved towards each other with the courtly ceremony of old Imperial musical circles. She was particularly fond of him. If there was one thing which moved her in others it was the fall from fortune and fame.

Another friend was an old woman who came round with flowers. Marguerite could never resist buying a bunch, no matter how costly or how faded. "The poor soul! She has such a hard life." Besides, she told herself, she adored flowers. Out of consideration to the old lady, she also told herself and others that these flowers were the best you could get in London. Once bought, the string still round the stalks, they were pushed into the nearest vase, sometimes with fresh water, sometimes with stale water, sometimes with no water at all, there to wither and die. She invited the old woman in and chatted to her about her rheumatism and what the doctor had said.

One of the Hoover men was also a special friend of hers. This one was middle-aged but she thought of him as a youngster. His manner was breezy and his cockney accent was overlaid with thin "o's". She thought him cultivated. If she was in when he called they had a cup of tea together. She said, "For the moment it's a little difficult. But when things are better I really shall need a vacuum cleaner." Fortunately he was not married and therefore there were no wife and children to support. But still, she thought, he must be dreadfully lonely and his life was no life for an educated man.

For many years a respectable-looking man had called from time to time, to produce from a good leather attaché case, packets of notepaper and envelopes. The containers imitated crocodile skin, the cardboard was raised in lumps of different sizes and varnished a rich brown. The notepaper was in sickly shades of pink, blue, green and yellow and had a powdery, over-absorbent texture. During her period of solitary unhappiness and drink, Marguerite had bought little off him and often told the maid to say she was out. Now she invited him in, looked through his wares with simulated interest and always bought two or three packets with the idea of selling them to lodgers. To avoid hurting his feelings by placing him under too great an obligation she mentioned this. "Oh, I shall soon get rid of them. The lodgers always want paper." But either she forgot to offer it to the lodgers or else they, quite understandably, did not like the look of it. Therefore as the man increased his visits the crocodile cases accumulated in drawers, on the bottom shelf of the bookcase and in a pile by the side of her dressing table. "They will make very nice Christmas presents," she thought. But when Christmas came, she had not the heart to give them as the only present and therefore had to buy handkerchiefs or eau-de-cologne to go with them. This man had a wife and children; the eldest boy had a scholarship to a "very good school" as he called it. She saw it as one of the major public schools. During each visit they had a long talk about the boy's progress.

She always accompanied these friends to the front door and waved to them from the step. Her manners with them were perfect.

Because no anxiety was created by them she was often quite humorous about them to others, revealing an unsuspected streak of realism. "That poor old Russian will never play properly again. That flower woman knows how to tell the tale." Seeing people as they are is, after all, a matter of removing emotional obstacles in most cases. She did not mind whether Mary laughed at them or not, even agreed that they were spongers, whereas she would have stood no word of criticism about Elizabeth, Lisa and the upper classes whose company she avoided like the plague.

10

Lisa was about to get married. Very soon after taking her degree she found a suitable husband and she was determined to marry him at the very earliest moment so that there might be no interim period of living at 52. Unfortunately it was necessary for the fiancé to meet the family—to have tea there once, formally.

The drawing room must have no trace of lodgers. The old Russian must do his practising in the morning. The maid must cut sandwiches and lay out cakes on proper plates and that sort of thing.

Everyone must be fully dressed and the place dusted. Marguerite was bored at the prospect. Elizabeth fussed and gave warnings and advice. Kathleen was over-excited and nervous. After all the girl was her daughter and she felt it was up to her not to let all this happen without registering that it was an important moment of her life.

It had to be done just once, thought Lisa. God alone knew how it would seem to Martin. But it would be over so quickly that whatever impression it made would be fleeting.

He was a socialist, although unmistakenly from the ranks of the professional classes, his father a Harley Street specialist, his grandfather a famous barrister. She had imagined at first that it was a good thing he was a socialist. But as the time drew nearer she realised it was not. She too was a socialist, having thrown herself into a larger view of the class struggle with the idea that somehow her family position might be explained to her or cancelled out. But was it? No.

She had said to Martin she was of working-class origin, scholarships and all that. But this was not the truth. It was no good thinking it was. One could make a clear case for it on paper because her father had been a humble clerk at the docks, but what had her father or his piano-tuner father to do with it? She had never known her father and old Treherne had seen her only when Kathleen waited at Cardiff for the boat to Lisbon. The convent and the feeling of the aunts was not that. She felt she had lied.

If only her uncles, Michael, and especially the one in the north, John, a miner—there was nothing like a miner—could be present! Their hands would be grimy with noble toil, their accents as plain and broad as could be, any deficiency or irritating mannerism justified because they were the exploited. They would have created the right setting and Martin would have been, not exactly at ease, but knowing where he was, able to fit it all into his view of life, of himself and herself.

But the real story could not be told. It was too long and too involved and she had not yet caught up with it and could therefore not see it clearly. Besides, private histories had a way of fitting into no pattern and ruffled people like Martin. The idea of the "working class struggle" had been presented to her during her last year at Oxford and with inexpressible relief she had jumped at it. "That's me. There I am. Now we know where we are."

The thought of revolution had stirred her, not that she believed she would do well out of it, but everything would be topsy turvy, the cards would be reshuffled, the nuns in the convent might all be clapped into prison and boarding houses might be abolished. Until the political conversion she had had no class; one moment a convent for young ladies, the next the basement kitchen with the maid, the next the Duchess's castle, the next the bailiffs and so on. She had no nationality; one moment Portuguese, then French, then English, then Irish, all of them and none of them. Now she could decide once and for all, plain English working class. But how unfounded and arbitrary the decision seemed when she thought it over.

Owing to Elizabeth's efforts the drawing room was packed with antiques and faded brocade for the tea party. Some very expensive-looking china had been produced from somewhere. In honour of the cultured guest a Beethoven sonata stood open on the piano. A shepherdess or two had got onto the mantelpiece and flowers were everywhere. It was the least working-class atmosphere you could have hoped for.

Elizabeth herself was in a tailor-made with a small string of real pearls, so refined that no one could believe in her, like a character in a British film with butlers and oak panelling. Marguerite was high-falutin' in a mood to use foreign words regardless of their aptness, dressed up complete with tilted hat and on her mettle. Kathleen was nervous and sentimental, her hair in small stiff waves after a visit to the hairdresser. No one was natural or plain or honest. And far from being delighted with this match they did not seem to care for it. Lisa had imagined they would be delighted. "He's doing frightfully well in documentary films," she insisted. "It's most fascinating work. And I should have thought you'd be glad his father's a Harley Street man."

They would have preferred her not to marry. This was not a marrying family. Clever women should have careers. They kept saying, "After you had taken your degree, too. It does seem a pity." Kathleen had looked forward to sharing a little flat with her daughter. Elizabeth had thought of Lisa becoming very respectable in some nice profession. Marguerite had hoped she would earn well and if she must marry, then she should marry a Catholic. Both aunts were worried because the wedding was going to be in a registry office.

Therefore instead of greeting Martin with the delight and admiration which perhaps he expected, all they could do was boast about the family and Lisa's promise.

Elizabeth did the handing round. "Of course, we're all very sorry to lose Lisa," she said in her cold high voice, laughing artificially, glancing archly. "It was a great surprise. After she's done so well at Oxford we imagined she would... well, make use of her brains if you know what I mean?"

"But I shall be using my brains. I shall be helping Martin in his work," argued Lisa.

"Yes, dear. I see," said Elizabeth, as though this was the silliest thing she had ever heard.

"We are every bit as good as he is," thought Marguerite, "better!" She was annoyed with him because his visit had meant such a lot of interference from the others, because it had tied her down for an afternoon. To her, he seemed exceptionally cold and reserved; there was nothing in him which made her warm and anxious to give pleasure, although he had the advantage of being a stranger and only here for a short time. His very accent and good suit irritated her, although on any unfortunate man who came to the door they would have called forth all her tenderness and the labels of "refined" and "cultivated".

Husky and drawling, with a fierce light in her level eyes, she held forth. "*Chère* Lisa has had an exceptional education. France, Spain, Portugal!" She waved her hands largely. "There is nothing like travel. We are one of those families who simply could not bear to be stuck in England all the time. Wanderlust, you know. But so few people seem to have the opportunity to go abroad these days! Have you been abroad much? To France and Germany, did you say? Ah yes, they all seem to go there nowadays. I prefer the south. Well, you've seen a *little* of Europe—*un tout petit peu!*"

Later, with gracious condescension she led the conversation to his profession. She thought very little of it; she had hoped he might be like theatre people, very ebullient and talkative, and seeing him as quiet as a mouse and very guarded she had soon made up her mind he would certainly not go far. "Films must be *very* interesting. What did you say you were doing? Cutting for the moment? Well, who knows, it may lead to something. I knew that famous director—I believe he's knighted now—Herbert Robertson, very well." She had nursed him for a fortnight. "Such a charming man. A very dear

367

friend of mine. And another person I knew very well was Alec James." She had seen the top of his head below the banisters in the Robertson house. "So brilliant we all thought. *Quel talent!* A great pity he died so suddenly. We were all very upset. A real tragedy. Did you know him at all?"

He did not. Fortified by this she went on unchecked. She had managed to take a little nip and she felt like talking. She listed famous actors and actresses (although Lisa had explained to her a hundred times that documentary films do not have actors she had not taken it in). "But most actors," she said, "the *real* actors do not really care for films. I personally think that they have no future because they seem to give everyone such a headache. And it is all this American jazz! So noisy." She returned to famous names. Each one was delightful and her personal friend. She believed it for the moment. She saw herself with them in a blaze of lights and evening dress. She made mistakes and jumbled names. Elizabeth and Kathleen looked anxiously at each other. This performance could not take in a four year old.

Lisa blushed. She wished to God they would not all keep glancing at each other as though giving signals. And why on earth didn't they sit on the chairs properly instead of jigging about on the edge? And why were their hands never still? Even while they were eating they scratched ceaselessly at their plates with knives or hands like three desperate birds.

Martin looked as embarrassed as he felt. He saw three middle-aged, fussy, nervous, tiresome, talkative women, two of them extremely snobbish and affected, the other a distracted shadow. In their different ways they were all trying to impress him, although all of them seemed to resent his existence. What a family!

Towards the end, having been unable to eat more than one slice of bread, carried away by her sisters and the occasion, Kathleen did an unexpected little act. Recalling vaguely passages from books she had read, she grasped Lisa's hand and dabbed her own moist eyes with a handkerchief.

"My little girl! To think she's going to marry soon! I shall miss her. You know, we haven't been like mother and daughter at all. We were always more like sisters. She told me everything. We were really good friends—chums. But as long as she's happy that's all that matters to me. I know you'll look after her. But I shall miss her. I lost my husband very young."

Martin wondered how long this would go on and wished he could be anywhere else in the world.

11

The night before the wedding the family was in full force in 52. Mary came round, with the children, and congratulated Lisa. She liked Mary; it was impossible not to. The children had been told great things of Lisa and were told to call her "aunt" even though she was their cousin. When they were taken away to be put to bed the rest of the family seemed tired, excited, despondent. The curtains had not been drawn and the swinging shadows outside sent a chill through Lisa. She felt it did not matter whether she married or not, stayed here or went away; the effect was the same in the end—you died and even while you lived you were isolated. It was best to go the whole hog like Marguerite, admit that you were absolutely on your own and have no illusions about being like other people. Everyone was really completely on their own and there was something exciting about those who acted on this assumption.

In the future *she* would not be acting on this assumption. She would be living with people who believed in groups and cliques and how they stimulated each other and how important it all was, the talk about life and the arts. It was called the exchange of ideas. It was like what the Principal had called "the life of the mind". She hoped to God she would believe in it again. She had before. You could take anything for granted if it was constantly with you. In any case those blasted street lamps would not be swinging. She found herself sighing loudly and it was as complete a physical act as a sneeze.

"I wished we could have booked a table at Hatchett's," said Elizabeth, "but at least we'll all have lunch together."

Lisa wondered what was happening now? Because she was marrying into the middle class they were going to pretend to her all that they pretended to others, as though she was unaware that not one of them had ever set foot in the restaurant mentioned. The aunts were not at ease with her and her mother was near to tears.

It was sad to them to think of this non-Catholic marriage. It was like watching her obtain a legal form to live in sin. And yet, now that

369

she had been to Oxford, now that she had gone up in the world, no one said a direct word against it. There were hints and sorry looks, there was a general feeling of disappointment but no more. Had Lisa looked the picture of radiant bride-to-be one of them might have tried to damp her, but seeing her glum and sighing they wanted to be nice to her.

Now that there was no remedy for it they might as well make the best of things. Elizabeth was anxious to give Lisa self-confidence so that she might face the future in-laws with assurance.

"She'll look very sweet in blue," she said.

"Very," said Marguerite absently.

"She was always very pretty," said Kathleen.

The past tense made Lisa smile. They might have been discussing her funeral.

The wedding lunch took place at an ABC. Elizabeth was paying and she said, "You must all choose what you like," as though on any other occasion she would choose for them. A small string orchestra played selections from musical comedies in one corner. The majority of the lunchers worked in offices nearby and knew the waitresses by name. It was not festive.

Their appetites were poor. They ate most of the grilled sole and left the potatoes in cold heaps at the sides of their plates. They tried to swallow part of the trifle. They tried to think of what you said at such a time. Marguerite in particular resented the flatness. She looked absent-minded and quarrelsome, although when she spoke her voice was soft and pleasant.

They rode on a bus for a certain distance. "You sit next to Lisa, dear," the two eldest told Kathleen. Then they took a taxi for the last part. It would look better to arrive at the registry office in a taxi. The ceremony took place and the witnesses signed. Martin and Lisa drove off in a car to his parents' house.

It was all wrong that *his* family should give the reception. Elizabeth had wanted to fight against it but she was so rarely in London and the others didn't seem to care. Kathleen could not have faced the rôle of hostess, let alone the cost.

In the Harley Street residence many guests assembled. Martin had sent invitations to all the film people, writers, artists and musicians that he knew. His parents had asked relations and medical men. The Reilly's and Treherne's had asked no one except two college friends of Lisa's. Among the distinguished throng

Marguerite, Elizabeth and Kathleen kept together in a huddle. They looked very small and lost. Martin's parents shook them by the hand, said that they were glad they had come, and left it at that. The men and women of art and letters did not approach them at all. Kathleen smiled hopefully at one or two faces, Marguerite glared and Elizabeth looked icy.

The champagne came round on a tray. Kathleen looked happier and Marguerite beamed. Elizabeth looked stern. She smiled graciously at the maid, waited till she was out of earshot and then whispered, "There's no need to drink it. You can just hold the glass."

While she looked away for a moment Marguerite drained her glass at one go. A rosy flush came to her cheeks, a sparkle to her eyes. If only she could find the maid with the tray again.

"Where are you going, *chérie?*" asked Elizabeth.

"We ought to move around and talk to people. It's very bad form to stay here like this."

"When they've thinned out a little, *chérie.*" Elizabeth looked worried. The soft creased powered cheeks showed red patches which did not match the rouge, the arched brows went higher, the exquisitely modelled nostrils tightened. She whispered to Kathleen "Don't let her drink any more, *chérie.* Please see that she is all right. I'll go and look for some sandwiches. On an empty stomach..."

"We had lunch..."

"I know, but she ate so little. Don't budge from here."

They were beside a long window which overlooked the street. Outside motor cars were parked and a few pedestrians walked in search of medical advice. The sky was grey and a cold wind blew. Kathleen felt that the parting with her daughter was final. Lisa would join all these fine people and even if she did ask her to the house sometimes what on earth would they say to each other? There would be all the business of looking tidy and not letting her down, just as there had been with her sisters' friends. To sustain herself she sipped a little. After all, Elizabeth had not measured the amount with a tape measure. And who had ever heard of not being allowed to drink at your own daughter's wedding?

The maid approached and Marguerite exchanged an empty glass for a full. "Do you think... ?" protested Kathleen half-heartedly.

"Do stop fussing," said Marguerite. "Elizabeth is bad enough." She knocked back the champagne and went on an excursion round the room. She hovered by groups as though taking part in their conversation, smiling at every face which turned towards her, shifting her weight from one sore foot to another. Her best shoes were a torment. Why did people stand like this for hours? She looked around for a chair. She pushed her way through the groups. "Excuse me. So sorry." It felt as though there were thousands of people here, thousands and thousands of standing forms in an impenetrable mass. Snatches of conversation came to her of which she could make neither head nor tail. She saw Lisa in the distance in her blue dress and with her hair fluffed. She had no wish to go and speak to her. She had never felt less interested in people than now. Another glass, a nice chair and let them get on with it.

She found an empty chair next to one which contained a frail old lady. This was better than nothing. Believing her neighbour to be a relation of the bridegroom she put on her social face and accent. "Very cold weather, is it not?"

Her companion nodded. "Yes, and what a wind."

"Do you not feel the draught?"

"No, I'm quite comfortable thank you."

"I am the bride's aunt."

"Oh, really?"

"Yes. I had to dash back from the continent—" (she must get travel in somehow) "—at a moment's notice to be here in time. We spend most of the time abroad." She caught sight of Elizabeth looking for her and this made her smile. Kathleen was still moping in her corner.

Another glass and Marguerite outlined a splendid new version of the history of the family with many foreign place names. She felt angry that Lisa had done nothing to glorify the family to these people. She might just as well have had no family at all. Anyone would think the man was doing her a great honour by marrying her. And she let him think so! Had she no pride? The thing to have done would have been to ask former patients—titled ones, famous ones. She, Marguerite, could have mustered them soon enough. Her anger, which naturally she did not mention, gave her family story a sharp tinge and made her aggressive to her listener, extracting from her every ounce of her attention. She didn't care who the woman was, she must listen. She used her hands and she used her eyes. She hypnotised her companion as a snake does a rabbit. Every now and then she suddenly bent down or moved her head sharply to the side. This was so that she might remain concealed from her sister.

Elizabeth had got into dull conversation with an elderly uncle. She said, "How lovely," and laughed when he said something humorous. She said "Really" and "Indeed" when he made an ordinary statement. Underneath her polite attention she was forming a plan. They must leave very soon. Goodness knew where Marguerite was, what she was drinking and what she was saying. Besides it would look better to say they had to dash off somewhere than to wait to the very end as though they had nothing better to do. Any moment too, some Harley Street man one of them had worked for might appear and this, though not distressing, would be tiresome. She had been to several parties in county circles and she knew it was best to slip away early, making no fuss about goodbyes unless the hosts were unoccupied. She would collect the others.

"I must dash off," she said to the uncle. "It's such a shame. But I have to be somewhere by four." He was a little put out. Now he must find another good listener.

She easily persuaded Kathleen to go. "It's Marguerite I'm thinking of. You find Lisa and explain."

She tracked down Marguerite, hovered by her chair. "So sorry to interrupt, *chérie—*" (a sweet smile for the old lady) "—there's someone who wants to meet you."

In the passage she explained. "*Chérie*, it looks much better if we slip away early. We don't want to look as though we hardly ever go out."

Marguerite was sorry to leave the champagne but this plea struck home. "No, we do not."

The three rode home in a taxi because Elizabeth believed Marguerite to be far more tipsy than she was. They were upset; the wedding was non-Catholic and contact with Lisa's future friends had galled each of them in different ways. Society contained many different pockets and when people got into one which was not yours they disappeared and even though you met them again they were like strangers. All the past years spent together counted for nothing. This was supposed to be a united family, yet they were all remote from each other. Kathleen had no friends. Elizabeth had never been able to put her heart into county life but lay awake thinking of her sisters and brothers and nephews and nieces. Marguerite had in the end found the company she wanted but the other two did not know of this.

Elizabeth told Marguerite she looked tired and suggested a nap. Having got rid of her she was particularly sweet to Kathleen. She was not unsympathetic and she was imaginative about social sorrows. "Don't be sad, *chérie*," she said, "I know what you feel. But you'll see a lot of Lisa. She's so fond of you."

The unexpected pity brought the lurking tears out. "I know, I know, but..."

"I'll get you a cup of tea."

Later she spoke of Lisbon when Lisa was a fat baby, of her first words in Portuguese, of Jacinta, the high flat and the sunny balcony. She drew that time and this one together as though the interim period had not existed and she and Kathleen had always been the closest friends. Marguerite she could do nothing with, but Kathleen might still be hers.

The reminiscences increased the tears and ended them. A real good cry, a sister you could trust and you felt better.

Elizabeth sighed. "Poor Marguerite. I wish she wouldn't."

"I think it's her weak head, *chérie*. I don't think it's the quantity." Neither knew that Marguerite seldom drank these days and that if anything led her to drink it was their presence.

"If only I could find the bottles," said Elizabeth. "I've hunted and hunted in every possible place. Then one would have an idea of how much... and also what."

"I've never seen a bottle yet."

"I know. I tried every cupboard. It's very sad, *chérie*."

"Mind you, I do think it's her head. After all she only had two glasses at the most this afternoon." They had got it wrong again. "And if only she would eat."

"Drink's a terrible thing, Kathleen. And smoking isn't good for one, either."

Kathleen looked down at her nicotine-stained fingers.

12

Soon after this Kathleen went away to Germany to give English lessons. Elizabeth had heard of new debts on 52 and was certain that now was the time to take over. She did not seek the appearance of power; her character was that of chief counsellor rather than ruler.

She always allowed Lady Watson to seem the monarch although in fact it was she, Elizabeth, who made all the decisions. She would leave Marguerite as the apparent head of 52 and controller of the family's destiny. She would treat her with respect.

All the same there was bound to be a scene and she was not looking forward to it.

"*Chérie*," she said, coming straight to the point as soon as they had exchanged the usual greetings. "As you know from my letter I want to clear up these debts thoroughly. What I want is this. All the money coming in must be put *every week* into my banking account. Choose a suitable day for it and always keep to that day. Then all bills must be forwarded as soon as they arrive. Otherwise I cannot take the responsibility of helping as I would like to do. You must have an allowance, of course. I'm sure we won't disagree about that."

She waited for protests. Each time the subject had been raised before Marguerite had stormed. She waited also for Marguerite to disappear into some other part of the house, determined this time to follow her, to dog her steps, to say what she had to say in front of the maid or one of the lodgers or whoever it might be.

But nothing was as she had expected. Marguerite remained still, smiling and gentle. "It's a very good idea, *chérie*. It's very kind of you. And there would be no need for you to come up so often, would there? I should like to spare you those long journeys. Yes, I shall forward everything as you suggest."

To make quite sure Marguerite had understood, Elizabeth kept repeating her terms. Having come here ready to worry and persuade it was impossible for her to take it easy. Each time Marguerite readily agreed. What did she care? She was past caring. She had a full life and she was happy. She was sick of bills and debts. If someone else wanted to worry about them, well let them. And as for power, she could still get her own way quick enough when she wanted it. It was not a question of power; Elizabeth was just the business manager.

Emboldened by her success, bent on anxiety, Elizabeth enquired into the moneylenders. Marguerite was silent for a short time and then told the truth as far as she could. It was difficult to remember details and it was boring. The position was not desperate; one man had been paid off altogether, the other had been half paid and the interest had been cleared monthly. She would find the papers and post them on. She would place everything in Elizabeth's hands.

Out came Elizabeth's notebook and she listed all the papers needed, placing the list in an empty drawer of the desk so that Marguerite should not forget where it was. They parted with great friendliness, Marguerite composed and dreamy, Elizabeth still waiting for the sudden storm and mistrustful of her victory.

Now Marguerite's life became really calm. She enjoyed herself. She ceased to worry. Free from anxiety she continued her visits to Curtis Street and the church. She looked ten years younger than she had and a good fifteen years younger than her age. Her devotion to little Margaret increased daily and frequently the baby was brought over to lie on the balcony while Marguerite looked at her from the window. She was not over-concerned to forward bills in good time. If they lagged behind a bit and there was a summons, well it was not her worry now. "Elizabeth is such a dear. A brick," she thought. She grew fonder of the lodgers now that they were not her direct concern and chatted to them for many minutes when she met them in the passage.

This was the real change; even alone she enjoyed herself. She picked up novels from the shelves, novels which she had never chosen herself but which had arrived as part of the auction lots from Elizabeth. She read them from cover to cover with interest. She screwed up her eyes and the print seemed faint. Often she guessed at the words, inventing as it were her own adjectives. Foreign surnames and place names she took over entirely. Anything with a plot, anything light appealed to her so long as the setting was comfortable. She hated what she called "sordid" books and that meant books about poverty and sex. Sex in very high places and discreetly done was all right. She hated what she called "morbid" books where the characters ran amok and became insane or violent. She skipped descriptions of scenery, paid attention to clothes and furniture, concentrated on the thread of the narrative, often getting through a book at one sitting.

There was nothing from outside which could alter the tempo of her days. The house was quite full and most of the lodgers were permanent. The Lisbon boys had long ago ceased their visits; some had died, some had gone to America and others had not enjoyed their stay in the house when everything had gone to pieces. The pilgrimages had also been stopped a long time ago.

In the past she disapproved of the wireless as vulgar and noisy but now she switched it on for company. When there was a play or a music hall show she turned it up and sat listening. Sometimes the jokes she heard made her laugh until the tears rolled down her cheeks and then the thought of herself sitting there all alone laughing would tickle her and make her laugh even more. Many things struck her as funny now, not that she had grown cynical about herself or her life but just that the humorous side seemed to predominate. She had no philosophy, as Kathleen had, that a good laugh did you good, but she would find the corners of her mouth twitching upwards and laughter would overtake her, because a cup had broken, because the geyser would not light. "A chapter of accidents," she thought.

She roared over the sayings of the children. She joined in the laughter round Mary's table. She was the most cheerful and easy-going of companions and landladies. She vied with the others in telling fortunes with the tea leaves and everyone said she was exceptionally gifted in this way. Through her jolliness came a hint of the great lady and Mary's circle praised. "She's a great personality. She's a fine character. And she's a fine-looking woman too. By all accounts she's had a very interesting life."

The children adored her. With them she exerted her charm, appeared to listen attentively although she never took in a word they said, entered into the spirit of their games although she got all the rules wrong. She made them feel that she was their best audience, the person who mattered. When she came in they ran to her and tugged at her skirt to drag her over to their latest treasure. She always brought some little thing for them and persuaded them of its merits as brilliantly as any professional salesman could have done.

When they came over to see her she let them have the run of the drawing room and the dining room. She sat and watched them complacently while they screamed. "Look, Auntie, this is the sea and this is an island. If I jump off I'll be drowned unless I can swim. Look, look, I'm going to jump. Look, do look, I'm going to jump."

"I'm looking."

Very occasionally there was a phone call from Lisa. Marguerite spoke to her affectionately and with her best accent. She was not interested in her niece's life and as soon as there was a pause began to tell her about William and Patricia. "We call her Paddy, but it sounds like a boy's name. She's so like you, *chérie*. She'll get scholarships and go to college. Willie's clever too."

Lisa asked her to tea one day when she knew her husband would be out. She wanted to impress her with her elegant flat. Marguerite forgot to come.

Lisa once went home to see her. "How's you?" said Marguerite and kissed her. "Lovely seeing you, dear. I must hear your news. Tell me about your flat. I want to know everything."

But as soon as Lisa began her description Marguerite darted out in pursuit of an illusory phone call, wandered up to talk to the carpet man, remembered that she must tack a cover on a chair upstairs and did not return.

"I'll have to be going now," said Lisa acidly when she found her. "I'm sorry I didn't have more time with you."

"It was lovely seeing you," said Marguerite. "Do drop in again. I do so enjoy our chats. I'm glad you're getting on so well. Perhaps next time the children will be here and then you can see them."

Putting new covers on chairs was one of Marguerite's favourite occupations. She sewed the pieces of brocade straight onto the old covering with large uneven stitches, cutting out as she went along. The children had evoked a late nesting instinct and she was always rummaging among the pieces of material Elizabeth had dumped there at different times to find something which would brighten up the place.

She also made very clumsy-looking clothes for dolls and teddy bears out of unsuitable material such as brocade and large-flowered cretonne, so that all the toys had the aspect of down-at-heel courtiers in a distant country. She had an unfailing way of making things look clumsy but distinguished. She had also a way of leaving no clues. Had any stranger attempted to judge her taste by her surroundings he would have had his work cut out. Beside an Elizabethan-looking settle there would be a Louis Quinze chair painted sticky chocolate and a phoney gate-legged table. None of these things was like her and yet the total effect gave a distinct impression of her personality. It was difficult to say why she kept certain pieces and discarded others; allowing for necessity and Elizabeth there was still quite a margin for her own choice.

On the walls of her bedroom hung the oval portraits of her mother and father, Portuguese bull fighting pictures, a mandolin with broken strings, castanets, a huge sepia picture of a lady and gentleman in an early nineteenth century drawing room, holy pictures, a coloured photograph of a Moorish city (very long) and a brightly tinted scene of some West Indian shore. This last she swore was San Sebastián. "But the sun never hung so low and orange as that and there were more houses and there were no tall palm trees," insisted Lisa.

"Perhaps not, dear," said Marguerite meekly. Nevertheless she told each newcomer it was San Sebastián. "I remember walking along that beach in that hot sun..."

When the question of taste arose she would say, "I like everything neat and dainty and everything to match. Just a small place but very neat." One might have supposed she hankered after a little bungalow with three-piece suites. To her it was very simple; you held views in order to air them but they did not affect your life in any way.

On the dining room walls was a dark red William Morris paper long past its prime. This, during the days of melancholy solitude, had been much criticised by Lisa as being gloomy.

"I know, dear," said Marguerite. "It's hideous." But she clung to it through all the redecoration, persisting in running it down to everyone.

Inside herself she had grown wise. Her surroundings and her companions were the ones which suited her. In her way she understood this. But she did not attempt to alter her pronouncements. She spoke as she had always spoken. Words, after all, were meaningless. They were noises you made to humour people, please people, persuade people or get rid of people. It was easier to fall back on the words you had always used, the thoughts you had always voiced.

One or two people found her excessively vague or contradictory or crafty and they were wrong. It was second nature to her to attach no importance to what she said, to forget what she had said in a moment, to pay no attention to what anyone else said either, unless they stated facts such as poverty and illness. What she now relied on were her own inclinations. No one could get at her; no one could influence her. It was out of their hands whether she liked or disliked them. She might for some reason take a fancy to you; for the very same reason she might dislike you. If you argued with her she agreed.

13

A fourth child was born to David and Mary, a boy. Marguerite busied herself with his welfare. Once more the mother was urged to breast feed. Her nipples were tender and suckling was agony. "Think of the child," said Marguerite.

Munich was approaching and people spoke of war. Marguerite, Mary and her circle were solidly behind Mr Chamberlain and did not mind what he did in his efforts for peace. They thought, as others did, that the next war would be Armageddon. "With the scientists inventing all those things sure none of us can know the half of what it will be," said Mary. The sky would be blackened with roaring planes and showers of bombs would wipe out the greater part of the population in the big cities on the first day. One of the cronies had seen an anti-aircraft gun in Hyde Park. "It's an enormous great thing and the Lord knows what they're expecting." They shook their heads at the thought. Unlike most tales of horror this one had no subtle charm. They prayed hard for peace and the safety of the children. They thought the world had become a wicked place, had deteriorated—from what?

"It's this younger generation," said Marguerite. "They're a hard, selfish lot."

"It's because they persecuted the Catholics over there—" (Germany) "—The priests have been saying for a long time it would lead to trouble," said Mary. "Every time in history the Catholics have been persecuted it's led to dreadful wars. So they say." She saw it like this: the Catholics themselves did not fight the wars but because they had been persecuted, God expressed his displeasure by making a war happen.

There was Munich, war was averted and they breathed more freely. They offered prayers for the Prime Minister and thanksgiving to God. Marguerite had taken no interest in politics beyond a one-time admiration for Clemenceau and always voting Conservative. Now she said, "Mr Chamberlain reminds me of Le Tigre." Perhaps it was the moustache.

In the uneasy winter Michael died of a haemorrhage. He had been attending a hospital off and on for years. He was regretted by his landlady and the clients in the pub. The publican said, "The best barman we ever had. Customers loved him."

Apparently, to the last, his white curls and handsome features had made him friends. He was the kind everyone took to and everyone felt sorry for. Of his children, only Anthony attended the funeral. The other boys were in Australia. The girl was in Canada married to a Canadian.

Anthony, who was now a grocer's assistant, was quiet and diffident. His gentle brown eyes looked timidly round at the group of relations and other mourners. He felt he had failed to get to know his father through his own fault. During the six months they had shared digs they had had nothing to talk about. Now it seemed that everyone else in Michael's life had found a lot in him.

Marguerite, in tears, spoke of his brilliant promise as a boy. "Poor Michael, he never had a chance. He was ruined by Hughes—thrown out of the house when he had a wonderful career before him. He was the cleverest of all of them. And such a nice nature. People took advantage of it. He had bad luck all along. After being gassed in the war he was never the same... Poor Michael."

The funeral was attended by as many of the family as could be got together and several friends of the dead man. Marguerite was surprised at the abundance of wreathes and crosses. All the regulars at the pub had subscribed to do "Mike" proud.

Michael had not done badly. Apart from the years in the trenches during the war his life had drifted on without major disasters and with many minor pleasures. He had had what he needed; unexacting company, drinks, regular though small wages and his pension. In his way he had been useful and successful; there was no more popular salesman at the vegetable market, no better-loved barman. As long as people did not expect too much from him they could find no fault with him. His slow words and soft smile, in the right environment, had given pleasure. His landlady had done what she could do in the way of providing nice meals. Other women had helped him to happiness in their way.

But Marguerite did not see it like this. To her it was a tragedy of unfulfilled promise and frustrated ambition. She forgot his air of dreamy content during their meetings of the last years. She pictured his unhappiness at seeing himself sunk into poverty, shabbiness and what she called a "low" job. She thought of him as endowed with her father's high purpose and crushed by circumstances.

"I knew him better than anyone," she said. "I know what he went through."

For a few days after his death she was disconsolate. But the call of the young was too strong and soon she was back with the children and the babies, cooing and laughing, playing peep-bo and hide-and-seek, organising a birthday party with crackers, streamers and candles on the cake.

Not long after, came news of the death of John. Elizabeth and Marguerite hurried north to attend another brother's funeral. Travelling back together face to face in the compartment, with bare trees, bare fields and telegraph wires flying past, thinking of possible war, thinking of the other family deaths, they were in sympathy, behaved naturally, forgetting their accents and style—just two pensive women.

"Three of them have gone now," said Marguerite. Not one of the boys had done well, she thought, not one had made a mark in the world. It did not seem to matter so much now. "Poor John," she said, echoing what she had said of Michael. "He never had a chance."

Elizabeth offered up many prayers during the journey. It soothed her and made her feel useful. To pray for a dead soul was like bandaging a wound. She had her rosary inside the flap of her handbag and her gloved hand could move along the beads in secret.

The international situation grew blacker. Elizabeth wrote to Kathleen in a prearranged code. *"Children expecting you for summer holidays. Do not disappoint."*

On reading these words, Kathleen packed her bags, took leave of the other mistresses at the school and came home. She was sorry. Of all the places she had ever been to, Germany was the most pleasant.

She loved the mixture of seriousness and sentiment, she loved the German interest in the human soul and the sad charged looks her colleagues gave her when she told them of her early widowhood. The Latins had been dry and their vivacity and bubble had spread itself over their different activities without ever coming to rest on her. They had made her feel lifeless and a bore. These Germans treated her with the same heavy intensity with which they treated their own lives and the arts, especially music. They pondered over her troubles and after much searching decided she had an inferiority complex. This struck her as very sound. They told her she had a deep love of music which had been suppressed and she agreed heartily. They were tall, big-boned, firmly padded women for the most part and she, small and thin, found herself provided with several mother-figures. They gave her treats.

"We heff a littell sorprice for you prepeert," her two favourite colleagues said to her on her birthday, smiling broadly and leading her to a display of presents.

They had daily jokes about pronunciation. She corrected their English and they corrected her German with much chuckling and twinkling. She found them very kind and humorous. They did what she had always wanted people to do; they marked your arrival with handshaking and good mornings or good afternoons; before you went to bed they said good night and sleep well. If anyone was going away for a short time everyone said goodbye and marked the occasion with advice and enquiries. They reminded you that you were not just a shadow, but that you were observed constantly by maternal eyes who reacted to your every coming and going.

The school atmosphere (it was a Catholic school in the Rhineland and therefore none of the teachers were Nazis though they had to be cautious and say nothing) with its celebrations of people's birthdays and feast days, its trips along the Rhine, its excursions in to the neighbouring town to hear concerts, had become a substitute for the home life she had never had. Her colleagues had been more motherly than her mother, more sisterly than her sisters. It had also had the feeling of domestication she had missed, with the labour-saving gadgets in the beautiful spotless kitchen and the special kinds of cake. All the teachers were interested in housewifery and all the girls had to learn it.

She had learnt that beauty was very important. Friends had pointed out to her the beauties of the Rhine. "Schön. Wunderbar. Prachtvoll." Sunsets and mountains had called forth quotations from famous poets. They had also told her of the "depth" of Beethoven, their favourite composer, and she had sat through many a concert, flanked by two massive friends, concentration written all over her small, peaky face, her head thrust forward, to show that she too had a soul. She had also been taken to a Wagner opera and although she secretly found it heavy and long-drawn-out, she tried to enjoy it and cheered up whenever a tune began, disappointed that it never came to anything. What she really liked was that these people took trouble with her, asked her to enjoy things, were full of theories about her, loved nothing better than personal conversations, looked at her so searchingly, their eyes on her eyes, communing.

From this aura of friendship and understanding to the indifference of Marguerite was a big drop. She knew in advance how cold it would seem. With every mile which brought her nearer home her mouth drooped lower and her eyes grew duller.

Back in 52 not only did she feel emotionally high and dry but also she noticed the dirt and the dust and the lack of up-to-date cleaning equipment and womanly touches. Here was no smell of baking or bedclothes spread hygienically out in the sun. Seeing the cleaner on her hands and knees she told her sister, "In Germany they never go down onto the floor like that, they have a special..."

"*Chérie*, you've already told me three times."

Marguerite thought Kathleen should make herself useful. She expected her to be devoted to the children, told her she was selfish not to volunteer to look after them and take them out, refused to talk about anything else.

"Do you not think Paddy's brilliant? A second Lisa?"

"I don't find her very like Lisa."

"You're always so sour, Kathie. I cannot think what's the matter with you. You're really unkind to the children."

"I haven't done anything to them. I only said Paddy wasn't like Lisa and I can't see the resemblance myself."

"Well everyone else can."

1

With attentive silence Marguerite, Kathleen and two lodgers listened to Mr Chamberlain's speech. They did not feel at war. They had hoped that every crisis would be solved by flights of Prime Ministers to foreign capitals and talks. War would always be averted at the last moment. People could always come to some agreement. Even now some leader might make a sudden journey and save the situation. The Pope in the Vatican might make a pronouncement. For the moment they were more sorry for the Prime Minister than for themselves.

Over at Curtis Street in the basement kitchen they found Mary surrounded by the children who stayed up till all hours. She too felt as they did. Her face was screwed in agonised sympathy for the poor Prime Minister. But there was apprehension there too. A last minute miracle was possible, probable, but supposing it did not come this time? They spoke of him and it was one of those conversations where anyone might have made any of the remarks for no one sentence was related to the personality or more private ideas of the speaker.

"He sounds a broken man."

"No one could have done more for peace."

"Those German leaders are a lot of maniacs. They say Hitler shouted at him when he went there and treated him like dirt."

"What that man must have gone through."

For the moment the gaunt moustached figure, stalking through their minds with his umbrella and hat, had the air of a saviour and messiah. But a very old, tired saviour who had reached breaking point and had no obvious successor. A few more weeks and he would change for them, becoming the elderly cautious gentleman whose dour presence could never bring victory.

On the following day they believed in the fact of war. The belief came suddenly when the false alert was sounded.

"They're coming, Kathie," said Marguerite. "Quick. Down to the basement. Bring the gas masks."

385

In the dark back room, afraid to have the light on although it was daytime, crouching below the dusty barred windows, the two sisters prayed. "Sacred Heart of Jesus, watch over us…" Pinned to their underclothes were medals and scapulars.

As soon as the last downward swoop of the siren had faded away, with clasped hands they waited for the throb of a hundred engines and the deafening crashes of tumbling buildings. Lorries rumbling through the street, shaking the foundations of the high houses, suggesting, as they had done for years and years, distant earthquakes, were now capable of a more sinister interpretation. Every footstep next door made the sisters hold their breath. Any moment now and they would be shot into the next world or emerge back into this one, maimed and with shattered nerves, to survive until the next onslaught, perhaps only for a week, perhaps only for a day.

No German bombers came that day. The weeks went by and still none came. The sisters, the lodgers, Mary and her cronies changed their minds.

"They won't bomb London at all."

"They wouldn't dare because we could do the same to them."

"They say they won't dare to use gas either."

"They say our air force is twice as big as theirs and we've great stores of poison gas just waiting. Not that we'd start a thing like that."

"If London was hit, the whole of America would be up in arms. It would bring them in in a day. Hitler knows that all right."

Anxiety and boredom came instead of major horrors.

Yards and yards of blackout material had to be bought. Days were spent hammering it to the tall windows. It tied back to the side in the daytime letting in a triangle of light. The glass above the door was painted black.

Long freezing nights were followed by grey days. In the streets the slimy, slushy, blackened snow thawed into slow trickles which made their way towards full gutters, or refroze into long murky streaks of ice. The permanently blacked-out windows were like sightless eyes. Indoors, pipes froze and cold draughts crept through every crack and chink.

Rationing came and shopkeepers grew tricky. "You cannot call your soul your own," said Marguerite.

Some lodgers moved out of London with their firms. Others joined up. Impoverished landladies of the district came together. Marguerite, who had previously had little truck with them because she had believed she was the most temporary of landladies and of a different order, now joined them and attended protest meetings against paying rates. She saw the Government no longer as a group of men round a table, some of whom one read about in the papers and might have nursed. The Government was really Ministries; huge office buildings full of cold, obstructive types surrounded by papers. She used the words "red tape" and "rights".

Bombers began to cross the Channel. Any moment and they might reach London. The four children had to be sent away. The platform was crowded with sad relations. Hot grubby hands waved from compartment windows. Marguerite wept.

"I miss the children, Kathie," she kept saying. "You know I do miss the children." She did. Her days had lost their last bit of brightness. There was nothing to look forward to, no sudden visits and high chattering voices. "I think about them all the time."

In the evenings David came over for a cup of tea and a bite of something. He was on his own because his wife had to go with the youngest. He ate what was put in front of him, tired after a long shift, too tired to think but not too tired to feel an overwhelming unhappiness. When he had finished eating he sat staring at the table.

"Sometimes one feels there is nothing left to live for," said Marguerite. "Why is it always gramophone records on the wireless?" she said. "And why do we get so little news?"

The paint brush had passed too lightly over parts of the glass above the door and therefore the hall was swathed in brown paper, crumpled and pinned. The sisters groped and fumbled. Would this be temporary? Was it worth getting it right and having a good light in the house? They asked these questions of themselves and each other and the answers varied. In the end the apathetic spell of 52 prevailed.

They smoked from rising till bedtime, holding cigarettes between their lips when their hands were occupied. They were hungry and yet had no appetite. Their insides rumbled and felt dry. They moped and lost weight. Kathleen's grey hairs increased. Marguerite's memory was failing. They said the same things day after day, simply to hear the sound of a voice, and because what they said was well-worn their voices were toneless.

"It will be over by next year."

"It can't go on for ever."

"They say it may last ten years."

"America will come in."

"Russia let us down."

"We don't seem to be doing very well."

The Russian professor came no more; flu had taken him off during the cold spell. The flower woman had gone to her married daughter in Dorset. The notepaper man had found some war work and the Hoover man had disappeared without farewell or explanation.

The two sisters had to talk to each other. If they agreed it did not matter. If they quarrelled it did not matter. Sometimes Kathleen was sensitive and harboured a grievance for hours. Sometimes a letter from the children made Marguerite excited and garrulous as she read and interpreted each line. But all feelings wore away to nothing within the course of the day. Their sight grew worse and their minds grew dulled.

2

Lisa appeared on Saturday afternoon. "What's happened to your phone?" she said.

"It's been gone for some time now."

"Really?"

"Well, with the house half empty. And the rent is quite an item you know."

Lisa looked tired, drawn, but full of nervous energy. She strode into the dining room, flung herself into a chair as though it too were against her and must be coerced into receiving her weight. She flung burnt out matches with a vicious flick into the grate. She had come to see her mother, not her aunt. She hoped Marguerite would disappear upstairs as she usually did and leave them alone together. She loathed this place. She might have guessed that Marguerite would pull off the fullest effect of gloom and hopelessness with the help of the blackout. The most comfortless, squalid place in the world.

They were glad to see her. Both of them welcomed the slightest distraction and Kathleen always longed to see her daughter. They fluttered round her, short-sighted, over-excited and small. How very small they were. She had forgotten that.

"You look a bit tired," said Kathleen.

"Do I?"

"And how's life been treating you?" Kathleen derived a feeling of security by using such a phrase. "Tell us all the news. How's Martin?"

"I don't know."

"You don't know? How's that, darling? Do you mean he's joined up? Have you had no news?"

"I don't know. I left him months ago."

At this they scanned her face for a sign. They were excited at the prospect of hearing a story and they were worried, ready to sympathise, ready to suffer, ready to protest and ready to agree. Had she suffered dreadfully? Was there a sordid story? What was her financial position? Both sisters wondered.

Marguerite took over the rôle of questioner. "It is true, Lisa? What does it mean?"

"Yes, I left him," said Lisa impatiently. "I told you twice."

"But why, *chérie*, why?"

"Because I wanted to."

"Did he, did he... ?" said Marguerite.

"Oh, he was all right." Fidelity was not essential to marriage in her circle. Martin was all right. She had married him for what he was and for what his friends and family were. And they had all turned out exactly as she thought they would. He was just what he looked like, the very image of himself from one day's end to another. She would have liked to blame him and she could not. He, with all his talk about the arts and temperament and personal liberty, was stable by the very fixity of his tastes. It was she with her ambivalent attitude towards everything who was bound to wreck any little haven of culture and rest, as she now called their home. Alternately she had swallowed and eschewed the Picassos on the wall, the books on the shelves, the special bits of furniture. These things were labels to proclaim, to every newcomer or familiar, without ambiguity, what you were. The idea that things were loved for their own sake was a myth, an unsophisticated pretence. As though these things had not been surrounded by words and associations by others whose path you followed! People who had once been to her pillars of culture grew simple in her eyes and unable to take an analysis far enough. At first it had been, "if only I could swallow it as they do, how happy I should be," as though all that was needed was a kind of religious conversion. Then came, "it's no use. I must clear out."

She had gone into her marriage deliberately and she found she could not stand the lack of surprise and mystery. Too long out of a groove she was ill at ease in any groove, much as she might yearn for a new one before she was in it. Since no one could be relied on to spring surprises she must drift from one man to another. She was fed up with herself. And the bloody part was she wanted security. Why had she got like this? What had made her like this? Marguerite, of course. Marguerite represented unreality, unreason, everything that made life a dreary mess. But Marguerite to her also represented the completely on-her-own person, the one who owed nothing to friends or books, the unpredictable, the unexpected.

Her present conversation could be a revenge, thought Lisa. She was unaware that the revenge was being taken against a person in the past. You never catch up with time. The time lag in reaction and analysis make actions of this kind irrelevant and unimaginative. "There'll be a divorce," she said, to annoy.

At this they looked shocked. Kathleen was silent; Marguerite was not.

"Ah no, Lisa. Think of the scandal. Think of the future. What will people say?"

"Which people?"

"Well, all our friends, *chérie*."

"And who are they?"

"Think of Elizabeth and..."

This made Lisa laugh. "It's Lady Watson, is it? Charlottte, who might have done so much for me—" (she imitated Elizabeth's mincing voice) "—if I had not been so ungracious. And Martin's doing the divorcing, too."

"No, *chérie*. What have you done?"

"Given him cause."

"*Chérie*."

Kathleen looked from one to the other. Conventions and scandals did not bother her so much but she was afraid. Would Lisa's life become a long, homeless pilgrimage as hers had been? Was this daughter, now so taut and malicious-eyed, to be a source of anxiety instead of the one safe spot in the family? And how menacing she seemed, ready to explode at any moment, full of the unhappy violence which had characterised Thomas! The nuns had said something about her having a terrible temper. But in Lisbon and Saint-Jules she had been such a good-humoured though wilful child. Kathleen did not know what to say and she longed to express something. She wanted to show that she was not shocked, that she would always be on Lisa's side, but Lisa would misconstrue any words at the moment and hurl them back.

"Lisa, darling," she said so timidly that one might have thought she was hoping to be inaudible. "Lisa, as long as you're..." She could round off neither the emotion nor the sentence.

"Poor mummy," said Lisa unexpectedly. It was not that she was particularly touched. She wanted to make it clear that the war was with the aunts only. "Don't be so upset. It's not so bad. I've got a good job."

"But darling, if you're not happy..."

Marguerite interrupted. "Well you will not have your job for long once your name is in the papers and there is a scandal."

"Nonsense. There are so many divorces now. Why should mine be singled out for publicity? Martin's not famous."

"But why did he not let you divorce him? As a gentleman..."

"Oh, he's all right."

"Perhaps his family..."

"As you say. It was his family I think."

A light came to Marguerite's eye. "But *chérie,* you too have a family. Just because they're wealthy they need not think they can get away with this."

"But Auntie, I've put myself in the wrong."

"You should not have done. You've a family just as much as he has. After all, what are his people? Nothing so wonderful. They made no impression on *me.*" Marguerite was angry and upset but the old intensity of emotion had gone. Despite her expostulations she felt calm enough. If one of the children had cut a finger it would have held her attention more firmly than this disaster could. However, there was the family to think about and she was head of the family. They were as good as Martin's family, better. She thought dreamily of famous Edwardian cases; Lady X not received at court; other ladies refusing to visit her; shunned by society. She thought of the plays of Pinero. She thought of the reception in Harley Street, a frosty business despite the champagne. There had never been a divorce in the family. She saw people in evening dress, whispering together in excited groups in drawing rooms.

"It will do you a lot of harm. Besides, think of the Church."

"You needn't worry about the Church. I wasn't married by it so it doesn't count, does it?"

There was a catch in that somewhere, thought Marguerite. It was not a nice thing to say. The drawing room groups dissolved, giving way to priests looking thoughtful, pained but comforting; the priest at the Cathedral, the parish priest, the Lisbon boys. They would certainly not agree with that. Divorce was wrong whether you were married in the Church or not. The break-up of a marriage was wrong too. She abandoned the idea of her family pitted one against another. She spoke quite gently. "Could you not make it up? Did you not love him?"

"Oh," said Lisa, exasperated by the word "love". What on earth could Marguerite mean by that? What romances had there ever been in the family? Had there been a single man in the lives of the three sisters, apart from her father? Besides, in order to love you had to have a proper heart. They had petrified her heart. They had induced in her that frantic wish to secure a husband which sprang neither from the heart nor the senses. And then they spoke of love as though it were the most natural thing in the world. As though they were natural! As though anyone was natural! They had never spoken of love before the marriage. It was the one word which had never occurred to them. But now, afraid of a scandal, the word came to their lips so pat. (To Lisa, Marguerite was often indicated by "they").

"And you had such a nice home together," continued Marguerite, not knowing how to interpret her niece's "Oh" and still hoping to persuade her. "I remember you telling me all about it. Is it not a pity to throw all that away?"

"You didn't listen to a word I said then or at any other time. You can't remember a word I said about that home." Again her aunt had said what would most irritate. Marguerite talking of "home" was absurd, since she, if anyone, had avoided all semblance of one for the rest of them. Yes, Lisa had wanted a home. At times she had thought that the only thing which mattered was to put down a root somewhere. She had thought of a house in the country surrounded by lawns. Lawns were the best thing in England, green and smooth, urging one to take root like a tree. She had dreamt of living there in solitude, the wife of a vague figure in trousers who was successful, popular but seldom at home. She had thought of better homes in places like Saint-Jules where the hot sun shone into the walled gardens. She had thought even more often of a house in Andalusia with a patio and large shuttered sombre rooms into which came strips of dazzling brightness. Always the husband figure had been of secondary importance. He must be successful and popular so that she need make no effort to provide him with friends or self-esteem. Apart from that he must leave her to lead her own life.

And now she was back where she had started. It was not so bad as 52 but still it was lodgings. She was surrounded by furniture which she had not chosen, hearing the footsteps of other tenants on the stairs, disliking every encounter with them, resenting the smallest demand of "Good morning" which human beings made.

"But why did you marry him, dear?" asked Marguerite, as though she really wanted to know. Kathleen too pricked up her ears for the answer.

"I would have married anyone to get away from 52."

Marguerite was hurt. Lisa felt exultant. "My one idea was to get out of this house."

There was a knock at the front door. Kathleen hurried out to answer. Aunt and niece looked hard at each other in silence.

"It's that old man who came last week," said Kathleen, putting her head round the door.

"What does he want?" said Marguerite.

"Well I suppose *de l'argent*."

"*Je n'ai que* sixpence." (They spoke in French to avoid embarrassing the man in case he could hear).

"*J'ai un* shilling."

"Have you got a shilling, Lisa?" said Marguerite in a whisper.

Lisa produced one. She was annoyed at the interruption. She also thought this day-to-day individual charity got no one anywhere. When the man had gone and her mother had returned she looked into the matter. "Does he live on what he gets like this?"

"I suppose so, *chérie*. Poor soul," said Marguerite.

"Has he no old age pension?"

"Perhaps he's not old enough."

"In that case he could surely get a job. After all there's full employment now."

"Well you never know. There are a lot of sad cases."

"I suppose you never asked him?"

"No," said Marguerite firmly and she turned her eyes until they looked straight at Lisa's. It was her grey, level, intent look. Her under lip came forward, tight pressed against the top lip. She found this examination tedious. She found her niece's concise way of talking jagged and angular. Marguerite's element was different from this, it was soft and shadowy. Lisa was like a creature from another world, a hard glaring place. She did not criticise the girl in any such terms to herself. She merely felt that sense of effort and frustration which comes when one has to talk to someone with whom there is no common ground of experience. Her mind drifted to something else and she turned her head away.

Kathleen led the conversation back to the divorce. Lisa replied mechanically. She was reacting to Marguerite's look. Her aunt thought nothing of her, less than nothing. She had looked at her with scorn and distaste. And why? After all she had handed over the shilling. She had handed over her ten pesetas. She had handed over her month's wages. But she had done it wrong. There had been no generous impulse behind it. She had been righteous, reluctant and calculating. She thought twice, three times, twenty times about every action, in advance and afterwards. Had she never had a generous impulse? Perhaps, when she was very young. Her marriage had been calculated. She turned her eyes away from the distress of others. She could not face it. A beggar's face would make her turn her head the other way and later she would justify it on the grounds of sensibility. "I could not bear to see him."

She was reading very much more into Marguerite's look than there was. She saw herself as her aunt might see her: a hollow shell containing a lot of arguments and reasons. Was she, after all, like Elizabeth? No, even Elizabeth was far more generous, far kinder. She tried to catch her aunt's eye but it was out of her reach. It was all so unjust. Marguerite had done the most ruthless things, things which Lisa would never have dreamt of doing and yet here and now it was Marguerite who was intact emotionally, yielding to her every impulse without question, despite the many years of illusion. Her flavour was like the wine she drank, rich and strong. You could get the better of her with words but her personality always won. And now what was she thinking of? Was she thinking of the man still? Was her mind a blank? Was she worrying about the divorce and Lisa? Lisa hoped so.

Marguerite was thinking about the children.

3

After that Lisa came to 52 no more. Elizabeth hurried to London on hearing the news. She questioned her sisters, went to far as to visit Martin and bombarded Lisa with letters and evening calls. "Terrible shock. Could not believe it. Keep Tuesday evening free. Must talk," she wrote.

"I have seen Martin," she said. "He seems willing to..."

"You should not have done such a thing," protested Lisa, white with fury. "I might have realise that *you* would stop at nothing."

Nothing came of Elizabeth's interference. Of all the family she was the most upset. She imagined what would be said in county circles if such a thing happened. She even raised the old story of being received nowhere. She was pleading and governess-like by turns, now saying she was thinking only of Lisa's happiness and future, now taking a high moral tone.

"After all I am a woman of the world. In nursing we come across all sorts of things," she said, expecting confidences.

"I could never have dreamt such a thing possible. Do you never think of God? Do you never realise where mortal sin will lead you?" she said as though a sudden horror of hell fire would do the trick.

Many an evening when Lisa got back from work she found her aunt waiting for her, ready for a further fray, having thought of new arguments during her consultations with others. Elizabeth consulted her mind as though it were one of her notebooks. "There are several points we have not covered. The first: who will pay the costs? The second..."

After these interviews, downcast but not despairing, Elizabeth walked with small brisk steps to the underground, along the dark streets. Back in the country she asked Our Lady and many saints to help her.

The news was kept from David and Mary and naturally not a word was said to anyone outside the family. Marguerite took it out on

Kathleen for a time, censored her maternal solicitude and sympathy as though they had caused the trouble, then forgot about the affair. Kathleen wept, wondered and kept in touch with her daughter, meeting her out from time to time for a cinema or meal.

The episode was forgotten when a greater tragedy occurred. David died of a sudden rapid attack of pleurisy. It took place within a week. Despite the most devoted nursing from his sister and wife (Mary had been back for some time) the temperature mounted and the end came quickly. He asked for the children, not because he thought he would die but because they were uppermost in his thoughts. "I would like to see them," he asked diffidently, as though he wanted to cause no one any inconvenience.

Ever since they had left London he had been lost. True there was more time for sleep and rest without them but he would gladly have exchanged the quiet Sundays for the Sundays before the war when he wheeled the pram round the park, underslept, overtired, while Mary prepared the dinner, when he gave a hand with washing and feeding, when stamping and screaming made it impossible for him to shut his heavy eyes.

Marguerite did not speak of him as having had no chance in life. She said, "What a tragedy," the words she had used when the others died. But when she applied them to the others she meant that the life was a tragedy. Now it was death which was tragic. With his devoted wife and fine children he was to her the most successful and fortunate of the brothers. Through his happy alliance had come the *raison d'être* of her efforts—the children. "He had everything to live for," she said.

Because he was the last of the brothers she had loved him the best. Without him she felt she was the sole survivor of her generation of the family because the sisters had never counted. She doubled her affection for his widow and widow's sister, Patsy, who now came to live in Curtis Street. In the Catholic Dublin atmosphere of their home her religious feelings grew. Now that death had taken the brothers, prayer was the remaining link with them.

Often she went to early mass and communion. Her charity increased. Any penny she had to spare she gave to the poor. She did not think of her own after-life. Any indulgences she gained she handed over for the souls of relations and strangers, a little to each sufferer in purgatory. She did without things in order to buy clothes for the children. "We must do all the good we can," she said to

Kathie, with a wild look in her eye and an impatient shake of her head as though someone were arguing with her. It was difficult to say whether there was a hint of reproach towards herself or whether she meant that the others must do as she did.

The children, her last brother's children, were her whole life. She was their father now. She was responsible for them. It needed only this sense of complete responsibility to keep them ever present in her mind. She thought of them through the day, she dreamt of them at night. She read each letter from them many times. She smiled at the rows of "X's" at the bottom. Photographs of them at different ages stood in a row on her mantelpiece, having ousted Jimmy and Anthony. She wrote to them weekly, a thing she had never done to former favourites.

Her one desire was to go and see them as often as possible. Whenever she could she spent a few days in the village where they were billeted. She called for them in the morning and let them lead her to the wooded edge of a field. She sat on the grass and watched them play. Interest and concentration made her observant and she noted the characteristic gestures of each one.

William, square and active, had her own straight brows. He spread his fingers wide and kicked any large rounded stone in his path. Paddy, feather-headed and lively, hopped from leg to leg and let her arms dangle by her side.

Margaret shrugged her shoulders and put her head on one side when she wanted something.

The baby Michael was engrossed in catching up with the others; when he cried because his powers were limited he stood still and turned his angry face up towards the sky; when he achieved something difficult he ran round and round in a circle laughing.

She no longer thought they were like her father, mother, Elizabeth, Lisa or anyone else. Her memory was no longer active and she had no need to connect them with the past. They were themselves. Each beloved character and appearance was its own justification. She put up with anything from them. Michael pulled her hair, pinched her nose and she smiled. Paddy tipped the contents of her handbag on the grass and she laughed and said, "You naughty girl," as though it were a compliment.

She was aware of them to the exclusion of herself and therefore she automatically adapted her speech to their various levels, switching skilfully from Michael's baby talk to William's tough monosyllables.

4

Marguerite looked up from the letter on her lap. "We must drop her a line to say we'll meet her."

The letter was from Elizabeth. In her anxiety to impress the directions on her sisters she had overdone it. "Not ABC but Lyons. ABC too far for later. Lyons more convenient. ABC convenient for other bus and less crowded but think Lyons this time. Know you do not like Lyons food and perhaps ABC food better, but..."

"Is it the ABC she means?" said Marguerite.

"No Lyons, I think," said Kathleen.

"Are you sure?"

"Yes, I'm sure."

"But she says ABC is more convenient and better food."

"I know, *chérie*, but you know what she is. I think it's Lyons."

They read the passage again carefully. "Yes, Lyons."

After mass at the Cathedral they must meet her at Lyons. Mass must come first because it would be a Holiday of Obligation.

Later came a wire. "Not Lyons. Wait outside Cathedral."

So when the time came and they waited by the steps Marguerite was muddled about the directions. She looked along the street, walked backwards and forwards with her little trotting steps and fretted. She forgot the order in which the orders had come. "Perhaps it was the ABC. Or was it Lyons?"

"No, the wire came later."

"Are you sure?"

The crowd had gone. They were alone on the steps. There was no trace of Elizabeth. Marguerite felt sure she was at one of the other places and Kathleen thought she might have missed her train. As Marguerite had the stronger will they decided to try Lyons. Finding no Elizabeth there they tried the ABC. In the end they boarded a bus for home. They quarrelled a little over the letter and telegram. Kathleen, though more clear-headed and in the right, got the worst of it. Peeved, she looked out of the window.

They were approaching a trim figure, familiar, in tweeds, a sober hat with a diamanté clip, spectacles, pearl earrings. They passed it. A second later the truth dawned on Kathleen.

"Elizabeth. We passed her. She was going the other way. I must get out at the next stop and run after her. She must have got the time wrong. She'll get there and we won't be there."

She jumped off the bus before it had properly halted. She swayed a little as she landed, frightened, panting. She caught her breath. With elbows out she half ran, half walked. Easily roused to anxiety she now behaved as though it were a matter of life and death that she should intercept her sister. Elizabeth had so little time in London and had to dash for trains. Her every moment was precious. She had to be at the sale early. It was very urgent she said. After a lightning meal they must go with her. Would there be time now? Would she perhaps take a bus and come back to 52? Would they meet?

Dear oh dear, it would be such a pity if she spent hours searching for them. She heard the sweet voice, "You let me down, *chérie*. And I was only doing it for your sake." Pity there was no phone. Kathleen came to a kerb but did not pause and did not look at the turning before her. Her eyes were looking out for every bus in the main street in case Elizabeth might be in one. A sudden grind of brakes and she automatically dodged a taxi, missing it by an inch. Her heart pounded. A narrow escape. She felt a sudden sharp pain in her back and a dreadful thud right through her. Then all was blank.

She thought she could hear the noise of an engine. It grew louder. She opened her eyes. What a peculiar light. She was moving. There was something she ought to be doing. Something very urgent? Had she done it and was it all right? Had she forgotten to do it? Who was that near her? Pain stretched from her neck to the small of her back, acute, unbearable. Her body felt strange and she was lying flat. The pain drove her back towards unconsciousness. She was inside a kind of bus. No, it was an ambulance. But surely she had dodged that taxi, it had swerved and sailed on. She turned her head, tried to speak. The terrible jab sent her back into a deep blank.

Conscious once more she groaned. She was still lying flat. There were people and nurses. Outpatients Department. "Please tell my sisters," she said, "then they can come and fetch me home." She gave the name and address. After a short examination she was taken to a ward.

The collar bone and thigh bone were broken, eight ribs were fractured. The surgeon set the collar bone in a flash without anaesthetic. The pain was frightful but momentary; the memory of it stayed with her. He strapped her up tight, her arm close to her side.

She was unconscious most of the time. During consciousness her worried mind hurried back to the central problem of what had happened. She had dodged the taxi and reached the other kerb. It was like thinking about the same thing all day but losing the thread suddenly and having to start again.

Her sisters were beside the bed. "Poor Kathie. No, not a taxi, chérie. A lorry. It came up behind you." But then she would have heard it, or was she too busy recovering from the taxi?

She bore the pain stoically. She was strapped to lie as still as the bed table beside her. She did not want to trouble anyone. She felt guilty. Her groans came out only after she had struggled to diminish them. She was trained to hospital atmosphere. A disciplined nurse becomes a disciplined patient.

Hypostatic pneumonia set in. Her pulse was taken four-hourly. When she woke sometimes it was light and there were flowers beside her. She had to move her eyes further to right and left than she had done before because she could not move her head. There was always a nurse nearby. She knew what that must mean. She must be seriously ill, in danger. Then another thing; her sisters seemed to spring up suddenly soon after she woke. Were they staying in the hospital somewhere?

She did not know that for two nights they had stayed downstairs in case. Neither did she know that the priest had anointed her. She had not heard their hushed voices, had not seen their solemn exchange of glances as they bent towards her watching for movement in the pale, thin face. Was it coma or was it sleep? Her slit of a mouth was closed so lightly that it seemed as though the lips would slowly draw apart to let out a faint sound. She looked very young, like a famine child old before its time. Experiences had come towards her, brushed her and gone away and therefore her face bore the marks of nothing but worried frustration. She looked very strained and very tired. She looked what she was; a person who had never done any harm, never asked for very much, never quite grown up.

Later, she could not remember when, she seemed to waken into darkness. It was not night, but thick shadow lay over the ward, thickest around her. She heard Elizabeth whisper, "She's going, *chérie*. I can't feel her pulse." And then it crossed her mind that she might be dying. She was too weak to mind. She thought neither of God nor Lisa. She thought it was like going under an anaesthetic.

When she returned to consciousness she was better. She could see the light and hear the nurses and patients. She was awake most of the day. Visitors came; the sisters of course and then Lisa, bright with lipstick and a bunch of flowers.

Kathleen had her hair parted in the middle and looped back in unbecoming plaits for the sake of tidiness. This gave her the aspect of one of the saddest members of the Victorian proletariat. She was concerned about her appearance and kept apologising. "I know I must look awful, dear."

"Oh no," said Lisa. "Not at all."

"Lisa, tell her about... you know," said Elizabeth. "Explain it."

"I thought you might be able to get compensation," said Lisa. "I've got a solicitor friend and he'll look into it for you. He wondered when he could come and see you about it."

"But do tell her what she must say," said Elizabeth.

"Well," said Lisa. "She looks a little tired. Leave it till later."

Elizabeth took no notice and her face came close to Kathleen's, conspiratorial, commanding. Kathleen could smell the face powder and lavender water. "*Chérie*," whispered Elizabeth. "Say your foot was on the kerb. You were just by the corner, half on the pavement. The witness said so. The driver had no right..."

"No. I think it was my fault."

"How can you remember? Poor thing, you can hardly have known what was happening. We heard everything from the witness. Remember, your foot was on the kerb."

"I don't want to get anyone into trouble."

"Don't bother her now," said Lisa.

Marguerite leant over from the other side of the bed. "This is for *her* sake. Now remember, Kathie, it was not your fault."

Lisa could see her mother's expression grow confused and anxious. They were, as always, making her wretched for her own good. They seemed determined to give her no peace of mind. "Leave the thing alone for the moment," she insisted. "Honestly it doesn't matter what she says. The solicitor will do his best."

Kathleen had been in hospital for ten days when the blitz on London began. Lying high up in the tall building, strapped, broken, helpless, she sweated with fright. She visualised the roof crashing in on top of her, crushing her. She had only one hand with which to protect her face. She imagined the glass from the big windows coming towards her in cruel splinters.

Sometimes they carried the patients down to the deep shelters below. The jolting was agony but it was worth it. Down there she tried to look brave, said, "I always say if it's got your name on it... No use worrying." But each bang and thud, no matter how distant, took the soothing words off her lips, made her eyes open wide, made her heart flutter beneath the mended ribs.

When there was little action they left the patients in their beds. "But, how can they tell nothing will happen?" thought Kathleen. To her every sound overhead was a German bomber. She was certain that the Germans would make straight for the big London hospitals with unerring aim. They were so thorough. She knew them. She had not clung to life when she thought she was dying but now she wished with all her heart to live, even in her present pain.

The bones healed. They told her she had made a marvellous recovery. She did not care very much about this. "Couldn't I go out of London?" She implored her sisters to send her away, anywhere safe.

"We have found just the place," said Elizabeth. "A convalescent home in Kent."

But in Kent it was worse than ever. The sky was never free of planes and to her every plane was an enemy plane. There was always an alert on. She slept little. She ate little. The accident had been the worst possible preparation for the present time. Her terror grew intense and obsessive, never leaving her. Fear absorbed all her energies, leaving no part of her mind with which she could read, look around her or think. When asked later what the place was like she said, "I can't remember. I don't know. I didn't notice."

She returned to London, to 52. After all there was a basement there and she could stay below ground except on those days when she had to venture as far as the hospital for further treatment and inspection. She dreaded hospitals, swore they were targets. "I know the Nazis. They are devils."

She could not use her left arm and she was left-handed. Marguerite performed many services for her kindly and willingly but her thoughts were elsewhere and she forgot when it was time to help. As soon as dusk came Marguerite joined her in the basement and they waited for the siren. They never slept during an alert. Both felt it was essential to listen for bombs, to make ready to dodge. They slept in the day time. Mary and Patsy came over to see them. Everyone except Marguerite looked ten years older. Why she did not was a mystery. She dreaded the bombs as much as anyone, slept less than anyone. Perhaps it was that she had become accustomed to strain and long inured to little food and little sleep.

Marguerite was more afraid for the house than for herself. 52 was almost empty now. Only two lodgers remained and they had moved down as low as possible in the house. 52 was not paying its way but must be preserved. If only she could hang on until all this was over and get it going again it would provide a future for the children. It would clothe them, educate them and even allot to each a small sum when they came of age. They must not have a struggle. For the moment Mary and Patsy went out as cleaners of Government offices to earn, but 52 would help them too in time. She told no one about her reasons for staying on in London through the blitz. "We have put so much money into the house," she said to Kathleen, "that we do not want to lose everything." Kathleen thought of "we" as the two of them and imagined that if anything happened to Marguerite she would inherit what there was. Now that she could not work she was worried about her old age. But Marguerite had lately made a will in which Kathleen's name did not appear.

One night the attack was concentrated on their area. The sisters lay under the bed in the back basement room, close together, silent. Bombs fell. Anti-aircraft guns burst out. A loud explosion followed by a rumble and rush of wind sounded very near. Another explosion came. That was nearer.

"Holy Mother of God," said Marguerite. "Pray, Kathie. Pray hard."

The plane, dissatisfied, as though it knew it had not got them yet, circled and circled, painstakingly, ineluctable, slow, regardless of the anti-aircraft, regardless of the searchlights. They could scarcely breathe. Marguerite could pray but Kathleen could not. She could only listen and wait.

It came. They heard it whizzing down straight at them. There was no mistaking the direction. They freed their hands from one another and banged them over their ears. The moment had come. Through their pressed palms came the sound, on top of them, all around them. The house shook, a chair fell to the ground, the windows splintered. Then all was over. They were intact. They remained where they were for some time then, shaking, they dragged themselves from below the bed, the smell of old carpet and damp walls in the nostrils, sudden flashes of light revealing parts of the room to their eyes. "Let's have a cigarette, for goodness' sake," said Marguerite.

In the morning, hollow-eyed, exhausted, they made a tour of inspection, Marguerite's jangled nerves quickening and sharpening her voice and movements, Kathleen following half out of her mind. The years of constant small anxieties had left her at the mercy of the past night. She wept and wept. "I can't stand another. I must get away. I can't stand it. It's too much."

The house two doors away had been hit. Next door was half down. The windows of 52, with the curious exception of one in the drawing room which would have appeared to be in the direct line of blast, were blown out. The front door had been pushed in and lay aslant on one hinge. Some of the inner doors were standing and others were not. There were cracks in the roof and outer walls. The two lodgers, both middle-aged men, clerical workers, abandoned all thought of going to their office for the morning and joined in the tour. The four moved out to look round the neighbouring streets, relieved to see the morning sky much as it had always been, the policeman on the corner, other tired sightseers. In one street, five houses were down, their contents spilling out into the road, the backs mapped out in squares of different wallpaper. In another street one house had been picked out clean.

"They say it's worse near the station," said one of the men.

Outside the newsagent they read the morning paper as though it could tell them more about their house and neighbourhood than their own eyes. It told them nothing. Apprehensive, they went along to Curtis Street and found Mary's house intact.

Mary and Patsy were in. They too were in no hurry to go off to work. Patsy had been to mass. "Thank God the church was safe," she said. In the kitchen the two sisters, the two men, Mary and Patsy discussed what to do and drank sweet, strong, scalding tea.

"It was a mercy we were spared," said Mary.

"I knew t'would be all right," said Patsy, whose faith in prayer was unshakeable. She alone was smiling and serene. "It does no one any good to worry," she said, as though this platitude would comfort all around her and stop them worrying any more. To her, death was a step between this world and the next and though while the raids were actually on she too was pale, the moment they were over she decided that death was really a blessing.

"We must phone Elizabeth," said Kathleen.

5

"Go on, Kathie. We must finish it tonight. After all, I'm tired too," said Marguerite.

"Why are you in such a hurry? And it's bad for me to keep lifting my arm."

"Well do it with your other one."

"You know I can't."

They were scraping away wallpaper in their cottage. The cottage had been condemned some time before but owing to the emergency they had been allowed to purchase it and live there. Kathleen's compensation had been used for this. Marguerite spoke of it as her cottage and intended to leave it in her will to the children as soon as she saw the solicitor.

"*Chérie*, do show a little spirit." Marguerite hoped the children would be coming soon. It must be made habitable for them.

The place was derelict. Outside, tall weeds knocked up against the lower panes when there was a wind. There was only one tap in the house from which came a slow rusty trickle. Black cobwebs stretched over corners. The rooms were poky, dark and damp. To reach the closet one had to go down a narrow path in every weather. Upstairs the rain poured in.

"It could be made very sweet and quaint," Elizabeth had said. Then she had dumped all the family furniture in the place. Every room had held so much furniture at first that it had been out of the question to sweep and dust. A decision was taken to turn all but the two rooms downstairs into junk rooms if it was going to be possible to move about at all.

They could not oppose Elizabeth although for once they were in a strong alliance against her and described her passion for collecting as a mania. She was supporting them. Without her they would have had nothing but the Public Assistance Allowance of eighteen shillings a week each. And that allowance was a source of misery. They had obtained it on false pretences, making out that they were

405

paying rent. At any moment they might be found out and asked to refund all that had been given to them. Each time the official came to the house Kathleen lost her nerve and left Marguerite to deal with her. "We shouldn't do it. You never know what will happen if they find out. We might be sent to prison. And then if they knew Elizabeth was sending money too."

Layers of wallpaper had to be scraped off, the last one dating back to goodness knows when. It was Marguerite's opinion that they could do nothing for the mouldering wall until they had exposed it and discovered all its wretched secrets. "Then the men can patch it up and put a nice coat of distemper."

"But where are we going to get the men and distemper? And if the assistance woman finds them here she'll ask where we got the money from."

Marguerite loathed the country and missed the town. She spoke of the pleasures of living in London as if she had always been quick to take advantage of them. But she was not unhappy. At least you could have the children to stay here and at least you were safe. Besides, after that sticky week in Lady Watson's house, it was worth paying any price to "call your soul your own".

Torn between her wish to spare her friend any inconvenience and her duty to her family, Elizabeth had listened to the dictates of her conscience and asked the two sisters to the country house. There she had told them, "It's so sweet of Charlotte. She doesn't like having people as a rule, you know. And of course the servants are being very awkward. It's difficult to keep them these days and I'm afraid our maid will be called up at any moment. Not that I mind, you know, but it's very hard for poor Charlotte. When you're used to these things. And one of her nephews has joined up and she's dreadfully worried about him. One never knows what may happen. So you will understand if as soon as something turns up you go on somewhere else. Any money I have of course... Do thank Charlotte. And try not to get in the way. She's an absolute darling really. Very kind and sweet."

"Obviously the woman doesn't want us here," said Marguerite after the first dinner. "And what does Elizabeth mean by begging us not to smoke?" (Charlotte could not bear the smell of tobacco). To be parted from cigarettes was one of the finest forms of torture that could have been devised for them.

"I'm going back to London," said Marguerite on the second day. "I do not care. I can go and stay with Mary and Patsy." She thought longingly of their easy-going kitchen.

Lady Watson was not unkind. She believed in good works and charity but she liked them to be at a distance. She had worked out a way of life which suited her and to retain it was her greatest desire. Any interruption in routine was unpleasant for her. She mentioned none of this but it showed through the placid expression of her large red face. She discussed with Elizabeth whether they should dress for dinner since the sisters had brought no evening clothes with them. She took this problem seriously. She wanted to offend no one and yet standards must not be lowered.

In her presence the three sisters spoke quietly and made a pretence of light conversation. An observer might have thought it a tranquil, uneventful life had he seen them only in the drawing room and dining room. But upstairs in bedrooms feelings ran high and sudden "Shh's" made raised voices sink again.

At first they had felt relieved to be safe. But to Marguerite, the preservation of her life was not everything. What irritated her most was that they were always being asked to feel sorry for Charlotte. "Poor Charlotte," Elizabeth kept saying, as though Lady Watson had been singled out among civilians for the greatest suffering. It seemed that she could not get the right food for the birds. It seemed that the billeting officer was not understanding and spoke of filling the house with rough children and, worse still, mothers. "After all poor Charlotte has done to get the school converted into a kind of camp for them."

Marguerite and Kathleen saw the well-ordered house, not a brick out of place, the neatly-kept garden. Kathleen, docile, said, "It's very good of her to let us stay here." Marguerite felt cramped.

Within a week Elizabeth had heard news of the cottage. Not disclosing to them how tumble-down it was she packed them off. To her it had the advantage of being in a different county and not too far from London. Therefore the sisters would not be in the way and all the London furniture could be taken there without too great difficulty and expense. She wanted to do her best for everyone. She had been supporting them for some time and she would continue to do so. She would try and meet the bills for repairs. She was communicating with the Government about 52. In return they must understand that Lady Watson's house was not her house and that she had a professional responsibility as companion. She made matters worse by being over-explanatory and never leaving the subject alone.

When they had come to the cottage, two hours before the furniture arrived, Kathleen had wept bitter tears. It was her money which had bought it and therefore this was to be her permanent home, she thought. Just as they had all been tied to 52 by that wretched long lease, so now she would be even more tied to this place by ownership. Nobody in the world would ever want to buy it off her, and having no money in the world, here she would have to stay. The floorboards were covered in sticky earth—someone had used the lower floor for potato storage. In order to clean the place up they had to boil water on a primus stove. And then, once the furniture was packed in, it was impossible to get at the floor anyhow until the two of them had carted most of it away upstairs. The heavy lifting sent pains across her chest, down her back and sides. Marguerite could not carry chests of drawers and tables alone and was a hard taskmaster. She did not spare herself and therefore no one else should, especially when a home for the children was at stake.

"I do not care what the place is like," said Marguerite, "so long as we are independent."

Independent she was. The nearest neighbours were separated by a field and a high hedge. There was no timetable. They ate when Marguerite felt up to cooking. They slept when she felt like it. There were many big tasks to be done and they went at these at any hour of the day or night when she felt energetic.

On cold evenings it was possible to keep the front part of your legs warm if you sat close to the small grate, but the rest of you remained chilled and damp. The wind whistled through the broken pane and under the door. One of the doors kept rattling in its frame, keeping up a dismal patter through which it was difficult to sleep. Marguerite wandered about in her stockinged feet, tearing them on unexpected nails. The sooty smoke from the fire gradually filled the room until they saw each other through a mist and their eyes smarted.

And now that the children were coming in a fortnight it was work, work, work. Tearing at the old paper filled their nails with bits of plaster. Fortunately neither was squeamish about insects and rats.

"I simply can't go on," said Kathleen crying.

"Oh, *chérie*, do stop snivelling. We'll stop then."

Marguerite understood perfectly well that such was Kathleen's nature that she would feel compelled to go on working as long as her sister did. She was trained "not to let them down". She might protest and brood but she would do as they said. Automatically she returned to her work, mumbling under her breath, letting the tears pour down, aching all over. She should have learnt by now that however piteous she might appear it made no difference to Marguerite, but still she fell back on the old useless form of defence.

They distempered the walls themselves. The children arrived and Marguerite went to the station to meet them, returning loaded with their cases but smiling from ear to ear. "We'll put the four of them in this room and you can sleep with me," she said to Kathleen.

In the company of their favourite and most indulgent aunt the children were exacting and tyrannical. They naturally adopted her attitude to Kathleen and treated her as an uninteresting skivvy. She was sent out to do the shopping, up the long village street to wait her turn in the queues. She was sent out to the stone-floored, barn-like kitchen to peel potatoes and wash vegetables. She was expected to be at the beck and call of the others. The only thing she was not allowed to do was cook. This was Marguerite's domain and she would stand no interference. While she cooked Kathleen was told to keep an eye on the children. She went into the living room and watched them play. They looked up, saw her, were disappointed it was not Marguerite and continued with their games.

She began to dislike them. She would have liked to be a child and have someone look after her. And if she was asked to do so much for them then at least they should be friendly and polite. She wrote to Lisa, now in the north with her Ministry. "They don't even say 'Good morning' or 'Please' or 'Thank you'. They're a spoilt lot and I shall be glad when they've gone."

What galled her was that when she had been ill Marguerite had never bothered about meal times, but now the children were here, there was hell to pay if the vegetables were not prepared in time. And the cottage was hers. It was she who had paid for it. True, the title deeds had been made in the names of all three sisters, but Elizabeth had promised that that was for a special reason and made no difference. But no one behaved as though it were her house. She was not consulted even about the colour of the distemper. Even the children seemed to think that she was being kept there out of charity. No one made allowances for the fact that she was partially disabled by her accident.

"How long are the children going to stay?" she asked at length, having plucked up her courage.

"As long as they want," said Marguerite vaguely.

"But when does their school start?"

"I'd thought of sending them to the local school here."

"Well in that case, I'm going."

"What do you mean?"

"I've had enough. I never have a moment to myself. I'm on my feet all day. There are the six of us in two tiny rooms. And I'm not well. You seem to forget that I'm not well."

"Very well then. I can manage alone."

"But this is my house. Why should I go?"

"You can stay here if you want."

"I don't want them here all the time, not unless Patsy or Mary can come and look after them. I've been the whole morning washing their clothes."

Kathleen wrote to Elizabeth appealing for help and threatening to go away somewhere on her own although she knew very well she could never carry out her threat. She wrote to Lisa. Lisa sent her some money telling her on no account to hand it over to the aunts, but she could do nothing else for her. She had no home to which to invite her.

In answer to the letter, Elizabeth came on a diplomatic mission. She knew how to handle Marguerite. "I quite understand, *chérie*. Of course you like them with you. But we must send them to good schools and I know you would not like them to be at an elementary school especially since they tell me the one here is very bad. They must be given a chance in life. Besides, quite frankly, you could get into trouble for having them here at all, all in one room. I have been very worried about that. Believe me, *chérie,* I know just how you feel and I do sympathise. But still we must try and think what will be best for everyone."

She even dissuaded her from keeping the two youngest. "When winter comes they will be bound to catch cold in this place. Until we can get it done up it's really only suitable for a summer holiday for them. We must think of their health." She sighed and looked sad. She held the purse strings. The children were sent away.

Marguerite returned from seeing them off, in a rage. She advanced on Kathleen as though she would have liked to tear her to pieces. "It's all your doing. It's all through your selfishness. You've never thought of anyone but yourself and your daughter."

For weeks the two sisters hardly spoke to each other. Repairs were discontinued. Until next summer there was little point in bothering about the place, thought Marguerite. "If only I could get really ill," thought Kathleen. "If only something would happen which would make them do something about me. If only I could get out of this."

6

Marguerite gasped, moved her head from side to side, shouted, "She's trying to poison me."

She opened her eyes and looked round with an expression of cunning and resolution. She was hot and flushed, her feet tingling against the stone hot water bottle, her one exposed hand freezing. She placed the icy fingers over her forehead. She felt thirsty. But nothing would persuade her to drink. She coughed and moaned and pulled at the cotton wool over her chest.

Through the door came the pale face of her mortal enemy, Kathleen. "Could you take some hot milk now? What about your medicine?"

Marguerite screamed. She knew what that meant. Kathleen was poisoning everything and then trying to get her to take it. "Go away. I will not drink anything. Go away, you wicked woman. I know you."

In the next room, Kathleen wrung her hands and waited. If only Elizabeth would come. If only the doctor would call again. If Marguerite went on like this she would be bound to die; she had taken nothing now for two days.

She heard a footstep outside and hurried to the door. "Oh, Elizabeth, thank God you've come. I don't know what's the matter with her. She's got some kind of down on me and won't take her medicine or anything. I can't even go near her to take her temperature but she screams the place down. And she's so ill. The doctor said it was pneumonia."

"Poor soul. Delirious."

"He says she must go to hospital. He says he won't be responsible for her if she stays here. I can't bear the responsibility, *chérie*. I can't really."

"I can stay a few days. Leave her to me."

Alone, with a gentle tread and a nurse's smile, Elizabeth approached the bedside. "Any pain, dear? I came as quickly as I could. How about some hot milk or bovril?"

Marguerite's eyes narrowed and her mouth set. Elizabeth did not want to poison her but she did not know Kathleen's ways. She did not know that every drop of liquid in the house had been poisoned. "No. I will take nothing. I know her. She's been at everything. I can hear her walking about, at it all the time."

Elizabeth pursed her lips into a disparaging smile. "I promise you I shall prepare the milk myself. Just a little."

"No. No. No."

Elizabeth shivered. There was snow on her brogues and her breath was like steam. The sensitive end of her nose was blue and her eyes had a look of migraine and insomnia. She looked at the Sacred Heart on the wall and was strengthened. "I shall prepare it now. Then I'm sure you'll take it."

But when the steaming glass was put beside the bed Marguerite looked at it with horror and shut her mouth tight.

"Well look, *chérie*," said Elizabeth. "If you feel like that wouldn't you be better in hospital? You could trust them there. If you don't want Kathleen near you—and I'm sure you're quite wrong to think of her as you do but still we'll say no more about that—then you would be right away from her."

Marguerite felt hot and cold. She had never been to hospital before in her life except as a nurse and she was certainly not going now. To think of being a patient, stuck in a ward, unable to do as you pleased, among a lot of other patients, at the mercy of every little probationer! She knew all about it. It was the final humiliation. She would sooner die, sooner let herself starve here. Also she knew her strength. No one could budge her against her will. She would fight to the last.

In the evening the doctor came and spoke to her. "I've told your sisters I can't be responsible for you if you stay here." Marguerite shouted, "I'm not going."

"It would be better," urged Elizabeth, disliking such a display of feeling in front of a doctor. "It's pneumonia."

Marguerite saw them as conspirators. This man who called himself a doctor was a creature of Kathleen's. Kathleen wanted her to die in order to get her out of the house. Kathleen with all her humble ways would stop at nothing. For two days she had been trying to poison her, bringing her one fatal drink after another. She knew what these country hospitals were like. And even if the man was a doctor he was only some little country practitioner. Marguerite had never thought much of doctors anyhow. She knew more than they did. She could have told him it was pneumonia without all the fussing and tapping. She knew her heart was not too good. She had always known the secret of her purple colour.

To speak at all caused her pain but her passionate resolve acted as an anaesthetic. She shouted at the top of her voice. She clutched at her hair, half clenching her fists as though ready for a fray. "I will not go. I will not listen to any of you. If you move me I shall die. I'm going to die. I know. I know all about it. I'm half dead now. If you lay a finger on me I shall die at once. Go away, all of you. I do not want anyone."

Kathleen, who had been hovering near the door, came forward to whisper to Elizabeth. She was afraid people might believe Marguerite. She could never believe that anyone could take her side. She felt she ought to mention she had done nothing wrong.

"What's she saying?" shouted Marguerite. "Do not listen to her. She tried to poison me. She tried to kill me. She wants me to die."

In the next room the doctor looked professional, wrinkled his brow, rubbed his hands together. "If you keep her here then it must be your responsibility."

"Very well, doctor," said Elizabeth. "I quite understand."

Marguerite was obsessed with her loathing for Kathleen. She had switched her loathing to make it represent Kathleen's loathing for her. By a long non-verbal thought process, a series of pictures of the children, of Kathleen's face when the children were there, of Kathleen's drooping shoulders at the sink, she had pieced together a chain of events, a series of emotions which led to one conclusion. At the bottom of it was something to do with the cottage, with ownership of the cottage and who should inherit it. Kathleen now represented the cause of every failure in her life. She remembered dimly that nephews and nieces had gone astray and because Kathleen now seemed to obstruct the present nephews and nieces, it was clear that Kathleen had undermined the others. Kathleen had been responsible too for the misfortunes of 52. And Kathleen's accident had become *her* accident. She felt that her sister had tried to push *her* under a lorry. (This revelation contained a reversed truth, for the cause of Kathleen's proneness to accidents on that morning had been the unhappiness of living with her sister; and now the sister could grasp her guilt and hand it back to the victim).

But above all Kathleen seemed to cast a shadow over the children. Even their faces were not very clear to Marguerite. There were four of them and they were hers and Kathleen hated them. Kathleen had in fact complained about their manners. Now Marguerite heard Kathleen hurling abuse at them, saw her maltreating them. If once she killed Marguerite she would have the children at her mercy. She wanted this just as she had wanted to undo all the other children—something to do with making Lisa the only one who survived or did well. But there had been some trouble with Lisa too. Probably Kathleen had wanted to do her own daughter harm as well. She was deep and crafty and her motives were wicked and selfish. With her in the house there had been the blitz.

She was haunted by Kathleen's face. She saw it as it was: frail, timid, questioning and then suddenly it darkened and took on an evil and strong expression and looked into her eyes and came nearer. She was not afraid of it. She was afraid of no one. She would fight it to her last gasp and as long as she lived Kathleen would not conquer. But if she died then who would protect the children from this monster? And yet she must die rather than accept the poisoned drink, rather than go into hospital. She must do her death in her own way. It was not dying which she minded. She must control her own destiny to the last; she would take no orders from anyone. It was as though the fight was not between life and death but between the death Kathleen chose for her and the death she chose for herself.

As she lay delirious, the sisters consulted each other. What should they do? How could they persuade her to take something? Elizabeth alone went into the sick room, for such it must be called although it had not the aspect of such a place. The floor was unswept because Kathleen had not been able to get in without screams. There was no medicine bottle or glass because they had brought forth such violence from the patient. The room was full of smoke and in great disorder.

"Why were all those clothes left about? What sort of people will the doctor think we are?" said Elizabeth.

"There's nowhere to put them and I've told you she wouldn't have me in there."

"But where are all the chests of drawers I sent here? I thought there were at least three."

"I know, but they're all so huge. If we had one of them downstairs we could hardly move at all. It's the same thing with the wardrobe. If only we had something small."

Elizabeth's face brightened. Here was another reason to purchase more. "I'll look out for one for you. There's a little antique shop near us which had quite a little pet."

Kathleen's face fell. Any more furniture in the house and life would be worse than it was. Besides, Elizabeth would never dream of buying just one chest of drawers; she would get inside the shop and pick up bits of this and that, all at bargain prices and therefore all with a missing leg or ravaged by worm and moth. And then it would all arrive here with many warnings and messages, the men would dump it by the front door and she and Marguerite (poor Marguerite—if she was here) would have another day of furniture hauling.

"By the way, where have you put all the furniture?" said Elizabeth. "Upstairs."

Elizabeth was horrified. Her precious pieces were exposed to a leaking roof! She began to remonstrate and stopped herself. Now was not the time. She must see to it later. However, she did not forbear to sigh and say, "We cannot afford to lose furniture through carelessness, you know. Apart from all I have spent—and it was simply so that we might all have a happy home together one day—it will be quite unobtainable soon."

At ten that night Elizabeth did a thing she had never done before, had never dreamt of doing and would never do again. She entered a public house. It would be wrong to send Kathleen. She must go herself. She put on her hat, gloves and slipped galoshes over her brogues. She wanted no one to make a mistake. She went straight to the bar, looking neither to right nor left, and produced an empty medicine bottle. "Would you be so kind as to fill this with brandy. It's for a lady who's desperately ill. Thank you." Her polite and quiet voice seemed to say to the barmaid, "I will not judge you but it amazes me how any young woman can bring herself to this life."

She was taut and impatient as she waited for her bottle to be filled. The smell of drink was unpleasant enough but the splashes of beer and the empty glasses with froth stuck to the side were odious. These places should not be allowed. Wrapping the bottle in brown paper, averting her eyes from the little bunch of standing drinkers, she hurried away. She did not know it but she had gone into the wrong bar, much to the amusement of the regulars.

Throughout the night Kathleen and Elizabeth watched over the semi-conscious Marguerite, feeding her small spoonfuls of brandy. They were both in coats and scarves and when they sat down they pulled old blankets over their knees. It was one of the coldest nights of the year and both dreaded the journeys to kitchen or closet.

In spite of discomfort Kathleen was amused. She later wrote to Lisa: "Who would ever have thought that Elizabeth would make M. take spirits? If M. had been conscious the bottle would have disappeared in a flash. As it was I think she enjoyed it. She was conscious enough once or twice and there was no going on about poison."

Whether it was the brandy or Marguerite's own will which brought about the recovery was uncertain. But two days later the fever had abated, the pulse was slow, the dark blueish purple of her face had reverted to the usual pinkish purple. She sat up in bed propped against a pile of freshly-covered pillows. Round her shoulders was a very fluffy pale blue shawl of Elizabeth's and her hair was neatly brushed back. She was a little dreamy and as mild as a lamb.

Elizabeth had not idled for one moment of her waking hours. The room was cleaner and tidier than it had ever been. A neat square of thick cardboard was tacked over the gap in the window. There was a smell of disinfectant and lavender water. The bed had been remade with clean sheets. The tiny entrance hall and poor Kathleen's room were filled with furniture brought down from upstairs to save it from the elements.

"Promise me not to take it up there again, *chérie*," said Elizabeth as she kissed Kathleen goodbye. "I was heartbroken at the condition! Still, we shall say no more about it. You have been a brick, dear. You've done wonders for poor Marguerite. If poor Charlotte hadn't been so stranded now that the maid has gone I would have stayed longer. But the corner is turned. You know God has been very good to us. I hope you pray every day, *chérie*. We need our religion more than ever at these times." She sighed and dashed away to catch a train by the skin of her teeth.

Marguerite took her milk, medicine and food very meekly from Kathleen's hands. Her mouth was soft and her brow was smooth. There was no suggestion of violence in her expression. And yet she never thanked her youngest sister, although she had been profusely grateful to Elizabeth. She said very little to her. She watched her every movement when she was in the room and she gave a straight, searching but non-committal glance when she approached the bed. The loathing had not disappeared. It had crept back to its hiding place and taken with it the fantasies which were both its cause and justification.

7

The daily question was money, money, money. The daily answer was that one of them or both must work. "Why did you never apply for the old age pension?" said Kathleen.

Marguerite was very cagey about her age and whittled down the years between herself and her youngest sister by leaving out of account the miscarriages of her mother and insisting that there was only a year between each of the children. She had a horror of the Old Age Pension; there were forms to fill in and then you had to wait in a queue with a lot of people who looked *really* old until your turn came and a sharp young woman was impertinent to you. She refused to be old. She did not look it. She looked younger than Elizabeth and sometimes younger than Kathleen. She had decided to stay forty-five, the colour of her hair.

Each was reluctant to work because each considered herself to be the invalid and resented the other's claims to be sick. In fact neither of them was strong. Kathleen had never felt the same since the accident. She mistrusted the top half of her body and felt as though something might suddenly collapse in her side. When she moved her arms she felt real and imaginary pulls.

Marguerite too felt low and mistrusted her heart and her chest. "We are a very chesty family," she said with frowning emphasis to Kathleen, as though if you were a member of a chesty family it was far worse to have your chest attacked than to be run over a thousand times. She continued to smoke heavily. She kept clearing her throat and turned dark purple as she coughed and spluttered. Her voice grew huskier and huskier. It was distinctive and beautiful.

"Talking of pensions," she said sharply, "why did you never get your widow's pension? You might have had it all these years."

"You know perfectly well we applied and they wouldn't give it to anyone who lived abroad."

"Well you should have said you never lived abroad."

"But supposing they found out?"

"Really, Kathie, you didn't even try."

One could not call either of them lazy. Given the right stimulus and the right incentive each of them had performed the most arduous work over long periods of their lives. Kathleen, when Lisa was at school, had taken case after case of night duty, had never had a proper holiday in order to ensure a good education for the girl and buy her what she needed. But they could not work for work's sake. Neither could they work, as Elizabeth did, for the maintenance of standards. Although their characters were different Kathleen and Marguerite had the temperamental similarity of needing excitement to touch them off.

The Public Assistance allowance had come to an end. The authorities had not failed to observe the installation of electric light, lavatory and bathroom and they had not been satisfied with Marguerite's confused rigmarole. Elizabeth's income had been used up for these installations, for the rescue of 52 and for the purchase of more unnecessary furniture and pieces of brocade and cretonne. (She persisted in her dream of a quaint, dainty cottage). Lisa sent money to Kathleen but Kathleen dared not disclose this because Marguerite would not only appropriate it but also take it for granted that the girl should send a sum regularly. Therefore Kathleen kept some idle and much needed pounds in a purse under the mattress and wondered how she could pretend she had just come across an odd pound somewhere.

Not that Elizabeth had left them without a penny. On the contrary, she had worked out a budget; they would need so much for food and so much for fuel; and she sent weekly what she considered to be the necessary amount. But Marguerite and Kathleen liked cigarettes, must have cigarettes. Because they could not do without smoking they had to do without food. They lived mostly on tea and bread and margarine. There was no question of buying new clothes for years and years and there was also no question of mending and darning. Marguerite had greatly diminished her former wardrobe by giving dresses away to people she was sorry for. Kathleen had never been allowed to buy anything new, had always been given Elizabeth's old suits. They were shabby and undernourished.

Living together did them no good. It was necessary for Marguerite to be with someone she could love. It was necessary for Kathleen to be with someone who took an interest in her. Each was all the more put out by the present arrangement because she had found the way of life which suited her and would have continued in it had the war not intervened. Marguerite had found a circle and the children. Kathleen had found her niche in the German school. Finding little comfort in blaming their present discomfort on the war in general, they blamed each other, sometimes openly, sometimes in secret. The resentments and grudges piled up with the dirt and the dust. The cottage became a symbol of all that was most unpleasant and pointless.

To escape from the cottage, quite apart from financial reasons, Kathleen found work. The local balloon factory needed hands. She rose at half-past six each morning in order to reach the factory by eight after a two-mile walk. Owing to the double summer time these early walks were taken in the dark. Changing into a dark overall she took her place at the long bench and gummed together strips of waterproof material. She was paid eleven pence an hour and she joined a Trade Union.

She got on well with her fellow-workers and rapidly absorbed their attitude to the management. Here as in hospital the ones who did the donkey work had the least power and the lowest wages. But in hospital no one had protested whereas here, from morning till night, the girls did spirited imitations of the authorities—from the chargehands to the works manager—and respected no one.

She was different from the other girls (in a factory, she learned, you are a girl at any age) because her accent was based on Elizabeth and her manner was quiet. From her sisters she had taken over the ideal of "refinement". From Germany she had brought back ideals of culture and sensibility. Also she prided herself on having travelled and learnt languages. The constant use of such a word as "bloody" jarred on her and she privately classed the girls into two groups, the coarse and the refined. But after that her difference from the others ended. She was no snob and she was on their side. She was grateful for the easiness and friendliness which they provided. Their moral lapses never shocked her—and many unmarried ones became pregnant by Canadians. As she put it to Lisa, "The poor things. They have nowhere to go. They've been brought here from all over England whether they wanted or not. They're in wretched diggings with rotten landladies. They work from morning until night and want a bit of fun. Then these men come along and get them drunk." Often she shook her head and told herself, "There's something very wrong somewhere. Things aren't fair."

Because she was a bench hand, Kathleen found herself lumped with the others and looked down on by the inspectresses. Automatically she took a dislike to the inspectresses. "Who do they think they are with their airs and graces and privileges? They haven't even travelled and most of them never went to a secondary school." She was furious to see hams and other nice things laid out in the canteen for the staff only. "If they don't want the girls to have it they shouldn't put it on view." Still, it was comforting to have so many natural allies. On private cases one had been at the mercy of the patient, the patient's relations and the patient's servants, alone and isolated. Now one could grumble without fear and answer back too. She was not so happy here as she had been in Germany but she was far happier than she had been as a nurse.

One day there was an accident during the stampede to lunch. One of the girls had a varicose vein pierced by a pair of scissors that fell from the pocket of another girl. As there seemed to be no one to take charge, Kathleen applied cold compresses to the wound. It subsequently came out that she was a trained nurse.

It was therefore decided to transfer her to a "clean" job so that she would be ready for other accidents. She was moved to the store room and given ten shillings a week extra. And she made a friend. There was only one other person in the store room, a young girl from the East End, and the two of them felt free in there, removed from the eyes of the supervisors, shut away in peace. Between sorting, listing and handing out material they talked. Kathleen described Portugal and Germany, said she had a brilliant daughter who had gone to Oxford and her companion—whose name was Nancy—listened with admiring wonder. These marvels gave Kathleen a reflected glory in her eyes. "Now I'm very fond of reading," she said. "Tell me what I ought to read."

Kathleen wrote out an impressive list in her childish hand, ranging from Dickens to Warwick Deeping, and gave it to Nancy.

Nancy confided all her love affairs and asked advice. She thought Kathleen learned and infallible and she loved her because she gave herself no airs. Nancy would not allow Kathleen to do heavy lifting. "Leave that to me," she said. She brought eggs and other titbits. She observed her every change of colour and size. "You're looking pale. You're getting thinner. Who looks after you?" she asked with solicitude.

No one looked after Kathleen and after years of nursing, where meals were provided for you, she was incapable of looking after herself. When she came home at night she found nothing prepared for her. Marguerite had not even bothered to put on a kettle. Marguerite had often forgotten to buy the rations and there was nothing in the larder. This meant that Kathleen must take her turn in a long queue on her way home to buy fish and chips. Marguerite had not attempted to tidy Kathleen's room or make the bed. Tired as she was Kathleen must face her chilly room, lay the fire and pull up the bedclothes. Marguerite expected to be handed the pay packet at the end of the week. The only thing she could be relied on to do was to keep plenty of cigarettes in the house.

"This isn't fair," said Kathleen at last. "You do absolutely nothing for me at all. You've the whole day to prepare a bit of food in. What on earth do you do with your time? After all, it's my cottage and my money. I don't grudge you, but you might..."

"The cottage belongs to all of us. We arranged that."

"You didn't put anything in to it."

"Oh, yes I did. All the electric light and the rest are coming out of what I get on 52."

"It's not fair. You took all my compensation. I didn't want the place. You made me buy it. And now you say..."

Marguerite brushed her aside. She did not want to go thoroughly into this argument. "I shall go out to work too."

Marguerite found a part-time job at a knitting factory. Here the workers were all part-time, most of them middle-aged housewives who had growing children to look after. The pay was small but by taking jumpers home to finish off the ends you could make a little more on piece rates. This appealed to Marguerite. She developed a passion to make money at home. Every week she brought home a great bundle of jumpers and every evening by the dim bulb she went at them, staying up till one or two. "If only we could do a hundred or so, *chérie*, it would come to quite a bit." Here was a gold mine if only she could work it.

Now when Kathleen came home from work she found piles of thick navy jerseys everywhere, the sleeves trailing on the dusty floor. She was expected to tackle them. "You sew them here and here. Just pull the thread together. It's very simple."

God help the sailors who got Marguerite's jerseys, thought Kathleen. She protested and grumbled. "I'm tired. I've had a hard day. I've been up since half-past six." But in the end she did as she was told.

"Oh, there's nothing to do in a store room," said Marguerite airily.

In her factory Marguerite made no friends. She was out of sympathy with the district. She was keeping her heart for the people who came to 52 and for the children. She neither liked nor disliked the other women. Neither did she feel particularly ashamed to be doing manual work. She called it "war work" and told herself that the highest in the land were doing the same. Also her memory and ambition had waned and her one concern was to have enough money put by for the summer to gratify the children's every whim. This was yet another period in her life which "did not count"; she looked on it as the hard prelude to one month of happiness. Thus she could dissociate herself from it in any but a material way.

Her eagerness to be earning and earning made her talk fast, push forward her head, keep her hands forever moving. While she worked the machine she thought of money. She would put it all in the Post Office. She would make Kathleen promise not to tell Elizabeth how much she earned. She had already told Kathleen she was only earning ten shillings a week—this was exactly half the truth. (Kathleen had also kept quiet about the extra shillings she was now getting in the store room). Then when the summer came, thought Marguerite, she would draw out the money, tell Kathleen it was some kind of windfall connected with the Government and War Damage, tell Elizabeth (if she happened to come at that time) that she had been given a special bonus and that Mary and Patsy had sent something, and have a wonderful time with the children.

Sometimes she greatly magnified her earning potentiality and thought of investing her savings in real estate in the neighbourhood, buying up houses and letting them, reserving for herself and the children a nice country house. She cursed the slowness of her fingers and the dimness of her sight. She could not understand why she did not go faster. Mentally she was always two or three jerseys ahead of the one in her hands. Even sacrificing every kind of neatness and firmness to speed, biting off the wool, making rough knots, she still lagged behind her intentions. And how slow Kathleen was, she thought. What was all this nonsense she kept saying about her poor left arm not being what it was and her right hand being no use to her? Kathleen took hours to do a simple piece of finishing off, over-conscientious, over-tender about the sailors. And then Kathleen seemed to think she should get the money for the pieces she had done. How ungenerous! How typical of her grasping, cunning nature!

They scrapped and grumbled, sent each other to Coventry. Each thought, "I will not ask after her health since she never asks after mine." And each thought, "How mean of her never to ask me once how I feel when I work so hard and my health is so poor."

Kathleen thought, "How rotten of her never to do anything to the house when she is only on part-time."

Marguerite thought, "How mean of her never to lift a finger at home when *she* has no home work to do."

They had one major quarrel. During the argument they rose from their armchairs, as though height would give the advantage, and their faces flushed and looked full of passion. They ended on an ultimatum. "If you won't let me have Nancy here for tea on Sunday," said Kathleen, "I shan't do any more of your jerseys. She's the only friend I've got in this country. I'm very fond of her."

Nancy had come once and Marguerite had made a fuss, saying the girl was common. Kathleen had brooded over this for a week, her resentment mounting. After all, she thought, what were Mary and Patsy but cleaners? Not that she minded that, because she was fond of them too. But where was the difference? What had the brothers been for that matter?

To Marguerite anyone poor whom she loved was either nature's gentleman or lady or else had fallen from high estate. Anyone poor she did not love was ordinary. She would stand no interference with her hierarchies either from the existing division of society or from the attitude of another person. Also, although she did not admit this, it galled her to see Kathleen taking on a protégée and even more to see the girl lost in admiration for her sister and her wide reading, treating her, Marguerite, as though she were the less important of the two sisters. In any case she did not like any outsider coming to

423

the cottage. When she was in a period which "did not count" she wanted to see no one in her territory.

8

"*Chérie*," wrote Elizabeth. "Government definitely requisition if no one in 52. Must be there by end of month. First aid done windows and doors. Have seen myself. Habitable. Could let now. Blitz finished for moment. D.V."

So Marguerite returned to 52. Alone she climbed the dirty front step, noted how dark green the brass knocker had become, inserted her key into the lock and went in. Above the door was black cardboard. The two top panes of the door—formerly glass—were of unpainted plywood. Inside it was dark and the electric light was switched off at the main. She found a torch in her bag and threw its thin beam onto a circle of the familiar carpet. Patsy and Mary had received the furniture the day before and had done their best to carry out instructions.

First Marguerite went to the front floor back. The portraits of her father and mother were still there, the frames more tarnished, the glass intact but dusty. They eyed her stonily but she did not notice this. Tears sprang into her eyes as she saw them. She did not know why. They were not her parents now. She was too old for them to be her parents or her past. She had severed all threads with her childhood except Sunday Mass and her prayer book. They reminded her not of Cardiff but of the lonely days she had spent with these pictures in 52. She did not remember the events of those days but the feel of them. She sat down beside a pile of folded blankets on the bed and looked around the room. Finally her eye paused on the back yards outside. They were filled with debris from the blitz. The workmen who had done the patching here and next door had flung any oddments out there: bits of wood, bits of piping, strips of rotting lino.

She must find the switch downstairs in the basement. Where was it? She had known for years where it was. The knowledge must still be in her mind somewhere if only she could find it. What had happened to her memory? Only yesterday she had forgotten

424

something very simple, very obvious, what was it? She could not remember even that.

Having found the switch, tired, curious to discover more about the house, she wandered into the front kitchen, looked out the area steps, the dustbins still filled with the builders' rubbish, saw above at street level a pair of legs pass by, female legs with wrinkled stockings, unfamiliar but part of the district.

For many minutes she stood by the window, her eyes now dry, one tear still on her puffy cheek. Mary and Patsy would be over in the evening or she would go over to them. Which was it? What had they arranged? Where had she put the letter?

The dresser was empty. An old grocery bill still hung from one of the cup hooks. Soot had come through the bars of the range—never used in her time—and lay in a heap on the stone slabs. There was a smell of stone and iron. There was no smell of people.

She must make a tour of the bedrooms, must see that each had a bed, a chest of drawers and so on, must get them let, must get the house working, must get money for the children. She had five pounds on her and she would keep quiet about that. Elizabeth must think she had not a farthing.

The dining room looked strange. The table was there and so were the chairs but they looked different. Was it too near the window? Or was it too far away from the fireplace? She had not realised to what an extent atmosphere depends on things being a foot this way or that. A very slight change in position and the room looks like a person wearing a new hat. She must solve this mystery and get it back as it was. It would have to be trial and error. She could remember nothing in detail.

The drawing room too had this feeling of strangeness. As though to fight it she pulled at the Elizabethan settle and drew the big armchairs near the fire. The piano was shut. She hated that. The rounded lid looked terrible. She lifted it to reveal the notes; to her they were like teeth disclosed by a smile. That was better.

The room known as the back of the drawing room, which had once been part of the drawing room when it stretched the full depth of the house in an L-shape, had a bed and a wardrobe inside. But this bed and wardrobe had been on another floor before? Or not? She associated them with a little mousy man, a regular who had stayed on for years. They recalled to her the parting in his straight thin hair. She, who had never seemed to observe him at the time, had observed his hair, uselessly, in secret, had even observed the colour of his eyes, brown. Her memory was going its own way, not obeying her commands any longer, filling her head with this little man but not telling her in which room he and his furniture had had their long acquaintance.

She was in a highly receptive, excitable state. The journey and the return to the house had left her feeling as light as air. She trembled and her eyes grew moist again. She was in a state where the slightest joke would have reduced her to hysterics, the smallest woe to unbounded compassion and grief. She was on the alert for something to touch her off in any direction. She seemed to hover and flutter like a bird.

Another flight of stairs, rather an effort. Short of breath, purple, she paused. Here began the chopped rooms with their speckled wallpaper and frieze. They had never seemed very familiar anyhow. When she had taken refuge on this floor with her bottle, the rooms had been large and whole. She looked into each, opened the proper door, opened the inner, frail, shoddy door the builders had made in the partitions. They could be let, they were usable.

On the next floor she continued her inspection. The two back rooms had once been one. Her memory did not remind her this had been Jimmy's room, but presented her with a sudden unexplained unhappiness. She knew there had been a disappointment, a dreadful disappointment; it was like when you tell a fortune with tea leaves and you say, "There will be a terrible disappointment," and you can shed no further light. It had been some kind of failure, the most important failure. She could not even tell whether it had been to do with herself in particular or with the family in general. Baffled, she allowed her misery to gather strength. Her face creased and she began to sob, leaning against the door. She tried to generalise, "We've had such a struggle. You struggle and struggle all your life and then what comes of it?" She told herself she was being sorry for the children because they were evacuated, for Mary and Patsy because they had to work as cleaners, for Elizabeth because she had sacrificed her independence, for Kathleen because she had been run over, for the brothers because they were dead. Every member of the family, whether she loved them or not, was her responsibility and a source of suffering.

And then she could not tell the time of this upsetting failure. Was it something happening now? It felt like it. It might well be, with the war disturbing the course of all their lives.

When she reached the top floor she was shaking violently, out of control, hysterical. She hoped no one would see her like this. Not only had these emotions been evoked which had Jimmy as their unknown source, but also the black cardboard in the windows, the broken rods of the banisters and the general smell of desolation had made their mark. She paused on the top step, swayed and then sat on it, her elbows on her knees, her hands supporting her head. Still sobbing she looked straight ahead of her at the cracked wall. She might just as well sit here as anywhere else. There was no place in this house now which was particularly hers. Often in the past, during those times when she was not trying to avoid pursuit, she had liked to see doors open, had left open the door of the dining room, drawing room and her own room, with the idea that you could move from place to place with no finality, no shutting yourself in as though for a stay of some duration, no differentiating between rooms, passages and stairs. When the carpet men had been on the stairs she had liked to stand there too. It was a no man's land.

Her sobs died down. She felt very tired. She must begin from scratch. There had been a lot of struggle and planning and it had come to nothing and now the lodgers and rents and bills must start again. Although she had not enjoyed the respite, nevertheless there had been a break. "If it was just myself I had to think of..." she began, but the thought was inconclusive. She rubbed her knuckles into her broad flat forehead.

Yes, she thought, it was really the children who were on her mind. But the next moment she remembered Jimmy. She saw him clearly, his smart suits and light eyes, his well-groomed hands, his man-about-town air. But she maintained it was not this which had caused her sudden sorrow. She wondered what had become of him, supposed he was the same age as when she last saw him and must therefore have joined up by now—a gallant officer, the right type for the Air Force. He needed someone to look after him, poor soul. He had had a struggle too. She included him in her general sympathy for the family. She pulled herself up and inspected the top rooms. A gas stove and sink had been placed in a cupboard on the landing—Elizabeth called it a "kitchenette".

On the downward journey she inspected the bathrooms; they were on the landings alternate to the rooms. The copper geyser was green, the enamel geyser was filthy. "The place needs a thorough cleaning out," she told herself, as she had often done before. But this time she had no illusion that the thorough cleaning would ever take place.

In the evening she went over to Mary and Patsy. They thought she looked a bit restless and they noticed that she kept repeating herself.

"Why not have the children back in London?" she said. "The two eldest can go to day schools. Very nice schools. The very best. Let them stay with me if you're too busy. And the two youngest might just as well be at home. They really ought to be at home. It's not right for them to be away. There will not be any more raids. Everyone says so. Why not have the children in London? Why not let them stay with me?"

"We'd been thinking of bringing them back."

"That's right. You're quite right. Let them come back. Let them stay with me."

"We'll wait till this term is over."

"Why? Why? What does it matter whether they finish their term or not. Some ordinary little country school. It makes no difference. Let them stay with me if you're working. We could bring them back next week."

That night she did not undress but rolled herself up in a blanket. She was ready to jump up if there was a raid or an intruder. She had insisted she did not mind sleeping in the house alone and in a way this was true. She was not frightened, she was on the alert.

She could not sleep. Neither could she dwell on any one thing for more than a few seconds. Pictures came to her eyes, the cottage, the kitchen in Curtis Street, the rooms upstairs, the pile of jerseys. She tried to say some prayers but after the first sentence or two of Our Father or Hail Mary there came a distraction. In the small hours she had a comforting thought, "I know where that main switch is," and fell asleep.

9

On a cold January morning, Marguerite thought she might have a temperature. There was no thermometer in the house so she let the matter drop. All rooms but the ground floor and basement were let, drawing room and all, to Poles.

She decided it would be nice to go and fetch the children from Curtis Street. Mary and Patsy had not sent them over for two days and they had put a stop to William and Patricia living with her. She imagined that this was because they thought it was too much trouble for her.

They had in fact been very tactful and hidden their real motives. They feared that with her present vagueness and oddness the children might get nothing to eat, might not get to bed till all hours, might never get to school in time.

She made her way along the streets lit by a wan sun. She ran into Eileen, her former maid whom she had tried to marry to John. She had often seen her at church during the past ten years and she now stopped and exchanged a few words with her.

She kept asking, "It is Saturday, is it not," because if not the four of them might not be there.

Her chest felt sore. She had had a cold for weeks without being able to throw it off. She had meant to spend yesterday in bed.

It was Saturday. The children were all there. Thank goodness. She kissed each one and asked for their news. "Would you like to come and spend the day with me?"

Mary looked worried. "Are you sure you can manage, dear? I mean the cooking and that. Won't it be a great trouble to you? Shall I give them dinner here and then send them over? You stay and have it with us."

Marguerite was mild but obstinate. "No, no. There's plenty there for them. No trouble. Now run and get ready all of you."

"You're looking well," said Mary. Marguerite did in fact look flushed and bright. "Is the cold better?"

"Oh, yes. Quite gone now." She did not want her cold to be used as an excuse for not sending over the children. "I shake these things off in a few days."

The drawing room furniture had been moved down to the dining room of 52. There the children romped and shouted while Marguerite went to look at the larder. A tin of spam, some bread and butter, that would do. As she laid the tray her head reeled and she was forced to sit for a while in the kitchen. She would spend tomorrow in bed. She would go to early Mass and then come straight back to bed, ask Mary to come over and have a look at her sometime during the day. She heard the kettle steaming. She had meant to make herself a cup of tea. That was all the lunch she wanted. But it was too much effort now and she fancied it no longer. She turned off the gas and sat down again.

She came into the dining room with her tray. The children said:

"What is it?"

"Spam."

"Good."

"I hate it. Isn't there something else?"

"Could we have jam too?"

"What will we have to drink?"

This reminded her. "William, do you mind running over to your mother's for some milk?"

"Oh, Auntie, I was just in the middle of a game. Why can't Paddy go?"

"I'm in the game too."

"You're not. You can be in it while you go because you're supposed to have gone out."

They both turned to her. "Auntie, why don't you go?"

This did not seem unreasonable. At any other time she would have done as they suggested. Their games should not be disturbed. Their happiness was precious. But she just could not face it. She felt ill.

"No, William. I must look after the others. You go. Now hurry along, there's a good boy."

She watched them eat, she watched them play, she watched them eat again. Sometimes they came up to her chair and asked her questions. She had no idea what to reply and they looked away impatiently. Sometimes the baby Michael wanted to sit on her knee but she felt afraid to have him close to her in case her cold was very bad, in case she gave him flu. They were used to being disappointed in her. They did not cling to her so much now because they had a home of their own in Curtis Street and because the country homes in which they had stayed had also been very happy. They prized her only for her indulgence. When she would not answer or made vague answers they said, "Oh, Auntie, why do you always say that? Why don't you listen, Auntie?" As the afternoon wore on and exhaustion made them fretful the two eldest criticised her openly.

"Doesn't Auntie look funny?"

"She's a funny old thing."

"Auntie, you're a silly old thing." Paddy gave a quick shriek of laughter, just in case this might be taken too seriously. But no one rebuked her so she went on.

The pain in Marguerite's chest increased. It would be difficult breathing tonight. She must remember to prop herself with pillows.

"Auntie, I wish you'd listen." Paddy stood straight in front of her. "You're a funny, silly old thing. Do you know what William called you?"

"No. What, dear?"

"I shan't tell you."

"You can tell her if you like. I don't care."

"He called you Aunt Maggie."

Marguerite was not offended. If anything she was rather pleased. She managed to smile.

Bored because she had obtained negative results from this experiment, Paddy turned to something else.

"It's time you went home," said Marguerite at last. "William, you look after the others. And will you remember to tell your mother to come in some time tomorrow." She could not be bothered to write a note and she did not want to tell the children she was ill. "Tell her to look in as early as possible. Try not to forget."

She had to stand while she helped them on with hats and coats and gloves. She thought it wiser not to kiss them goodbye. She walked with them to the front door and waved. Now she was certain she had a temperature. The bedroom would be icy and so would the bed. She could not go down and boil a kettle for a bottle. She could not even clear away the tea things. She would lie down on the sofa and try to get some sleep. She turned off the light and lay down after making up the fire. She propped her head high; the red reflections of the dancing flames flickered over her face. The fight for breath began. She should not have smoked so much but one had to keep going somehow.

One of the children had left a glove behind on the floor. It looked like Paddy's. That child had plenty of character. Lovely children. She heard the front door open. One of the Poles coming in for the night. Better not call out to him. He understood neither her English nor her French. If he came in then he would have all of them down interpreting and fussing. If only she could have a real, good sleep tonight she would be better in the morning. And in any case, if she did not feel better Mary would be over to look after her.

She could not remember ever having felt so weak, except perhaps last year when she had that bad attack and Kathleen was so rotten. But then it had been much more serious. The doctor had given her up. And she had had much more pain too.

She shut her eyes and dozed off. Her mouth fell open and her face smoothed out. The dirty white blanket slipped towards the floor, uncovering all but her legs.

She looked very smart in her new costume, the only one she had bought for five years. And her hair was done in the latest style—she had done it herself. Every since Bordeaux she had mastered her hair completely. Now it was lifted into a high swirl above her forehead and it shone and looked reddy brown in the moving light. Below her ears one could see a curled strand or two, part of a loose roll. Anyone aged between sixteen and seventy might have worn their hair like that at the present time. She had kept abreast of fashion as a matter of course.

Some women tend to stay in a fashion to which they become attached at a certain date. So Elizabeth had always retained a look of the twenties, always keeping her chest low and compressed, never emphasising her waist, wearing her hair in a flat shingle with a tight curl or two, pulling her hats well over her head. By small and grudging concessions to changing fashion she managed not to look completely out of date.

Kathleen had never looked smart at any time, had allowed the others to dress her. Yet she too seemed to cling to a past time, a time before the first World War. Her thick unmanageable hair automatically fell into the bird's nest coiffure of her youth.

But Marguerite, without consulting any lady's magazine, knew the line of the moment. When she had gone out today her hat had been tiny, high-crowned and tilted forward. The costume she was wearing now had padded shoulders and a nipped-in waist. Lying on the shabby magnificence of the Elizabethan settle, in spite of her open mouth, in spite of the dirty cups and plates only a few feet from her head, she not only looked elegant herself but also lent a fine air to her surroundings.

She fitted the settle exactly. Her feet were one inch from the end. Above the high, tarnished gold-brocade back stretched the dark William Morris paper, the centres of the fabulous flowers looking down on her like a hundred eyes.

The flames had gone and the dying embers turned slowly from red to grey. The room was in total darkness. Marguerite woke suddenly and groped with her hand as though to find the blanket. She felt cold, she felt hot, she felt colder and she felt uneasy. She stirred and said one Our Father and three Hail Marys. She shut her eyes and slept again. Sleep turned to coma and coma to death.

10

"*Deus cui proprium est misereri et parcere...*" gabbled the priest in Irish Latin.

Lisa looked at the translation in the right-hand column of her booklet. They had all been handed a booklet, pale mauve, black bordered: Mass for the Dead and Burial Service.

O God whose property it is always to have mercy and to spare, we humbly present our prayers to Thee in behalf of the soul of Thy servant N. (here the priest must have said Marguerite Reilly. She could not remember hearing the name in Latin.) *which Thou had this day called out of the world: beseeching Thee not to deliver it into the hands of the enemy, nor to forget it for ever, but command it to be received by the holy angels, and to be carried into Paradise; that, as it hoped and believed in Thee, it may not undergo the pains of hell, but may obtain everlasting joy.*

Lisa knelt in a row with Kathleen, Elizabeth, Mary, Patsy, Eileen Stebbing (the former maid) and a woman she did not know (one of Mary's cronies). Between them and the altar, the coffin lay under a pall and the heavy rounded folds swept gracefully down to the grey marble. The pall was the most beautiful thing in the chapel, the deep, deep lightless black throwing into relief the wide silver bands of the central cross.

The small side chapel was hygienic-looking. The marble and mosaic had probably been rich and Byzantine in the mind of the designer and yet, even with tall yellow candles and black vestments, the result was like an expensive kind of operation theatre. The altar was bare of flowers. The colours present were black, white, silver and grey.

It was as well, thought Lisa. It kept one dry and with a sense of proportion. And so did the priest's rapid progress and expression of unconcern. A tall handsome young man, probably not long over from Ireland, he no doubt had many years of holy life before him. He had not known *Thy servant N.*, he was helping her to get to Heaven; why should he worry? He handled the large black-bound book and the holy receptacles with marvellous dexterity. When he turned from the altar to face the kneelers he swivelled round on one foot in a single swift movement, smooth, like a top. Even priests had a professional touch. Their movements were always under public observation, that was why.

She felt cheerful enough but a little bored. She looked round at the others. They were all praying hard or pretending to. Kathleen was wearing a black hat several sizes too large for her tiny head. Elizabeth must have produced it from somewhere. It was a very old-fashioned hat with a wide brim. Kathleen looked absolutely buried in it. The two men from the undertaker's—were they Catholics?—were kneeling on the broad marble steps which led into the side aisle and they looked most devout. Their heads were bowed. They too were professional. They must have knelt through many a funeral service in this attitude.

Now she came to think of it, Mary's and Patsy's hats looked odd. Had Elizabeth produced those too? Had they once graced Lady Watson? Had they been bought at a jumble sale? Did Elizabeth have a drawer full of things which would come in handy for funerals? It was very likely.

The priest spoke softly to the altar as though confiding to it his holy secrets. He turned and faced them and raised his voice. "*Orate fratres.*" It was cold here. Her hands were numb. She turned the pages until her eye was caught by a list of names. She had forgotten them since the convent. *Peter and Paul, Andrew, James, John, Thomas, James, Philip, Bartholomew, Matthew, Simon and Thaddeus, Linus, Cletus, Clement, Zystus, Cornelius, Cyprian, Lawrence, Chrysogonus, John and Paul, Cosmas and Damian.*

These names did not sound dead. Eight hundred years or more after your death and you did not seem dead at all. You had taken on a new life, not a holy one in heaven, but an earthly one like an old stone or picture. How very dead these Apostles and Martyrs must have seemed a few days after they died. She did not think of her grandmother as dead any more either. How many years was it before you did not seem dead any more? You were never so dead as during your funeral!

At the end of the Mass the priest put on a black cope. His fresh young face seemed to grow sterner and he had a look of the sixteenth century; perhaps it was the slope over the shoulders, from neck to spreading hem, which suggested dignitaries of the church in paintings. The adolescent acolyte held out a bowl of holy water into which the priest dipped a brush. Slowly the priest walked round the coffin throwing the holy droplets thrice on each side of the corpse, shaking them off the soft bristles with a quick yet solemn flick. Then taking the censer he walked round once more wafting small aromatic clouds of incense over the pall.

Mary was crying and as they left the side chapel Patsy put her stout arm around her. Elizabeth kept an eye on what was happening, held herself ready to give instructions. Kathleen walked slowly, very anxious not to be the first to reach the street. The two men had carried the coffin ahead in the hearse. The crony had disappeared.

In a black car the mourners followed the hearse. They were packed tight, six of them. Mary was crying quietly. Elizabeth looked tense and filled with responsibility. Kathleen looked nervous. Patsy and Eileen were smiling. Lisa looked grumpy. She had not wanted to come and it would go on for ever. Kathleen had implored her, "You must go to the funeral, dear. Elizabeth will make such a fuss and she'll go on at me about it and it would look odd for Mary and Patsy. Please, dear. After all, it's just an hour or two and then it's all finished with."

Suddenly, as though the idea of breaking the silence had occurred to them simultaneously, all three began to talk. One word or two came from each and then they withdrew.

"So sorry. What were you going to say?"

"No. You go on. It was nothing."

"No, you say what you wanted."

Patsy took the lead, smiling, with a steady voice. "After all she'll be in Heaven. She's better off than any of us. And she's left a wonderful memory behind her. Do you know what the nuns were saying to me about her?"

"You must hear this," said Mary through her tears. "You must listen to this."

" 'There's no one like Miss Reilly,' they said. 'She was the soul of charity,' they said, 'and she'll be long remembered in the parish.' Half the people came up to me after mass yesterday and asked me about her. There'll be many praying for her for weeks to come."

435

"They will," echoed Eileen.

They were moving at a moderate speed along blitzed streets. People on the pavements turned to look at the hearse; the more curious eyes attempted to pierce through the shine on the glass of the following car to see the family. Down a long shopping street they went; a clothes shop, a big greengrocer, a cinema, a butcher, another clothes shop. Lisa was amazed at the pace. She had imagined they would crawl along and she had also imagined the others would be silent and praying to themselves.

Now Patsy was laughing. "It's we sinners who are left. The best go first." Not that she felt a sinner at all. That was the joke. She saw Lisa's puzzled face. "You're very quiet there, Lisa. Now don't be fretting. She had a lovely peaceful death and she's better off than any of us."

Lisa had not been fretting. But, as sometimes happens, the sympathy started her off. She began to feel as she had done when a child, that there was a thick dark cloud inside her. Her facial muscles were slipping out of her control; her eyes screwed up, her mouth trembled. Her throat was full. She knew that if she attempted to smile back at Patsy a dreadful sadness would overtake her. She could feel it ready to pounce on her. She had little realised it was there and therefore she had not bothered to stave it off, and now it was too late. She held her breath and counted slowly. As she looked round on the living, the two sisters, the two sisters-in-law and the former maid, all past their prime, all lined, all tired, it conjured up in her a feeling that Marguerite was in the car too. And then she knew that Marguerite was gone, quite gone, gone for good. She thought, "Auntie". It was too much. It was too final.

Lisa thought that she must get through this moment, push back the feelings which menaced, climb back onto a plane of indifference and all would be well. It would be as Kathleen had said, "Just an hour or two and then it's all finished with." But the knowledge that her aunt had gone had spread through her and unable to fight it any longer she let out a sob. Having done that, her sudden grief overcame her and she put her black-gloved hands up to hide her hot distorted face.

At all costs she must not let in any visual memory. She must not see her aunt's face. One could cope with words but not with pictures. It was no use. Before her shut and brimming eyes came Marguerite, small, her behind sticking out, her chin forward, her handsome profile in the air. And then, worse still, came the front face, the wide forehead with the square hair-line, the fanged mouth and, alas! the level, deep, grey, wide-set eyes, looking out so straight, so intent, telling such tales of a large warm heart, no matter how much her actions might belie them. It was no use.

Lisa tossed back her head as though that would hold in the tears. She did not care whether the others saw her cry or not. Why was she so upset? What had happened to her? These tears felt as though they had been withheld for years and years. What could she mean by it? Had Aunt Marguerite been alive this day she would neither have written to her nor gone to see her, would not have done so for months and months, perhaps years had she survived, would not have given her a single thought. Therefore there was no loss at all.

Patsy did not believe in crying at funerals. Hers was the faith which welcomes the entry into the next world. But she liked others to cry so that she could hearten them. She leant forward and put her hand on Lisa's knee. "It'll do you good to cry. You'll feel better after. You must have been very fond of her and no wonder. And she was always talking about you. It was Lisa this and Lisa that. And each of the children was to be like Lisa. She thought the world of you."

This caused pricks of conscience. Had her aunt thought so much of her? Had she misjudged the degree of Marguerite's interest? Had she, Lisa, seemed horribly cold and ungrateful? She put these questions aside for the moment. That was not what she minded. Neither was it a sense of loss. What was it? As though to answer her came memories.

She was by Marguerite's side in a London street, queuing up for a matinée. A notice went up, "Standing Room Only," and half the people went away. Then someone shouted, "Full up, no more room," and the rest of the people, grumbling, made off. For a moment she felt disappointed and then she realised that this did not apply to her. Her aunt was different from other people and if she wanted to get in she would. She looked up at her and Marguerite bent down with the light of battle in her eye and a knowing smile—for at that time Lisa was the favourite—and she said, "By hook or by crook we'll get seats."

Lisa was small then and her aunt seemed very tall and broad. She held on to her hand. Sure enough they reached the bright crowded gallery, her aunt saying some clever words to each attendant on the way. The orchestra was playing and they were among the standing

437

audience at the back and, gripping Lisa's hand tight, Marguerite began to worm her way down the side stairs. There was whispered talk to the programme girl, the lights were lowering, she could not catch what her aunt was saying, in a way did not want to know, it was all part of the magic, but she knew it would work, knew that the other was weakening and melting. They ended up in seats in the front row and although she had known that would happen it was marvellous. Her aunt was a magician and could never be defeated. How happy she felt to have such confidence in her. How fortunate she was to have come with her rather than anyone else.

Lisa remembered another scene, one which caused her shame and embarrassment. She was in the dining room with her aunt and she was explaining to her how the mother of her young man (her first young man just before she went to Oxford) had given her a pair of gloves. "I had to take them," she said. "Why do you think she did it? She said something about my not having gloves last week. Oh, I wish I hadn't accepted them. But what could I do?"

And Marguerite was livid, walking up and down with fury, a dramatic expression on her face. Up and down she walked, jerky, taut. "No, you should not have taken them. Does she think you come from the gutter? Does she think you have no family, no one behind you? How dare she tell you she was amazed you had no gloves like that? How could you let her think such a thing? Why all the young girls nowadays go about without gloves or hats either—girls of the very best families." Here her voice softened as though she were talking of the daughters of her personal friends. "And do you mean to say you never said a word? Never said you did not choose to wear gloves? Did you allow her to think we could not afford to buy you a pair?"

Then suddenly Marguerite's face brightened. "I know what we'll do. How much did they cost? Let us say about ten shillings. Well I'll give you ten shillings, and you must have some flowers sent off to her at once, with a short note, from a very expensive shop. I'll find the money." And broke as she was, she rifled the gas meters and counted out the ten shillings into Lisa's palm.

When the flowers were dispatched she smiled with satisfaction and hauteur, contemptuous of Lisa, contemptuous of the woman, raising one side of her mouth. Money was well spent on family honour and no wealthy woman would ever get the better of her. And at that moment Lisa had wondered: is Auntie right? Should you bluff it out always? And even if you shouldn't, isn't it marvellous to have so definite an attitude, to make so confident a gesture?

Why had anything got the better of Marguerite? Given all that fight, all that fearlessness of other people and given the conditions of her later years Marguerite must be considered to have failed. But if Marguerite had failed then nothing was worth an effort, nothing mattered any more.

If only Marguerite had ended up rich, eminent and admired. Given all that pride, had she felt humiliated by her life? Lisa, not knowing her aunt's inner development, dwelling only on those occasions when she had been dominated by ambition, concluded she must. It was like a sum which had added up to a minus. It was all a waste.

At this conclusion, in a panic, her mind kept running to and fro. If... if... if. If only she had had just a few years of living in grandeur with a big income and a house free of lodgers and holidays abroad in hotels. That would have done. It would have framed the picture. If only she had acquired the setting for her manner and voice, her soft, husky, rich voice. If only the spotlight had been turned on her for a short time. If only she could have said to herself, "I achieved all I meant to and now I can pause, satisfied."

But there she had been, still in that boarding house, probably in squalor and without a penny to spare, probably still living in hopes and it had all ended before the finale. But then was it something in Marguerite herself which had gone wrong? Would she perhaps have continued to live for the future even if she had lived to be a hundred? Ambition was a curse if it prevented you from enjoying the present. Had her aunt ever lived in the present at all? Had she, for example, enjoyed those matinées, or had they been merely some preparation for a future occasion? If not, could the thought be borne? Didn't it make her death a thousand times worse than anyone else's and her life nothing but a prelude? It was like saving up for a treat, doing without every pleasure to save, and then never having it.

By now Lisa's sorrow was so obvious that Elizabeth was patting her knee and Kathleen, upset, had to say something.

"I'm sorry, darling. I hate to see you so unhappy."

"Oh, if only..." Lisa began, hoping that if she told them what was on her mind, they might know the answer. But the words choked her

439

and the very thought of bringing them out was so overwhelming that she flung her head downwards into her hands.

It is more soothing to blame anyone, even yourself, than to remain with a feeling of hopelessness and despair. It keeps enough anger pouring in to dilute the sadness. It enables you to focus and direct your grief, creates an illusion of control, a belief that some good will come of it. Therefore Lisa turned on herself with reproaches, half knowing that she was moving away from the heart of the problem.

Was it true what Patsy had said? If so she, Lisa, had been a beast. Her aunt had thought a lot of her and in return she had hurt her, had tried to make her think she was responsible for the marriage and divorce. That was a wanton piece of cruelty when her aunt had so many failures on her hands. The word "failure" was terrible in connection with her aunt. It did not matter if other people failed. It did not matter if she, Lisa, failed. But not Marguerite. On the point of appealing to her childhood's God, Lisa was begging that somehow the sum should come right, that her aunt's life should not have been a shapeless chaos, that her aunt should have got something out of it.

She could never make it up to her now. Being an unbeliever she could not even pray for her soul. Even this small act of respect, the attendance at the funeral, had been wrung out of her and she had grudged it to the last. They had both been living in the same town for the past months, within easy reach of each other, and she had never bothered to go and see her aunt. To keep the picture black and white, Lisa naturally forgot how her aunt tended to disappear when one did go to see her. Perhaps it was because she wanted to feel she had played an important rôle in her aunt's life, even though this were an unpleasant one.

Patsy was talking, partly because she felt talkative and partly to cheer up Lisa. "There's nothing like a Catholic burial," she said. "I've been in service with Protestants and I've seen them buried. There was one old girl I laid out myself, the poor soul, and their parsons just say a prayer or two, no expression, you know. I thought that priest looked so kind, so full of pity. And the words are a consolation and the holy water. Wasn't it young Walter Carter who was serving? He's a fine lad. He had such a solemn look on him. Wasn't it his father who was telling me he was thinking of making a priest of him? It's a great thing to have a vocation."

"That was not Walter Carter," said Eileen, "that was the other one. Now what would his name be? They're very alike but this one's darker."

"I think she's right," said Mary, who was feeling happier, "young Carter's hair is lighter."

Elizabeth smiled sadly at the conversation. Soon she would be taking control of Patsy's and Mary's lives, telling them what was good for the children. She was wondering about the will; not so much what was in it as where it was and which solicitors were likely to know about it. She herself did not want to inherit anything, she was far better off than the others, but obviously she would be the executor and poor Marguerite had been a little absent-minded about things at the last and it might be in a mess. There might very well be no will at all.

In fact Marguerite had made several wills and they would soon be found in her top drawer. She had left everything to the children, regardless of whether it were hers to leave or not, even Kathleen's cottage and piano and Elizabeth's furniture.

Suspecting something of the sort, Kathleen was feeling uneasy. If she had been done out of everything and if Elizabeth also took the line that the children should have everything because they were young and the young must come first, then what would become of her in her old age? How would she live? Would she have to ask Lisa to support her? Would all the money she had poured into the houses never return to her in any form? She could go back to Germany and give English lessons after the war, but who knew what Germany would be like then, and who knew what had happened to the Catholic schools already?

Patsy was good-natured but stubborn. "It *was* Walter Carter. Don't I remember him from the choir? He used to sing soprano. He had a beautiful voice like a bell. They say those who had fine voices get them back again later on. The boy who made the records, now what was his name? They say he has a beautiful baritone now."

Elizabeth's thoughts were divided between this world and the next. Between plans about the children and their mother, she prayed for her sister's soul. Lisa's tears touched her; it showed the girl had some ties with the family after all. Very kindly and simply she gave her a wan smile and patted her shoulder.

This started Lisa off again. Even Elizabeth reacted at once, without complication, to the unhappiness of others. In spite of her flavourless, faded, governess-like exterior, there was a small fount of kindness intact in her heart. She had given her money to the others. From now on she would look after the children too. Only she, Lisa, was heartless. When she saw others crying her one idea was to remove herself from their tears. When Marguerite had been unhappy she, Lisa, had made no movement of sympathy; she had resented and reasoned. How bloody she was! What was the use of a brain if you had no heart, if you reserved your heart for special occasions? No, Marguerite had not been a failure because she had kept her heart open and that had given a glow to her activities. Even though she had dreamt of the future she had loved in the present.

Consoled by the thought that it was she who was the failure and not her aunt, Lisa dried her tears. She felt almost happy at having reached this conclusion. To strengthen it she recalled a hundred little sins of omission. Had she ever sent a card for Marguerite's birthday? No. Had she ever sent her a present or a note at Christmas? No. She might say that her aunt never sent her anything either. But that was quibbling, that was a mean-minded, petty-minded answer. Marguerite did not give presents to people because they gave her presents. She acted on impulse.

But then if (no, she wasn't excusing herself, she really wasn't) if she had sent letters, would they have been read? Would Marguerite have registered anything? She thought of her aunt during the drinking period. Marguerite seemed to her like a wounded animal, wounded long ago and not knowing where the wound was. There had been some desperate grief in her which she had buried. She had, for brief and rare moments, when she was free from day dreams or drunken exhilaration and fuddle, looked so empty, so in a void. But as soon as the look struck you it was gone. Now Lisa could see her aunt's face with only that look on it.

If all her nephews and her niece (yes, she was now swallowing the legend of Marguerite's heart being broken by their ingratitude) had sent her letters every week and cards and presents on special occasions, what difference would it have made? Well, it would have added up to something, some sensation of pleasure.

They descended from the car by the gates of the cemetery. One of the funeral men, the ginger-haired one, helped them down, keeping his eyes fixed on the house across the road. The coffin had been carried on ahead. They walked up a gravel path in silence.

If she had had plenty of money, thought Lisa, what difference would it have made? Debts and money worries had tormented her it seemed. But had they? Was it really them?

"That's the Catholic part over there," said Patsy.

They stepped onto the grass, in single file past old tombstones, past new ones which were straight and ugly. They saw the two men by a freshly dug square hole and went towards it, grouping themselves around, three on either side. They waited for the priest. It would be a different one who said the Burial Service, the one who was attached to this place.

It was cold and windy. Each woman's face was blueish and the contraction of the skin emphasised the lines. The grey light became no one, drained their eyes, lips and hair of colour. A few yards away the cemetery ended abruptly with a fence, beyond which a grass bank sloped down to railway lines. Over the way were poor houses. Everything seemed dirty and poor.

Lisa felt the tears pouring down her cheeks, some reaching the side of her mouth, a soft salt taste. Really it was too bad burying her here in the most squalid part of the cemetery. Was it cheaper here?

She looked down at the coffin, a very plain coffin covered in a sticky varnish, and so tiny; it looked as though it could contain only a child. On it the name was "Margaret Reilly."

The priest advanced with wide steps and a flutter of robes. He was elderly, white-haired and thin. His voice was the voice of an English parson. The coffin was lowered. Looking at their books the watchers murmured. "*Benedictus Dominus Deus Israel...*" Lisa read on:

> *Eternal rest give unto her, O Lord,*
> *And let perpetual light shine upon her.*

The priest held a mounted, perforated silver ball which contained holy water. Having sprinkled the coffin he then passed the ball on to the next person. This was Kathleen. Taken by surprise she hurriedly worked out which was her right hand and tugged off her glove. She sprinkled wildly with an anxious expression. The drops fell on the turf. Her arm worked away as though she were pumping. Glad to be rid of it she thrust the ball towards the next person.

A train passed by, hissing and roaring, to drown the words of the prayer. All were covered in smoke. The priest coughed. As the smoke dispersed, all eyes were turned towards the coffin as though they could see Marguerite lying there. She had never liked to be watched. How often when she was doing something and one had looked at her, she had said, "Now run along, *chérie*. You go into the other room. I'll be there presently." How she hated people about. "People get on top of me."

And here, thought Lisa, how would she ever find rest, crowded among other graves, with trains rushing past every few minutes? And any flowers placed above her would be quickly sooted over and lose their brilliance and the grass around her would always be blackish and gritty. How few wreaths she had been given! Oh dear, she, Lisa, had not sent a wreath of any kind, had not thought of it. It was a bad time of year. There were only chrysanthemums to be had and dark evergreen leaves. Who had chosen the chrysanthemums? Why were they all so brownish and niggly and drooping? Why did everything look done on the cheap? The windows of the houses on the other side of the railway had darkish lace curtains and a look of despair. Small slum tenements they must be.

If only it could be true about heaven just for this once, just for this one person, thought Lisa, what a comfort it would be. Thank goodness Marguerite had believed in it. How had she visualised it? Was it lovely for her? Did it seem very real? *And to be carried into Paradise... Everlasting joys...*

The others were praying aloud, in English, Patsy's voice louder and racing ahead of the rest. It was the De Profundis. Lisa joined in at the end. *Amen.*

It was over. There was no more to be done. Patsy said something to the priest. The others looked at each other. Elizabeth took the lead. They retraced their steps to the car, over the grass, along the gravel. The ginger-haired man and his companion had driven off with the empty hearse. Another man, the driver of their car, held open the door. He seemed to be a chauffeur only, dissociated with the coffin.

They drove back the way they had come. Lisa noted the same greengrocer's shop with its stalls coming out onto the pavement and the beautifully arranged rows of potatoes and Brussels sprouts. Marguerite's death had not created the slightest ripple in this part of London. Without the hearse they sped along like a family on an outing.

Patsy was smiling. She did enjoy funerals. "Well, she's gone to her rest at last, she's better off than any of us," she said, as though it was only at the cemetery that the soul had finally been freed to speed upwards. "And wasn't it a wonderful thing to have the same priest that David had?"

"Poor David," murmured Elizabeth, absently.

"That'll be four of us in the first grave," said Mary. "First your mother, then Michael, then David and then myself when my time comes. The three sisters will be all together in the second grave. It's a fine thing when a family can be together."

As Mary spoke she displayed a row of large yellowish false teeth. Mary, Patsy, Elizabeth and Kathleen had false teeth. In Cardiff slums and Dublin slums they had been malnourished. Mary, Patsy and Kathleen lost their teeth early on, all in one go. Elizabeth's had gone one by one. Lisa wondered, do they bury a person with her false teeth in or not?

Eileen was talking about Marguerite. "And I met her the day she went, in the street, looking flourishing. And she asks me where I'm going and I says to work and she laughs and says, 'You haven't changed, Eileen. They all say *business* these days but you still say *work*.'"

Lisa was taken aback. Had Marguerite really been so observant of the use of words? This remark of her aunt seemed out of character. And yet she could hear her aunt saying it, especially using the name of the person to whom she was talking—that very personal touch. She knew just how it was said. She knew it had been said. Marguerite had probably spoken out of character. People who were inarticulate about their real feelings often did.

She looked through the window at the cold January sky. Her feelings had abated and her thoughts seemed to come from a distance now, through an enveloping glaze of melancholy. She remembered the middle-aged cashier at the tea shop yesterday saying, "How's everything?" to a regular customer. And unaware that what she heard was an echo of Marguerite's "How's you?" the memory of the cashier's words moved her extremely and she found them rich in concealed sympathy, humanity and interest. The inarticulate were the poetic ones and they were wise and good. All the everyday sentences spoken by typists in the office, by a pair of shoppers on a bus, by people in shops, Lisa invested with a new significance. And as she sighed for Marguerite—forgetting that she had resembled none of these people—she sighed for them all and envied them.

445

A smart car rushed past them, honking impatiently, causing them to swerve. The bloody rich, thought Lisa. Outraged as though her own aunt had been affronted, she recalled many scenes with bitterness; upper-class people on buses; a silly female painter who laughed at the cockney accent of her maid; the mild, cosy, humdrum life in a pub brutally shattered by the entry of two young members of the intelligentsia who spoke, self-listening, in BBC accents ("Good evening, Charlie") to the barman, their tone proclaiming that all must now abandon the dimness of their dull privacy to marvel and give thanks for the matiness of the newcomers.

Only melancholy and bitterness remained. She was dry and she was empty. She was as little able to help herself as the grey houses in the grey streets, the heavy lifeless sky above.

As her thoughts ran on it never occurred to her to praise her mother. Kathleen had a genius for life in the fish queue, the bus and the factory. From her lips came many of those phrases which Lisa so admired. No, all Lisa's bitterness must be presumed to be a defence of her aunt. If you love a person you spare no pains in building your system around them and your feelings provide the logic.

The ancestry of her thoughts was unknown to Lisa. She imagined that they had sprung from herself. But she was repeating Marguerite's, "We are as good as they are—better," extending the "we" to cover all who had struggled for a small income and the "they" to cover her husband, the class from which he came, his friends, their friends and the people they admired. And she was voicing Kathleen's long resentment against the people she nursed.

"It's a wonderful thing," said Patsy, and she leaned forward and looked at Lisa as though what she was going to say would be of the greatest comfort. "It's a wonderful thing, a Catholic burial. Did you see the priest's face? The old one, I mean. You feel someone is looking after the dead. You feel they are not forgotten by the Church. You feel the Church is like a mother. Did I ever tell you about that old lady I was in service with?"

"No," said Lisa politely. Patsy's vitality was pulling her into consciousness not only of Patsy herself but of the other four. "Do go on."

"A Protestant but she was a dear old soul. God bless her. Well now when she died her daughter was over from the States and she had her cremated. I went to the place with her, a dreadful place. And there wasn't a prayer, nothing. And coming back in the car, as we are now it might be, she turns to me and says, 'Take it. Take it.' And she hands me the urn, a little plain stone thing. 'And you can do what you like with it,' she says. 'Scatter the ashes where you like,' she says. 'You can do anything.' Did you ever hear of anything so heartless? She must have had a heart of stone."

Lisa's love of reason came up. "But it might not be that. It might be that she was so upset that she couldn't bear to have the ashes with her."

"Sure and she was heartless," said Patsy, "real heartless."

Mary agreed emphatically. "I never heard the like. What a terrible thing."

"Now while I remember it," said Elizabeth, "I know it may sound a little too business-like, but these things have to be mentioned, and after all we none of us know what may happen, especially at times like these. I want you to write down the name of the firm who did the funeral." This was to Kathleen. "They have the papers about the grave and know exactly where to find it. You have to show the papers, you know, when you want it opened again. I know this sounds very gloomy but we must think of everything. If anything should happen to me... A new grave is very expensive, at least fifteen pounds, but to have it opened only costs thirty shillings. You've bought the plot already, you see. Lisa, you too had better make a note of this. If I should go and then your mother you would know who to get on to. It seems dreadful to have to say this but one must think of everything."

"Very well, *chérie*," said Kathleen meekly. "But I haven't a pencil on me. Wait until we get home."

"No. We might forget." Elizabeth took out her notebook and fountain pen and wrote. "And do keep it in some safe place, *chérie*. Try not to lose it."

"It's a terrible price they charge for graves," said Patsy.

Also available from The Clapton Press:

SPANISH PORTRAIT
by Elizabeth Lake

ISBN 978-1-9996543-2-0

Set principally in San Sebastián and Madrid between 1934 and 1936, this brutally honest, semi-autobiographical novel portrays a frantic love affair against the backdrop of confusion and apprehension that characterised the *bienio negro*, as Spain drifted inexorably towards civil war. It was described by Elizabeth Bowen as "A remarkable first novel [revealing] a remorseless interest in emotional truth".

Elizabeth Lake was the pen-name adopted by Inez Pearn, a girl from a working-class background who won a scholarship to Oxford in the early 1930s and later joined the campaign for Britain to provide support for the Spanish Republic. She went on to produce five novels.

Along the way she was briefly married to Stephen Spender and subsequently, more enduringly, to the poet and sociologist Charles Madge.

This edition of Spanish Portrait includes an afterword by her daughter, Vicky Randall.

Also available from The Clapton Press:

BOADILLA
by Esmond Romilly

ISBN 978-1-9996543-0-7

Esmond Romilly (1918-1941) was Winston Churchill's nephew and rumoured to be his illegitimate son. Already notorious as a teenage runaway from Wellington College, Romilly was among the first British volunteers to join the International Brigades in Spain, cycling across France to fight on the side of the Spanish Republic against Franco's insurrection. He saw intensive front line action in defence of Madrid, culminating in the battle of Boadilla del Monte in December 1936.

Written on his honeymoon in France after eloping with Jessica Mitford in early 1937, this is his personal account of those events, in which many fellow comrades lost their lives. As well as a highly readable and moving memoir, it has served as a primary historical source for many leading scholars writing about the Spanish Civil War, including Paul Preston, Hugh Thomas and Anthony Beevor.

This annotated edition includes an introduction and an appendix with three poems written in Spain by the poet John Cornford.

Also available from The Clapton Press:

MY HOUSE IN MÁLAGA
by Sir Peter Chalmers Mitchell

ISBN 978-1-9996543-5-1

In 1934 Sir Peter Chalmers Mitchell retired at the age of 70 from a distinguished career as Secretary of the Zoological Society of London. During his tenor he had been the driving force behind the creation of the Whipsnade Zoo, which opened in 1931.

He moved to Málaga "for what I expected to be a peaceful old age" and spent his time writing his memoirs and translating novels by Ramón J. Sender. Then came the rebellion of 1936. While most other British residents fled to Gibraltar, Sir Peter was one of the few to stay in order to protect his house and garden, and his servants.

Although an open sympathiser with the Anarchist cause, he provided a safe haven to the wife and five daughters of Tomás Bolín, members of a notorious right wing family, eventually helping them escape across the border.

He later offered shelter to Arthur Koestler. When the Italian forces sent by Mussolini to support the rebellion took Málaga, they were both arrested by Tomás Bolín's nephew, Luis, who was Franco's chief propagandist and who had vowed that if he ever laid his hands on Koestler he would "shoot him like a dog".

This is his memoir of that period, first published in 1937.

Also available from The Clapton Press:

SOME STILL LIVE
by F. G. Tinker Jr

ISBN 978-1-9996543-8-2

Frank G. Tinker was a freelance US pilot who signed up
with the Republican forces in Spain because he didn't like
Mussolini. He was also attracted by the prospect of
adventure and a generous pay cheque. Once over in Spain,
Tinker chalked up the largest number of acknowledged
enemy kills, shooting down a total of 8 Junkers, Fiats and
Messerschmitts.

In their free time he and his colleagues roamed the bars
and hotels of Madrid in search of champagne and a hot
bath, befriending fellow Americans such as Ernest
Hemingway and Robert Hale Merriman, Commanding
Officer of the Lincoln Battalion of the International
Brigades.

When Tinker returned to the US he was unable to rejoin
the Armed Forces and, depressed by Franco's victory, he
was found in a hotel room in June 1939 with an empty
bottle of whisky by his side and a bullet in his head. This is
his account of his experiences in Spain.